Family Outing

Alison Habens was born in 1967. She is the
author of *Dreamhouse*, 'a truly astonishing feat
of the imagination . . . a writer to watch and
cherish' *Sunday Times*.
She lives in Portsmouth.

Also by Alison Habens
and available in Minerva

Dreamhouse

Alison Habens

Family Outing

Minerva

Published by Minerva

1 3 5 7 9 10 8 6 4 2

First published in Great Britain by
Martin Secker & Warburg Ltd 1996

Minerva
Random House, 20 Vauxhall Bridge Road, London SW1V 2SA

Random House Australia (Pty) Limited
20 Alfred Street, Milsons Point, Sydney
New South Wales 2061, Australia

Random House New Zealand Limited
18 Poland Road, Glenfield,
Auckland 10, New Zealand

Random House South Africa (Pty) Limited
Endulini, 5a Jubilee Road, Parktown 2193, South Africa

Random House UK Limited Reg. No. 954009

A CIP catalogue record for this title
is available from the British Library

ISBN 0 7493 1767 1

Typeset in Perpetua
by Deltatype Ltd, Ellesmere Port, Cheshire
Printed and bound in Great Britain
by Cox & Wyman Ltd, Reading, Berkshire

For Viv and Jo, the other two Graces;
Ian and Fred, for the other cover;
and all at 95 Warren Avenue

One

There was no beginning. It had always already begun.

There was light, alright; before I knew I had eyes, I was blinded by it. But there was no flash. The bright spark that blew me into life came from a fire started before I was part of it. All it took was a slightly whiter moment in the molten orange, a relatively insignificant puff of smoke.

There was no beginning, as far as I can see. Something was always there before me. I opened my eyes and saw other eyes already open. I arrived in a strange new place and found I'd been expected. My very first words fitted into the conversation that someone else had initiated.

I say this because I'm trying to find out how the stuff that's happening now started. A truck-load of seriously silly shit is about to dump on my doorstep, and if I can work out where it came from I might be able to send it away again, still laden. I thought there might have been a beginning to this mess, an original hot spot, and I've tried to get back there to see if I could change it; but the beginning never comes, not as far as I can see.

I can't remember being born.

I expect it was like dying, my very first breath fusing with the last one like a bridge to span a lifetime. I suppose I started the incredible journey alone, passing through a tunnel without air; and hands must have helped to pull me out, and members of my family must have greeted me. I suppose I passed from black oblivion to luminous awareness, like stepping onto a moving bus.

But I can't remember this. It was always already light. As soon as life dawned on me I forgot about the darkness. A certain person would smile and there'd be no such thing as night. Before I'd even got the hang of the language, he'd flap questions in my face, pull answers from hats, and follow me around like the sun out of orbit, to keep me in constant day.

At first his face was so close to me I thought it was my own. I marvelled at his eyeballs, prized them like marbles. I loved his hair as if it were my teddy bear. His mouth I associated with music, and couldn't keep my hands off it, tinkering with his teeth the way I tinkled on the keys of my tiny plastic piano. He moved around me with such ease of mobility I assumed he could fly.

I wish I could remember the first words we spoke. Perhaps there'd be a clue in them, something important, of great portent. An annunciation, before I'd got the proper pronunciation.

But probably, it was just small talk. Unformed ideas falling out without much thought, much as it is now. The idle chat of companions so at one with each other there's no need to make much meaning; sentences that don't have to go anywhere so long as you both know where they're coming from. The significance lies in what is left unsaid.

It has never been different to this. But it wasn't always the same. There used to be shadows cast on the hearth rug, bold lines across the carpet like cage-bars. There used to be a fireguard in front of the fire.

'What's that?'
    'It's a fireguard.'
'What's it a fireguard for?'
    'To stop you sticking your fingers in the fire.'
'Why can't I sticker my fingies in the fire?'
    'Because it's hot!'

That was not the beginning. I was only two years old, but it had already started. The match had been struck. The conflagration was underway.

The fireguard is not there any more. I have unrestricted access to the temperature control. I'm sitting on the hearth rug with Eugene Bloom and the fire's full on. We can get as hot as we want. Everything is different now, but something is still the same.

We're sitting on the mat, having a chat. We've had ones like this before. There's a bit of a recurring theme to our after-dinner discussions. They're all about the chicken and egg situation. Which came first. The origins and beginnings of things. This one is a conversation about Genesis.

'If Adam and Eve were the first people on the planet,' Eugene says, 'their sons and daughters must have had sex with each other. The entire human race is raised on a hotbed of incestuous relationships.'

He always talks like this when he's had a drink or two. Like he's eating words that have taken hours to prepare. Most people snatch at sentences like fast food, but Eugene's last as

3

long as a sit-down meal. They're all lip-smacking nuances and slow-roasted meaty matters.

'A hotbed of incestuous relationships. It's the best-kept secret in history,' he is saying.

He leans towards me, gleaming wickedly, fringe clinging damply to his glistening forehead. Joining in is irresistible, though his argument is unscientific.

'It's a load of old baloney,' I tell him. 'If we're all descended from the same couple, we must be so inbred by now, we're a completely different species. Degenerates. Increasingly removed from the Garden state of perfection. That's the very opposite of evolution.'

'No, it's not,' he says.

'Yes, it is,' I insist. 'Adam and Eve would have to be something else to start the whole human race between them. They'd have to be more and less than we are. Subhuman, or superhuman.'

'Well,' Genie beams, 'that would explain the existence of this God everyone keeps going on about.'

Baloney.

'It's nothing to do with God,' I say. 'It's genetics. By the time Adam and Eve were great-grandparents, the newest additions to the family would be disgusting slugs crawling in slime.'

'Primordial slime?' Eugene asks.

'Possibly,' I shrug.

'Then I don't see your problem,' says Eugene. 'Everything evolved alright in the end, didn't it?'

The firelight is doing amazing things to his eyes. They're glowing, and the shadows of his eyelashes touch his cheek like the bars of a cell. When he looks up at me his eyes are as bright as the prospect of being freed from prison.

'You mean, we've been here before?' I ask. 'We came, there wasn't anybody else to play with so we had to play with ourselves, but we did it too much and our hands and arms wore down to stumps till we were disgusting snake-like things . . .' Eugene is slapping me playfully so I break off to slap him playfully back. 'But after lying in the slime for a few generations our limbs started growing again and we got up and boogied at the highly populated party this planet had now become?'

Eugene has captured both of my hands.

'You've got the soul of a poet and the spiel of a philosopher,' he says.

There's a big bead of sweat on his brow, a ball of reflecting firewater.

'Are you too hot?' I ask him.

'Don't change the subject,' he smiles.

'I'm not!'

'Some people would remember the time in the slime though, wouldn't they?' Eugene persists with his theory. 'They'd remember the secret, the original sin. They'd know why the dinosaurs died out.'

I watch him wipe his forehead with an expressive hand, but take no notice of his words. Those who talk in riddles don't deserve straight answers.

'I'm wondering whether to turn down the fire,' I say.

'Only if you'd prefer to date the fake coal scuttle.'

That is Eugene's idea of a joke.

'I don't think I can stand a whole weekend of this,' I say. 'You're going to drive me mad.'

'You don't need me to drive you,' he replies, 'You could walk it in five minutes.'

'I'm only five minutes away from madness?' I laugh, despite myself. 'But you're so fast, you're one step ahead of me. You'll be mad first.'

'Why did the dinosaurs die out?'

His face comes so close to mine I can see he really wants me to answer the question. But I don't know what to say. I look at his lips, still open, softly inviting a response.

'They didn't fancy each other,' I suggest.

'Don't you think so?' He sits back in surprise.

'They weren't very attractive.'

'They might have been to each other.' He sounds hurt.

'They were awkward shapes. Spiky.' I almost spit at him in my excitement. Verbal sparring is how I get my kicks. I collapse backwards on the mat.

I can smell the carpet dust baking in the heat, dust of burning school books and hot cross buns, dead verrucas and African violets. Dust from the pyre of my childhood. A ridge of worn woollen tassels at the edge of the rug runs between my shoulder blades in a line across my spine. I'm longer than this rug now, but long ago I was short enough to lie underneath it and completely disappear from view.

'Can you see me?'

    'Shhh.'

'Can you see me?'

    'Shhh. I'm reading.'

'Can you see me?'

    'Shut up!'

'But can you see me, can you, can you?'

'Yes.'

'No, you can't.'

'Yes, I can.'

'Can't.'

'Can.'

'Can't, can't, can't!'

'Right, I'm telling my mum of you.'

'No, find me, go on, find me, find me!'

'I already know where you are.'

'No, you don't.'

'Yes, I do.'

'Don't.'

'Do. You're under the carpet.'

'No, I'm not.'

'Yes, you are.'

'No, I'm not.'

'Shut up!'

'I'm indivincible. You can't see me.'

'You're a babyish big-job and you can't say your words properly. I hate you.'

'I'm not under the carpet.'

'I'm telling my mum of you.'

'I'm not under the carpet.'

'Well, in that case, Grace, you won't mind if I jump up and down on the carpet, will you?'

'Ow! OW! I'm telling . . . MUMMY!'

I remember being small enough to hide underneath this hearth rug, while that big boy jumped up and down on top. He was a bit of a bully. He taught me a few lessons I'll never forget. He educated me privately, in crime and punishment, in pride and falling, in bossiness and boots.

I sit up abruptly, twenty-five years of carpet dust in my nose, a sneeze released like the persecuted from my mouth.

'Bless you,' says Eugene.

'Thanks,' I smile.

Through watery eyes he looks good enough to talk like a vicar. His face radiates blessing. His smile is so warm.

'What are you thinking?' he asks me.

I'd rather not tell him about the boy who taught me I'm too bumpy to hide under hearth rugs by bruising one of my ribs. It will hurt him now as much as it hurt me then. I open my mouth to say 'nothing', and nothing comes out. I can't lie to Eugene, but I can make light of the matter.

'I had a flashback,' I say. 'This carpet may be full of holes, but it's got a better memory than I have. It keeps reminding me of things.'

The hearth rug and I have shared experiences. It's close to the heart of my family home. I haven't actually lived here for years. I haven't lived here since I left to go to college, abruptly one autumn. If I had died, the haste with which my parents removed all traces of my presence from their house would have been called indecent. I came back at Christmas to find my bedroom a spare room, full of pictures down and possessions packed up. But they had to do it, they said. They had to bury the body of my belongings, or my absence would have screamed at them in the night, and all the empty spaces would be shaped like me. They thought that leaving home was a suicide of sorts.

My mum and dad are at a psychoanalytic conference this weekend. And while they're away, I'm playing mouse in their

8

house. I've got a new flat now, but I miss this old home. Many of my memories are stored here, lying dormant in rugs, hiding behind curtains, collecting dust on the mantelpiece. My childhood hopes are still hanging around in the hallway or sitting on the windowsill, watching for the postman; my childish fears are lurking on the stairs, unleashed with every angry flush of the toilet or bang of a door; my childhood joy is still dancing barefoot on the summer lawn and bouncing on beds on Christmas morn. I don't want to lose these memories. I've come to find them while the house is quiet. Mum and Dad know I'm here; I'll stay and have tea with them when they get home tomorrow.

Eugene will, too. I didn't invite him. But he's got the right to invite himself.

'What was your flashback about?' he's asking me politely. 'When did you flash back to? Where did you go?'

I don't want to tell him. He's so keen to hear it, it seems he must already know the answer. He's testing me, having sneaked a look at the back of the book. But it's my memory.

'Was I there?' he says.

He's taking up too much of my head-space. I can feel my privacy shrivelling.

'Eugene, please,' I implore him. 'Give it a rest.'

The reprimand is thrown like a stone into the smooth pool of his face. Frown lines crease his forehead.

'Sorry,' he says.

It's okay. Now that I've told him where to get off, there's plenty of room on top again.

'I'm sorry,' says Eugene, 'I know I'm the bane of your life. But you're the bane of mine, too, if it's any consolation.'

'I don't know what a bane is,' I say.

9

'It's everything,' Eugene replies.

I reach out and touch his hand and a feeling like the snapping of shiny plastic passes between us. Things have grown up so serious between us. But I remember playing with toys on this hearth rug, in front of this fire.

'Action Man is at the Mouth of Hell.'

'So is Sindy.'

'That's not fair. You said she was going shopping.'

'She's been.'

'What did she buy then?'

'Sweeties.'

'Where are they then?'

'She's eaten them all up!'

'Well, that's not going to help Action Man much, is it?'

'Yes.'

'How?'

'They were special sweeties. Sindy is strong now, and . . . and . . . her head goes all the way round.'

'So?'

'She can save Action Man from the . . . what? The Mouse of Hell.'

'How?'

'Well, first of all, you've got to push him further in. Like that. See. His legs go between the bars.'

'Put his arms in, too.'

'Yes! Arms in, too; arms in, too! There. Will his head fit?'

'No, the gaps are too small. Don't! You'll pull it off.'

'Sindy's head comes off. Look.'

'No, don't. Sindy's going to the rescue. Come on, quickly! Poor Action Man is in great pain.'

'Okay. Oh.'

'What's the matter?'

'He won't come out.'

'Pull.'

'I am pulling. He's stuck.'

'Oh no! Mummy! Grace has got my Action Man stuck in the fireguard!'

'Sssh! I've got his arms out. It's just his legs. They're too fat.'

'Get them out this minute or I'll call my mummy again.'

'Okay. Oh. Oh no!'

'Oh no! Mum! Mummy! Grace has broken my Action Man in half and his legs are still stuck in the fireguard!'

Poor boy. His Action Man met with a sad end. I can still see those disembodied legs caught like the remains of a soldier on a barbed-wire trench fence. I can still see the scorch marks creeping up his calves and smell the burning rubber.

I'm still holding Eugene's hand, and there is electricity between us.

'This is killing me,' he says. 'I'm trying to be cool, but I don't know how long I can last. If you don't say something soon I think I'll explode.'

With these words, he blows my mind to the size of the dome of St Paul's. An unreal ringing resonates around the space inside my head and echoes in my ears. From this height, there's a whole new perspective on things. I'm standing in the whispering gallery, a place for hearing secrets, if ever there was one.

'What do you mean, Eugene?' I ask.

He leans toward me and sweat drips like a tear onto the knee of my jeans.

'Don't you remember?' he says.

11

'Remember what?'

'The secret.'

'The secret what?' I'm watching the wet sweat dry before my eyes, fading back to the true blue of my jeans, as if it had never been any different.

'The beginning,' says Eugene.

'There wasn't one,' I say. 'Believe me. It was always like this.'

'Was it?'

'I can't remember anything else.'

'Can't you?'

'You're older than me. Why don't you remember it?'

'I do.' Eugene gives me a look that goes right through me and leaves me forgetting to breathe.

'Well, tell me then,' I say after a pause.

'No,' Eugene shakes his head, 'I'm not going to tell you if you don't already know.'

'Why not?'

'Because it will be a shock.'

'Oh . . .'

'A big shock.'

'But . . .'

'I can't tell you. You'll have to tell me. If I go first and you've forgotten it, you won't believe me.'

'I might . . .'

'You'll think I'm making it up.'

'Are you sure . . .'

'You'll be really shocked.'

'Maybe we shouldn't . . .'

'Talk about it? Yes, I'm sure we shouldn't talk about it. But listen, I slammed my brakes on two minutes ago and show no signs of slowing down yet. My tyres are wet. I can't stop.'

'Eugene . . .'

'I can't stop.' He really does seem to be out of control. 'Once upon a time, everything changed between us in the blink of an eye. In a twinkling, everything was different. If you didn't notice that, you might have seen me running away afterwards. I hitched a lift on the motorway to Madness and Lies, and I've been living in Lies ever since. And now, you know, it's time to hit the road again, but it seems there's only one way to go.' He gives a hysterical giggle. 'I can see the outskirts of Madness and I don't like the look of it much, but I hate living in Lies. By the way, are you in town or are we talking on the telephone?'

'What?'

'Are you living in Lies, too?' he says.

'Er, no. Hello. I'm hailing from Highly Mystified.'

'But suddenly the fog is clearing.' Eugene is calming down now. 'I know when you're lying, Grace. You're not highly mystified at all. You remember what happened, don't you? You do remember what happened.'

I'm on the spot, roasting in front of the fire. We're going round and round in circles. We could go on like this forever, but there has to be a way to stop.

'Nothing happened, Eugene,' I say. 'That's what I remember.'

'Do you think I started it?'

'Nothing was started, silly.'

'I know I was a bit of a bully . . .'

'But . . .'

'I didn't mean to abuse you . . .'

'You didn't . . .'

13

'Grace, let me finish.'

'You don't need to finish,' I cry. 'There was no beginning. It had always already begun. We were only children. We were not to blame.'

But I don't know who I'm trying to kid. There was a beginning. I know there was a beginning, because after it everything was different. Once upon a time everything changed between us in a twinkling of an eye.

I have trouble remembering it because I tried so hard to forget. Or maybe I forgot it easily because it was too difficult to understand.

The beginning looks like a series of photographs, black and white photographs. It doesn't move through my mind, it's not an animated sequence; but if I think fast, like flicking through the pages of an album, it jerks with an automated life of its own.

Sometimes I remember it with my body, instead of my mind. Then I remember it slowly, graphically, in glaring technicolour. Then the sound is in stereo, the sensations are crystal clear, the smells surround me. The present moment grows dark, a shadow of my memory, a facsimile of the original. I'm living in the past, and it's a problem, because every time I feel like this I'm supposed to be fucking someone in the here and now.

Truly, the story tells itself best when I'm making love.

The rest of the time, it's not even as real as photography; the images are drawn in pen and ink. They're illustrations, pictures from a book that's a cross between Enid Blyton and William Burroughs.

And we were only children.

14

Eugene's thirteen, I'm eleven.

It's a Sunday night in late autumn, time caught loosely between baths and bed, made all the merrier by the threat of school tomorrow, a final hour of fun snatched from the satchel of the setting sun.

We're wearing our dressing gowns. Mine's pink and fluffy with applied rosebuds, Eugene's is rather like his father's, in Black Watch tartan with a great tasselled bell pull of a belt. His slippers are imitation-adult, too, high-sided and sober-soled, while mine are a mini riot of purple and pom-poms.

We're sitting in front of the fire, waiting for wet hair to dry. The air is warm and fragrant with soap and cocoa. The television is on, a semi-religious programme of the nineteen seventies, which manages to bring light ale and sheepskin and someone standing up in a speedboat right into the centre of Christianity. We're not watching it. We're playing a game.

It's one of those games that gets made up as it goes along. It starts as a fight: Eugene pushes me over and pins me to the ground and I have to struggle to get free. So then I do the same to him, though his greater size and strength make for more of a challenge. It's like trying to stay on a bucking bronco. A see-sawing, hee-hawing situation follows.

We take it in turns to splat flat on our backs, sat on by a bouncing bubble-bathed bottom. It's all hands, knees and a boompsadaisy. But fingernails soft from soapy water do not scratch, and sweet teeth do not bite; this is a friendly match with much laughter. We are well balanced; he's bigger and stronger, but I'm better at tickling and making funny faces.

One of my faces is more frightening than funny and it works every time. I can roll my eyes round in my head so only the whites show and still appear to be staring right at him. Eugene surrenders immediately. When I tease him afterwards he says that for all he knows I might have 'really gone like that', and he didn't want to provoke me. He's seen a horror film called The Evil Dead at his friend Quentin's house, in which the terrifying special effect had occurred, and he couldn't bear to see it happening at home.

A cup of cocoa gets kicked over. We don't even notice at the time, though with hindsight I remember a wet warmth spreading up the backs of my legs. I'm writhing under Eugene. I could roll my eyes and he'd rock off in an instant, but that's too easy now. It's boring. I tickle him and he laughs helplessly. His tummy rubs against mine, our legs are tangled up in twisted nightwear. And then, on a wild irrational impulse, I blow gently in his ear. It works wonders. Eugene has braced himself for a massed attack, but I find a tiny chink in his armour. He shrieks, piercing my ears, and leaps into the air.

I wrestle him to the ground before he has time to draw breath. I'm good at this game and Eugene's getting a proper thrashing. Now I'm on top of him again, riding like a jockey, and I can't resist giving a whoop which resounds like a whipcrack. Then I give another, which breaks off abruptly, as something unheard of happens.

Something unheard of happens. I don't know what it is. I've never come across anything like it. There's a sensation like two pieces of a jigsaw puzzle snapping together. I feel full inside; satisfied in a way that no amount of sweets or meat has ever made me feel. I feel like I've eaten a horse.

I look at Eugene. He's looking at me. I look guilty, but his eyes are enormous and innocent. I've stopped moving, but he's only slowing down.

Are we still playing?

There's a pregnant pause. And then a can opens and fizzy drink bubbles up, corn pops inside my body. My heart bangs like a balloon. The moment of silence and stillness gives way to an internal circus, with trapeze wires twanging, a breathtaking turning through high space,

16

then a burst of applause or white noise. I stay in the air. The act isn't over yet. I'm not coming out of the arc.

But Eugene pushes me off him, roughly now. The game was exquisitely pleasurable, but we're not playing any more. As we separate, I feel him pulling out of me, long and thin and soft and sticky, like a snake shedding its skin, or regurgitating an egg whole. This is serious. Something was inside me, and it's coming out prematurely, unformed as poo, too soon to survive. Something's being born that is going to die. The disappointment overwhelms me. All I can hold onto is my breath.

Eugene gets up and leaves the room without looking back at me. I don't see his face so I don't know if he's sad or happy, but I can tell from the tension in his shoulders that he's holding his breath, too.

I try to shout after him, but I'm speechless with shock. Where are you going? Don't go. Are you going to tell anyone? Don't tell Mum. She won't believe it. I don't believe it. We didn't . . . did we . . . we didn't have sex. Did we?

Scared to death, I sit by the fire, and shed some scorching tears. This is bad. If we tell anyone, there'll be big trouble; bigger than when Action Man lost his legs in the fireguard, bigger than when Eugene broke the arms off my Sindy in revenge. I've forgiven him for that, but will he ever forgive me for this? He's got up and left the room without looking at me.

From that day forth all I really want is to get him back. All I want is to go back to the beginning and get him.

That was the beginning. I'd forgotten it until tonight. It was out of my mind, except when I had sex with someone else; then I was out of my mind, so I never remembered it in the morning.

All I want is to hold Eugene, long enough to know that he

17

doesn't hate me after all. And suddenly, for the first time, he seems within reach. Now that I'm aware of the memory I'm only aware of when I'm making love, it is us making love, which means he loves me, which means he doesn't hate me.

I hold my arms out to him. They're not like Sindy's. It's as if the limbs are growing back after years of lying snake-like and unconscious in the slime. We're sitting on the hearth rug where it happened when we were children, but we're grown up now. We're sitting on the hearth rug where it wasn't supposed to happen but it did.

It was an accident. A freak accident. A happy accident. I'd rather be a happy freak than an astral philosopher. Slowly as planets our heads are moving into alignment. Our eyes are guided by the stars. Like the hands of a clock as it grinds to midnight, Eugene and I come face to face.

'Now?' he asks, the incredible question.

'Or never,' I say, decidedly.

The time that is now has been waiting for us, it has always been here, by the fire. It has been happening here invisibly, all along. We have altered ourselves to meet this preordained moment in history. We have arrived at this point breathless and battered, but we were never going to be late. We came too early once, and often we didn't come at all, but it just wouldn't have been possible to be late.

Because, once it starts, the kiss is continuous.

Our lips come together soft as slow-motion pillows fighting in the night. But unlike children misbehaving beneath the bedclothes, they stay put. Because this kiss has been coming for ever, and once we lock into it, fate is sealed. Slightly parted, our lips stay in place while we breathe in each other's air and feel each other's hair on first-time faces.

It's the taste that makes my pulse race. Some biochemical substitute for cocoa is tingling on his tongue and ringing bells all over my body. What is this big boy made of? Sugar, spice and puppy dogs' tails. He is not altogether nice.

But his kiss comes from the heart. It beats me why we've never done this before. No, I tell a lie, I do know why. Our electric defences have never been turned off. And when they are on, they're more of a deterrent than jaws barbed-wired with dental braces, mouths like minefields. All hostilities are on hold today.

This kiss is a conversation. We're speaking in depth. I didn't know a man could be so talkative. He's got so much to ask me, so much to say; so much in common with me that I want to clap him, toot him, trample all over him like a dog myself in the joy of discovering that actually, he's a bit of a lady.

Our lips stick, his eye lashes my brow, my nose lies snoozing in the broad shadow of his. The closeness is catching; along the length of our bodies the touch is spreading, the heat is rising. Arms wrap around shoulders and legs are wound around legs; chests, bellies and pelvic girdles come up against their opposite numbers, fuelling with friction the furnace that burns between us.

His kiss is dribbling down my chin now. It dives off the jutting, and slides down my throat. My head is back so far that my neck is breaking, but then his lips hit some lymph glands, and my neck goes limp. The improbable angle is no problem.

There are hands, too, two hands, hands full of a handful. Overflowing flowery bra kneading immediate release. It's a miracle. He is making five thousand loaves and fishes out of a single pair of breasts. I'm a disciple; the one who made the cock grow three times, I hope. I grope.

19

Clothes brush naked flesh. The eyes at the back of my bra are unhooked, and I am unhinged; a loose woman, with a tightening in key places. My flesh is crawling with pleasure, all over him. There is a titanic heaving.

A titanic heaving. And then it is going down. The *Titanic* is going down; no, hang on, it's him. He is going down. I swallow hard. My mouth is full of feathers.

But there are button-flies in his mouth. This guy is a genius, undoing my denim trousers with his teeth. This can only mean one thing.

Oh, you French-kissing fannyface, get lost between my great white thighs. Risk pressing those perfect lips to my hungry maw, though they may be stretched out of all proportion by the strength of my yawning. Dare to caress this time-switched ticking clitoris with the tip of your tongue, though the subsequent explosion may tear it out by the roots. Be prepared to drown in my juices, brave boy; for fingers in dykes never held back a flood of this magnitude.

Orgasm: black water breaking on a black beach with phosphorescence like fucking fireworks.

When it subsides, the protagonist is washed up at my ankles, panting into damp pants. Slowly he crawls back to the breast. I see him coming cross country, over the storm-shaken landscape of my body, head first. The glare from my whiteness lights up his face.

I see the sublime smile which he applies to my nipple. Lips, plump as bees, sting. Pain and pleasure are the same thing. Both cause swellings.

Sweet mothersucker. There is such ancient asking in this young man's mouth, such timeless thirst, as he drinks me to the brink, as he brings me to baby talk, as his lips make me bare, make me lisp, make me swear to fully fill him.

Orgasm: somersaulting rainbows in a spinning sky.

When it's over, he's still got his jeans on and there's something trying to get out. Something hard in all this softness. Shaking fingers fumble with stiff flies. Our four hands touch at his crutch and clutch each other; serious supporters of this silly sport. We cling together for safety, like we've clung on a hundred other occasions; but we've never been a danger to ourselves before.

Suddenly he lets go. He can't hold on any longer. Rising up, he lowers his trousers in one graceful swoop; and underwear in the seven colours of the spectrum slides down to earth, over the sunspots and rain shadows of his curved body.

I stare at him. Not his face. At the other part that has an eye to see me looking. Wild thing, snakestick, heat-rashed violet, indigo and red. How very different to my own dear indignity.

How it stands up on its own, with no visible means of support. How it strains at the seams. With the ease of a seamstress, I fold it in my fist and feel the threads throb, feel steel through shifting silk. This won't hurt. Though my strokes slowly get harder and faster, I don't have the strength in my swan-neck arm to break him.

But the movement stirs up a watery aroma, something steaming, something seedy. I bend my head to the source of the smell, and saliva pours. For a moment I pause, kneeling at his knees. I know you're supposed to shut your eyes when you pray, but I want to see if he's a believer. I look up at his face.

His eyes have undressed while my gaze was averted. I've never seen them naked before. Scantily clad in suggestive

21

underwear, yes; but naked, no. They look back at me in awe and devotion as I start to slaver over his hot stave.

I'm starving. I gobble at his gooseskin till I gag. I'm cavernous inside, hollow ribbed and echoing like a cartoon whale. My darling Eugene's dick slips salty as a ship's mast between my lips as he sinks slowly to his knees.

And down below, his hands are still to the pump. He's got half a shell-white buttock in each, clenching my muscles. His fingers are forward; they force their way into my private places and personal spaces without waiting to be asked. His touch is delicate and dangerous as glass.

Orgasm: I shatter, I splinter. Only my orifices stay in one piece. Only the holes are whole.

This is the beginning, the middle and the end. There is nothing except this. My eyes are closed but there's brilliant light. My body is part of someone else's. It's him, the man of my dreams, awakening me, totally heightening my sensitivity, taking me to levels I've never had the pleasure of experiencing before.

It's him. Eugene. In the flesh. Really doing it to me. I wish I could pay more attention to the graphic details, memorise the exact order of events, but I'm mesmerised, in a sort of trance. There's power surging through my body but my eyes and ears have turned themselves off and rerouted it all to my sense of touch. All I can feel is the feeling.

I wish I could see, too, but somehow it seems that the graphic details, the actual acts, are not where the beauty lies. In fact, they're somewhat grotesque.

If we could see ourselves, we'd stop. We might watch, but we'd no longer be lost in the being, the feeling. But I do want to see Eugene. I want to look at him. He is what I love.

I open my eyes and see his eyes already open. His eyes and my eyes are the same. When our gaze meets there's an explosion of energy that feels like a new sun has started in my stomach. The look he is giving me, the look that is going into me, knocks me flat.

I lie like a bed spread on the floor. He kneels between my knees. I hold out my arms to him, and my legs, and I will him towards me with my eyes and my Ohs.

He comes closer, as the strings of our attachment contract, winding tight around the spools inside us. He comes weaving between the strands of my being, plaiting with the pattern of my very DNA.

It probably feels like penetration to him, when his penis parts my petal-lips and starts to probe. But at this point, it's all done by suction. I'm magnetic, me. I'm pulling him in. I'm easily as strong as he is. Easily as long.

Oh.

It feels like penetration to me, too.

I'm impaled on him. Crown and sceptre. I'm full to the brim, and beyond it, full to kingdom come. But kingdom's not going to come yet.

We're still kissing, a continuous kiss. We're kissing at both ends, now; kissing on a continuum. It's a conversation, a long conversation, with all sorts of ins and outs. We can't speak properly, we're pre-verbal and just making silly noises, but we know what we mean.

If we could hear ourselves, we'd stop. We're not supposed to talk to each other like this. Our wordless words are expressing an inexpressible bliss. Our sightless sight and speechless speech is bringing us to a mindless understanding of each other. Our bodies are conducting the conversation. It's all in the rhythm.

The togetherness is shaking me.

It's overtaking me.

Orgasm: tambourine.

Orgasm: trumpets.

Orgasm: tuba. Only a big man can make this happen. The earth is as unstable as a makeshift podium under a full orchestra coming to the finale. The earth is moving, but I don't even notice, because I'm in heaven.

Then Eugene leaves my body. Like an untimely death, like in an accident, he is there one minute and gone the next. I try to catch him. I snatch with arms and legs struck numb. Contrasting senses of *déjà vu* and shock hit me as he pulls out prematurely. I've crashed. I'm as crushed as a mini in a motorway pile-up, and my mouth's making a noise like something slammed against the hooter.

'Oh, no, why did you go?' I whine.

'Gracie, my baby, we can't do it without a condom,' Eugene replies.

I know. I would have been thinking the same thing, if I hadn't been blissed out of my head. I sit up sticky and shaking. Reality comes back like a bucket of whitewash and I notice our nudity for the first time. Eugene's standing up.

'We shouldn't be doing it at all,' he says.

If his body were not so beautiful I would be tempted to agree. What we're doing is dangerous, and we never should have started it. But Eugene's erection has got my name on it, and it's going to take a lot of rubbing off.

'Have you got any condoms?' I ask, and sound like I'm paralysed.

'There's one in my bag,' Eugene mutters.

While he's looking for his bag, I try to collect my thoughts. I seek them out and destroy them, because they're spoiling everything. I've dreamed and hardly dared to dream of this evening, I've thought of nothing else and sworn to never think of it again, it's sent me to sleep and kept me awake, caused exam failure and flashes of winning inspiration. But the moment I've been waiting for is happening now, and this is no time to be wasting it.

At last! Eugene sees his bag behind an armchair and bends over to pick it up. His buttocks part like lips for a kiss, and his balls look like a lovely uvula in the deep throat between his thighs. It sends my passion surging again. I get to my feet and rub up against him while he rummages in his rucksack. His back fits my front exactly, but his sides are wider.

'Found them,' he says.

The sound of a struggle with cellophane and cardboard fills the room. I try to lead Eugene back to the fire because he's cooling off. He keeps his back to me, his shoulders towering, his hands wrestling with skin-tight rubber and a fast-shrinking member. It's a race between the clock and the cock. He's got himself in a right state, ending up with two inches when he really wants eight.

I open my mouth to encourage him. But before I can speak or do anything else to him, I hear car doors slamming in the drive outside the house. I hear high heels on the front door step. I hear a key slipping smoothly and easily into the lock.

'Godfuckandbloodyshit!' I say. 'It's Mum and Dad!'

The voices in the hallway ring clear as bells, then the lounge door opens slowly and my mother's face appears. Eugene and I finish our frenzied attempts to get dressed; we stand frozen but try not to look stiff.

'Hello, you two,' Mum says. 'Not in bed yet? It's so late.'

'We were just on our way,' I answer breathlessly. 'What's happened? Why have you come back so early?'

Mum walks into the room, wafting cold night air and the whiff of car rug and travel sweets. She's bright-eyed and excited.

'There was an accident,' she informs me. 'A cow fell through the ceiling. I've never seen anything like it, though your father says it's a sign of the times. It landed on the speakers' platform and killed an important delegate, so the whole conference was cancelled. It'll be in all the papers tomorrow. I posed for photos with a piece of splintered lectern. We'd already given our speech luckily. It went down very well.'

'What?' I can't take this in.

'It was a hit,' she says. 'Is that so surprising?'

'How did it fall through the ceiling?'

'Sorry?' She eyes me suspiciously.

'Was it on the roof?' I ask.

Eugene comes to my rescue, better late than never.

'Was it a protest?' he says.

'No, there was no protest,' Mum smiles and shakes her head at him. 'They loved it. Don't you believe me, you unkind children? They lapped it up. Ask Garth if you think I'm telling a porky. I'll ask him myself. Garth!' She goes to find my father who's struggling with luggage in the hall.

I take a tentative look at Eugene. He's looking back at me with his face dead. When it's alive and kicking, his articulate eyebrows convey ironic messages as clearly as Morse code.

Now it is morose, clouded over, with no hint of a sunny twinkle to save us from the seriousness of the situation, and no wink to keepsake our secret.

'Tell them I was good, Garth,' my mother is still in earshot. 'They're saying that people protested. They're ganging up on me.'

The sound of Mum's voice is giving me a sinking feeling in my stomach. She's already scared me witless by coming home unexpectedly, and now she's piling all this paranoid shit on top. I pull back my shoulders and take a deep breath.

'The cow,' I say calmly as she drags Dad into the room, 'I only questioned the cow.'

'Good grief!' Dad spots the flushed face behind my cool façade at once. 'Look at the state of Grace. What has she been doing?'

'I don't know, dear,' Mum shrugs, but I see her eyes slide from me to the drinks cabinet and back again. 'They said they were just going to bed.'

I hate the way they treat me and Eugene like figments of their own imagination. It's very undermining. No wonder we're such shadowy charcoal-lined characters.

'All I want to know,' I try again, 'is how the cow came to fall through the roof of the conference centre.'

Dad smiles at me so self-indulgently that it's not really me he's smiling at. 'Who are you calling a cow?' he says.

'Mum said a cow crashed onto the speakers' platform and killed someone,' I say. 'I just want to know how it happened. Actually I couldn't care less how it happened, but that was how the conversation started and I'd like to get it over with as quickly as possible so I can go to bed.'

'I'd like to know if the cow died,' says Eugene.

'What on earth is the matter with you two?' says my father, heading for the fire. 'It wasn't a cow. It was some heavy office machinery from the room above. The burden of bureaucracy.' He squats to turn the fire down, and sits accidentally on a tea tray from hours ago. 'Oh, good,' he says. 'Is this tea hot?' He feels the pot. 'No. Never mind. I'll make some more in a minute.'

'Mum said it was a cow. I'm going to bed now.' I leave the room abruptly. I don't get very far.

'I did not say it was a cow, Grace. Come back and acknowledge the fact!'

Another thing that annoys me about my mother is she always acts like more of a child than her own children do. This makes her impossible to disobey, but piss-easy to punish. I turn on my heel at the foot of the stairs and go back into the living room. I know what I have to do. It's what I've done since time began, and I'm amazed she hasn't learnt to see it coming.

'Tell her what she said, Eugene,' I say.

His sigh fills the silence that follows, like air in a balloon. I can hear the agony of his indecision, an aural inflammation. It's cruel of me to ask him. He's often told me not to. But he also says that the truth is always right, and for some reason, in this house, he's the only one who's allowed to tell it.

'You said it was a cow,' says Eugene to my mother. Then he looks at me as if I'm the thorn in his side.

The balloon bursts.

'Did I? Did I say it was a cow?' Mum gasps and giggles. 'Aren't I a silly girl? But I remember why it was now. We were talking about them, weren't we, Garth, as we drove into the drive. The cow, everyone's favourite bit of meat, is itself a vegetarian. Isn't that Zen? No wonder they're sacred in the East. Anyway, it must have been a slip of the tongue . . .'

She breaks off suddenly and stares hard at my jeans which are half undone, which I hadn't noticed till now. I start to back away, covering the inches of exposed pink with my hands.

'I'm going to bed,' I say. 'Goodnight, Mum. Goodnight, Dad. I'm sorry your conference got cancelled.'

'Grace,' my mother calls as I leg it up the stairs, 'aren't you going to say goodnight to your brother?'

'Goodnight, Eugene,' I say. The words are like sickness in my mouth. My head spins like heads spin above toilet bowls. I feel as pale as porcelain, as low as kneeling. Dirty.

My brother doesn't reply.

Two

By the next morning I hate myself so much I don't wait for the shower to warm up before stepping in. Water like a stream of spite hits the top of my head and spits at my shoulders, a hail of tiny stones, of ice. Cold water starts coursing down my spine. I stand still as a dead person, blue as a black person, silent as a deaf person in the splashing. When it reaches my bottom I take the thrashing. I don't flinch from the flow, because it's just what I deserve.

I nearly fucked my brother last night. And not for the first time, either. I think I would have finished it properly if our parents hadn't interrupted us. Eugene and I are over twenty-one, so we count as consenting adults, but no matter how grown-up we get, we'll still have the same Mum and Dad, and we'll always be related.

The water is running down my legs. It's tepid now and gushing, warm and fast as urine, and I feel as stupid as a child wetting myself in public. I'm overcome with shame.

One day, long ago, I asked my mother why I was called Grace. She said it was because I had good table manners. I wasn't satisfied with her answer so I went and asked my father.

He replied that I could glide like a ballerina, and gave me a book to balance on my head. I asked my brother next. He said I was called Grace because I smelled like an old lady. I cried at this, so Eugene took the book, which was a dictionary, off my head and told me I was a gift from God.

I've always wanted to have sex with my brother. Ever since we had it by accident because we didn't know what sex was yet, I've wanted to have sex with him. I've never admitted it before, not to him, not even to myself; not in so many words. But it all starts to make sense now, our ridiculous love–hate relationship, the endless miserable merry-go-round of attraction and repulsion.

Eugene's fourteen, I'm twelve. We're waiting outside our martial arts class for a parent to pick us up in the car. Our teacher is waiting with us. He wants to have a word with Mum or Dad.

They arrive, both together, in their embarrassing red Cortina. Eugene and I get shamefacedly into the back. We bundle in, hoping to make a quick getaway, but Lee is knocking politely on the passenger window and Mum winds it down.

'Hello,' she says.

'Hello, Mrs Bloom,' says Lee.

'How are you?' Mum asks.

'I'm fine, thank you,' says Lee. He pauses, then sits down on the pavement, squats in a martial pose he adopts with ease, so that his face is level with my parents in the car, and his white trousers don't touch the ground. 'I feel the time has come to speak with you about Eugene and Grace.'

'Oh?' says Mum.

Dad revs the engine.

'I fear there is a problem,' says Lee.

Dad's revs fade away.

'Eugene and Grace work very well,' smiles Lee, 'with the other children. They are coming along nicely, they are committed to the art. However . . .'

Dad turns the engine off.

'When they pair up, when they work together,' Lee continues, 'something goes wrong. You see, ours is an art of self-defence. It is designed to be used only in case of attack. With deflective moves all blows bounce off the body, and the violence of the aggressor defeats itself. We do not fight.'

'No,' says Mum. She looks at Dad. He looks over his shoulder at me and my brother in the back.

'This evening,' says Lee, 'I had to forcibly separate Eugene and Grace. I had to physically restrain them. They were fighting,' he says, 'as if they wished to kill each other.'

'Oh,' says Mum. She looks back at Lee. 'Thank you for letting us know. We'll talk to them about it. I'm sure it won't happen again.'

'It already has,' says Lee, sadly. 'Over the last few months, it's been building up. At first it was just a slap, but it seems that as soon as they get their hands on each other they can't stop. They abandon the etiquette and lose themselves in a deadly serious wrestling match, Mr and Mrs Bloom.'

Mum and Dad are silent.

'I haven't said anything till now because I'd hoped to be able to resolve the matter myself,' Lee sighs. 'I'd hoped that the art would answer the problem. It's not just a physical thing, not just a sport; it's strongly spiritual and it induces a certain state of mind. Peace pervades as a person's mental energy grows. I'd hoped Eugene and Grace would no longer feel compelled to overpower each other, once they were aware of their own inner strength.'

'Okay,' Dad says. He starts the car.

'Thanks,' Mum nods at Lee.

'Wait,' says Lee, 'what is to be done for your children?'

'We'll talk to them about it,' says Mum.

'I think perhaps it would be better if they did not work together for a while,' says Lee. 'I run classes every night of the week. Perhaps it would be best if Grace and Eugene came separately, until such time as they can discipline themselves to the natural laws of the art.'

'Okay then, thanks, bye,' says Mum, winding her window up.

We drive off. Mum and Dad don't take Lee's words very seriously. The only thing I remember about the talking-to they gave us was Mum saying, 'And you thought we were hippy old sticks.' We didn't go to separate classes after that. I went to the same class and Eugene didn't go at all. He took up a new hobby. He got his first computer.

The water is getting hotter. I think it's going to scald me. I turn to face the shower head, and sleepy dust, though I didn't get a wink all night, is dislodged. My dry eyes are bedewed. In the warmth and wetness I'd be blooming like a rose washed by summer rain, if I wasn't just a daisy or a dandelion, ready for weeding. Like any flower, my heart is also my head. I can't lie to myself. If my heart says I'm a disgusting piece of compost, my head can't persuade me otherwise.

The water starts to burn, but I make no attempt to adjust the temperature. I firmly believe I need a telling-off of the first degree. I've been asking for one for years.

When I was thirteen, I had an experience in my Religious Studies class. Halfway through the lesson I came over all fervent, and had to sit on my hands to stop myself sticking them up, because I had a question to ask the teacher. Somehow I managed to contain myself till playtime, when at the sound of the bell the other pupils rose as one and rushed off to eat apples.

I sidled up to the desk at the front, and shyly addressed Mrs Smith.

'Excuse me,' I said, 'is it wrong to think about your brother in bed?'

Mrs Smith was shuffling a stack of exercise books. She looked up at me and smiled.

'It's perfectly alright. It's right to remember everyone you love,' she said. 'But remember, too, Grace, bed is not the only place to pray.'

I think I said thank you, and backed away, but I knew she hadn't answered my question. She didn't understand that I'd meant it sexually. My bid for salvation, my unspoken plea had fallen on deaf ears. I remember the confusion I felt at this, because it is strongly connected with what happened next. I went to the toilet block, a grey concentration camp place, and in a grim cubicle found that my first period had started. The shock at the sight of the blood has stayed in my mind. Every month it comes like the anniversary of a murder to remind me of my secret feelings for my brother, and the awkwardness of expressing them.

With the tight and painful passage of time, these feelings for Eugene have grown. I've kept them in the closet, where the cramped conditions cause deformity, and the darkness makes them pale. I've tried to grow out of them, to grow without them, to be a strong-limbed, beautiful and sexy individual with healthy skin and no heart murmurs; but I've remained attached to him, all weak and watery; a toadstool, a toad, a stool.

My first boyfriend only lasted five minutes. It was a case of mistaken identity at the sixth-form disco. Eugene was there, too, with his 'behind the bike shed' boys; the whole gang of them, not dancing with girls. He and I had a little chat while my young man was buying me some orange squash. I was only asking if he could supply us with some of the vodka his own plastic beaker was spiked with. But Eugene had drunk it all, so I returned to my partner empty-handed and found him in the grip of a jealous fit.

'Don't be silly, he's my brother,' I said.

But my boyfriend didn't believe me.

'People don't dance like that with their brothers,' he said.

'We weren't dancing. We were talking,' I laughed.

'You were smooching,' he shot back. 'Touching and talking and moving to the music.'

The Hell's Ballerinas were playing their latest hit, with an insistent rhythm thrusting away beneath an insinuating melody.

'I was just trying to get some vodka,' I said.

He threw the cup of orange squash in my face. It stung for a moment, but was mainly sticky.

'He's my brother,' I protested. 'Eugene.'

'Grace, people don't behave like that with their brothers,' said my boyfriend and walked away.

That was the last I saw of him. He'd only lasted five minutes. I still couldn't fathom out what I'd done wrong, so I went home with Eugene, who didn't seem to find anything amiss; and either didn't notice the unsightly orange-squash stains on my white ra-ra skirt, or politely pretended not to.

Scenes from the darkness of my past; the skirt, the stain, the hurt, the pain. Yes, I even stooped to writing poetry at one point. But really I'm a mathematician. I do things by numbers.

When I was sixteen and Eugene was eighteen he went away

to university. He went as far as it was possible to go. He went to Glasgow. Mum and Dad drove him up there, on a dismal Saturday in early October, but I didn't go too. I'd been invited ice skating with some friends.

I stood on the doorstep in my dressing gown at eight o'clock in the morning. The car was loaded. Dad was manic, Mum was depressed. I just looked at Eugene.

'I'll see you at Christmas, Grace,' he said. 'Until then, have a succession of nice days. Stay up late and eat cereal to save waking for breakfast, sit around in my room and have imaginary conversations, kick the shit out of my spare football and get into trouble with your girl gang; but on no account look in the old shoe box at the back of my wardrobe.'

The first thing I did when the car containing Eugene disappeared from view was to go upstairs and into his room where I opened his wardrobe doors. The sparseness of its contents made me gasp. It used to bristle with overcoats and jumpers, burst with the scent and colours of my brother, but now only a few faded or unfashionable garments were hanging there and it smelled of old wood.

I took the shoe box out and headed for the bed. Again I stopped short. The bed was so freshly rumpled, still warm. As I sat down on it, I could feel my heart breaking. Deep in bereavement, living only in the past, I hardly had eyes for what was in the shoe box. But it turned out to be a present for me.

This is why I thought my brother was a god. He had the power to rewrite the Pandora myth completely. In her story the box not to be opened was full of evil, in mine there was nothing but good.

That's no comment on the actual contents, which were a pair of enormous pink fluffy bunny slippers, a tiny boxing glove on a key-ring and a bottle of cider; more a statement about the nature of the gift, which came as a pleasant surprise to cheer me up.

I was, however, inconsolable. I went ice skating with my friends as planned, but due to a lack of concentration on my part I got run over by someone's blade and lost the top of the little finger on my left hand.

It's amputation was symbolic. Eugene had left home to go to university. He'd left me, and I was incomplete without him. I had a bit missing. I didn't realise this at the time of course. I had a vague sense that the bottle of cider he'd left me wasn't deep enough to drown my sorrows in; but I had girlfriends to go out drinking with, all of whom had bits missing, too, and anyway, there were loads of other boys to play with.

So the start of Genie's academic career was marked by my blood spurting like red ink across the ice. I'd forgotten that until today. This scalding shower seems to be stripping layers of memory away, sloughing off the dead stuff like skin, to reveal the long-past moments still pulsing with a life of their own deep in my unconscious mind. Now I'm remembering when I was in the final year of my maths degree, and Eugene phoned to invite me out in a foursome with him and his new girlfriend.

It was the first I'd heard of her. I'd had a string of short-lived things since I was fifteen, a succession of one-night stands, but I'd never introduced a boyfriend to my brother; and because I'd never met any of his conquests, I'd assumed Eugene had even less success on the romantic front than me.

That may have been the case so far, but suddenly there was this Sharon. We arranged to meet, to have a drink, very sophisticated, in a pub in town; Eugene and her, and me and my latest escort.

It was like seeing Gandhi in a pair of glittering earrings. I'd never seen my brother with another woman and it came as a shock, coming across him so out of place, coming into view through the lush plastic foliage of an Embankment pub. It seemed so strange to be the one who wasn't already there with him, the one just arriving, with a law student on my arm like a sensible handbag.

Sharon had dark hair and a face so bright I could hardly bear to look at it. She was all over Eugene. When he introduced us she turned to me and smiled, and said she'd been looking forward to meeting Eugene's sister, as if he belonged to her and not me. She'd only known him a few months and already she thought she owned him.

I sat opposite them across the square table while my partner went to get a round of drinks. I was pinned in place at the point of a triangle, with Eugene and Sharon at the other corners, and I could really feel the tension between us. I was used to being just me and Eugene, one to one, a simple exchange of energy; but now Sharon was in the picture, too, and she was distorting it, because she thought she was his number-one woman.

I tried to pretend not to notice, to just be nice and polite and normal, but Sharon said she was an actress and insisted on being the centre of attention. She wasn't a proper working actress, though she kept tossing her hair back and talking about some fringe play she'd been in: she was just one of the army of unemployed, whose ghostly professions, the jobs they would be doing if they could, continue to haunt them.

I was drawn into a debate with her.

'I've never understood the attraction of acting,' I said. 'Wouldn't you rather be yourself?'

Sharon replied that it was the best way to find yourself, up there on the stage, artificially lit so you can't see the audience, allowed to shout and scream without getting told off.

'But you can't use your own words, can you?' I protested. 'You have to say what's in the script.'

Sharon said something about there always being room for improvisation, but I was adamant. Actresses are people who have no minds of their own, just dumb bodies to fit the parts some superior individual has crafted.

Eugene came to Sharon's defence, but instead of simply challenging the argument I'd put forward, he launched a personal attack on me.

'You act, Grace,' he said. 'You act all the time. You're acting now.'

I was taken aback. All I could manage was to splutter, 'I'm not,' before turning with a very false smile to the law student who'd just got back with the drinks.

The evening was not a resounding success. By the time we'd downed that first round I was ready to go home. I'd dropped out of the conversation entirely, and was trying to hold back the tears. Eugene and Sharon were talking to the law student about law and students, but I could tell they were only thinking about themselves by the way they were feeding each other peanuts.

Every so often Sharon gave me a veiled glance, and I would feel myself flush with rage as I imagined her marvelling inwardly how unlike my brother I was, instead of realising that actually we were one and she'd never be able to come between us. Eugene ignored me completely, and when we left the pub, at the unnaturally early time of ten past ten, he didn't even say goodbye. The look he gave me said he was livid, but he shook the hand of the law student, put his arm around Sharon, and strolled nonchalantly in the direction of the river.

I wanted to be an actress at that moment. I wanted to shout and scream without getting told off. I wanted to say 'Stop! Sharon, you boat-rower to Hell! He's mine! He's not dead yet. You can't have him.' But instead, I went back to my hall of residence with the law student, limping arm in arm like a pair of unbalanced scales.

This water is too hot. Much as I hate myself, much as I want my sullied flesh to melt, I have to adjust the dial. I twist the slippery white plastic in the direction of a blue arrow and the relief is instant. The water is still hot but not boiling. The water is warm. I hold my head under again, and a whole new cascade of memories fall upon me like a fit; flashing lights, defamiliarised feelings that seem to come from dreams. Memories come flooding back. A scene from a long way away suddenly zooms into close-up: a move that makes me so dizzy it seems that I must have been distant, on my travels, and this was here all along.

We went on holiday one summer in a threesome, me and Eugene and my first proper partner. Nigel was a real boyfriend, even though he was a lot older than me, and I was discovering the joys of regular sex for the first time. We stayed in a caravan on the Isle of Wight, which seemed like a good idea at the time. Actually it seemed like a great idea, sleeping with Nigel every night for a week.

At bedtime on the first evening though, I went cold. The walls of the caravan were paper thin, and as Nigel and I climbed between the sheets, I could hear Eugene creaking into his bunk next door as clear as day. The separate bedrooms, a double for me and the tiny children's for Eugene, were merely an illusion, insubstantial as the cardboard walls dividing them. If Nigel and I had sex, Eugene would be able to hear us, as if he were in the same room; he'd be there with us, every inch of the way. The caravan would shake and, uncomfortable in his bunk, he would be carried along with our rhythm.

So I couldn't do it. I was thinking about Eugene, so I couldn't have sex with Nigel, because it would have been like having sex with Eugene if I wasn't thinking about Nigel. I'd known all along that thinking about your brother in bed is wrong, but thinking about your brother while in bed with another man must be worse. I had to put Nigel off, pretend to fall asleep, and lie there overcome with frustration which focused tight on Eugene.

The same thing happened the next night, and the next. It spoiled the holiday. Three of us in a caravan was too intense. Eugene's presence loomed large in the darkness, bigger than Nigel's expectant form, and sex would have been the size of a lie. I was not an actress. I couldn't play Nigel's lover when I really wanted to be Eugene's. To do it silently was impossible. I was full of feelings I couldn't release. They had to be kept secret.

And I haven't whispered a word of this to a single soul. I haven't shouted and screamed it, I haven't sung it, I haven't written it down and pretended it was just a story. I have kept it completely to myself. But not even my ordinary everyday self has known about it. My ordinary everyday self is innocent. It's the self kept for special occasions that holds the key to my guilty secret. The self that's unlocked once a year at most.

Eugene's twenty-five, I'm twenty-three. It's Christmas and I'm drunk at dinner time. Not so drunk I don't know what I'm doing. Drunk so I know what I'm doing but I don't care. Eugene must be drunk, too, because he doesn't seem to know what I'm doing till I've been doing it for ages.

We're sitting at the family dining table, with the white lace tablecloth dangling down around the edges. There is Mum and Dad on one side and me and Eugene on the other, all wearing brightly coloured paper crowns as if to say everything's okay for a day.

I'm out of my head though. My concentration has slipped under the table. I can hardly see what's happening above the white lace layer; pudding, I think, more drinks being poured. My entire focus is on the fact that our legs are touching, mine and Eugene's, not just our knees, not just by accident, not just bumping into each other as our bodies above table level respond to the cut and thrust of conversation and food.

They're glued together, from the knee to the hip, held tight by sheer magnetism as we sit close enough to be girlfriend and boyfriend, or Mum and Dad. My thigh is pressed against Eugene's and his thigh is pressed against mine.

I can barely contain my excitement. Every breath I take tells me I'll burst, because this shouldn't be happening; but with each exhalation there's a great letting go, a surge of strength of feeling. I go on talking and laughing and I guess I must be getting louder and louder for suddenly I make Eugene jump. He jerks away from me, head first, turning to face me as he tries to get his ear away from my mouth, and then seems to realise what's going on below the table, for I see a fleeting look of horror in his eyes before he lowers them. He moves away completely, chair and all, clumsy and clearing his throat. It's just a new note in the family dynamics, an eddy in the ebb and flow of interpersonal communication, and I don't suppose Mum and Dad *notice anything but a slight change of position around the dinner table; but to me, something earth-shattering has happened.*

My eyes are filling with tears now, tears and tap water; and the see-through walls of the shower cubicle have steamed up so I can't see through them. I can't see a thing. I can only feel the earth-shattering event that happens next. I get a space-age sensation as the door of the shower capsule opens and vacuum seals again at the speed of light; it's fast, but not quite fast enough to prevent a blast of hostile air and an alien body entering my self-containment, my solitary confinement.

Eugene is in the shower with me. I can tell him by touch. He is big and cold, all goose-pimpled flesh, bone-dry but slipping on the wet floor. They say that blind people can see colours with their fingers: if I didn't know that Eugene was white I'd swear he was green, the green of copper oxide, the green that grows corrosive on ships' bottoms, and appears as if by magic, especially in the spring. Eugene is the colour of chemical reactions, with a smell to match. Salt and spice pour from his pores and cling to him, like perfume oil on his skin. It's impervious to water, even to the ocean of water produced by this power shower. The volume is overwhelming. We're surrounded entirely by a pounding sound. I don't think I'd hear if he said anything.

But I don't think he's saying anything. There's no room for two in here, so we have to stand close enough together to become one. The only place for him to put his arms is around me. As our bodies touch, the green seems to turn to gold. This is alchemy.

Eugene puts his arms around me, but I thought he was going to hit me. Ever since that first night by the fire when he walked

43

away without saying why, I thought he was angry with me. Ever since that first accidental sex session, I felt as if there was a fight started, an argument unfinished, between us.

This morning it dawns on me that he may have been feeling the same way as I have all along; shocked because what we did was wrong and sad because we'd never be able to do it right. His every ambiguous expression seemed to blame me, but I suppose they could have been guilty looks. I was so convinced that he was angry with me that I never stopped to consider me being angry with him. Today, in this state of shower-blindness, I seem to see more clearly. I can feel his heart beating, and it's fast but not furious.

I hear the rattling of plastic, the lifting of lids, the squeezing of scented air. When we were kids, he used to pull my hair. Now he is washing it. He squirts shampoo onto my scalp and gently massages it in. I don't deserve this kindness. I'm too full of sin. I'm surprised he can't feel it, so sensitively do his fingers caress the contours of my skull and tease the tangles out of my hair. Maybe he can feel it. Maybe the cap fits him, too. I sigh as my brother holds my head right under the source of the water, and dirty bubbles rush away from me in soapy waves, leaving squeaky-clean hair.

Maybe it's me who's squeaking. This is a bit of a baptism. I can't help feeling born again. Very vulnerable. It's dark with my eyes shut and the water's fall is deafening. I could be anywhere, but I should have faith that the situation is safe. Eugene must know what he's doing. He's older than I am, and he's got better qualifications. Admittedly, they're not in midwifery, but he wouldn't do anything stupid.

Eugene smooths conditioner over the crown of my head. Holy water's all well and good, but a dip in the font can leave

44

your hair flat or frizzy or flyaway. Most men are afraid to use a conditioner, bar barbers. Actually even barbers fight a bit shy of it, so it certainly sorts the sheep from the type of guy who isn't embarrassed to call himself a hairdresser. My brother perceives the need for bounce and body, manageability and shine; and it makes him so much more of a man. I'd look up at him but my eyes would sting if they were open, and with them closed I'd look like a baby. So I bury my head between the twin twitchings of his male breasts, where a pair of token nipples – sticky with mingled sweat and steam – are the next best thing to the possibility of suckling.

My big brother may be a complete freak of nature, but he sure knows how to nurture me. He's slapped a second helping of creamy conditioner onto me. But not on my head. Not even on my shoulders. He's slapped it on my bottom. With a blob of the pearly substance in each hand he is smearing my buttocks. From the small of my back to the fat of my thighs he is buttering me up and greasing me down. He's getting the measure of my body, he's weighing it in his hands, and he's going to pay for it one way or another.

But it doesn't feel wrong when Eugene touches me rudely like this. It doesn't feel perverted, and I can't understand why. There's generally believed to be a chemical incest-repellent, released in our bodies to make our relatives sexually repugnant to us. That's the popular theory. But I don't feel this incesticide, it's not being sprayed on my desire till it dies. The locusts of lust are still swarming. Eugene might be any man with his arms around me, watery romance in his eyes, and his erection hot and dry between our bellies.

Oh, I wish I could get my brains wet. They're in a terrible tangle, a knot of 'to be's and 'not to be's. What is the question?

Whether to nobble my brother. Will anyone else mind? Will anyone else suffer, or sling arrows, or take arms in outrage, if Eugene and I have sex in the shower, if he caresses me under a waterfall, kisses me in the thundering stream, looks at me naked in the gleaming eye of the storm? Fortunately, no one else can see us; and what they can't see won't hurt them.

Eugene moves me, pressing me up against perspex, into the apex where the shower walls meet. My buttocks warm holes in the cubicle's condensation, like big hot pennies on a frosty windowpane. Higher up, my shoulder blades make pound signs in the steamy surface. But there's no purchase, my feet have got no grip on the wet floor. I grab at his hips and he dips and his dick slips into me. It happens suddenly but it stabilises me.

I've never done it standing up before. I've always thought sex standing up was a myth, in which the princess needs a goblin, a magic footstool, a pre-kissed prince the size of a frog, in order to do it properly. I'm a different height to most of my lovers and it just hasn't seemed possible. The angles are all wrong. The lines get broken. The path less travelled turns a corner and proves to be impassable; not so much overgrown, as underreaching.

It seems that I've been missing something breath-hissingly sharp and sweet. Slow and lengthy, he slides in and out of me. I feel forty hands high on horseback, taking the cross-country route.

We're eye to eye and smile to smile. We're kiss to kiss. I open my mouth and Eugene's tongue comes in to shelter from the storm; a shivering slug, covered in strawberry pimples. I'm out of the water's line of fire, but it's still running through Eugene's hair and streaming over his shoulders. The odd trickle is conducted down his arms and onto my back where his hands lie, then trickles down some more. It's getting hotter and hotter. I don't know where it's going to stop.

But stop it must. Once again, we're caught without a condom.

My body is such a bastard. The minute I think about contraception it brings me to the brink of a rubber-ripping orgasm. As soon as I think how Eugene and I must on no account have a baby, it gives a series of convulsive vaginal gulps, as if I'm trying to drink him in. My thrusting overrides my thinking in a burst of primeval passion.

A drone as long as a didgeridoo issues from my throat and resounds around the bathroom, interspersed with wild animal noises and whoops and wails.

But Eugene doesn't come too. He has more self-control. I remember him telling me once, out of the blue and with no follow-through, that children born of incestuous bondings have very big heads. I myself read in a magazine that such kids may be mentally handicapped; but my brother has more of a sense of genetic responsibility than me, and he unselfishly stems his own urges.

Down below Eugene is withdrawing, pulling his penis slowly out of me, for good. As he goes, a little panic flutters like a trapped butterfly in the pit of my stomach. My heart starts falling like a dead bird. The feeling of bereavement is getting all too familiar.

But I smile bravely. And Eugene kisses me, in a way he's never kissed me before. It could in no way be considered brotherly. He is pulling slowly away from me; but once we get far enough apart for him to have a panoramic view over my shoulder he starts to pull away faster, his face shutting up like a telescope, his eyes shrinking into tiny dots as the lenses zoom in on something.

Something over my shoulder. He's seen something through the steam, through the cloudy shower cubicle, where clear streams course through condensation, making peepholes in the perspex walls. He's seen something in the bathroom.

But it's worse than that. Something is only a nameless horror until it sees you, too. For Eugene, the apparition has just become someone.

'Mum,' he merely mouths. 'Mum!' No sound comes out. Then he whisks away from me, whirling wet through the shower door.

I take a while to work out that he's gone. My hands are still tingling from his touch, my tits are left hanging where his hands were. I'm in a state of post-orgasmic shock. My head is still ringing from the primordial screaming.

Mum must have heard me cry out. Of course she did. She's my mother. That's what she's for.

'Quick,' pants Eugene, appearing at the shower door in his underwear, 'get out.'

I don't want to. I want to stay in the warm and wet. I want him to still be inside me.

'Come on,' Eugene says, turning the taps off, 'get dressed.'

I wring out my hair, and listen as it echoes the last splashes of the shower. I listen as the water drains away. It sounds as sad as a life-support machine being turned off.

'Get out of the shower,' says Eugene.

'But I want you to come inside me.'

'Just shut up and get out, Grace.' Eugene removes me from the cubicle. 'We're in trouble.'

'Mum saw us,' Eugene shoves a fluffy towel in my face.

48

'Are you sure?' I say. I take the towel, wrap myself up in it and feign feeling secure.

'Yes,' Genie addresses the pair of jeans he's struggling into.

'I didn't see her,' I say.

'You were facing the other way,' he replies. 'But your arse was bared at her in a grin split from cheek to cheek. She must be having a fucking heart attack.'

I don't like his tone at all.

'If you'd thought to lock the door before you stepped into the shower . . .' I say.

'I thought I had locked the door,' Eugene interrupts me angrily.

As far as he's concerned, thinking that he locked the bathroom door is as good as actually locking it, and vindicates him from all further blame. I turn away, still smarting from the blow to my buttocks. The picture Eugene has painted of our mother's angle on the accident is not a pretty one; it portrays my backside as some sort of gargoyle. So to be brutally honest, I'm less upset about our mother's horrifying discovery than I am about the horrible way Eugene's behaving to my bottom. I'm jealous that Mum is suddenly the sunshine centre of his attention.

'Did you speak to her?' I ask, in the ice-cold voice usually reserved for adulterous spouses.

'No, she'd gone.'

'Are you sure she was really there?'

'Do you think I imagined it?'

'She seems to be looming unnaturally large in your mind.'

'Are you questioning my perception?'

'Does Leonard Nimoy wear stick-on ears?' I say. Something

about my sarcastic answer seems to lift Eugene's spirits, and the corners of his mouth.

'Look here, Grace old girl,' he smiles, 'arguing is futile. Shortly, we'll find out for sure whether she saw us or not.'

This wins me over. Now I know we're on the same side. I notice how differently the word 'she' sounds when he applies it to me and my mother. When he's talking about her the 'sh' could easily go on to become sheep or shit. But when it means me the tone is softer, used sparingly, like sugar. I find this strangely reassuring.

'Listen,' Eugene opens the door a crack and puts his ear out. 'I can't hear a thing. There'd be shouting if she'd seen us.'

I agree. In my mind's eye I can see Dad sitting quietly in the kitchen with the Sunday papers. I can see Mum rushing in with the unbelievable truth burning a hole like a Polo in her tongue. I can see her screaming her headline off at him. It's a grainy black and white picture, with flashcubes exploding like fireworks.

I can see it, but I can't hear it.

Eugene's opened the bathroom door some more. He sticks his head out and listens for a long time.

'Nothing,' he says, as he ducks back inside. I'm nearly dry now. I drop my towel on the damp floor and slip into my dressing gown.

It's a special dressing gown that stays at this house for me to wear when I visit. It's different to the one I've got at my own flat. Today it feels a bit like slipping into a sick joke, so I don't want to describe it in too much detail. Let's just say it's pink, with appliquéd rosebuds, and it puts Eugene in danger of pricking himself.

He waits till I've tied the girdle then wilfully grabs it and tries to untie it. But my double-knotting doesn't yield, so he gets me by the fluffy scruff of my neck and wrestles the thick fabric from my shoulders. My breasts appear like a pair of cherubs floating on cotton candy clouds of the stuff. He tries to catch them.

'Stop it,' I say.

Eugene snatches his hands back.

'We'll have to tiptoe to the top of the stairs and try to hear what's going down,' I say, shrugging myself back into the dressing gown.

We leave the bathroom in silence. We must have been in there for hours. The light on the landing has changed completely. It's mid-morning; sun the colour of honey is spread thinly on the carpet, dripping from a trickle through the window. There's a hush, as if the upper storey of the house is sleeping now that the night shift is over and the people have gone out to work or play. By this time of day we shouldn't still be up here, unless we're ill.

Halfway along the landing I hear someone coming up the stairs. The tread is strangely unfamiliar. I can usually tell whether it's Mum or Dad by the sound of their footsteps, shuffly in slippers or slippery in shoes. I can even tell what mood they might be in by the pace of their progress. But today, with my breath held and my heart missing beats, there's nothing reliable to measure the time by.

Eugene and I realise that we're holding hands, and let go of them without looking at each other. Our eyes are fixed on the point where a parent is about to appear, the top stair. Freed from his clutch my hand falls to my side, and the way it slaps my thigh expresses an emotion which is as hard for me to put into words as it would be for a spider to spin this sentence in cobweb thread on the ceiling.

Everyone always talks about the thrill of discovery. In all the modern myths and legends of illicit love that's the big *frisson* of excitement: for the milkman who delivers a teaspoonful more than a pint to the bored housewife; the trouser salesman who hides in the wardrobe when the lady's husband comes home; the night nurse who makes her rounds as deep as her favourite patient's night is long; the student and the teacher, the secretary and the boss, the politician and the vicar; they all get a buzz from the possibility of being found out.

I can't understand that attitude. For me, it would be much more exciting not to get found out. I can only assume that the milkman, the night nurse and the vicar secretly want to be discovered. They might not have the courage to come out of the wardrobe, but once the door is open it's all a big relief.

The head appears first. Before the feet reach the top stair, the head pops up above the banister. It's our father's. He's acting suspiciously, keeping down, levelling his eyes along the landing.

He jumps when he sees us standing there.

'Not dressed yet, Grace?' he says. He doesn't seem to notice my frozen expression, my stone pose, and Eugene standing statuesque beside me. Eugene's got his clothes on though, so he may be cloaked in invisibility.

'Er, no, I'm not,' I answer the question carefully, desperate not to be caught out.

Dad sighs at me, but only like he always sighs at me, I think.

'Well, get a move on,' he says. 'We're leaving in ten minutes, and I don't suppose you've had any breakfast yet.'

'Leaving?' I say cautiously.

'Yes,' Dad smiles, 'we thought we'd go on a family outing, seeing as we're all in the same place at the same time for once in our lives. I knew there had to be a good reason why the conference was cancelled, other than the tragic death, of course.'

'When was this decided?' Eugene doesn't bother to disguise the anxiety in his voice. He's allowed to sound a bit strange, though. Always has been. I'm not. I don't know whether it's because I'm the youngest or because I'm a girl, but I always seem to be carrying the container for the rest of the family's sanity, and that means keeping a steady gait and a level head.

'It was decided on the spur of the moment,' Dad says, 'Your mother had a brain wave.'

'When?' says Eugene.

'Just now,' says our father. 'Why? Did the pair of you have other plans for the day?'

Only screwing each other senselessly, Dad.

'No,' we whoop in unison. 'Oh, no.'

Eugene and I don't look at each other before speaking as one, and Dad doesn't seem to notice. I can't help feeling that if I were a parent, and my two children seemed to be in telepathic communication with each other, I'd notice. But Dad seems to suspect nothing. He lifts his head briefly above the banister-rail and gives us a normal smile, before disappearing downstairs again. We hear him whistling unconcernedly in the hall.

'He knows,' says Eugene, under his breath. 'He's acting weirdly.'

'He's always like that,' I whisper back.

'He kept darting glances at the bathroom door,' says Eugene. 'His eyes were everywhere.'

'Perhaps he was just shy of me in my dressing gown,' I reply. 'Don't be paranoid.'

Neither of us have moved a muscle since Dad disappeared. We are speaking without using our lips.

'Perhaps Mum didn't tell him,' Eugene says.

'Listen,' I whisper, 'if Dad doesn't know we were in the shower together then Mum didn't see us there; because if she had done, running to tell him would be the first thing she'd do.'

'What?' Eugene mutters crossly.

I grab his hand and pull him along the landing, away from the top of the stairs. He's got me flustered now. If Mum and Dad knew what had happened between us there'd definitely be shouting; not unconcerned whistling and invitations to go on a day trip. Eugene thinks everything's weird.

'You,' I say, 'are reading too much into Dad's darting glances and sudden desire to go for a stately stroll round some old church.'

'Grace,' he replies, 'I swear Mum saw us in the shower.'

I do believe him.

'But our parents are as blind as bats, and as belfry stupid,' I say. 'We must have dropped some clanging clues over the years, made more Freudian slips than we can remember; but even though Mum and Dad are trained psychotherapists, they never noticed a thing.'

'This time . . .' says Eugene.

'They didn't see a thing,' I say. 'Now, what shall I wear?'

Three

Going on a family outing is the last thing we should do. It would be better to stay indoors and clean up the skeleton cupboard instead.

But the secret which, until yesterday, Eugene and I were even keeping from ourselves, is not about to go any further; even though we are all climbing into Mum and Dad's car and driving off down the road.

They have decided to take us on a day trip to Durandal Castle. When they told us, Eugene gasped.

'That's a symbolic venue,' he said.

'Yes, it is,' they nodded and smiled, thinking that he just meant it's a nice place. But I saw the expression in his eyes and knew differently. He meant that it's a significant location. He thinks that Mum and Dad know about our incestuous relationship, and that the place they've chosen to take us, to play out the next stage of the story, really means something.

I don't think things are that serious.

I'm sitting in the back seat of the car, and there's no quicker way to travel back to childhood. I get the urge to turn around and make faces at the driver of the car behind, sticking my tongue out so far it leaves smears on the rear window. My head is full of the songs Eugene and I used to sing on long journeys, endless improvisations around misheard pop tunes and mispronounced operas, while memories of the trips repeat on me: packets of sweets and the sour taste of motion sickness, playing hangman and sleeping in neck-breaking positions, fighting and tickling and generally wriggling around on the sticky plastic of the back seat of the car. I remember being told to shut up, sit up, cheer up, wake up and wind the window up, from the space between the two front seats, the gap between Mum and Dad, through which all that could be seen was the road ahead.

My parents never appear so clear as they do when I'm staring at the backs of their heads. I seem to see them best when they don't know that I'm looking. It's how I see them in my dreams, always from behind, following them blindly into the distance.

They've both got red hair. Mum's is Pre-Raphaelite red, long and wavy, the same style as Botticelli's Venus, the same style as mine. Dad's is post-middle-age red, brittle and twisted, like little batches of Brillo gone rusty.

From behind, Mum looks really beautiful. But if she turns around, the Venus comparison shatters like a mirror. Her face is a shock. The nose is an enormous carrot. Her eyes are small and watery grey, sheltering under eyebrows the shape of haystacks. Her cheeks are turnip purple, round and rough. I love my mother, but I swear on her life that she resembles no one so much as Worzel Gummidge, the scarecrow.

We never say anything about her strange looks, in the same way that you don't mention the war in front of Germans. Once Dad caught me goosing behind her back and was so sad that I never did it again. His eyebrows met in a frown, and the corners of his mouth turned down, till he had a clown face, too.

Normally my father's eyes are like swimming pools on a sunny day and when he looks at Mum I assume he only sees her in the best light. There's a meeting of minds. They're bright, my parents. The pair of them have written a book together. They're a husband-and-wife team, with minor celebrity status in the world of psychoanalysis. They're called upon to give conference papers and occasionally talk on the radio.

I never listen. The way I see it, if they were any good at family therapy I would be a lot happier than I am today. Especially now that I know what I know about me and Eugene, and they're still oblivious to the fact of our sexual developments. It's been going on for years, since he was thirteen and I was eleven, if not before; and they've noticed nothing fishy, nothing amiss. We must have sat on the back seat of this car in various states of shock and trauma, in horniness and dilemma, and they've carried on driving regardless.

That's why I'm cynical about shrinks, who keep themselves sane by doing all the diagnosing and drawing the dividing line between reason and delusion. The psychological profession are just backs of heads, faceless drivers of the family car. They're taking everyone down the same road, but only one person is behind the wheel, and no one else can see the signposts.

Sometimes I think I'm wrong and my parents are going the right way after all. They certainly seem to have found the key to a long-lasting marriage. After all these years being lawful wedded husband and wife, they're still as thick as thieves. There's no chance of them filing for divorce. They're not bored, they don't argue, I never see them look twice at other men or women. They've always got their heads together in a book, cooking something up; even doing their tax returns makes them giggle like best friends over school homework. They never disagree with each other's answers, and they always complete each other's sentences correctly.

It's the perfect partnership, and that's why I think there must be something wrong with them. Is it natural to remain in wedded bliss for a quarter of a century? Is it normal to stay in bed all day with the same person you've been sleeping with for twenty-five years? Don't they ever spring up in the night, hot-flushed and full of fancy for a fresh conquest, a complete stranger, someone who doesn't know what they're going to say before they say it, and do before they do it?

If your spouse is carved so hard, engraved so deeply on your heart, your heart must be made of stone. That's what I think. Call me new-fashioned, but I believe people change, and even the perfect partner becomes impossible to live with in time. Perhaps my parents are in love with the backs of each other's heads, the snapshot, the dream image, the silhouette, the shadow, the outline with no infill. They've saved their marriage by throwing away their little differences, emptying their separate lives, recycling their personalities. They're all front and no faces.

And facing front in the back seat of the car, looking at my mum's head, I am reminded of that Magritte painting; the one where a man seen from behind is looking in a mirror at himself seen from behind. He looks not at a reflection but a repetition.

It's time to break the spell of this motionless hurtling through space. Car sickness makes me slump soporific on the seat, with strange thoughts that are getting me nowhere fast. I glance sideways, look sidelong at Eugene sitting next to me. I turn to take off my safety belt, to wake from the spell, and get a better look at him. His face is averted, staring through the window at the surreal suburban streets of our childhood. Porch and Porsche, lawn of grass-stained children and rockery of stone gnomes, house fronts with facial expressions, the wink of a pink curtain, snooty, double-glazed, too many smoking chimney pots. I wonder what Eugene is thinking. All I can see is the slope of his cheek bone, and the brush stroke of his eyelashes. I think he's feeling faint.

'What's the matter with you two then?' says our father suddenly. 'Aren't you speaking to each other?'

'That's right, dear, they are very quiet,' Mum says to him loudly. Then she looks over her shoulder at Eugene and me and says, 'Talk.'

Now that I know they've heard our silence, its grip on me tightens. I panic, and clutch at something secure, my parents need to treat me like a child, because I don't feel capable of an adult conversation with my brother while they're listening. I thrust my head between the two front seats and say, 'Are we nearly there?'

This is an old family joke. It all started when I was five years old and asked if we were nearly there as soon as we'd left the driveway, though we had a long day's journey to the Isle of Wight ahead of us. The response was so good – Eugene practically pissed himself laughing – that I revived the joke regularly every summer holiday till we left home for ever. Today, Mum and Dad smile as politely as they did the first time, but as I sit back relieved in my seat I see that Eugene hasn't even managed a twinkle.

He's letting me down. We're supposed to be in this together, getting out of it together, snatching for handholds in midair, catching each other like a trapeze team in spangly tights. But Eugene didn't even try to stop my joke falling flat on its face.

I stare at him angrily, but he doesn't look at me until we really are nearly there; and then it is without recognition. If he thinks pretending not to know me will solve anything, he is very much mistaken, the silly boy. He ought to be more like me, and behave normally.

The car slows to a halt, grinding across the gravel of a car park.

'We're here!' Dad sings over his shoulder, slamming the vehicle into reverse and swinging it into a parking space.

We get out. My parents squall over small change and make heavy weather about finding where to pay. I try my land legs, standing around stiffly, sulking deep enough to drown in. Eugene bends down to tie his shoelaces and stays there for ages.

All around me I see happy families flooding toward the castle gates; proper families, with parents who aren't speaking to each other and kids shouting. Ours isn't like that. Eugene and I aren't speaking to each other and Mum and Dad are miles away at the moat-side, putting the price of parking in a slot machine, but I can see their heads turning like dials as they look in our direction. As they walk back arm in arm with a sticker to display on the car they're whispering about us.

Or am I being paranoid? Eugene's silent panic is rubbing off on me. The whispering stops as soon as they get within earshot, and Mum says, 'Let's go back in time.' Then they lead us two by two across the drawbridge. The shadow of the portcullis falls on my face, and a sense of dread settles on my shoulders. Am I being paranoid or are we about to be beheaded?

As Mum and Dad join the queue at the ticket kiosk, Eugene

punches me on the arm and pulls me away from them. We melt into the crowd and hide behind a batch of Brownies, in a battlement-patterned patch of sunlight. He's pale as a ghost.

'I think they know,' he says. 'Don't you?'

'It's not my fault,' I snap. 'It was a dead giveaway, you not laughing at the "nearly there" joke. You always laugh at that joke. It's traditional.'

'I couldn't help it. I kept catching Mum's eye in the rear-view mirror, and she looks like she knows. I'm scared, Grace.'

My anger goes. The rock-hard emotion is eroded by Eugene's stream of words.

'Don't be scared,' I say. 'They can't do anything to us. We'll deny everything, okay?'

'Deny everything. Okay,' he says, looking more like a little brother than a big brother. Then he doesn't look like a brother at all, as he adds brazenly, 'So we won't tell them I love you.'

Bombshell. Eugene's never told me he loves me before. I'm not sure that he really said it now. In the buzzing of Brownies I could have imagined it.

'What did you say?' I ask him.

'I love you.'

I got an electric shock once. It was only a little one, from the Christmas tree lights, but it still felt like some unseen being had come up behind me, grabbed me off my feet and flung me across the room. It left me feeling like I was covered in glistening blue jelly, an unearthly colour.

Eugene has never said he loves me before and it gives me a shock akin to the electric one. I no longer seem to be standing where I was, nor is my skin tone monochrome. The sun comes on stronger and the buzzing in my ears sounds like music.

Extraordinary chords, changing as I breathe; in and out like a squeeze-box, but more beautiful.

Eugene loves me. Not brotherly. Not greeting-card sentimental. He loves me like a real person.

I hope I didn't mishear him.

'You love me?' I stutter.

'I love you.'

'I love you, too.'

The Brownies have gone. I didn't see which way they went. I didn't even notice them go. All I know is that Eugene and I are suddenly standing alone, in the middle of a medieval great expanse of empty space. Our parents are approaching, waving the tickets and looking a bit more cheerful. Obviously our last words were not unfurled above our heads on banners for them to read.

'Mum! Dad! Hi!' Eugene tries to act natural.

'Hi, guys. Shall we?' Dad casually takes Eugene's arm and gestures to Mum to do the same to me.

Walking arm in arm with my mother is like being a paper doll in a chain. I feel flimsy and two-dimensional, losing my identity to the family resemblance. But Dad's a supporter of hands-on parenting, and hurries Eugene on ahead up a long tree-lined avenue.

'We'll take the high road, and you take the low road,' he calls back over his shoulder. 'Let's meet at the tea shop at three o'clock.'

They've split us up. Eugene's going off with Dad, and I've got to stay with Mum. This must mean they plan to quiz us, woman-to-woman and man-to-man. But they have made a big mistake. The plan is doomed to failure. Mum won't get a confession from me; not because I won't give her one, but because she won't be listening. The only one of us she'll want to hear the facts from is Eugene. And Eugene can fob Dad off with bullshit till the cows come home, but he can't look Mum in the eye and lie. Meanwhile, I might, just might, have confided in Dad because he might, just might, have been genuinely interested in my plight.

If Mum had taken Eugene and I'd got Dad there could have been a result. As things stand, woman-to-woman and man-to-man, they're guaranteed to get a no-score draw. Over my shoulder I watch Eugene and Dad till they disappear, still staring over their shoulders at me and Mum. Then there's nothing else to do but relax and enjoy the scenery.

In the watery autumn sunlight, the castle looks grey-gold. It climbs up one side of a small hill and slides like treacle down the other, with the keep clinging on at the top. Walls aren't built like that any more. It's very old; parts of it date from the tenth century. Today it is run by elderly people who stand around waiting to name-drop about dead people.

Inside, fantastic rooms are furnished erratically. First, there's the great hall. All along its length, an assortment of tenuously linked objects are lined up against the walls. The incongruous display includes a dummy dressed in sixteenth-century papal robes, and stiff photographs of the current Duke and Duchess of Durandal meeting the present Pope in Rome.

Then there's the armoury where an array of inappropriate weapons – pistols, crossbows and pikes – wait for the invasion of tourists; for the Spanish, French and American inquisitions.

Next is a book-walled library, where time seems to stand still, though clocks softly tock. The books are behind red tape, in locked golden cages and stifling velvet drapes. There are thousands of them, holding their breaths, holding their tongues, till someone opens one to air its opinionated pages. There are four centuries' worth of first editions, the world's finest writing, philosophy and politics, poetry and plays stored in this room; and the only volume the lucky owners have seen fit to leave lying open on a desk in a red-curtained reading recess is the latest copy of a certain glossy magazine; a horse-riding, house-buying, hob-nobbing periodical, an antique-loving, arse-licking publication, as if this were the sitting room of a semi-detached in Surbiton.

Nevertheless, it's the best bit so far. The kitchen is a complete anomaly. You couldn't cook anything in there, not even crab-apple crumble and peacock pie. It seems the Duke and Duchess have cobbled together a few things that are old, expensive and have something to do with food, and left the rest to the general public's imagination. There is no stone oven, no flag floor, no ice chest, no meat hooks, no water pump; none of the conveniences of early modern living. This is history from a textbook with the pages torn out, and stuck back in the wrong order. It is a patchwork of mismatched pieces.

But it is here that my mother and I start to talk as we walk, exploring our own lives as well as those of old kings and queens.

'So,' says Mum, 'did you get a swing-bin for your kitchen?'

'I certainly did.'

'No more bulging carrier bags hanging on the doorknob, then.'

'No, there's still a bulging carrier bag hanging on the doorknob.'

'Is there? How come?'

'Well, Mum,' I say, 'to cut a long story short, I bought the bin but as I was carrying it home from the shop, I heard a strange sound. At first I thought it was just a baby crying in the house I was walking past, but something made me stop. I stood on the pavement and listened. It was outside one of those big squats at the bottom of my road, with broken windows and bits of motorbike in the front yard, and there was this weird wailing coming from the dustbin on the doorstep. I was scared, but I lifted the lid anyway. And what do you think I found? A litter of little kittens, bedded down in a black bin liner.'

'Oh, no!'

'Two of them were dead already, but the other four were still breathing. Only one had the strength left to miaow for its life. It stopped the minute I lifted it out of the stinking bin, as if it knew it was safe now. I didn't bother to knock on the front door and find out who they belonged to. Obviously it was not a good home. So I put the surviving kittens in my bright red kitchen bin and took them back to my place.'

'But you haven't got room to swing a cat.'

'I don't swing them, Mum. They moved in with me that very day and I haven't had to sling them out yet. They live in the bin. They love it. It lies on its side and it's full of straw and the swing-top is like the revolving door of a posh pussy hotel. They sleep in there, and in the daytime they come out to play. There are three girls and one boy. The girls are called Wynken, Blynken and Nod, and the boy's called Wankin. Their names come from that poem you used to read us when we were kids; do you remember, ''Wynken and Blynken are two little eyes, and Nod is a little head''?'

We're climbing an elegant staircase, and to my surprise Mum suddenly runs on ahead of me and strikes a pose at the top, saying:

Wynken, Blynken, and Nod one night
    Sailed off in a wooden shoe —
Sailed on a river of crystal light;
    Into a sea of dew.
    'Where are you going, and what do you wish?'
    The old moon asked the three.
    'We have come to fish for the herring fish
    That live in this beautiful sea;
    Nets of silver and gold have we!'
        Said Wynken,
        Blynken,
        And Nod.

Wynken and Blynken are two little eyes,
    And Nod is a little head,
And the wooden shoe that sailed the skies
    Is the wee one's trundle-bed.
So shut your eyes while mother sings
    Of wonderful sights that be,
And you shall see the beautiful things
    As you rock in the misty sea,
    Where the old shoe rocked the fishermen three:
        Wynken,
        Blynken,
        And Nod.

'Well remembered!' I catch up with Mum at the top of the
stairs, flabbergasted by this blast from the past. She recited it
rapidly, but recaptured all the slow-falling magic of this night-
song. I'd forgotten the hours she spent at the end of my bed,
singing me to sleep.

'What a sweet little lullaby,' I go on. 'It fits my kittens like a glove. I could hold them all in one hand at first, they were so small. They didn't even have their eyes open, which is how they got their names.'

'The poem doesn't mention Wankin.'

'No. But you must meet them, Mum. They're bundles of fun.'

'You've got no garden, Grace. What sort of lives will they have, cooped up in your top-floor flat?'

'They'll be sky cats. They'll rule the roofs. When they're bigger I'll let them out of the kitchen window, and the whole world will be their oyster. It's all narrow ledges and drainpipes and fire escapes out the back there. They'll make flying visits to every garden in the street and still be home in time for tea.'

'How will they get up to your flat again?'

'They'll climb. Cats can do that. They're a lot cleverer than we are.'

'What?'

'Well, they're a lot cleverer than we give them credit for. They'll probably work out a little route. There're plenty of trees. But if they really can't find a way, I'll send them down in a bucket or a basket on the end of a piece of string. I'll rig up a rope and pulley.'

'You can't do that! They'd panic and jump out. You'd be forever scraping their remains off someone's patio.'

'No one's got patios round my way. But that's beside the point,' I say. 'If they want to panic it's their problem. Having pets is a matter of facilitation, not total control. I saved their lives, but I can't live them, can I?'

'I don't know. I don't know what you mean, Grace. If you really want to keep your kittens you'd better find somewhere else to live. A house.'

67

'Yeah. In my dreams.'

'Well, if I remember rightly, Nigel asked you to move in with him.'

'So?'

'He's got a garden.'

'So?'

'Your cats would have somewhere to go.'

'That's no reason to move in with Nigel.'

'How long have you been seeing him now?'

'Ages. Four years.'

'Has he ever proposed?'

'He wouldn't dare.'

'But it's natural to want to, you know, marry the person you love. To be with them all the time.'

'I don't think so. It's my idea of a living nightmare, sharing your bed with someone every night, even if you've just had an argument and wish they were dead. Engaging in social intercourse as soon as you wake up in the morning. To have every hour of your day accounted for in a jointly held diary. To cook meals you don't want to eat, watch bollocks on television because there's nothing to talk about, sit on the sofa every evening because you can't go out because you want to go to different places but you're supposed to stay together. Anyway, I'm not in love with Nigel.'

'You're not?'

'No.'

'But he's in love with you.'

'I know. I've tried to talk him out of it, but it's hopeless. He's helplessly in love. They all are.'

'They? Who are they?'

'My lovers. They're all in love with me. I know it's silly, but they just can't separate it from sex. Don't get me wrong, I do love them, too; but only in the way that I love my kittens, or you, or the way the sunlight falls on this stone floor.'

Mum and I have walked to the end of the long thin corridor, a corridor flanked by vacant suits of armour trying to look occupied, and have come to a window where the light shines through coloured glass in diamond and cross and crescent shapes. I stand in its shifting kaleidoscope beam.

'I love them,' I say, 'but I'm not in love with them.'

'Good God, Grace. How many are there?'

'Only four.'

'Four!'

'Yes. Mum, I've told you this before.'

'No, you haven't.'

'Yes, I have.'

'No, you haven't.'

'Yes, I have. I knew you weren't listening.'

'Ssshhh. Keep your voice down. You've got four lovers?'

'Yes. Only one at a time, though. It's not a gang-bang.'

'Don't they fight each other?'

'Who?'

'Your four men.'

'Did I say they were all men?'

'Hey, look at that!' Mum is distracted. 'The bedroom where Queen Victoria and Prince Albert slept. How amazing! Come on, let's go in.'

The sign says it's the bedroom where Queen Victoria and Prince Albert slept, but I don't think the royal couple could have got a wink. The furniture's enough to have kept them up all night. The wardrobe and chest of drawers are so startlingly encrusted in raised detail they're positively hallucinogenic.

69

The real knobs to open the doors and drawers could only have been grasped after several false attempts. The bed itself is a ghostly apparition, a four-poster draped with gothic shrouds. But despite the obvious authenticity of this furniture, its careless arrangement in an otherwise bare room gives it all the style and character of a cheap DIY suite in a council flat.

Because the lifts aren't working, Mum and I make our way up the spiral staircase to the keep. We don't speak. Mum goes in front. I watch her rear view moving away from me while I follow at the same pace. It's just like being in the back seat of the car again, though a car would balk at the steep gradient, the sharp bends, the climbing curves.

We emerge at the top of the keep and look down on the garden. The trees are green and going gold and shivery silver as autumn sets in. The air is white with cold. The grass and paths and little walled flowerbeds slope away from the foot of the tower where it touches down on the knoll. It's the loftiest perch for miles around and we've got a bird's-eye view of the neighbourhood; fields and fields and fields, the sky and the sea.

If an English person's home is a castle, an English person's castle should also be a home. The stone cladding's quite classy, but the turrets are a bit over the top. In the days when the only ways to fight were with bows and arrows or boiling oil, living on a hill with a moat and a high wall between oneself and the bleeding obvious advancing army was as safe as suburbs. You could single the buggers out from the built-in archery bays, thin slits in the solid brick of the battlements. It must have been quite cosy up there.

But from what I've seen of Durandal, the Duke and Duchess might as well live in that semi-detached in Surbiton. What's the point of being able to lay your dining table for a hundred people if you've only got a handful of friends? Who needs a banqueting room when all that's on the menu is a quick crossword and a couple of surreptitious sherries before supper? What's the point of living in a castle, a bastion at the edge of British soil, when your poison's Spanish, your car's a BMW, and you spend your holidays in France. If you've got a keep, you've to keep something out.

As we stand there, Eugene and Dad come into view, on the long and winding path which wends its way all around the castle grounds and ends up at the lichen-licked bottom of the keep. Their talk is every bit as long and winding and obscured by trees as the path they walk on. I can't hear it, of course, but Eugene fills me in later. It goes something like this.

'How's work?'

'I'm on the dole, Dad.'

'I didn't mean it like that. You told me about some job you're doing on the side, last time we spoke on the phone.'

'No, that's just playing.'

'What are you playing at?'

'I'm trying to save the planet.'

'Having any luck?'

'Oh, yes. I could do it in theory. I could start tomorrow.'

'So what's stopping you?'

'The money, really.'

'Is that all?'

'There's also the small matter of persuading everyone I'm right.'

'Persuade me,' says Dad. 'Go on, try. What would you do?'

'The way I see it,' says Eugene, 'two problems are threatening life as we know it. Growing unemployment, and dwindling energy resources. Honest to God, we need a renewable source of light and heat, and fast. So what I'd do is get everyone who's out of work to help me save the world with nuclear fusion.'

'You're pro-nuclear?' says Dad. 'But it's so dangerous. The radiation . . .'

'No,' says Eugene. 'Fusion, not fission. Joining things together, not breaking them apart.'

'It's different, is it?'

'Completely different. Fission is dirty, smashing up atoms, scattering debris. Fusion is clean. It's two identical things coming together, creating energy, to power the planet,' says Eugene.

'It doesn't sound very natural to me,' Dad replies.

'But it is nature,' Eugene insists. 'That's how the sun works. It's the most natural thing there is.'

'Are you talking about solar panels?'

'No,' says Eugene patiently, 'I'm talking about making a bit of the sun in a box.'

'How on earth do you do that?' gasps Dad.

'Two positively charged protons,' says Eugene, 'usually repel each other, but if you give them enough energy to get extra close, they will bond. Their union releases vast amounts of potential power. But it's got to be really hot for this to happen, as hot as the sun. So the chances of it occurring naturally on Earth are phenomenally small. What you have to do is make some steaming proton soup and suspend it, spinning, in a magnetic field.'

'Not a simple wooden box, then?' says Dad.

'Regrettably, no,' shrugs Eugene.

'Nevertheless, I like the idea,' Dad says. 'Two identical

72

things uniting, their act the very freak of nature that got nature started in the first place.'

'I wouldn't put it quite like that.'

'Not scientific enough?' teases Dad. 'Who cares? Think of the psychological implications. This could be the subject of our next book. People are protons.'

'What?'

'We repel each other. Except on the rare occasions when two of us get close enough to release enough energy to light up our lives.'

'Oh, don't,' says Eugene.

'What?'

'It's not about therapy, it's about saving the world.'

'Love could do that,' says Dad.

'Well, you can think that if you like,' says Eugene, 'but we're talking about completely different things.'

'And fission,' Dad exclaims, 'that's hatred. That's when people blow themselves apart with the power of their emotions, resulting in severe psychological disruption.'

'Dad, you've got this way out of proportion. You're on a different scale. We're talking atomic disruption, here. Really serious shit in the intimate matter of our existence. Listen. There are things so small we're not even sure they're there: quarks, they're called, and three of them allegedly make a proton. People aren't nearly so important,' Eugene says. 'If you think about it, the smaller something is, the more intrinsic it is to the whole; and that's why I'm interested in nuclear fusion not nuclear families.'

'You think about it!' Dad is too excited to listen to Eugene's argument. 'If more people were walking around with halos instead of mushroom clouds hanging over their heads, the world would be a much better place.' Then he pauses. There is a stone in his path. He stops, not sure whether to pick it up, or stumble round it, or what. 'Wait a minute,' he mutters, 'nuclear families, you said?'

'No,' Eugene shakes his head.

'Yes, you did,' says Dad.

'I'm not talking about that,' Eugene quickens his pace. 'Too much fallout.'

When Dad catches him up he's gone all evangelical.

'Don't you want to shout it from the rooftops? Maybe your formula for fusion is the answer to our prayers. You could be the man of the moment we've been waiting for.'

'Don't be silly,' says Eugene.

'The messiah. You could be the second coming,' says Dad, to the surprise of a couple of passers-by.

'Shut up, Dad.'

'I'm serious. Look here, Eugene, someone's got to be the saviour and it might as well be you.'

'But angels would have appeared to me by now, and in heavenly chorus informed me that you're not my real father. They'd have told me to expect some divine intervention towards the end of the week, and to look out for an advertisement for the post of Christ child in my local press.'

'Very funny. Have you been spending a lot of time alone?'

'Most of it.'

'Are you bored?'

'I don't know. It's hard to tell.'

'It seems such a shame. You did so well at school. Everyone had high hopes for you. Are you quite sure you can't get a job?'

'You know what the situation is, Dad. You'd be unemployed, too, if everyone stopped behaving like it's a new age

74

before we've got to the end of the old one. Investment in science is the only way to change things. Otherwise, society is just digging its own grave.'

'Son, you could do worse than get into psychotherapy yourself. It's a boom industry.'

'But all you do is help people accept the fact that they're going to die.'

'No, you're wrong,' says Dad.

'Why?' demands Eugene angrily.

'Because you can't see past your paranoid delusions. You're neurotic. You're in a state of denial.'

'Fuck off!' Eugene blows his top.

'Don't take it personally,' Dad says calmly. 'Everyone's like that before they've had therapy.'

'You would say that though, wouldn't you,' shouts Eugene. 'Dad, you're the one who's deluded.'

'But we're not talking about me, son. We're talking about you. How's your girlfriend?'

'What sort of question is that?'

'An innocent one. How's Trudy?'

'Alright.'

'Still working at the hospital?'

'Yes.'

'Any closer to that promotion?'

'No. She's had a lot of time off.'

'Why's that?'

'She's not very well, if you must know.'

'Oh, dear. What's the matter with her?'

'We're not sure. She's having tests.'

'What sort of tests?'

'Hard ones.'

'What do you mean?'

'She undergoes an excruciatingly embarrassing and painful process, and then has to wait ages for the results.'

'And what do the results say?'

Eugene stops walking and stares at the ground.

'Eugene,' Dad asks again, 'what do the results say?'

'I really don't want to talk about this.'

'Have you told anyone? Your mother doesn't know, does she?'

'No.'

'Does Grace?'

'No.'

'You haven't told Grace?'

'No.'

'You haven't told Grace? But you're so close.'

'So?'

Eugene starts to walk again, faster.

'Calm down,' Dad says. 'Is it cancer?'

'No.'

'Aids?' Dad quavers.

'No.'

'Is she pregnant?' Dad is light-hearted with relief, but Eugene fixes him with a heavy look.

'It's some sort of mystery virus,' he says.

'What are the symptoms?'

'None of your business,' Eugene's voice cracks. 'I don't want to talk about it.'

'But I want to help you. Turn to your family. You're going to need a lot of support.'

'I'm fine. It's Trudy who needs support.'

'Is she at home?'

'Yes.'

'On her own?'

'People are popping in. I'll be back tomorrow.'

'Does she need nursing?'

'Not quite. But it's beginning to look like she will. It's so ironic. Being a nurse was the first thing that attracted me to her. Now I might end up being one instead.'

'You are allowed to sound bitter, you know,' says Dad. 'I won't blame you. Often, when one partner is taken ill, the other can feel angry or abandoned. Worse still, you might realise that the relationship should have been over a long time ago, but now there's no way you could end it. Feeling like that is nothing to be ashamed of.'

Eugene is walking one pace ahead of Dad. He looks angry and abandoned, but doesn't sound bitter.

'I don't feel like that,' he says, 'and if I did, I would be ashamed of myself. I promised to follow Trudy to the ends of the earth. Though secretly I knew that it was round,' he adds quietly.

'I can't believe you haven't told Grace,' says Dad.

Eugene is silent, snatching at a falling leaf.

'You're obviously not as close as I thought.'

Eugene still doesn't speak.

'Are you?'

Something in his father's tone makes Eugene turn.

'Am I what?' he asks.

'As close to Grace as I think you are?'

'Oh, look! There they are! Up in the keep. You can see Mum's head between the battlements. Wave, Dad, wave!'

Up in the keep, Mum and I see him waving. Mum waves back. I try once, but can't keep it up. There's too much weight on my shoulders. I lean on the balustrade as if this cold stone tower were an Italian balcony and Eugene were my Romeo. Our eyes are meeting though our faces are masked. We're star-crossed lovers, and no mistake; not from two different households but from one. Irreconcilable similarity is our fatal flaw. If only I were a Capulet, I'd catapult myself at him, quick as lightning.

'Let's go down,' says Mum suddenly and, disappearing through a trap door, starts to descend the spiral staircase at breakneck speed. We pass some people on their way up, a couple of women, panting and pushing each other. They're laughing and joking, and Mum says hello to them, but she doesn't utter a word to me all the way down.

At exactly three o'clock, we meet up with Dad and Eugene outside the castle's café. Dad is squinting through the leaded window and doesn't see us coming, but Eugene watches our approach with a white, washed-out expression. The sleeves of his jacket are hanging so limply by his side that his arms don't seem to be in them. As we get closer Dad catches our reflection in the glass.

'Hi there, female half of the family,' he says, turning with hands held out to greet us.

'Hello,' says Mum. 'Were you looking at those cakes?'

'I've spotted a white chocolate gateau,' says Dad, and without another word, he and Mum stampede into the café.

I don't want anything to eat, but at the check-out desk I'm compelled to choose a bag of Twiglets just to avoid suspicion. Eugene opts for an egg sandwich, and we get a big pot of tea between us. Mum and Dad have coffee and cake. They carry the trays to a table in the window, which looks onto the castle's courtyard. Eugene and I stay behind to collect the cutlery and serviettes, buying just enough time for the following conversation:

'Are you alright?'

'Yes. Are you?'

'Yes.'

'Really?'

'Yes. Are you?'

'Yes.'

'Really?'

Then we follow our parents to the window seat. The courtyard is the heart of the castle, enclosed on four sides with brick walls and windows but with the sky for a ceiling. They used to have executions here, hangings and beheadings and the burning of witches; now there's just a lawn, neatly cut as a cricket pitch. In my mind's eye I see a ghost scoring a century, his severed head a ball, his wife's charred arm the bat, and sundry stumps as the wicket.

'This is an interesting place,' my father is saying as we sit down. 'Has anyone learnt anything they didn't know already?'

'Yes,' says Mum with a curt laugh, 'my daughter has four lovers.'

'Grace?' gasps my father.

'I only have one daughter,' Mum says.

'She's got four lovers?' Dad's cake fork is frozen in the air a foot from his mouth. The layers of light sponge and fluffy mousse are quivering with indignation. 'Four lovers?' he repeats, and the forkful of white chocolate gateau falls onto the tablecloth. 'All at once?'

'Apparently so,' says Mum.

'Anyone we know?' Dad looks at me this time, but Mum answers again.

'Only Nigel,' she says.

I didn't tell her that. It's not the truth. They know another of my lovers very well indeed. But I'm not about to admit it. There's a sticky silence as Mum scrapes the cake off the table with a knife. Eugene is chewing his egg sandwich like it's chicken-shit. There's a tough expression on his face as he stares out of the window. Dad is still looking my way, with a fluffy white mousse moustache and moist eyes.

'Extraordinary, Grace,' he says. 'How on earth do you manage it?'

'What?' I suck a Twiglet as though it's a cigarette, narrowing my eyes as the Marmite tingle hits my tongue.

Dad laughs. 'These four lovers of yours,' he says. 'Do they know about each other? Aren't they jealous? Don't you have trouble keeping them apart?'

Trust Dad to be genuinely interested in my affairs. He's shocked, but he's not going to tell me to stop. 'How did it all start?' he asks.

'Garth, that's enough!' Mum says sharply.

He takes hold of her hand. He takes the knife out of it first.

'It's alright,' he says, 'I'm only asking.'

'Grace doesn't want to answer you,' Mum replies.

'But she's in an ambiguous position. Promiscuity is both frowned upon and fêted by society; and anyone engaged in polygamous acts is likely to encounter difficulties. I'm sure she needs someone to talk to.'

'But you're her father.'

'Darling, don't panic,' Dad pats Mum's hand. 'I'm not condoning her behaviour, but neither can I condemn it without hearing her side of the story. Things may not be as bad as we think. We need to have a bit of a chat about it, don't we?'

'She needs a good therapist,' says Mum. 'Pay for her to see a professional if she can't afford it, but don't try and do the job yourself. The cobbler's kids are always the worst shod. Now let's finish our drinks and go back to the car. I'm tired of the whole bloody business.'

I drain my teacup, feeling terrible. I seem to have caused a bit of a stir. Mum and Dad leave the café with the cake still unfinished on their plates, and rush off down the long tree-lined avenue to the drawbridge at the bottom. They no longer seem to be trying to eavesdrop on Eugene and me, but we hear snippets of their heated conversation, as we follow them slowly down the hill in the early-setting autumn sun. The number four features frequently in their debate.

'Nice one,' says Eugene.

'Sorry?' I say.

He sidles closer.

'It's put them right off the scent.'

I hardly hear him. I'm overpowered by his perfume, the natural aroma of him, enhanced by the surroundings. He always smells woody, but under these trees it's specifically oak. He always smells musky, but in this dusk it's definitely time for bed. I wish we could sneak back to the castle and find a place for the night in that vast space, anything rather than getting back into Mum and Dad's claustrophobic car. I just want to lie down quietly and go to sleep with his arms around me.

'How did you think it up?' Eugene interrupts my train of thought.

'Think what up?'

'Your tale of four lovers. It's sent Mum and Dad right off the track.'

I answer him without thinking. 'It's true,' I say. 'It's not a story. It's true.'

'Pardon?' says Eugene. But he heard the first time, I can tell by his tone, I can tell by the way he's looking at me. I try to smile reassuringly at him.

'You've really got four lovers?' he asks. 'Four lovers?' The way he says it makes it sound like leprosy. I clench my fists, but speak kindly.

'Why so surprised?' I say. 'You already knew about Nigel.'

'Yeah, Nigel,' Eugene shrugs, 'but not the others. Who the fuck are they?'

'Oh, you don't want to know.' I use a steady tone to counterbalance Eugene's shaky one, but it doesn't work.

'Keep your secret, then,' he cries. 'Pretend I know you upside-down and inside-out because we're one in spirit, when all along you've been spinning the same line to more stupid flies than I've had hot dinners.'

'You're not making sense,' I say. 'Don't be jealous, Genie. It's silly.'

'Oh, come now,' he says sarcastically, 'I'm sure you're no stranger to jealousy, little Miss Four-Lovers. I'm sure you're not shy of it.'

'I don't know why you're making such a big deal of this,' I say. 'You live with Trudy. And I can handle that.'

'Of course you can handle that; harmless Trudy you've known for years, transparent Trudy I've told you almost everything about already. But how would you feel if you suddenly found out I was seeing some Madonna-faced mystery chick with feed-the-world breasts and a PhD?'

I can't help laughing. It's the way Eugene's mind works. In his insecurity he assumes that my secret lovers must be much better than him, brighter and more beautiful with bigger reproductive organs. He's conjuring up gods to taunt himself with, thundering chaps. I could tease him with them, too, for a while, but we're approaching the drawbridge and beyond it our parents will be waiting for us in the car. I have to tell him the truth before we get there, or the wind might change, or we might have an accident on the way home, and he'd never know.

'Listen,' I say, 'until this weekend I never believed you could be my lover. It took four other people to fill the gap that I thought would be left for ever. The lack of you hacked out such a wound in me, it took four other people to lick it better. They didn't ease the pain, they didn't soothe or satisfy me much. But that was the form of relief I chose, from the nagging need to be shagging you, and I don't see why I should apologise. It's no worse than you living with Trudy, who is incompatible with you in every way.'

'Three,' says Eugene.

'What?'

'Three other people. You said four.'

'What?' I turn to look at him as we duck under the portcullis and cross the drawbridge. I can't work out what he's talking about.

'If you've got four lovers including me there have only been three others licking your axe wound, as you so tastefully put it. I thought you were meant to be good at maths.' Eugene sighs impatiently, but everything is going into slow motion for me.

'No, sorry, let me explain,' I say. 'The last thing I wanted to do was give us away to Mum and Dad, so I didn't include you in my reckoning. I've got four lovers excluding you. You're actually number five.'

83

Eugene doesn't hear me. He's jumping out of his skin and pointing a scared and skeleton finger at Mum and Dad, who are emerging from a dark alcove in the castle wall. Eugene doesn't hear me say how he makes my number of lovers a nice round five, but Mum and Dad do. I'm not sure whether they were hiding in that damp alcove to surprise us or whether they'd got themselves lost in a snog, but one thing is certain; they know I've had sex with my brother.

Four

So it all came out in the end. Family outings are like that. We thought we were getting away from it all, but it all went with us. And then it followed us home again, our close personal storm; too late to be tight-lipped, we had a strained and silent car journey nevertheless.

Mum and Dad are now having a humdinger of an argument, downstairs. Through the walls, through the floor, I can hear the shouted sentences rise and fall; Dad rumbling like thunder, Mum shrieking in streaks like lightning.

I'm lying on the bed that was my bed when I was a child, in the room that was my room but is now a guest room. It looks like a ghost room to me. There's still the same wallpaper though my posters are gone; and on its darker patches I can still picture the pop stars, teenage surrealism and political icons of my heyday. There's still the same furniture, and I can remember how every scratch and scuff mark was made.

I'm lying in the foetal position. There's an ache in my stomach and a breathlessness in my chest. It looks like all the trouble I've ever caused is about to catch up with me.

When I was growing up, I got off lightly. I got smacked a bit, and grounded; but my parents were so deeply into discussing the social and moral implications of what I'd done wrong, that telling me off was normally as far as they got. Their form of punishment was mental, not corporal. Endless Freudian analysis, that was the price I paid for my crimes; episodes of *Scooby-Doo* completely drowned out by my parents' psychobabble.

But I've never done anything this bad before. I dyed my hair blue, I went on the pill, I gave school a miss and stayed at home all day sniffing joss sticks with someone who thought he was Johnny Rotten and wasn't far wrong. Like all parents, Mum and Dad reacted to my adolescent rebellion as if it were murder; and yet they managed to persuade me to mend my ways in the course of two or three tea times of conversation. By merely talking to each other, they convinced me to drop the jerk and catch up on my school work, and I wasn't even really listening.

This is different. I can't help hearing them raging down below. The storm is too distant for me to make out detailed words and phrases, but I'm in no doubt about the subject.

Is this what I've secretly always wanted to do, provoke my parents to a proper display of anger? None of that heated debate while holding hands deceit; this is an honest to God-forsaken stonker of an argument.

This is the first family crisis to affect our hearts as well as our heads. Did I devise the scenario specially? Mum and Dad have turned on each other. Their caring co-counselling has turned into a one-to-one Gestalt frenzy. It's out of control.

No, I'm sure I never wanted this to happen. I'm curling up around a pain in my middle, feeling sick and sorry. I wish they'd hurry up and punish me. But what can they do? If they throw me out of their house, I've got my own home to go to. I don't even have to run away, I could walk it.

I don't have to lie here on this scared childbed, trembling like a toddler, waiting with bated breath for the sound of a parental footstep on the stair and the confrontation which follows.

I could go out for a drink.

It seems that you can get Dutch courage from the anticipation of alcohol, as well as its actual consumption. Suddenly, I'm leaping off the bed and picking up my bag. Light-footed and high-headed I could walk right out of this nightmare bedroom and go for a drink, and Mum and Dad would not be able to stop me.

Drunk as a lord on adrenalin, I reel along the landing, bouncing off the walls, but I clutch my handbag like a lady. It contains my survival kit: sweets and little sums on scraps of paper, doorkeys and tampons, loads of lovely money, the phone numbers of all my friends, silly plastic things I've picked up off pavements; and if I can get it and me out of here we'll be safe. Then I come to the top of the stairs, where Eugene is sitting.

His image is so permanently etched on my retina that sometimes I see him when he's not really there, and don't when he is. My reaction to the sight of him is always delayed, as if my mind thinks at first he's just me reflected in a mirror. I often reach up to brush his hair out of my eyes, before I realise that there's two of us and we're not both the same one.

'Where are you going?' asks Eugene.

'Hello,' I say.

'Are you going?' he asks again.

'No.'

'Why have you got your bag?'

'Well, I thought I'd pop out for a pint. Would you like to come, too?'

'Can you hear what's going on down there?'

'They're taking each other to pieces. I've been waiting for them to come up and talk to us.'

'Shout at us, more like. They've never been so loud. I've never heard Mum so much as snap at Dad and now she's screaming her bloody head off. It's scary.'

'I bet they're more scared than we are,' I say with bravado. 'We're so weird, Eugene. We're, like, their monstrous progeny.'

'Can you make out what they're saying?'

'No. There's lots of booming and hissing but not many high notes.'

'I bet they're trying to decide whether to call the police,' says Eugene.

'The police?' I reply. 'That's a bit strong.'

'But incest is against the law.'

'Is it?'

'Of course.'

'You've never told me that before.'

'I thought you knew.'

'What can the police do? Take us away in handcuffs?' I start to giggle. 'That could rather defeat the object. Hang on, they wouldn't put us in prison, would they . . . ?'

'Sshh, listen,' says my brother.

Mum and Dad must be pacing up and down behind the closed kitchen door. For a moment, they become more audible.

'No, I don't think the terms bitch and bastard are gender specific,' we hear Dad say.

Mum, muffled, replies, 'You've never called me a bastard before.'

'I've never called you a bitch before,' shouts Dad, 'but you've never acted like one.'

I think that's what they're saying. It seems rather improbable.

'Do you think the terms bitch and bastard are gender specific?' I ask Eugene.

'Handcuffs, eh?' he laughs, and grabs my ankle.

'Do you?' I say.

'If a man calls another man a bitch he's probably camping it up a bit, and if a woman calls a man a bitch she's probably perceiving his true nature,' says Eugene. 'A man will call another man a bastard as soon as look at him, but if he's talking about a woman he'd sooner call her a bitch.'

'I wouldn't call another woman a bitch or a bastard unless she'd called me one first,' I inform him. 'And I wouldn't call a man a bitch unless he'd been bitchy to me, or a bastard unless he'd been a bastard to me.'

'Oh,' says Eugene. He's stroking my calf.

'Let's go for that drink,' I gulp.

'Okay.' His hand slides up to my thigh.

I grab the banister for support.

'You make my knees weak,' I say.

'You make my dick's month!'

I sit down next to Eugene on the top stair and his hand stays up my skirt. I laugh and, in the face of stiff opposition and upper lips, it feels like a mouthful of champagne. I could still do with a real drink though.

'Listen,' I say, 'let's go. We don't have to stop at the pub. Let's stop at nothing. Let's go on the run.'

'Why?'

'Because the police could be after us. Let's go to a hotel and call ourselves Mr and Mrs Smith for the night. The Bonnie and Clyde of illicit sexual relationships.'

'No,' says Eugene.

'Go on! In the morning we could steal away to another city with matching bathrobes and start a whole new life together.'

'What, pretend to be married?'

'Yes.'

'You don't want to be married. You'd be married to Nigel by now if you wanted to be married, Grace.'

'But we might as well be, we've already got the same surname. Mr and Mrs Bloom.'

'Don't be silly. You're always saying that marriage drives people mad.'

'It wouldn't be like that with us.'

'Why not?'

'Well, we're mad already.'

We're mad about each other. I smile like a cat as I remember the scene from this morning, our conversation at the castle, when Eugene said he loved me and I said I loved him, too.

'But I don't want to be mad,' he is saying now. 'And anyway, there's something else. There's something I've got to tell you. It's about Trudy.'

An awful thought crosses my mind. If she's pregnant I'll kill myself. But luckily, until I've had a drink or two, there's no danger of saying what I really mean.

'What?' I ask.

'She's . . . she's . . .' says Eugene, then he stops, struggling for words.

'Pregnant?' I suggest.

His laugh leads me to believe that she isn't; one horrible irresponsible HA! and he subsides into silence.

In the silence I hear something: the shouting downstairs has stopped. It's all gone quiet on the domestic front. Eugene and I look at each other with widening eyes, then cock our ears at the kitchen door, straining to catch the slightest sound of a marital row, like red setters watching a rabbit hole.

When the door suddenly opens we jump out of our skin. Eugene's hand extricates itself quickly from my skirt as Mum steps into the hall. She gets to the foot of the stairs before she looks up and sees us at the top, but she doesn't look surprised. Her face is fixed around the fathomless pits of her eyes; smooth, shiny, rock-hard.

'Eugene, Grace, come down please,' she says. 'We need to talk.'

I have to remind myself that I'm an adult as I follow Eugene unconsentingly down the stairs, because my legs are wobbling like jelly and my teeth chatter like ice cream. I feel like I'm being forced to attend a children's party, or a firing squad, when I really want to go to the pub.

In the kitchen, Dad is standing at the sink, looking like he's about to be sick. Slowly, he turns to face us and his mouth seems to move in a mute rehearsal of words. He's nervous, clutching at a potato masher as if it is a prop. He clears his throat.

'We've got something to tell you,' he says.

I double-take like a Marx Brother. My brother does, too.

'You've got something to tell us?' I say. 'I thought it was the other way round.'

'Listen,' says Dad, 'we should have told you this years ago, as soon as you were old enough to understand. Now everything has got out of hand and it's all our fault.'

My mother is smoking a cigarette but I smell a cigar, and see Groucho spectacles and a moustache. In the tension of the moment, my mind plays tricks on me, turning tragedy into comedy.

'What have you done?' I ask.

They don't answer.

'Mum? Dad?' I say. I'm bursting to relieve their silence with a rugby song. Something must be seriously wrong.

'Go on, Garth,' Mum blows out smoke.

Dad shakes his head.

Mum clears the smoke cloud between them with a wave of her hand and says, 'Go on, Garth,' again. Dad doesn't want to speak, it's obvious, but it seems he doesn't want to disobey Mum either.

'We're not your real parents,' he says.

'What?' I think it's me who says that.

'We're not your real parents.' He sounds robotic. 'We adopted you.'

'When you were babies,' adds Mum.

'But you didn't come together.'

'We got you separately.'

'You're not related to each other.'

'You're not really brother and sister.'

'Not in blood.'

I think that's what they say. Everything has exploded in my face and I'm out of it, going like a rocket, faster than the speed of sound. All I can hear is the shrieking and screaming of my own ears as I leave the Earth's atmosphere, but I don't think anyone else can.

Mum and Dad are not our real parents. They adopted us when we were babies. We're not related to each other. Not in blood.

'Who are we then?' I say.

I think that's what I say. No one answers me though. Dad bursts into tears and Mum runs towards him, arms flung wide, sending a saucepan crashing to the floor and making all the cutlery clatter.

'Who the fuck are we then?' I ask again, trying to be louder this time, and more specific. 'Who the fuck are you?'

They still don't answer me. I can't believe it. I can't believe what they're telling me, and I can't believe the way they're telling me. All this disbelief is having a draining effect on me, making me feel like I'm not really here.

'Hello?' I say tentatively.

Dad doesn't stop crying. I hate to hear him cry. He sounds like a child and that scares me. I mean, it used to scare me. If he's not my father, there's no reason why he can't be a child. And this is some immature stunt he's pulling. What a pranker. What a schoolkid trick to play on me, pretending I'm adopted.

'Liar, liar, pants on fire!' I sing at him.

I think I do it aloud, but he doesn't seem to hear me. Nor does Mum; no, not Mum, some complete stranger. They're locked together, rocking to the rhythm of my chant; fire, fire, pants are liars. I can't be singing this out loud, surely. It's an inner jam.

Things are getting sinister now. My heart starts to beat faster. I'm half expecting Jeremy Beadle, Beelzebub himself, to appear. It's got to be a joke, surely. Someone from the real world of television has got to come out of the kitchen cupboard with a microphone and say I've been framed.

I start laughing. Actually, I say it's laughing but it could just as well be crying. It's an awful sound, but I can't stop. My parents are not my parents and I'm a little orphan baby. I'm gasping for breath.

Mum glances over her shoulder at me.

'Sit down, Grace,' she says.

Luckily there's a chair right behind me. I fall into it. All the breath goes out of my sails, with the wind-whispered words, 'Why are you telling us this?'

Dad's face appears above Mum's breast. It bobs up. His eyes are swimming pools of tears.

'Because it's true,' he says in a deep voice.

He looks at me through water as if he's drowning, but I start to lose consciousness first. I drift away.

Some weird sort of dream winds me up for a while. It's in black and white but there are no pictures, just long strings of words whipping past me, looping round me, taping my mouth shut, tying me down. The words go something like this: We're not your real parents real parents are we not We adopted you adopted you adolf he adopted you as babies You're not our real babies we got you from a catalogue a second-hand stork a flamingo with one wing a Chinese takeaway You're Chinese babies different blood don't belong to us we're just doing a favour Different flavour babies jelly black ones Hoped you wouldn't notice.

Slowly the sentences start coming to full stops again. Slowly they start to make sense. I find myself lying on the kitchen floor. I don't know how much time has elapsed since I collapsed. Dad's stopped crying but Mum and Eugene have started. I can only see their feet, but I can hear them speak.

'We didn't tell you sooner,' Dad, that man, is saying, 'because we didn't want to tell you at all.'

'Why?' That's a small sob from Eugene.

'I suppose we thought that if we hid it for long enough, the horrible truth need never come out.'

'Why?'

'We love you,' says Dad, 'we love you like our own. It doesn't matter that there's no biological bond. Blood may be thicker than water, but love is a pure white light, and there's nothing to stop us basking in it.'

'And anyway,' sniffs Mum, that woman, 'to all intents and purposes we are your real parents. We did all the things that parents do, from teaching you the alphabet to taking you to the zoo. We changed your tiny nappies and took your teenage shit, too.'

'But we're not complaining,' says the man. 'You've done us proud. You're smashing youngsters, the pair of you.'

'But you've got nothing to complain about either,' says the woman. 'I've cooked and cleaned and clothed you both, while juggling a career, and seen that you've wanted for nothing. Good schools, ideal home, the best universities . . .'

I sit up to interrupt.

'But surely,' I say, 'our academic achievements are due to our own genetic make-up.'

Mum looks like she's bitten her tongue. I spit another mouthful of bile into her bloody silence.

'If we're adopted, you can't claim copyright on our DNA,' I say. 'How will you impress people, now that taking the credit for our qualifications is out of the question?'

She gives me a dirty look. A dirty look is often the easiest sort of look to see through. That's one good reason why the eyes can't be the windows of the soul.

'I've never done that,' she says. But it's not the only lie I can see in her eyes. I'm still finding it very hard to believe that Eugene and I are adopted.

But Eugene isn't. Well, he's finding it hard, but he seems to believe it. He's been sitting with his head in his hands for ages, as if he's afraid his face will fall off if he looks up. He speaks slowly, as if he's coming to terms with the terrible truth.

'Who are we really?' he asks.

'Exactly who you think you are,' says Mum, her tone, as ever, softer and more comforting for him than it is for me. 'That has not changed.'

Eugene lifts his head. I turn away before I see his face.

'Is Eugene my real name?' he asks.

That is the saddest sound I've ever heard. It's like a lost lamb, bleating at the edge of the fold. I turn my face further away.

'Yes,' says 'Mum', 'of course it's your real name.'

'Where do I come from?' he says. 'Why didn't my real parents want me?'

'They did! Oh, my baby, they did!' She responds to Eugene's plea as if she were his real mother. 'They wanted you more than anything else in the world. They loved you, from your nose to your toes. But they . . . they . . .'

From my position on the floor I see 'Dad's' hand tighten on her knee. I see her smooth American Tan tights wrinkle in his grip. 'No, I don't know. I'm sorry. I don't know any more,' Gaynor finishes lamely.

Garth gives her another helping hand. 'The adoption agency didn't provide us with much personal information,' he says.

'Would they tell me?' says Eugene, in a tiny voice.

He believes them. He believes they're not our real parents. He believes that they adopted us when we were babies.

He believes them. And if he believes our parents' story then I will be forced to agree with him. There's no way we can have a disagreement, not in the face of such extraordinary adversity.

I believe him. Therefore I believe them. They're not our real parents. They adopted us when we were babies. This is the truth. Our whole lives have been a lie.

Gaynor gives another sniff and her lips start to tremble. She's going to cry again. She's going to cry harder than me and Eugene. It seems that the idea of us looking for our real parents hurts her feelings; they're so fucking fragile, and we've spent our whole lives creeping round them for nothing.

'You cow,' I say to her. 'All you can think about is yourself. How do you think we feel? You've just turned our world upside-down and we're not supposed to notice. You've just revealed that there's no one looking after us, but we're still supposed to look after you. Shit!' I believe I am standing up to leave.

The man, what's-his-name, Garth, stands up, too.

'Look, Grace, and Eugene, listen,' he says. 'We know you're sleeping together. We don't know how long it's been going on for, but your . . . Gaynor saw you in the shower this morning and we heard your conversation at the castle. We couldn't let you go on thinking your relationship was incestuous, and feeling strange and ashamed, when we knew there was no real reason why you shouldn't have sex with each other if that's what you wanted.'

97

'What?' I say. He's holding his hand out to me, but if we touch I'll scream.

'Obviously our revelation comes as something of a shock, but at least now you know there's no blood between you and your . . . Eugene, you're free to be together if you choose. It's safe to have sex. You can love each other loud and proud, and I hope you'll still love us, too. Tonight it's hard to get your head round, but maybe you'll forgive us in the morning.'

Garth's liberalism bounces by me like a bright orange rubber ball I've got no hope of catching. I'm still seeing red with sharp corners like triangles and squares, and endless aching blue. His glib words are so far removed from my early ABC of agony at the loss of my mum and dad that I can hardly hear them. I think I start to speak before he has finished.

'You crap bastards,' I cry. 'I'm going to find my real parents and tell them of you!'

I rush from the room and up the stairs and fall onto the spare bed. I don't sleep a wink all night, but I'm not awake either; I pass out before my head hits the pillow and lie there, deathly and dreamless, until the dawn warms me back to life.

Five

It's early when I wake, and the day looks grey and unshaven. A mist rubs rough as stubble against the window pane. There's a heavy silence, as if all of nature is having to hold its breath and heave to lift a sullen sun into the sky. It is an unsmiling morn.

I leave the house without even cleaning my teeth. I am dressed already, because I collapsed on the bed in my clothes last night. Opening my eyes to find myself still on top of the covers feels like Christmas Day without stockings. No one came down my chimney while I slept, to gently tuck me in; no fantasy figure came in the night, to kiss me or comfort me. But I don't dwell on the disappointment. I throw my belongings in a bag, and go down the stairs and out of the front door without bothering to slam it behind me.

On the way to the station my eyes begin to water. This makes the streets glisten and houses seem insubstantial; wet façades, liquid moments I've never noticed moving before. By the time I get to the bottom of the road my old home has melted. No oasis, but a mirage image, now the illusion has worn off. Home is where the heart lies, but mine is broken. My eyes water, but when I get to the station, sweet tea in a paper cup treats me for shock.

During the jolted and jilted train journey I stare out of a window. It's backsides of houses all the way to the city, behind the scenes of people's lives, with kitchen doors open so I can see what they're having for breakfast. Tightly lined up in rows, they grow extensions as the family inside them grows, pink plastic playthings spilling like entrails onto their patios and the tiny green handkerchiefs of their lawns.

There's no room to keep secrets in houses as small as this. But in a semi-detached, like my so-called parents', there's space for things to go unspoken. There's so much privacy, you can lead a double life without anyone knowing; in a spare room or under the cover of the shrubbery. All these years we've been living a lie, a normal family, connected like the branches of a tree. I always suspected we weren't entirely normal, but at least I thought we were a family.

Now I live alone in an attic flat. I don't even have a garden. Still the place is full of flowers, drying a slow death, their colours dusty. There are pot plants, too, dying for a drink after my weekend away. The first thing to do, when I arrive back, is water them.

The first thing to do is water them. I stand on the doorstep of my flat for five minutes, thinking that the first thing to do is water my plants. Then I wander from one pot to another, from rubber to umbrella plant to weeping fig, till ten more minutes have ticked away. I stand in the kitchen, watching the pots on the windowsill, the parsley, sage, rosemary and thyme, my indoor herbaceous border. Their leaves will fall off and flavour the linoleum, if I don't give them a drink. I turn to the kitchen sink. There's a blue china jug on the draining board. It's what I usually water my plants with. Why aren't I using it now?

The next thing I know, I've fallen to the floor. I'm lying on the kitchen lino crying. I cry a bucket of tears, bitter like someone's horrible home-brew left fermenting for far too long. Foul stuff, thick as syrup but sour as shit; I hold my head under until I'm drunk on it. At the end of my crying, when the beer barrel is empty, a smile comes. Pissed on my own unhappiness I start to laugh.

I'm adopted. (Ad-*op*-ted.)

I would have killed to be adopted when I was still at school. The prestige of it. Persuading the other kids I was a princess or a pop-star's daughter. There was a girl in my class called Amy Dag and she was adopted. It was the first time I'd come across the term. She was away from school one day and the headmistress made an announcement about it to the whole assembly. She said that Amy was special because her parents had chosen her, they had singled her out. I thought this was why all babies were born, so when I got home I asked my mum what the headmistress had meant.

The next day Amy was back in class. I'd never taken much notice of her before, she was a quiet girl obscured by a screen of dense black hair, but suddenly she was screamingly obvious. I spent the morning swivelling in my seat, staring at her with my eyes on stalks. And then, if the reports of my teachers are true, I spent the lunch hour torturing her. I pinned Amy Dag up against the wall of the playground, and asked why her real mummy and daddy didn't want her. Then I proceeded to perform Nazi experiments on her. My only tools were the contents of my pencil case, but you can be very nasty with a compass and protractor. For some reason I seemed to think

Amy was alien, a changeling child, and that if I prodded her hard enough the impostor would pop out. I don't know what on earth my mother said to give me such an idea.

She's not my mother. I'm adopted.

I never heard Amy Dag say anything like that, though from the day I first tortured her until we left school at sixteen we were the best of friends. In fact, she seemed to believe that her adoptive parents were the real thing. She had no trouble calling them Mum and Dad.

'Not he who sows the seed, but he who tends the sapling,' she used to say, 'should reap the fruit.'

I was always rather in awe of her wisdom, still secretly believing that she was from another world; not realising that her open-heartedness was perhaps a product of the family who'd chosen her to be their child. She was the first girl in our year to have a boyfriend, even though she wasn't particularly pretty.

When I was a teenager, the idea of my parents not being my parents was very attractive. I wouldn't have kept it in perspective like Amy did. I'd have had all my friends wishing they were adopted, too. I'd have had them all guessing which front-bench politician was my real father, which TV newscaster was my mother. On second thoughts, I might have opted for ordinary parents, a young unmarried mother, a scallywag of a dad, because by this time my actual pair were becoming prominent in the world of psychoanalysis and it was doing my head in.

So why didn't they tell me the truth, way back when I asked what 'Amy Dag is adopted' meant, the same day Amy's adoptive parents were telling her? It would have been easy then. In my formative years the skeleton of personality was so supple, I could bend almost double without breaking it. A complete change of address would not have left me lost completely. But it's too late to learn a new identity now; I don't go to school any more, and there's no kind headmistress to make an announcement in assembly. I'll have to tell everyone myself that Grace Bloom is adopted; and even though I won't be pretending that I'm really an African princess, I don't think anyone will believe me.

I can't believe it myself.

I bash the lid of the red plastic bin that's lying on its side beside me on the kitchen floor. It swings in one full revolution, before settling into an irritating pendulum motion. Irritated by the pendulum motion, I smash it again. I wish there were some kittens curled up asleep inside, then I wouldn't be so angry and aggressive. If they were here, my furry family could soothe me quickly with quiet cuddles and soft stroking. But I sent them to stay with friends while I was away for the weekend; and bringing them back could involve noisier cuddles, firmer stroking and more insistent soothing than I can stomach today.

The problem is that by pure chance, I had four kittens and four lovers. On Friday evening, inspired by the seeming symmetry of all things, I allocated an animal to each of my sexual partners to care for until Monday morning. On Friday evening I was feeling horny and it seemed like a good way to secure some sexual relations for the following week. But now the time has come to collect the kittens, I'm not in the mood for human contact. My symmetry has been thrown, and I'm all off balance. I've got five lovers.

I leave the flat in a rush but can't leave that thought behind me. I can't believe that I've got five lovers. To contemplate them all at once is too much. Too many faces to fit into my head, too many bodies to get into my bed. One of them would be perfect, but in conglomeration, they're a great misshapen monster, unsexy as the elephant man.

I leave the flat in a rush, grab a bag and stagger out, but I've got to take this morning one step at a time.

Nigel's house is only a short walk away. His front door is ice blue with panes of frosted glass, but it's warm on the other side. I arrive on the tiled doorstep and knock. I knock again. I thought I was early, but maybe I'm late. I knock a third time, impatiently.

Nigel comes to let me in at last, with a blast on his hooter, a bright red nose.

'You're early,' he sniffs, stuffing a handkerchief into the pocket of his old faithful dressing gown. I love this dressing gown in a snuffling animal way. It smells, deeply, of musk and fluff and flakes of dandruff snow. It's been a Saint Bernard skin to me and has saved my life many a cold night. I've borrowed it and I've burrowed in it.

This morning I brush straight past it on the doorstep, and down a hall like a wormhole where time lasts longer. Perhaps because I've been this way so often and spent so much, there's extra time, a discount for regulars. Nigel's hallway is a historic passage, and as I walk down it I see that yesterday wasn't over when I woke up this morning. Yesterday was way too unwieldy to fit into an ordinary twenty-four-hour cycle so I've had to bring it with me today. It's getting stuck in the bottleneck of the hall, and only with the greatest of effort do I eventually pop into the kitchen like a cork. I'm trying to keep one step ahead of Nigel, because he thinks he's my only lover, and Genie is only my brother.

'Have you had breakfast yet?' Nigel asks, following me into the kitchen in furry slippers.

I shake my head. I haven't even had yesterday's breakfast yet.

'Sit down then,' he says.

I sit in a chair and stare at the cloth of old gold roses which covers the tabletop. This has been the backdrop to many a meal. It gives Nigel's kitchen the look of a nineteenth-century cook's; the food is Fanny Beaton. You . . . Eu . . . Eugene's eaten here a hundred times, and drunk wine, and waved his hands around in after-dinner discussion. He and me and Nigel have sat in our places for hours putting the world to rights, but now it seems that familiar scene will never be set at this table again.

I look up as Nigel opens a cupboard containing everything from Indian aubergine pickle to Coco-Pops, Victoria sandwich mixes to mustard and mayonnaise. I love this cupboard; the bazaar aromas are therapy for me, inducing a sense of well-being. Nigel catches my eye.

'Good weekend?' he asks.

I shrug.

'Did you have the house to yourself?' he says. Nigel is making fried Brie and black pepper sandwiches, which are my favourites. I watch in silence as he butters bread, cuts cheese, and constructs delicate triangles in the smoking pan, while putting together a pot of tea with his other hand. He beams at me, over his shoulder.

'I had a houseful,' he says. 'Kristen came with the kids. Beth and her new baby and Mark, Michael and Chris. It was complete chaos. We had to eat our meals in the garden, lounging around on the lawn, bundled up in blankets, because there wasn't the room for everyone to sit down indoors; and I slept, would you believe, in the bathroom, with those old green curtains from work as bedclothes; but we all had a good laugh. The baby is brilliant.'

Nigel drops the spatula on his foot.

'Whoops!' he says. 'Friday night I hardly slept at all. We grown-ups got into a bit of a session and didn't go to bed until about four, absolutely fubar, Fucked Up Beyond All Recognition. Then, of course, the children were up at six and sliding down the stairs in their sleeping bags. They're so healthy; it must be going to bed early and abstaining from alcohol that does it. The adults staggered through Saturday with screaming hangovers and fixed expressions, while the kids ran the gamut of emotions from serene to ecstatic, full of the joys of spring. Kristen is pregnant again. It's her fifth. Yes, her fifth. She says it was a mistake, but I saw a twinkle in her eye. Mass fatherhood is taking its toll on Chris though. He smacked one of them, Polly it was, just because she didn't finish her toffee apple. She licked all the toffee off then said she was full up. I didn't blame her, I'd had one, too, and the apples they use are really rank. In fact, I'd thrown half of mine away. I tried to tell Chris that, but it was too late. Now, Kristen is completely against corporal punishment, I've never seen her lay a finger on any of her children, she hardly even tells them off; but when Chris hit Polly, Kristen grabbed him by the tie and said she'd cut his dick off if he ever did it again. And Chris had the cheek to look relieved.'

Nigel gives me a cup of tea and a wry smile. I try to ask him if Chris and Kristen are Catholics, but he isn't in a position to listen. He can't stop talking. He's on a roll.

'Beth's baby is beautiful,' he says, 'as good as gold. But he hasn't got a name yet. Beth doesn't know what to call him. She says she was so sure it would be a girl she didn't think about boys' names at all. She says she didn't believe she could give birth to a boy. She's totally in awe of his masculinity. That's why she can't decide on a name. She doesn't want it to be one that a man's had before. Everyone was making helpful suggestions. The kids were calling him Babacious and Swaddlington. Mike chipped in with Dicola and Stiffenie, male versions of popular girls' names. Chris suggested Bark or Meth which combine the names of the baby's parents. Beth said that the problem was boys' names don't seem to mean as much as girls' names do, so there's less chance of them being character-forming. I said that Mark means a lot, and Beth muttered something about stubborn understains that no one quite caught. This led to a long debate about whether a rose by any other name would smell as sweet, and eventually Beth broke down and told us the root of the problem. She'd wanted to call her child after a flower. She had a long list, a chain of Daisy names, Rose, Lily, all forms of Flora. They were unambiguously female, and the only masculine equivalent she could find was Leaf. Even Ivy, fast and strong, has been appropriated by the ladies. So we compiled a list of all the tree names we knew, and the upshot of the story is that she's now thinking along the lines of Oak.'

Nigel hands me a hot plate with sticky edges. There are four golden sandwiches upon it, cooked Brie oozing between crisp crusts, cracked black peppercorns like sweet coals. I dig in. I don't say thank you, or anything.

'Poor baby,' says Nigel. 'But I'm sure Beth knows what she's doing. She's going to be a good mother. She's so gentle. Radiating warmth. It's amazing how women change when they have children, almost as if a switch is flicked on overnight. Beth was such a wild one before. She used to drink like a fish, but now she only touches water. We went to the pub on Sunday lunchtime. I was doing a roast but we all fancied a quick pint beforehand, so we went to the Bouncy Castle, as the kids call the local. While they were making themselves sick on inflated orange plastic and Kristen, Mark, Michael and Chris sat and watched, I stayed at the bar with Beth and the baby because it was a bit cold outside. We had a long talk. She told me about the birth, and bonding with her little boy, and how she felt fulfilled though prior to becoming a parent she'd poo-pooed the notion that she was at all lacking . . .'

Nigel stops abruptly and looks at me. I give him back the empty plate.

'Thanks,' he says. 'Everyone sends their love, by the way. They were sorry not to see you.'

I look pointedly at the teapot.

'Would you like another cup?' Nigel asks.

I nod.

'What's the matter?' he says.

I shake my head.

'What's the matter?' he asks again.

I get off my chair and pour the tea myself. Nigel comes up behind me and envelops me in the arms of his paper-brown dressing gown.

'I missed you,' he says.

I shrug him of. He makes a muffled sound, small as a disappointed child, and turns away.

'Do you want to see your kitten?' he says.

It's time for me to stop the silent treatment. I only started it by accident, when Nigel wouldn't let me get a word in edgeways. But now I can't speak, though I want to, though I have to, to get my kitten back. I open my mouth to try, but only manage a violent sigh.

'Oh, Grace,' says Nigel, 'tell me what's wrong.'

I can't.

'Please?'

I can't. I'm sorry, Nigel, I can't. My heart's too heavy to heave into my mouth and pour out. I need some help.

'Has something happened?'

Don't ask me. Do I have to do everything for you? Do I have to be your dream woman and speak, too? It's true, Nigel thinks I'm his dream woman, but that's only because he doesn't know who I really am. He often bangs on about babies, and it always sends me into a sulk. It's the easy option, sulking. The alternative is serious conversation. Although he never comes right out and says it, Nigel wants me to be the mother of his children; and acting like a kid is my way of avoiding having to give him a grown-up yes or no answer.

'Grace?'

Shut up. She's not here. There's no such person.

'Grace!'

Suddenly a thought strikes me, sharp and sweet as a labour pain. If Eugene isn't my brother, I could have babies with him. I've always sworn that maternity isn't for me, but at the thought of having babies with Eugene I suddenly feel the stirring of some soft new life, and a love which surpasses all understanding.

I shake my head in surprise.

'What's going on?'

I forgot that Nigel was watching me. I don't know what's going on. I still can't speak to him, though my head is now as

109

full of nappies and teddy bears and tears as he must be. Nigel is ten years older than me, and the time on his biological clock is running out.

He tuts impatiently.

'Well, go and find your kitten then. I've got to get ready for work. Do you want a lift?' he says.

Yes, I do.

The kitten is in the conservatory. It's Wynken. It's in a wicker basket, with a little wooden handle and a door. The basket is full of straw. Wynken wasn't in it before.

'Kristen's kids helped me choose it,' says Nigel. 'It's safer and more secure than that swing-bin you were lugging them around in. And less surreal.'

Oh no. It's happening again. My bottom lip begins to wobble. I'm going to cry. Nigel has brought a wonderful wicker basket for my kittens, and he shouldn't have done, because I don't deserve it. He's always so nice to me, and I'm never anything but nasty to him. I start to cry. Sometimes I hate myself for not loving Nigel.

'Sweetheart,' he says, 'don't cry. Tell me what's wrong and I'll make it better. Grace, angel, it's alright, Nigel's here.'

I cry harder. He's making it worse.

'Tell me,' he says.

I can't. But I really need a cuddle. My body is aching all over from the weekend's emotional exertions.

'What happened?' says Nigel.

How shall I put it? Well, Nigel, I spent the weekend with my brother, who I've secretly been in love with since we were children, and on Sunday morning our mother caught us having sex in the shower, and told us that we were adopted. It's a bit of a blow, I can hardly believe it, but at least it means I can be legal with my best man now and possibly have a baby. Oh, Nigel, you've stopped cuddling me. Now you're crying, too! Why are you looking for ropes and daggers? Oh, Nigel, you're trying to commit suicide!

That's why I can't tell Nigel the truth. I don't want to kill him. I want him to hold me still and steady and call me an angel. I don't want him to let go of me, or see his angel fall. I open my mouth. My nose starts to run. My tongue races.

'It's my parents,' I say. 'They're separating. Dad's a drug addict. Mum wants a divorce.'

What am I saying? I only meant to make up a little white lie, substitute a sad story so Nigel would cuddle me and I could cry; a personal problem that wasn't too private, a social sin that wasn't too incriminating. But I've gone and told him a blockbuster. Nigel looks shocked. Nigel looks sick.

'Drugs?' he says, his face white as a sheet. Then he opens his arms and offers me an unconditional hug with no hint of bed.

I screw Nigel for every ounce of comfort I can. He's held me like this a hundred times and soothed away the smallest problems and imagined slights. Now the problem is overwhelming, I can't bear to let him go. I'll miss him most of all my lovers, when I give them up for you . . . Eu . . . Eugene.

I make a snail trail of snot on Nigel's dressing gown collar. That's how long he hoids me for. That's how close we are.

He's been like a father to me, better than a father, and all I can do is abuse him. I'm abusing Nigel and his unconditional love, making a mockery of it, taking the mickey out of it. To love someone unconditionally doesn't mean you don't mind being lied to. It means you still love them no matter what truth they tell.

111

'My dad's on drugs,' I cry. 'He's not my dad any more. How can he be? He's in a different reality.'

'I know,' says Nigel, rocking me gently. My face is buried in his shoulder. He can't see my lies.

In the car on the way to the sixth-form college, Nigel becomes philosophical. He shouldn't really; he's a maths teacher. It's not his place to be Plato. But he's calmed me down and cleaned me up, so I let him carry on placating me.

'You won't always feel this bad,' he says.

That's true. I'll feel a lot worse when he finds out I've lied to him.

'And you know, Garth still loves you,' he says.

That's true too. It applies to my real predicament, as well as the one I told Nigel: my father was my hero until I found out he was on heroin.

'He's the same dad he's always been,' Nigel continues. 'You just know more about him now. Whether you still love him or not is up to you.'

That's a load of rubbish. I open the door of the glove compartment and slam it shut again with a bang.

'My father is a complete stranger,' I say, for my own benefit as much as Nigel's. I just can't get it to sink in. I can't believe I'm adopted. I can't believe I don't know who my real father is.

'Don't be silly, Grace,' Nigel says. 'You know him better than ever.'

'I don't know him at all.' This stupid argument is of my making, not Nigel's, but I kick the underside of his dashboard anyway.

He puts his hand on my knee.

'How's your mother taking it?' he asks gently.

'Search me,' I say.

'Divorce?'

'Complete estrangement.'

'That surprises me. She's always struck me as a cling-on, your mum.'

'Oh yes,' I say, with bitter significance, 'she's an alien life form alright.'

'Are you angry with *her*?'

'Chance would be a fine thing.'

Nigel faces my cryptic clues bravely, as he tries to work out where I'm coming from, but he misses the mark.

'They're still your parents,' he says.

I look away from him and down, at the seat, at my feet, at despair. The next thing I know is darkness, my head is in my hands, my face hidden, my eyes squeezed tight.

I'm not acting. I may be telling stories, but they're semi-autobiographical.

A suffocating feeling is wrapped around me like a school scarf. A headache sits on my head like a black beret, old school badge stuck in with a rusty pin. But Nigel is driving through the gates of a sixth-form college, and up the drive.

A dense and seething mass of young insect life suddenly surrounds us. Workers scurry by with worried frowns, drones comb overblown hairstyles, leather jackets prowl with animal smell, prides of high heels try not to fall, anorak nits watch with uncool admiration. The college is crawling with arty types, buffs and boffins and gothics and scruffs. We drive through honey, highly perfumed and stuck, as in Help – I can't do my homework.

I'd play truant today, if I were a student; I'd go for a game of hookey, or hide behind the bike sheds. Unfortunately, I'm the teacher. I'm only a part-time teacher, but this is one of my times. If I don't go to the lesson, the whole class will grass me up to the headmaster.

Six

The classroom is full of bright orange chairs and tables, but they don't make it feel any warmer. The frozen stiff faces of twenty teenagers greet me as I walk through the door and up to my desk at the front. Actually, there are only nineteen of them. I see this at a glance, but not because I'm good at maths.

'On your feet,' I say.

They leap up with alacrity. They think I'm about to call the whole class off and send them all back home to tea, toast and breakfast television. They are sadly mistaken.

'Everybody jog. On the spot.' I start to set an example.

Now the students are looking at me as if I've asked them to drop their subject entirely, to run right out of the Maths Block and into Arts and Humanities, where all that seems to be studied is depression, self-expression, and how to dreadlock your hair.

'Come along,' I say, 'your brains won't work if you don't warm your bodies up.'

Reluctantly, they start to follow my lead. My holistic approach goes right over their heads; it seems I'm just treating them like children.

In the second row, someone says, 'She thinks we're in the infant school.' I don't, actually. I was talking to myself. I personally cannot think if my brains are shrivelled with cold. I personally am standing at the teacher's desk feeling too small to see over the top of it without jumping up and down. But my class think they're big. They think I'm making it too easy, they can take something harder. Their wish is my command.

'Have you done your Integration homework?' I shout, over the sound of shuffling feet.

The shuffling slows down.

'No, don't stop,' I say. 'Kulvinder, you start. What do all integrals have in common?'

'Constants,' Kulvinder says, 'at the end.'

'Yes!' I declare, punching the air. I love it when they get the answers right. 'Lois. Functions. What's the integral of the F of x if $F(x)$ equals cosine x?'

Lois looks at her best friend Heidi before she replies.

'Sine x,' she says.

'Heidi,' I ask, 'what if $F(x)$ equals sine x?'

Heidi looks at Lois, jogging along beside her.

'Minus cosine x,' she says.

Are these two reading each other's minds? It can happen. Once, when I was with Eugene, he suddenly started singing the song that was playing silently in my head. He came in loud and strong; right on time, in the right key, with the right lyrics. We found this fascinating, and told all our friends, but none of them seemed particularly impressed. But I'm a listening teacher, the sort that students can really talk to, so I give Lois and Heidi the chance to open up and share their spooky psychic story with the rest of the class.

'How do you do that?' I ask.

116

'We did it together,' says Heidi.

'Did it? Did what?' I say.

'The homework,' says Lois.

'Oh,' I say. 'Okay. But you've got to be able to do it apart, too, because you won't be sitting on top of each other in that great big exam room. Ray, what's the integral of one over x?'

Ray stops dead. He's the only bloke in the front row, and he's only there because that's where Debbie sits. Debbie's his girlfriend and she's deaf in one ear so she has to sit where she can hear.

'Don't stop jogging, Ray,' I say, 'just tell me the integral of one over x.'

A look of panic is fixed on Ray's face though his eyes flicker as he searches inside for the answer. Then, like a heart patient being jump-started by a massive electric shock, he jerks back to life.

'Log x, log x,' he says.

'Mmm,' I reply like a doctor. 'Let's have a closer look at that log. What exactly is it?'

Ray pounds the floor behind his desk, panting.

'A natural log?' he says.

'Yes, it's a natural logarithm. But what is it a natural logarithm of?' I ask him.

Ray is sprinting, face red and veins standing out on his temples, as he attempts to answer the question. Debbie's looking at him in alarm.

'x?' Ray suggests.

Something inside me snaps.

'I want more than that,' I say. 'Get down on the floor and stay there until you've given me either a thousand press-ups or the correct response, whichever comes first.'

117

Ray gasps.

'Go on,' I say.

I'm serious, but the class are laughing. They don't know I'm serious because they've never seen me so serious before, because I've never been so serious before. I watch Ray get slowly into the press-up position. He's groaning.

'Go on,' I say again. I'm really pissed off with him. I don't know why.

Ray does his first press-up and stops, ready to drop. It's a strain for him, a struggle, his arms are not very strong. His second press-up could be his last. The rest of the class, except Debbie, are laughing. She's looking at me as if I'm cruel, but I've never made a student suffer like this before.

'Let me give you a clue,' I sigh. 'It begins with "m".'

Ray's face is obscured by a dark wing of hair, so I can't see if anything dawns on it. But something is enlightening me as I stare at the long fringe, a memory is stirring. There's something I know about Ray that someone told me in the staff room once. He's adopted. (Ad-*op*-ted). And I'm torturing him like I tortured Amy Dag, with maths as my tool. Oh, God! I've got to let Ray go. I've got to get him off the floor.

'What's that you say, Ray?' I ask him, stooping to put my ear to his lips, as if he's whispering something. 'The modulus of x? Congratulations. The integral of one over x is indeed the natural logarithm of the modulus of x. Well, class, respect is due to this student.'

Ray stumbles to his feet and Debbie catches him in her arms like a Hollywood starlet whose partner has just escaped from the Blob. She eyes me suspiciously. She knows that Ray didn't really know the answer.

'So what's the integral of the tangent of x?' I ask her, trying to smile reassuringly.

Debbie takes a step backwards.

'Minus tan x,' she says.

'Try again,' I reply, gently, to regain her confidence.

'Two arctan e to the x?'

'You're just guessing,' I say. 'Think about it. It's a natural log.'

'Oh, yes!' gasps Debbie. 'It's the natural log of secant x.' It's third time lucky but it's such a relief. The poor girl looks as if she could weep. She probably thought I was going to make her do backflips.

'Cotan x?' I say.

'The natural log of sine x!' Right first time. Debbie gives me a tentative smile, before turning her brilliant full beam on Ray. She's such a sweetie.

'Ewan Cleaweyton,' I say, because he's dying for me to ask him the next question. 'How would you integrate a constant?'

'The constant times x plus a constant,' says Ewan Cleaweyton, at once. He's one of those anorak-obsessed train-identified spotty intellectuals without which no class is complete.

'It's the constant multiplied by a single factor of x plus an undetermined constant. Always be as specific as possible. Small distinctions may make a big difference,' I say. Ewan Cleaweyton blushes and, still jogging on the spot, starts furiously flicking over the pages of his textbook. I don't think he's looking up anything in particular. He just wants to avoid my see-through-you stare. Ewan isn't quite as brainy as the rest of the class think he is. He spends a lot of time doing homework because he hasn't got a social life.

I turn to see through someone else. 'Jason, what's the reciprocal of a function multiplied by its differential?' I say.

'You what?' says Jason.

'What's the reciprocal of a function multiplied by its differential?' I repeat.

'The cat was sick in my bag so I couldn't put any books in it, then my grandmother died and my pencil case accidentally got locked in her coffin. I couldn't go and borrow one from a mate because I've got athlete's foot.' Jason trots out a list of lame excuses, smiling all over his face. He's a fit bloke so the jogging's no problem, but the maths is a bit much. He's the class comedian; but it's mainstream rather than alternative comedy, Benny Hill as opposed to Ben Elton.

I slow down so he can catch me up.

'$F'(x)$ divided by $F(x)$,' I say.

He grasps it at last.

'It's log $F(x)$,' he says.

'Tell me more,' I say. I'm always mock-seductive with Jason, almost a Benny Hill girl, but only because this seems to stretch him to the limit of his learning capacity. He's prepared to pump up his brain as well as his brawn to impress the ladies.

'The natural log of the function of x,' Jason beams.

'A natural log of the modulus of the function,' I make it sound obscene. This is my tried and tested method of fixing things in his memory.

The whole class are sprinting now, all together rhythmically, ready to snatch the baton as I relay the next question.

'Neal, what's the integral of sine $n x$?'

'Minus one over cosine $n x$,' he says.

Nice one, Neal!

I'm just about to ask his neighbour the last and nastiest

question, when I'm suddenly gripped with embarrassment. It is as if a part of me has stood back with arms folded, watching the rest of me bouncing up and down, breasts flapping in the faces of the front row of my breathless class. I stop jogging abruptly.

And at this moment, the classroom door opens, and Simeon comes in.

'Sorry I'm late,' he says, his eyes sliding sideways when mine try to meet them. Has he been watching through the window?

'What's the integral of x to the power n?' I say.

Now Simeon looks at me with eyes which have only just got out of bed, dusty with sleep but bright with dream-light. I can't hold his gaze.

'Careful!' I say, turning to the class. 'This is a hard one; the only integral with strings attached.'

'It's one over n plus one times x to the power of n plus one, when n does not equal minus one,' says Simeon.

'Er, okay,' I say. 'Go and sit down. Sit down, everyone. Let's begin the lesson proper.'

Between the scraping of chair legs, the banging of bags on tables, and the clatter of calculators coming out, there is some chatter. I hear one of the good students say earnestly to her neighbour, 'Doesn't Ms Bloom mean "begin the lesson *properly*"?' Behind them, a naughty boy says, 'Bum deal! She laid a detention on me for being late last week.'

I clear my throat. The class become silent.

'Sim, you're in detention,' I say quietly, looking at the books on my desk.

Someone gives a whispered wolf whistle, soft but unmistakable, and because I've got my head down I don't see who it was. For a fraction of a second, I can't look up, in case my flush of anger is taken for a blush. But then I raise my head, full of the righteous rage teachers know how to fake, ready to roar at the whole damn lot of them until the culprit owns up.

As I open my mouth, there comes a loud miaow from under my desk. It's Wynken in her wicker kitten carrier. It's a very loud miaow.

'Miss, that was a cat!' cries one of the girls in the front row.

'Don't call me Miss, I'm not a milkmaid,' I say automatically.

'A cat, a cat!' chorus the class. 'Here, kitty kitty! Puss puss puss!'

Sheepishly I lift the basket onto my desk. Wynken appears. Her ears are big as sails above her pointed little boat-face. She smiles a winning smile, which gets all the girls wet on their plastic seats.

The whole class is softening up, in fact. The suspicious wolfish whistling has been silenced by the sight of an innocent kitten in a little kitten carrier.

But Wynken wants to be free. She's pleading 'Me-out! Me-out!' She wants to play with the big children, sit on their laps and get stroked while she listens to Mummy teaching sums. Wynken puts her face right up against the bars of the basket door and shouts 'Me-out! Oh, wow, Mum, it's really bad in here, let me-out!'

I toy with the idea, but it's silly. My students aren't children and nor, for that matter, is the cat. I can't get her out in class. I don't know what else I'm going to do though. I meant to prepare a lesson plan at the weekend, but I forgot. I was too busy trying to screw you . . . Eu . . . Eugene. Now I'll have to improvise.

'Maths is stupid. It says nought is a real number,' I begin. 'It says nothing is real.

'We can't count to zero, can we? Science says we can't encounter it at all; no physical apparatus can measure it, it's not a place we can actually go. Even the integers that seem to signpost the way to zero are abstract, not concrete. Five four three two . . .

'There is only one number you can trust. The number one.'

Simeon stays behind afterwards. He sits scoring lines on his desk with a compass-point, a design whose perspective changes with each new stroke. It has a shifting centre, and the inside and outside are interchangeable. I pretend not to notice his drawing, the demonstration of his mental ability, while I pack the class's homework books into my bag; but eventually the sound of splintering formica and splitting wood starts to wind me up.

'Stop it, Sim,' I say.

Simeon looks up.

'Was that a real detention you gave me?' he asks.

'You can't expect special treatment,' I reply.

But he's already had it. He smirks at me.

Seducing this seventeen-year-old student was one of the stupidest things I've ever done, and one of the easiest. On the first day of term he sat in the back row of my class. He looked a bit slippery but I could see that he was gasping for a grasping. His need for some sex seemed so razor-sharp I pictured him with a sword instead of a penis, and thought he'd cut his hand off if he had to satisfy himself manually one more time.

But that was just my opinion. I wouldn't like to give the impression that all teachers are as sick and psychedelic as I am, or that they all have such swashbuckling ideas about their pupils. In my defence I would like to add that this thought was as close to the back of my mind as Simeon was to the back of my classroom. But as the term progressed they both worked their way forward.

Simeon stood out. It's not that he was unusually bright, though he could be brilliant if he bothered to do his homework. It's not that he was unnaturally beautiful, though he would be if he brushed his hair, had a bath every once in a while, and drank more water than beer. It's just that there was this silence and stillness about him. It drew my eye every time, away from the antics of the rest of the class, the distracting hairdos and the who-loves-whos, the silly questions and the stupid answers.

Simeon never said a word until he was spoken to. He just sat there like a pool waiting for me to fall into, as I got closer and closer to the edge. One day my foot slipped. I asked him one question too many. He never stuck his hand up or squirmed in his seat like the other students did, so I could never be sure whether he knew the answers or not. He was inscrutable, and unscrabbling him had become a bit of a game for me. That day he finally won me over with his reply.

'The question is as close as you will ever get to an answer,' he said.

I don't feel secure as a member of staff at the best of times, and if a seventeen-year-old speaks to me sternly I'm willing to believe I've still got a lot of learning to experience. Simeon reminded me of myself when I was at college, eyeing the teacher from behind a textbook, mentally undressing him with arithmetic. This was in Nigel's classroom just down the corridor. Nigel was that teacher. And I came from the back row, too, with bold advances and admiring glances. I came forward. That's why it was so easy to seduce Simeon. I'd crossed the generation gap while I was still a student, so there were none of the guilt trips that other teachers go on. Actually, the headmistress of my conscience was nagging me incessantly; but the more I thought I couldn't have Simeon, the more I felt I must.

He moved closer to the front of the class, drawn by long slow eye-contact and revealingly brief glances, until he was only a paper plane's throw away from every schoolboy's dream of making love to the teacher. He came to every lesson. The tension was mounting.

In the secretary's office I checked, furtive and flushed and fully prepared to protest too much, for records of his attendance at his other classes. He wasn't going to any other classes. In his files were a series of letters spelling serious trouble. Simeon was inches away from expulsion.

The same day, I kept him behind after maths. I stammered like he should have done, and shuffled the sheaves of paper on my desk.

'Why don't you go to your other classes?' I asked.

'I don't like the teachers,' he replied.

'Is that really a good enough reason?'

'It's good enough for me.'

'Aren't you worried about the future?'

'I have no future.'

'What about going to university?'

'What's the point? Why wait three years to be unemployed and in debt, when I could start being unemployed while I'm ahead?'

I should have known better than to embrace the disinherited

youth. No good could come of it. Most people in my position would have turned away from such fleeting fancies as butterfly-fresh buttocks, poppy lips and puppy eyes.

But not me. I gave him a kitten to look after while I went home for the weekend. And now I've got to go home with him to get it back. Luckily, I've done my day's teaching, and he doesn't go to any of his other classes, so we can slip straight away. While I'm waiting for him to put his compass in his pencil case and his body in his jacket I calm myself by chalking on the blackboard the proof that two and one are the same:

Let a and b be two numbers

let a equal b:	$a=b$
multiply by a:	$a^2=ab$
subtract b^2:	$a^2-b^2=ab-b^2$
factorise:	$(a+b)(a-b)=b(a-b)$
cancel $(a-b)$:	$a+b=b$
substitute $a=b=1$:	$1+1=1$

Therefore: $\qquad$ $2=1$

We leave the college grounds separately; Sim invisible in beetle-black jacket, iridescent eyes turned toward the ground; me glaringly obvious with orange hair and an aloof air. When I first came back here to teach I was often mistaken for a student, but not any more. I pass Nigel's car in the car park and have to look twice at it, it seems to have come from a different dream: it conveyed me here, but having done so, it should have disappeared. It's out of place, the only real vehicle in cartoon city.

We walk some distance on opposite sides of the road before I deem it safe to cross over and walk with Simeon. There's always the possibility that someone from work will see us together and tell Nigel, but I never get my knickers in a twist about it. There's also the possibility that I could lose my job on the grounds of Gross Moral Turpitude, but I can't quite bring myself to give a toss about that either.

Simeon lives on the edge of town with his parents, who are out earning his keep. He leads me down a draughty hallway with a black and white checked floor. In the kitchen there's a plate of stale prawns but no sign of my kitten mate. A horse is looking in through the window.

'King!' shouts Sim, and throws his satchel on the floor. He unbolts the stable-style door and rushes into the back garden. I stand on the stone step, with old sand-castle buckets and ground-in palm leaves, and watch.

The earth is a patchwork of tiny plots, wearing their winter colours; the off-white of wormwood and old-man's-beard, the blackened aftermath of bonfire night. A picket fence marks the end of the garden and the start of a small cold paddock, but the sticks are thin, and no match for a big horse.

Sim is splashing through brackish water and burnt leaves to the place where the fence has fallen down.

'Come on, King,' he calls, 'you cunt.'

I don't like that word.

I don't like this picture, either. High above Simeon's head, in the vast tramp's vest of a shapeless grey sky, rooks the size of fleas fly. In the paddock, on the rise, a tree stands in stark silhouette; bewitched as a broomstick, stripped bare as a cross. The wind is screaming like a woman in childbirth, squeezing a few raindrops or feverish tears.

The whole atmosphere is making me shiver.

'Where's my kitten?' I call.

Simeon doesn't answer me. With a hand on each of his horse's buttocks he is busy easing it back where it belongs. But my Blynken had better not be out in this banshee-singing and blustery back of beyond. She'd better be in the house, curled up on a feather pillow, in front of a radiator, safe and warm.

I turn around and go back inside to find her. First, I come to a dining room, with a cool colour scheme and a chilly air. I drop to my hands and knees and look under the functional furniture. There are no soft folds, no pleats or padding on this table and these chairs; nowhere for a pussy-cat to pull in her paws and hide from sight. I go through double doors into the living room. This is a glorious muddle of plant life in pots and high piles of magazines, knotty knitting and saggy seating, mugs making rings on the coffee table and photographs on the mantelpiece.

There's Simeon as a little boy. I stop my search and stare at the photos. Lined up above the fireplace he is six, ten, thirteen, and sixteen, in quick succession. Different times, different school ties, different places, but the same face stares back at me. I'm used to seeing his features in the frame of early adulthood; the leather jacket, the long greasy hair, the smoke and the sulk and the stubble. But now I can see a rosy smile, bright eyes and short curly baby locks, a whole new light is shed on the subject. When Simeon's with me, he's as grown-up as he gets. At home here with his parents, he's still their little boy.

This time last week, that thought would have given me an unspeakable thrill. It would have made the hairs on the back of my neck tickle with inexplicable excitement. Today, it makes

128

me feel sick as a paedophile. Because now I can explain the excitement. I can name the tune.

'You Can't Always Get What You Want.' Looking at these choirboy pictures of Simeon reminds me of that old Rolling Stones song. My whole life has been an attempt to get what I want. Seducing my student, and my teacher, Nigel, was just my way of plucking the forbidden fruit.

The only one I really wanted was Eugene. The only one I really couldn't have. But now as the angelic chorus soars inside my head, it seems that the words are proving untrue. I can always get what I want. If Eugene isn't really my brother, I can have him for a lover: a parting gift from my dear departed parents.

I'm still staring at the photographs of Sim but my eyes are misty and brimming over. The photos look like Eugene now, and they're taking on a new life, like photos do when the person in them has died. If Eugene is not my brother he is just another man for me to be obsessed with.

I get down on my knees, lifting the frilly petticoats of the lounge furniture and looking underneath for a flash of kitten. There's still no sign of Blynken. On the floor, balls of wool lie tightly rolled, untangled with.

I run upstairs, swift and silent, though I'm sure there's nobody but me and Simeon here. The first room I burst into is the master bedroom. Despite the sexist implications of its name, this is a place where the male and female principles combine. It is done out in an uneasy mix of pink and blue; midnight carpet and sky walls, dawn-colour quilt and curtains, ottoman and cushion covers in queasy pink candy stripes. It smells of damp, dried semen and talcum powder. Ghostly white footprints are trodden into the dark carpet. Apart from these I can barely sense a presence in the room. There are no personal effects, no ornamentation, no entertainment. Simeon's parents are authentically adult: they live their lives in the living room and never play upstairs. I suppose I should have suspected that my mum and dad weren't real sooner; they spent too much time alone, independent of their offspring.

Blynken isn't in the master bedroom. I leave, and can't remember whether the door was open or closed so shut it on the grounds that it could have been blown closed but not open by a draught during the day. I'm feeling like an intruder and need to cover my tracks. The next door looks like it leads to the bathroom. A sign on it says Disabled Toilet, and a series of glamorous rock stars, clutching their crutches in postcard poses, appear to be queuing.

It turns out to be Sim's room, dim and gloomy. A thin shaft of weak light fights its way through a crack in the curtains and fingers a dusty corner of the room. It settles on some shelves where Just William, Jennings and Biggles are lined up alongside *Men Only* and *What Bike*. Oil-black bottles and jars of greasy screws sit next to a box of white tissues; tiny plastic trolls coexist with fossilised sharks' teeth and real dinosaur bones; a chunk of amethyst crystal and a yo-yo lie on top of a Levellers CD.

I stumble in the darkness on a Doctor Marten boot, bicycle wheel, a beer bottle. This is one way of life but it's not my own. It is not a bedroom as I know it. This place has more in common with my father's garden shed or a boy scouts' bring-and-buy sale than a haven of peace and rest and possible sex. Having said that, I'm sure my father's garden shed is a place of peace and rest; and you know what they say about Lord Baden-Powell. But I like light and air, a honeysuckle-scented breeze breathing on net curtains and making them dance in the moonlight. I like fine art, reproduced in miniature on the walls, I like music everywhere, and a pile of books by the bed.

I stumble across Simeon's clumsy floor to the window and try to pull the curtains open. They're stuck, or maybe they're not meant to move. I draw one up like a stage drape and tie it in a dramatic knot, then turn to survey the spotlit scene.

Blynken's on the bed, rolled up in a sleepy ball, not stirring. Something about these kittens fills my heart with a simple, uncomplicated love that I wish I could feel for humans. It's tender and it asks for nothing in return. I pick Blynken up, and she squeaks and stretches as I tuck and tickle her under my chin.

Suddenly, an enormous sentence in my own handwriting catches my eye. YOU CAN DIFFERENTIATE AND INTE-GRATE BUT IF YOU WANT TO INTERPOLATE AND REALLY STAND OUT FROM THE REST OF THE CLASS SEE ME AFTERWARDS. Now Blynken's not the only one who's blinking. DO IT AGAIN PLEASE. AND AGAIN. AND AGAIN. I can hardly believe what I'm seeing. THIS IS A LOAD OF HYPERBOLIC FUNCTIONS BUT I CAN HELP YOU HANDLE THEM. Blown up as big as banners, hung like bunting above his bed, these are some of the comments I've written while marking Simeon's homework this term. I don't know what shocks me more; my inappropriate sexual innuendo, or his photocopying it out of all proportion.

That's not all. Giant ticks and huge crosses, unmistakably mine despite the skulls and bones he's drawn on, adorn Sim's headboard, chest of drawers and wardrobe door. Brightly coloured, hectic-eclectic, Simeon's made art out of his maths book and a mural of my marking. It's piracy!

While I'm still standing there, staring in shock, Simeon comes in. He doesn't seem upset by my invasion of his privacy, his personal space; but that gives me room to be pissed off with him.

'What do you think you're playing at?' I ask.

He doesn't understand the question. He looks me up and down, lingering on the kitten under my chin. I can see him wondering if the answer is to do with the real world of school, or the dream world of sleeping-with-teacher. He gets on the bed and hedges his bets.

'Dunno, Miss,' he says.

'This,' I say, staring over his headboard at the blown-up sentences, 'is supposed to be a secret.'

'It is a secret,' says Sim, 'anyway, who cares?'

'Plenty of people would care about our little affair,' I reply crossly. 'The board of governors, the college principal, the teachers, your parents.' I myself could not care less for parental concern or staff assessment. Except perhaps Nigel's. 'You'd better not be shooting your mouth off,' I say.

'I'm not!'

'Well, why was there wolf whistling in class this morning?'

'It's you . . . if you don't mind me saying,' says Simeon.

'What on earth do you mean?'

'You're giving it away,' he says. 'You blush when you speak to me, and you ask me all the really significant questions. The whole class think you've got the hots . . .'

'Oh, God,' I gasp.

'I haven't said anything. Honest!'

'So it's me.' I'm staring in despair at the wall where one of my ticks has turned into a prick. It looks like it only took a stroke or two. 'I'm a terrible teacher,' I declare.

'You're the best I've ever had,' says Simeon.

'I'm so unprofessional.'

'I think you're doing a great job.'

'You don't understand,' I say. 'It's not easy for me.'

'It's not easy for me either,' Simeon protests. 'I don't even like maths!'

This has got nothing to do with maths. It's all about Eugene. I didn't realise how far off the rails I'd gone, how far out of my tree I was leaning to reach that forbidden fruit. I've broken the oldest rule in the book – twice! Once with Nigel and once with Simeon I've violated the unspoken agreement between student and teacher, the bond of trust that makes learning possible. I've seriously overstepped the mark, and now it turns out it was neither of them I really wanted, it was you . . . Eu . . . Eugene.

His eyes have been in the back of my head all morning. The feel of him watching me is to the forefront. Now it turns out that my every action is solely to entertain thoughts of Eugene, the whole show is performed with him in mind. I wonder what he would think of me today, standing here, cat in hand, attractive young boy stretched out on the bed. I think he'd call Sim a bimbo. He'd talk to him politely enough, but he'd only ask trick questions to catch him out and prove he's a bit of a sprat.

'How many women have you slept with?' I say.

'Only you. The others were girls.'

'Did you idolise them too?'

'No, their breasts weren't big enough.'

'Do you know what idolise means?'

'Oh, yes,' Sim says.

I don't believe it. He's giving me trick answers. That's such

133

a Eugene thing to do. I notice something else, too. His eyes are the same colour as Eugene's. It's an identical shade of pigeon grey wood speckled faraway cloud feather peacock blue. I look and find myself reflected in them, in the moonstones. I'm in the moonstones, the moodstones. I'm in the mood.

'Come here,' says Simeon.

I put the kitten down. Something is stirring in the loins of my mind and the heart of my trousers. Something is turning me on. But as I look into his eyes, the feeling fades. It's just a memory, a pressed flower of the desire I used to have for Simeon.

His eyes are nothing like Eugene's. They don't give when I look at them. They take.

Simeon squirms on the bed.

'Come on, Miss, I mean Grace,' he begs.

'If you call me Miss one more time I'll hit you,' I say.

Then something unexpected happens. We don't have sex. I don't hit him either, of course; I'd never do that, it was just a joke. But we've had sex before, three times, and he was fully expecting to try for a fourth.

I can't shag him, suddenly. It would be like doing it with my brother, if I had one, or another member of my family. I can see the erection in his jeans, and it looks lovely, but, like a vegetarian offered a bit of beef, I'll have to turn it down.

The abstinence makes me light-headed, and the emptiness takes me high. Moving away from the bed, almost floating above it, I have a revelation about my relationship with Simeon; one that applies to Nigel, too. It's sexy being a teacher, and it's sexy being taught. Both parties know it's sexy, but neither is prepared to admit it. As soon as the word is spoken the illusion shatters; as soon as the nod or the wink is given, the roles can't be played any more.

I pick Blynken off the bed, and fly backwards through Simeon's bedroom door. She sticks her claws out in protest; I'm shaking my head in surprise. For the first time in my life, it seems, I know what taboo feels like: a burst balloon.

With the bang still resonating in my ears, and the rest of my body in shock waves, I make up some wild story about a staff meeting I'm meant to be at. Simeon settles down quite contentedly in front of *Playbus* on children's television; and I rush off like a postmodern milkmaid with my briefcase in one hand, and the kitten-basket in the other.

Seven

It's a bit of a bad trip, taking public transport to the place where Wankin, my third kitten, spent the weekend. It's nearly lunchtime by now and the bus is full of shoppers with happy bags and tired feet. I hold the wicker basket on my knees, and hope the rocking from stop to stop will send its occupants to sleep, but Wynken and Blynken are wide awake and making more noise than the traffic. Children peep over the backs of the bus seats and wriggle out from under their mothers' arms, watching as Wynken and Blynken play their favourite games; eight-paw fisticuffs, tickle my whiskers, and which-of-these-darn-tails-is-mine? Children come to fawn around the wicker kitten-carrier, and stare in awe and ooh and aah until I feel like a cross between the Pied Piper and Hamleys.

And then a woman near me gets cross and smacks and shouts at her son and spoils everything. For no apparent reason, with no redeeming rhyme, she screams a torrent of abuse, whirls him off his feet and pulls him back into his seat. She punches him to punish him, but what was his crime? Just curiosity, which might kill cats but was never meant to hurt children.

I wish I could do something to stop her attack, to crack open her anger like a coconut and let her mother's milky love flow free. But her fury frightens me as much as the confused little boy who cowers in her shadow. I grab the kitten-basket and get off the bus two stops too soon in case she turns on me. I'll have to be careful from now on; anyone could turn out to be my real mum.

I walk the rest of the way, stuffing my face with chocolate brought from a small corner shop. At the end of the road, when I've come too far to turn around and go home again, it strikes me that I might have eaten too much.

Fat and flapping I arrive on Kelly's doorstep. It's strewn with pink petals which have fallen from a rose bush arching overhead. I press them with my footprints and they bleed. Then I knock three times, and hear the sound of carpet slippers slopping on shag-pile as Kelly comes to let me in. As the door opens, my mouth closes. I'd planned a speech, something gushing, but the chocolate rush has sent it out of reach.

'I've come for Wankin,' I say.

I don't realise what I've said until Kelly's smile hits me.

'Then you'd better come inside,' she says.

All fuss and fluster, I stumble on the doorstep.

'I mean, I've come for the kitten,' I say.

Kelly is beaming.

'You're just in time for lunch.'

'What is it?' I ask her.

'A dirty great meat pie that I made with my own fair hands.'

I look at her blankly.

'Steak and kidney,' she says.

'But . . . but . . .'

'You're a vegetarian,' she says, slapping herself on the forehead.

I'm not, actually. I'm a chocolatarian.

'Well, let's see what's in the fridge,' Kelly continues. 'We'll find something nice for you.'

'I've already eaten,' I intervene. I've eaten a shit-load of the brown stuff and I'm only just starting to pay the price. I'm feeling a bit sick.

Kelly gives me a funny look.

'Are you okay?'

I swallow.

'I'm feeling a bit sick,' I say.

She holds out her hand to relieve me of the kitten-carrier and I lean against the banister. There's sweat on my face.

'What's up?' she asks me. I look at the stairs, into the distance. 'Would you like to lie down?' she says.

'I think I would.'

She helps me to the bedroom. I could walk unassisted, but my head's spinning so it's hard to go in a straight line. When we get there, I crash-land on the bed.

'You're in a bad way,' Kelly says, taking my shoes off. 'Where have you been?'

'At work.' My feet are throbbing.

'How was it?' she asks.

'Fine.'

'Have you got to go back this afternoon?'

'No.'

'Oh. How was the weekend?' Kelly is taking my skirt off.

'Great.' Released from the grip of the waistband, my stomach expands. I take a deep breath and stretch and start to feel a bit better.

'Really?' she says.

'Yes.'

'What's the matter then? Time of the month?' Kelly is unbuttoning my blouse.

'No, I'm just feeling a bit sick because I ate my . . . my lunch too fast.'

'You should have waited,' Kelly strips me completely naked with a smile. Then she puts her hand on my stomach and rubs it gently. 'This'll aid the process of digestion.'

I don't know about that. I close my eyes and feel her touch on my drum-skin. Maybe I'd be better bent double in the bathroom. I know she's only trying to loosen me up but I'm getting tighter by the second. Although her hand is soft and sweet it hits me like a toffee hammer right where I'm most brittle. I flinch.

She rolls me over and strokes my back instead. I bury my face in her pillows for a moment's peace. I wish she'd go and eat her lunch and let me recover quietly. But it seems she wants to stay and see me restored to my senses.

Her hand slides down to my bottom.

'What did you say you'd come for?' she asks. 'Spankin'?'

I sigh.

'Now that you come to mention it,' I say, 'I do deserve a good smack.'

'Why?'

'Because I'm bad.'

'No,' says Kelly softly, 'you couldn't be.'

'You want to bet?' My voice sounds hard. She doesn't know the half of it. I'm a bitch. A bastard. A double-bastard: not only do I have no father, I don't know who my mother is either. I'm thrice thrash-worthy. I've been screwing around too much, with no regard for social mores. I've had my brother, a man old enough to be my teacher, another young enough to be my student; and hey, I don't even draw the line at members of the same sex.

'Tell me about it,' Kelly says. 'You can talk to me, you know.'

I can't. The first thing I ever said to her was a lie, and now I'll never be able to tell her the truth. The very first time we spoke I implied that I am a lesbian, though imply is probably the wrong word: she asked me if I'm gay, and I said yes. She said have I ever slept with a man, and I said no. I gave these answers for fear that the conversation would be over too quickly otherwise. I gave these answers because at that moment I wished they were true, more than anything else in the world.

And in a parallel universe, every word I said to her *was* true. In another dimension Kelly is my steady girlfriend, and I haven't slept with a man since that off-putting experience with my brother when he was a little boy. There, I've practically moved into her house, which is the safest place to be. We talk for hours about everything, always in tune with each other, almost telepathic. We probe deep into matters of mutual interest, and never end up watching football on television.

In real life, I can't tell her anything, so we end up having sex. Normally this is the next best thing to a satisfying chat. But Kelly and I are having sex in the same way we had it last time, which was also the first time.

In real life I've never been with another woman, so I don't know if it's normal when Kelly blindfolds me and ties me to the bed. I don't know if it's natural for her to bind me with silk stockings that she never wears on her legs. I don't know if it's

140

ethical of her to force me to relax and unwind. But the position she puts me in is not uncomfortable, so I lie still and listen to her undressing. There's the sound of change rattling as she drops her dominant jeans, and a whoosh as she lifts her sweatshirt over her head.

I've never seen her naked but I know what a woman's body looks like. Peaches and cream by candlelight; orange peel, blood stains and broken veins in the cold light of day. Blindfolded, I can only picture her standing over me, breasts and belly distended by the angle. She's silent now but I can hear her getting closer, eyes burning black holes in my bright white body.

I'm overexposed. My legs are spread as wide as they go. She's put pillows under my hips so they're raised in the air as if I'm aching for it. There's no alternative, I can't cross my legs and pretend not to be interested in what's about to happen. It's obvious my legs are open, but I don't realise my mouth is until I feel her put something in it.

Her nipple. I don't know if it's right or left, but I suck it like the most satisfying cigarette I ever smoked as a substitute. Before I've got halfway through, Kelly takes it away. She's gone for ages, but just as I'm beginning to wonder if she's gone for good, I feel her tit touch my lips again. It's hanging, full moony, above my face, and her nipple is in the middle. I open my mouth and catch it, but just when it's beginning to seem that she dare not snatch it away again, she does. This is giving me withdrawal symptoms. I lift my head off the pillow to follow her breasts. She lifts them out of my reach.

'You have to ask, Grace,' she says. 'You won't get it unless you ask.'

141

'Give it to me,' I say helplessly. I don't know what else to say.

Kelly still won't keep still.

'What's the magic word?' she says.

'Abracadabra.'

'Don't try to be clever,' she says, 'it's too late for that now. You've stupidly let me tie you up, so don't try to be clever. What's the magic word?'

'Please.'

One nipple touches my lips briefly, then the other one. She's kneeling astride me, her seat almost on my stomach, and her breasts are swaying from side to side in a pendulum movement across my face. I give chase, but Kelly is in a jockeying position so it's not a fair race. Eventually I have to say please again.

'Please,' I say, 'give me one.'

She gives me one. I suck it like a newborn baby, badly like I don't know how to suck. I suck for ages, until I get it sussed, until it feels like I'm really getting sustenance. I suck until she doesn't want me to stop, yes – *she* doesn't want *me* to stop, because it's satisfying her too now. I suck her tit until her legs give way and she sits like a split watermelon on my stomach, red and juicy. Her nipple pops out of my mouth with the movement, but neither of us notice because we're having a multiple orgasm.

Then her lips are around my nipple. I'm so disorientated by the mutuality I'm not sure which of us is which, and for a moment it seems as if I'm still sucking. But this is a completely different sensation. Now I'm full and she's empty, I'm the maid with great jugs of milk and she wants a drink. The cow is still in control though. She won't actually clamp her lips on my tit, she just kisses it and pisses off again, teasing me like a breeze. Our sameness makes this sex seem insubstantial. Because we've both got breasts, I'm not sure what I want.

'Go on, ask for it, Grace,' she breathes.

'No.' I hate asking. I never normally have to ask. I normally get it without asking.

'You won't get it unless you say it.' As she speaks her lips brush my breasts.

But I hate saying it. I never normally have to use the words. It makes me feel like I'm in a porn film or a radio play, where sentences that normally go unspoken are called on to fill the gaps in the art form. Suck my nipples. Kiss my tits. I can't say such clichéd phrases without sounding like an actress. But I'd really love her to do it.

'Liposuction,' I say. 'Oh, give me suction with your lips!'

Kelly laughs. Then she does as I ask. And when there's a moist trail off the slopes of my breasts she follows it onto my stomach with her tongue, licking and sticking all the way down till her face is between my legs. She hovers at my entrance, with a mouth like the nozzle of a vacuum cleaner.

She stays there, only inches out of reach. I can feel her breath on me, but no touch. I'm straining against the ties that bind and nearly sprain my wrists trying to get physical contact but she keeps her distance. She has the sporting advantage of not being blindfolded. I start to see red in the darkness.

'Remember,' Kelly murmurs, 'you only have to ask.'

But this isn't a parlour game any more.

'Just say please,' she says.

Nor is it a public service announcement.

'Why should I beg,' I shout. 'I'm not that desperate.'

143

'Aren't you?' she says, and flicks my clitoris with the tip of her tongue.

I give a great Amazon jungle cry, something more Tarzan than Jane; a testosterone rush that's my own silly fault, I suppose, for sleeping with a woman. As it dies away, I start gibbering like a chimpanzee.

'Oh God, go on, do it, please, do it again, don't stop,' I say.

'Do it?' she breathes sweetly from between my legs. 'Do what?'

I scream at her. 'Put your face in my fanny and shut the fuck up!'

Kelly isn't into sadomasochism, she says; it's politically incorrect. She's decoded the power relations, and deconstructed the dialogue of master and slave, and found that pleasure itself can be so exquisitely painful that the introduction of actual pain is unnecessary.

She says she doesn't do S&M because it hurts; but I think her mind games are just as damaging.

Okay, so my body is happy to join in, jerking around like it's being electrocuted on the bed, soaking wet from the waist to the knees and trying to swallow her head. But I don't really like subordination. It makes me feel sordid. And I don't really like humiliation. It makes me feel silly. Sex as a reflex action doesn't give me a lasting inner glow. There's no love involved. It makes me feel like a laboratory animal, routinely examined for my responses.

However, if this is a test, I must be doing pretty well. I've reached double figures on the orgasometer. I've achieved such heightened sensitivity that Kelly's slightest touch sends seismic shudders through me. She's speeding things up now, no recovery time between each climax, no languid troughs between the peaks, no time to draw breath. I'm in constant seizure.

'Stop,' I pant.

She doesn't.

'Stop,' I gasp. 'I'm having a heart attack.'

Still she doesn't stop. Surely she can hear me? Surely she can't want to hear me say please?

'Please stop!' I can hardly speak. Tears appear in my eyes and are blotted immediately by the blindfold. Am I to die at the hands of a lesbian sex-murderer? Will I live on in history as the victim of a crime publicly abhorred, but privately thought horny? Luckily I've got no parents to be pictured in graphic grief on the front pages of national newspapers; but what on earth will my poor Eugene do?

The thought of Eugene gallops into my mind like a handsome prince on horseback, a knight in shining armour.

'Help!' I silently mouth to him.

His steed thunders to a standstill.

'Save me!' I scream. In my head I see him slowly lift the visor of his helmet.

He's smiling. Hair is sticking to the sweat on his forehead, and he's smiling, the swine. I suppose he finds it funny, seeing me stark naked and strapped to the bed, and Kelly almost killing me with cunnilingus. Most men like the idea of girls kissing, so I suppose a knight might have room for an erection in his armour.

Will he untie me? He shakes his head. It's not that he enjoys seeing me suffer, though he'll admit that the sight of my plight will keep him entertained for many a long and lonely night; it's just that his hands are tied as tightly as mine are, being a figment of my imagination, and thus having no physical presence or power of his own. There's only one thing he can do to help me, and that's to remind me of the password, the special way to say stop when you really mean stop; the emergency password that Kelly told me about, just after she said she wouldn't do anything dangerous.

I'd forgotten about Kelly. I know she's still there, because my body is still struggling against her, but I can't feel any pain. This S&M isn't all it's cracked up to be; it doesn't hurt nearly as much as how much I love Eugene.

I stop dead, plop on the bed, no longer doing a limbo dance, lifeless. I lie still.

'What's up?' says Kelly.

'Mercy mercy, Uncle Percy,' I say.

That's the password. I've remembered it. Don't know who Uncle Percy is; doesn't sound like a feminist, more like the name of a penis. Anyway I say it once, then I belt it out again in a strangled tone. I'm so angry I don't care if there's a penalty for improper use.

Kelly's limbs buckle and she drops onto the bed beside me. I want her to untie me so I can go to the loo, but it takes ages because she's got butterfingers. Every time I tell her I can't hold on any longer, I'm going to wet myself and saturate her mattress, she says it wouldn't be the end of the world. She thinks this is Noah's ark, but I'm feeling like St Joan.

By the time Kelly takes off my blindfold I've forgotten what she looks like. I didn't expect her to be smiling like a blooming bride. She tries to come to the toilet with me. That's so honeymoony. I know we're both sticky with sweat and stuff, but we're not stuck together. I tell her to stay in bed. I piss privately and it burns, it makes my eyes water and as soon as I finish I feel like I need to go again. My flesh has melted but there is something solid and knotted inside me.

I walk back to the bedroom on stiff legs to get dressed. Kelly is stretched out on the bed, smaller than she seemed before. She should never have tied those tights round my eyes; blind to her actual image I saw her in pictures of greater magnitude.

'That was amazing!' She props herself up on some pillows, her chest damp, her face blotchy.

'Yeah. Where are my clothes?'

'There. But don't put them on yet. Come under the covers with me.'

'I can't. I'm sorry. I haven't got time.'

'What? You're not leaving?'

'Yes. Sorry.'

'But we haven't finished yet. I want to make love. Talk about wham bam thank you ma'am!'

I zip my trousers up.

'You were the one doing all the whamming and bamming,' I say.

'How was it?' she beams.

The button comes off my trousers as I do them up.

'Bollocks!'

'What? It was bollocks?' Kelly says.

'No, the button's come off my trousers.'

'But the sex was bollocks?'

'I think we've chosen a rather unfortunate word,' I say. I put the button in my pocket. Kelly puts her glasses on.

'Are you trying to tell me you didn't like it?'

I'm trying to find my shoes.

'Grace!'

'What!'

'Didn't you like it?'

I'm under the bed.

'Come on,' Kelly says, 'yes or no.'

'Maybe.' I put my shoes on. 'I don't really like being dominated. It doesn't turn me on.'

'Did you want to be on top?'

'Side by side would have been alright.'

'Are you making a political statement?'

'It just wasn't very personal.'

'But we'd hardly even started,' Kelly says. 'It would have been your turn next. You could have done anything you liked to me.'

'I don't like playing around with people.' I pick up my bag.

'Yes, you do.'

'Shhh!' I say. 'I told you that in secret.'

'I haven't told anyone else,' she protests, 'but I'm allowed to broach the subject with you.'

'Look,' I reply, 'I'll see you later. It's not a very good day today.'

'The spheres are in commotion,' says Kelly.

'What?'

'The planets. They're doing strange things.'

'Are they?'

'Yes,' she nods, 'Saturn's entering Uranus.'

'Well, I'd best be off then,' I say.

She follows me down the stairs, wrapped in a duvet. 'Why have you got to go?' she asks. 'Where are you going? Can't you stay a bit longer? Have some lunch with me. A bottle of wine. You're leaving me most unsatisfied. It's not really the done thing.'

I turn on her angrily at the foot of the stairs.

148

'I don't know what the done thing is, do I?' I say. 'You scared me.'

'How?'

'You didn't stop.'

'I did!'

'But only after I'd asked you three times,' I shout. 'When I say no I mean no.'

' "Mercy mercy, Uncle Percy" means no,' she says calmly. ' "No" is just a sound you make when you're having sex.'

'But it wasn't sex,' I protest. 'It wasn't me having it. Honestly, Kelly, I feel like I've been in a fight.'

'I'm sorry,' she says. 'I didn't realise.'

We go into her farmhouse-style kitchen, and find Wankin breaking through the crust of the steak and kidney pie. It's not hot enough to scald him, but Kelly tries to. She chases him off the table and drops the duvet on the floor.

'Oh, shit,' she says. 'Grace, have you been abused?'

I look at her naked. There are scars on her body. There are so many scars her body looks like it's been written all over. Scores of red and pink and white lines, intersecting as they go from place to unimaginable place; it's a road map of transgression.

'Why do you ask?' I gasp.

'Well, I seem to have touched a raw nerve,' she says.

My eye follows the line of one of the scars as it ribbons around her thigh.

'Did you do that to yourself?'

'More or less,' she says.

'Is that why you use a blindfold?' I ask.

'Probably,' she says.

'But if you stopped cutting yourself up,' I say, 'you wouldn't have to blindfold your lovers, or tie them down.'

'That's like saying stop breathing, then you won't have to live,' Kelly replies. 'Why are you so angry?'

'Because people keep doing things to me. Taking things away from me.'

'Breasts,' says Kelly.

At first I think she's using the term as a feminist dismissal of my argument, in the way that one might say bollocks or bullshit.

'No, it's not,' I protest. 'You wouldn't believe the weekend I've had.'

'What happened?'

I blurt it out. I didn't think I could tell Kelly anything, but on the spur of the moment I just blurt it out, and immediately feel better; a bit purged.

'I'm adopted,' I say. 'My parents told me I'm adopted. They're not my real parents.'

'Breasts,' says Kelly, nodding sympathetically. 'That's what they've taken away from you. They've metaphorically withdrawn the breast. And that's why you got so cross when I literally did it upstairs.'

'It was awful,' I say, 'I felt powerless. Nonexistent.'

'I'm really sorry,' Kelly sighs. 'If you'd told me sooner, I wouldn't have teased so.'

Wankin is slinking past my ankles so I pick him up, quickly brush him off and thrust him into the basket with Wynken and Blynken. They pretend not to remember who he is for a while, but they can't cold-shoulder him for long. Soon they're batting him about the ears and treading on his tail as if he'd never been gone.

'There's one more cat to get yet,' I say to Kelly. 'Nod. I have to leave now. I'm sorry.'

'Can I give you a lift?' she asks nicely.

'No. It's right across town. It's quicker by train. Thanks all the same.'

It's quicker by train, but there's a snag. I stare through the smeared window at a vaguely familiar landscape and wonder whether my parents telling me I'm adopted counts as abuse, when the scene behind the window grows suddenly more familiar and the train grinds to a halt at a station. To alight here has always been my delight. This is Eugene's station.

I jerk in my seat as the train stops, absorbing the shock. It's Eugene's station. My mind is blown into several pieces. Part of it actually leaves my body, just gets up and gets off the train; a blithe shadow of my former self leaps onto the platform and makes eagerly for the exit. Another piece of my mind keeps me in my seat, freezing me with the realisation that I'll never leap without looking again, I'll never get off the train here so lightly. A third fragment is flapping around the carriage like a trapped bird, desperate to find a way out but flying into windows every time.

Suddenly all the kittens in the basket beside my feet start miaowing at the same time. I get to my knees on the filthy floor and look through the holes in their door to see what's up; and the next thing I know the train is moving again and I'm travelling with my head and shoulders under the seat, and my bottom shaking in the faces of some bemused fellow passengers. I get to my feet and spend the rest of the journey pacing the length of the train in the direction of travel, so that

151

when I look out of the window I seem to be walking at a hundred miles an hour.

Every time I knock on Dave's door someone different answers it. I don't know how many people live in his house, and whenever I ask him, he says he doesn't know either. They're mainly men, and sometimes I engage in a bit of banter with them, but I'm not in the mood for that today.

'Hello,' I say to the fish-faced guy in the doorway. 'Is Dave here?'

The man turns and shuffles down the hallway to a low door under the stairs. He opens it and, holding back his long, lank and tangled hair, shouts into the darkness: 'Dave!'

'Yo!' comes Dave's deep reply.

'Visitor.'

There is the sound of hippy footwear on concrete steps, and Dave slowly appears at the top of the cellar stairs.

'Gracie-baby!' His greeting rings like a doorbell.

'Hi,' I say.

'For sure. Come on down, something's happening!'

That's right, Dave, take me straight to the basement without so much as a cup of tea or a digestive biscuit in the kitchen first. I follow his bad-mannered backside down the stairs and into a room which smells of eggs, and not just because its walls and ceiling are lined with old egg boxes.

'Listen to my new song,' he says, picking up his electric guitar and starting to play. Dave's a consummate musician, but as far as I'm concerned he might as well be farting. It's not that I don't appreciate his complete mastery of the instrument, I just think the way he never stops to ask me how the hell I am stinks. I wouldn't tell him anything, of course, but it would be nice to be asked.

I've known Dave nearly all my life. He used to be my brother's best friend, when I used to have a brother. He spent an entire summer holiday pretending to be Gary Glitter in our back garden, but he was called David then, and had short hair and a snotty nose. We lost touch with him in the great sea of faces at big school and I forgot he ever existed; but Eugene bumped into him again after university and one day he said to me, 'Remember David Poppins? His band's playing at Glastonbury. Do you want to go?'

Going to Glastonbury with Eugene was my idea of bliss, and it would have been even if David Poppins still had short hair and a snotty nose. But the bloke on stage, standing barefoot amidst a tangle of leads and basking in spotlights, had long blonde ringlets. At first I thought he was a woman, but then I looked through binoculars and saw that he was quite clearly a male member of the band.

Poppins and the Pills didn't have a vocalist, but they didn't need one because Dave was the best guitarist we had ever heard and he was making it sound like an opera singer on acid. He didn't just play G, he played green or grief or Geronimo. He didn't play D, he played daisy or daddy or dirty. Each note sang like a word, each phrase ran like a sentence. He could play a scale so fast it sounded like the whole of the Bible in sixty seconds. He could sustain it so slow we thought the earth had stopped moving.

I've heard that the way a pop hero performs on stage is a clear indicator of his sexual prowess. The ones who thrash about, grabbing at their crotches and missing out the quavers, are more concerned with their own satisfaction than anyone

153

else's. But Dave had the quivering stillness and minimum show of a sophisticated soloist. He stood quietly, head bowed, eyes closed, while his hands were possessed by whirling dervishes and danced in a trance.

Dave is skilful between the sheets, too; his stamina is laudable and his enjoyment is loud. He's good with his hands, but he doesn't kiss me much and sometimes I feel he'd rather be with his guitar. Sometimes I feel that my body is wooden, my neck is long, and my strings are tuned to concert pitch. When he fingers me, strums me, plucks me, I feel that it's all rhythm and no soul.

'Yeah?' Dave finishes playing his new song and looks up at me for a response.

Yeah, Dave. Well, maybe. I don't really know if I liked it or not, because I didn't hear a sound. I didn't hear the electric guitar inches away from my ear in an egg-boxed cellar. Why not? I was miles away.

'Your brother liked it,' says Dave. 'Arse-end of last week he came round and danced so hard we all thought he'd got a new girlfriend.'

I get a sad feeling like a guitar string snapping inside. Whatever Eugene is doing now, I bet it's not dancing.

'Fancy a shag?' says Dave, putting down his instrument and lighting up a cigarette.

I haven't told Eugene that I'm still sleeping with Dave. It all seems a bit too close to home. Having said that, home just got so close to itself that it imploded and now there isn't one. But I still won't tell Eugene that I've been sleeping with Dave.

He knows about the first time, of course. Well, he was there, too. It was that same night at Glastonbury; I'm a fast mover when I want to be, especially under the influence of intoxicating substances. But even so, the dawn was breaking before me and Eugene and the boys in the band were ready to wend our ways to bed. I remember walking in a row, slow as elephants, hands held on either side like trunks and tails, along a winding path between burnt-out campfires to our settlement at the top of a hill.

Eugene and I had a two-man tent, but tonight there was only room for one. When we got there I stopped him unzipping the entrance flaps and said: 'I'm going to roger Mr Poppins. It would be jolly nice if you could wait outside for a while.' I spoke politely – I was so high on drugs I had to enunciate very carefully to convey my extreme clarity of vision – but my words seemed to offend Eugene. He took a step backwards and banged into a big gong standing behind him with an angry clang.

'What about Nigel?' Eugene said.

'He's not here.'

'You've got no respect for him. He's faithful to you. He told me he's so determined to avoid other women he won't even stroke a female animal.'

'Nigel is mad as a mongoose. Where's that sensible Dave disappeared to?' I said, peering into the group of bombed-out musicians who'd sat down around the damaged gong and were either trying to repair it or turn it into something to do more drugs with.

'He disappeared at the mention of your boyfriend,' says Eugene.

'No, he didn't, he's been eyeing me up all evening, and now I'm going to get him into my snaking bag, whether you and your beloved Nigel like it or not.'

On this trip, we were walking and talking through treacle;

words were hard to say, and ways were hard to see. Luckily, Dave hadn't disappeared at all. He'd merely fallen to the floor. He was still holding my hand.

'Aye up, matey, in we go,' I said, lifting the flaps of my tent and helping him in. He got a bit stuck in the doorway and I had to apply my boot to his bottom before he was fully inserted. As I was following him in, Eugene sat down firmly right outside.

I turned to look at him.

'I don't know why you're so upset,' I said. 'You told me you don't even like Nigel that much, and Mr Poppins used to be your best friend.'

As I turned away again, I caught a desperate look on my brother's face and I didn't understand it. I understand it now. If you want to sleep with someone, Eugene's look said, sleep with me. Fuck Nigel, I don't care if you're faithful to him or not, but if you want to be with anyone else, be with me. We could be brilliant together, and the longer you leave me sitting outside the tent listening to you screw Dave, the more I'll know I'm right.

I think I understood it then, deep down, but it had been such a weird day, full of hallucinations and unreal sensations, that I couldn't trust my perception. My mind was mashed up and messed with. My heart was lying in my ribcage like a dying rabbit, and to realise what Eugene was saying might have been too much for it.

But that might have been the night, that might have been. If Eugene had come into the tent with me, would we have gone to sleep separately, or would we have slept together? And come the morning, would it all have been forgotten, buried deep as a dream? For I remember nothing of that first sex with

Dave but the dim inverted V-shape of the tent and the fact that Eugene could hear us through the canvas.

'Grace. Wake up.'

I'm doing it again. Dave's talking to me and I'm taking no notice.

'What?' I say.

'Do you fancy a shag?'

'No, sorry,' I say, 'I'm not into sea birds. I just came to collect the kitten.'

'Collect the kitten?' says Dave. 'What does that mean?'

'Take it back.'

Dave doesn't look convinced. He starts singing the words 'Take it back' to the tune of the Beatles' 'Get Back', and when they don't quite fit he shakes his head in confusion. He can be so stupid sometimes.

'Where is it?' I ask him.

'What?' he says.

'The kitten.'

'The kitchen?'

'In the kitchen? Okay. So can I go up and get it?'

'Go up and get it? Yeah.'

'Do you want to come too?' I say. 'Then you can make me a quick cup of tea.'

'Tea. That's all you ever want from me.'

'Now you know that's not true, Dave. It's just that I'm in a hurry today, on account of my weekend away.'

'Alright, Grace, I'll make you a cup of tea. Ain't got no milk though.'

Shit.

Dave and I go up the concrete stairs and through the door to the hall. There's a powerful smell of cooking coming from the kitchen. We go in.

'Dudes,' says Dave, greeting the group of talented musicians and complete twats gathered around the table.

One or two of them grunt in response. They never talk much when I'm present, though there always seems to be great hilarity behind the closed door, after I leave the room.

'What's cooking?' says Dave.

'You make raw foodstuffs hot and eat them and they're easier to digest,' says a thin man with a skinhead sitting on the windowsill.

'So what's in the oven?' says Dave.

'A dead animal,' says the bloke standing by the stove.

I go cold.

'Where's my kitten?' I ask Dave.

Before he can answer, the skinhead says, 'It's in the basket,' in a silly voice, and everyone laughs except me and Dave. 'Where is it?' I ask him again.

Dave looks blankly at the kitten-carrier in my hand.

'Not these ones, the other one,' I say. 'The one I gave you to look after for the weekend.'

Slowly his face changes and realisation dawns.

'So you did!' he says. 'Oh Jesus, so you did!'

Dave turns and runs out of the kitchen and up and down the hallway. 'Where is it? What have I done with it?' he shouts, racing to the top of the stairs and down them again straightaway. The thin skinhead comments that he hasn't seen Dave do so much speed since New Year's Eve. Then he reappears, pulling at the collar of his shirt.

'What did this kitten come in?' he pants.

'A box,' I say, 'a little brown cardboard box. Full of straw.'

Dave stands still on the spot, his eyes straining as if with second sight, and slowly his gaze crosses the kitchen and stops in the corner where the swing-bin is. The floor around it is littered with crushed beer cans and crumpled pizza boxes and a little brown cardboard box. Full of straw.

Dave rushes across the kitchen and picks it up.

'That's the one,' I say. 'Now where's Nod?'

Dave lifts the box to his ear and listens carefully.

'No,' I gasp, 'you didn't leave her in there.' I shake my head in denial, but I'm only delaying the shock.

Dave hands me the box.

'Sorry,' he says.

My hands are shaking as I open the box and look inside. Little Nod is shaking, too. She's as scared as I am. She's crouching in the dirty straw of her incomprehensible prison, eyes closed against the first light she's seen for three days. She must be starving. She looks worse than the first time I found her, in the dustbin.

'Nod,' I say. 'Oh my God.'

The skinhead gets off the windowsill and goes to the sink.

'Let's give her some water,' he says.

'Maybe it's too late,' says the bloke by the stove.

'No, bring some, quick,' I say. I tip Nod out of the box and onto the table because I'm frightened to touch her. She's so thin and shivering and her legs aren't holding her up properly. 'Quick. Oh, God.' I snatch the saucer of water from the skinhead and put it down beside Nod. At first it looks like it's been so long since she's seen a drink that she's forgotten how to do it, but soon she starts lapping and doesn't stop till there's not a drop left. Then she falls over. 'Fill it up,' I say, handing

159

the saucer back to the skinhead, 'and find some food, too. I did bring some tins for her.' We both look at Dave.

He shrugs.

'I'm sorry, Grace,' he mutters, 'I'm a cunt.'

'No, you're not,' I shout. 'Cunts are nice.'

'What can I say?' Dave shrugs helplessly.

'Ouch!' I inform him.

'Ouch?' he says. 'Why?'

By way of an answer, I pick up a kitchen chair and swing it at his head.

Only when I'm satisfied that I've hurt Dave as much as he's hurt my kitten, is it time to leave, and not before. Nod is at death's door, and while Dave is being helped to bed, I pick her up and cradle her to my chest. Her fragility makes my heart beat faster. Her quiet acceptance of the awful situation makes me feel so ashamed.

'Put it in with the others,' says the skinhead. 'They'll lick it better.'

So we put Nod in the nest. Wynken, Blynken and Wankin seem as shocked as I was at the state of her. They go really quiet and back off to watch her from a distance. I put some food in, too, and they don't even notice. But she crawls towards it, and eats a little bit, and then the others creep closer, to crowd round her and ask questions and cry.

'Can I give you a lift home?' asks the skinhead, whose name is now Steve. I gratefully take him up on the offer and give him the address. He hands me his spare motorbike helmet.

'On a motorbike?' I say. 'What about the kittens?'

Steve smiles and takes me outside. His fine old-fashioned motorcycle has a side-car.

'My girlfriend's got kittens, too,' he says, 'only hers are of the human variety. Put the basket on the seat there. It's safe enough.'

I have visions of the tiny side-car disappearing beneath the wheels of a lorry, it's so low to the ground it seems highly dangerous, but once we've started my fears are crushed. Steve is a sensible driver. I've ridden pillion to some complete plonkers in my time, who push their luck and pull the speed limit behind them like caravans, and hug the corners so tight I've stopped breathing. Sometimes, riding a bike is like flying, and I swear it's possible to reach orgasm from the buzzing black leather seat between my legs. But today I sit still and look at the kittens through the scratchy perspex of the side-car and have an imaginary conversation with them in which everything is going to be alright.

'We've arrived,' says Steve, switching off the engine.

That was quick. I look up. Where are we?

'Why have you brought me here?' I shout, through my helmet. This is Eugene's street. We're parked outside Eugene's house.

'What?' says Steve.

I struggle to undo the strap under my chin.

'This isn't where I live,' I say.

'But this is the address you gave me.' Steve looks a bit confused.

I look up at the top floor of number 27, Eugene's windows. One of them is open, he must be at home.

'It's my brother's,' I say, then bite my lip so hard I taste blood on my tongue. I hand Steve his spare helmet.

'I can still take you home,' he says. I read his lips through his visor.

161

'No, it's okay,' I say, 'I'll stay here.' I lift the lid of the side-car and get the kittens out.

'I hope it's alright,' says Steve.

'It could be touch and go,' I sigh. Eugene's not actually my brother any more, so he may not even want to see me. 'He might never speak to me again!'

Steve shakes his head, and starts the engine. It's not until he's driving away that I realise he was talking about Nod.

Eight

I've got my own key to Eugene's flat, but I don't know if it will
fit his lock any more. Standing in darkness on the landing,
because dusk has set in and the lights don't work, I knock on his
door. I'm hallucinating a warm glow, a halo around its edges,
so desperately do I want to find him behind it.

The light widens as the door opens. He's there. I'm here.
We're both in the same place at once. My mind clears like a
mirror.

'Where have you been?' Eugene asks.

'Chucking my lovers,' I say. 'Every single one of them, well
and truly told where to get off. Given the elbow, the big heave-
ho. I've rebuffed them, repulsed them, spurned and dismissed
them; finished with them, once and for all.' I pause for breath,
like a carol singer on the doorstep.

'Come in,' he says, holding his hand out to take mine.

Because I'm the image of him I hold my hand out, too. But
my feet don't move.

'Do you believe me?' I say. 'I'm free!'

'Okay,' he laughs.

'And you can be, too,' I add.

Eugene's face falls, but before he can speak there's the sound of someone shouting in the living room.

'*Who is it?*'

A door bangs behind him.

'*Who is it?*'

Footsteps come down the corridor.

'*Who is it?*'

It's fucking Trudy. Eugene's girlfriend. She comes into view beside him, and for the life of me, I can't figure out what he sees in her. She's so fucking ugly. And so fucking stupid. Even now she's in full sight of me she's asking Eugene who it is again.

'It's Grace,' he says gently. 'Come on, let's get you back in the warm.'

Instantly overwhelmed with jealousy, I turn to leave. The way he speaks to tiny Trudy fills me with a rage so great I can't contain it. She's just a bead, a mere button on my bursting blouse; but she's wearing Eugene's jumper and it seems to make her bigger than me.

'Grace,' says Eugene, 'come on.' He takes hold of me with one hand and Trudy with the other, and ushers us down the narrow hall to the living room door.

'In you go,' he says, and we both get pushed inside. 'I'll make some tea.'

When he's in the kitchen I smile coldly at Trudy. She looks back at me. My smile turns to ice and cracks. Trudy looks like she knows something. Has Eugene told her about the adoption, or anything else that went on over the weekend?

Something looks different about Trudy, very different indeed. I haven't seen her for a month or so, but she is years older than I remember her. Last time she was pretty and nursey-pert; all blonde and blue and whiter than white. Now her snub nose has grown gnome-like, and the mouth that was once so starchy-smart is dotted with cold sores.

'Are you alright?' I say.

She doesn't reply, just shrugs almost imperceptibly and carries on standing in the middle of the floor looking me up and down as if I'm something the cat dragged in. We've always been a bit hostile towards each other but this is ridiculous.

'Would you like to see my kittens?' I ask. 'There're three girls and a boy.'

I put the basket on the carpet and open its door. Wynken, Blynken and Wankin tiptoe to the edge of their territory and peer out, whiskers quivering, whole bodies shivering with excitement as the light bounces off a sea of new smells. With a hop, skip and jump they're on the floor, daring each other to go further, with shy glances and sly shoves. But Nod stays inside, lying down.

'That one isn't very well,' I say. 'I gave her to a friend to look after for the weekend, but he forgot. He just left her in the box. No food, no water, no air.'

This would have turned the old Trudy into a pool of tears but the new one is harder to melt.

'That's nothing,' she says nastily. 'Look!' And she puts a hand to her head and pulls out a clump of her own hair. She doesn't pull very hard; the tresses come away effortlessly.

'What?' I say.

She holds it out to me.

'Look.'

I am looking. It's real alright. The hair is really in her hand.

'Why?' I say, staring from the limp golden strands to the bald patch on her scalp. 'What's happening?'

'Hello Peter,' she says.

165

'What?'

'Allo Pecia. Alopecia. My hair is falling out.' Trudy slaps her hand to her head.

'Oh my God,' I say.

Trudy pulls out another length, and waves it in my face.

'Go away,' she says.

I go into the kitchen to find Eugene. He hasn't got very far with the tea. He's sitting on the floor with his head in his hands.

'Trudy's hair is falling out,' I say.

He nods slowly.

'Why?' I say. 'What's the matter with her?'

'I don't know,' he shrugs and stands up stiffly. I'm about to suggest that it might be stress when he goes on. 'Nor does the doctor. He doesn't have a clue. None of them do. She's seeing three.'

'Three doctors? Because her hair's falling out? She'd be better off seeing a shrink.'

'No,' says Eugene, 'it's not just the hair. Didn't you notice? The way she's acting.'

'Well, yes,' I say, 'but I thought that was because her hair's falling out. I'd be pretty upset, too. It's one of the worst things that can happen to a woman.'

Eugene drops a box of tea bags on the floor. 'She's not just upset,' he says, as he bends over to retrieve them.

'I'm getting a saucer of water for my kittens,' I say at the same time, and try to give him a clumsy hug on the way to the sink. He's still stooped and the corner of the tea bag box stabs me in the stomach as he stands up. Shocked at the awkwardness of our touch, I start to stammer an apology. 'Sorry,' I say, 'I'm a bit upset myself, as it happens. One of my kittens is sick. She got left in a box over the weekend with no food or water and now she's not very well. Do you know how long it would take, under those conditions, for a kitten to, you know, become terminally ill?'

'No,' says Eugene.

'Can you have a look at her for me?' I ask. 'See if you think she'll be alright?'

'Yes,' says Eugene. 'How did it happen?'

'Oh, I gave her to someone to look after and they forgot about it.'

'Who?'

'No one you know,' I say. But he does know Dave. Since finding out about being adopted, I may have lost a surname, but Liar is my new middle name. I also told Eugene that I've severed relations with all my lovers, which is not strictly true, though it's what I fully intend to do.

'Well, give it a drink.' Eugene sounds distracted. Usually he'd have got all cross about cruelty to my kitten, and jealous of the secret lover who was supposed to be looking after it. I watch him pouring boiling water into the teapot with a shaking hand.

'What about Trudy?' I say, suddenly.

'Huh?' Eugene half-turns toward me, shrouded in steam.

'Have you told her?'

'What about?' he says.

'About us. Not being brother and sister,' I say.

'No!' Eugene holds the teaspoon up to stop me, almost as if it's a crucifix and I'm a vampire.

'I don't understand, then. Why has her hair fallen out?' I say.

Eugene gives me a long look. Then he taps himself on the forehead with a teaspoon.

'No one knows,' he says. 'That's the thing. We've been to Harley Street to see the main man, and even he didn't know. Mystery Virus, he said; or in plain English, "Dunno, mate." '

'What does Trudy think?' I ask him.

'Interesting question,' he replies, 'and she's given me no end of interesting answers. As soon as she tries to tell the doctors though, they start going on about Alzheimers or mad cow disease. But honestly, Grace, it's way crazier than that. There are all these seemingly unrelated physical symptoms. Some, um, lumps growing and . . .' Eugene stops and swallows with difficulty.

'And what?' I say.

'Some other things,' he says turning back to the tea, and stirring it slowly. 'You'll see, I expect.'

'How long has this been going on?' I ask.

'Six months,' Eugene replies exactly.

'She's been ill for six months? Why didn't you tell me?'

'I didn't want you to know.'

His answer triggers a bullet of anger from me.

'That's what Dad said when I asked him why he didn't tell us we were adopted sooner,' I shout.

'Well, I admire his honesty,' says Eugene.

'I don't,' I say, 'but I was raised on a foundation of lies.'

'There's no need to take it personally,' Eugene says wearily.

'So why didn't you want me to know she was ill? Did you think I wouldn't care? Do you think I'm that callous?' I fire questions at him.

Eugene looks me in the eye. He'd never let himself be blindfolded. He faces up to things.

'I'm the callous one, Grace,' he says. 'I was planning to seduce you, see.' My mouth drops open but it doesn't stop him talking. 'It's all that's kept me going the last six months, the thought of this weekend, the thought of you and me; and I thought if you knew Trudy was ill you wouldn't care to two-time her, even if it was only once. Now, it's time for tea,' he adds abruptly, popping a cosy that looks like a cottage on the pot.

His efforts to make a lovely cuppa are wasted, sadly. He carries it on a tray as far as the living room door, where he drops it, crash and splash, on the carpet.

'I don't believe you wanted to do that,' I joke from behind him, before I realise that he's not laughing; he's standing and staring at something in the living room in an attitude of extreme shock.

'What's up?' I say, rising on tiptoe to see over his shoulder. There's a big pink billiard ball, a big bald egg, in the place where Trudy's head should be; the bare outline of a baby or an old man. All Trudy's hair has fallen out. Her head is naked.

'Trudy? Where's it gone?' Eugene walks toward her, treading softly, his voice grave.

I follow him, managing not to drop my saucer of water but to put it down by the kitten-basket instead.

'Where is it?' Eugene says to Trudy. 'Where's your hair?'

'It came out,' she says defiantly.

'Did you pull it?' asks Eugene. I don't blame him for being suspicious, there's a very dodgy look on Trudy's face. But she doesn't reply. 'Where did you put it?' he says, starting to look on the floor around her. From where I'm standing he seems to be looking everywhere but at Trudy's staring scalp, as if he can't bear to see it. I don't blame him for that either. It looks strangely obscene.

'Does it hurt?' I ask Trudy.

'There're kittens on the curtains,' she says.

There are, too. I turn and see them, clinging desperately to burgundy Dralon; Wynken, Blynken and Wankin arranged in an ascending scale across the deep red expanse like those flying geese in awful murals.

'What are you doing up there?' I say, in the tone of voice reserved for things that aren't going to answer back. But there is a response. There's a faint rustling of straw and a weak miaow from the cat-basket. Nod is coming out for a drink at the saucer of water. I watch as she emerges at the entrance, and gasp with surprise. Nod has got long blonde hair. She looks like nothing so much as Dougal from *The Magic Roundabout*, doped up on sugar lumps, as she comes into view, moving stiffly on hidden legs and peering blearily through the fringe of her wig. Nod is wearing Trudy's hair; it's stuck on with Sellotape, a long strip in a slick centre-parting.

I look back at Trudy.

'Why did you do that?' I say. I feel like crying, on behalf of my cat. Nod looks so sad, so beaten when she's down. She's drowning under a golden waterfall and she can't get a drink. I kneel down beside her and gently peel the Sellotape off her fur. 'Blimey, Trudy, you're mad, you are,' I say.

'Don't, Grace,' mutters Eugene.

'I can't be milder than that,' I say.

'I know,' he says, 'but . . .' He looks pointedly at Trudy.

'My kitten's sick, too,' I say.

'I know, Grace, but can we be a bit grown-up about it?' Eugene replies.

'I want to go to bed now.' says Trudy.

Over her shoulder I see Eugene repress a sigh. He looks very

170

pale and tired. I was too busy being pale and tired myself to notice this sooner.

'Okay then, off you go,' he says.

'No,' says Trudy, 'carry me.'

'You can walk,' he says.

'No. I'm tired. Carry me.'

'Let me take your arm.'

'No. Carry me. Like you always do.'

Eugene looks at me.

'She's tired,' he says.

He lifts Trudy into his arms. She looks light as a feather.

'Do you want to say goodnight to Grace?' he asks.

She just laughs.

Eugene gives me an apologetic shrug, and carries Trudy towards the door. 'I'll be back in a bit,' he says.

'No,' says Trudy, 'come to bed with me.'

'Trudy, it's only eight o'clock,' he says. 'Can't I stay up and talk to my sister for a while?'

When he says 'my sister' I give a start; I didn't think I'd begun to take our estranged relationship seriously, but him calling me that already sounds unfamiliar.

'No,' says Trudy, 'I want you in bed with me.'

'But . . .'

'I want you, Eugene, I want you.'

Eugene looks at me again, blushing darkly. Trudy sounds like a cross between Arnold Schwarzenegger and Zsa-Zsa Gabor; she's definitely trying to seduce him. I'd have thought she was too ill for that.

'Not tonight,' Eugene mutters. 'I need to see Grace.'

'No,' says Trudy.

'I can't leave her sitting here all alone,' says Eugene.

171

'Tell her to go home,' says Trudy.

'No,' says Eugene. 'Look, you'll be alright in bed on your own for a while. I'll come in later.'

'Now, come now, oh please, please,' Trudy is hanging round his neck like a baby but I don't think her motives are pure. She is wriggling about in his arms so much that her skirt is rising to her thighs. Then I see one of the lumps Eugene mentioned, a growth the size of a golf ball on the back of her knee.

'I've got to go anyway,' I blurt out. 'Better get the kittens home where they can be comfortable.' I start picking the three of them off the curtains. They're sticking like burrs. I'm panicking a bit.

'But you haven't had any tea yet,' says Eugene.

'Tell you what,' I say, putting the kittens in the basket and fastening the door, 'I'll come back tomorrow. I'll see you then. Okay?'

I stand up to go. Eugene looks relieved. For the moment, he doesn't have to choose between me and Trudy.

'Sleep tight, don't let the bugs bite,' I say cheerfully as I go; but I gasp for air in the stairwell, and buy a packet of cigarettes at the station.

When I come back at ten the next morning Trudy is still in bed. The windows in the living room are open to a cold grey sky, and the smell of winter city. Eugene's cleaning the tea stain from the tray crash on the carpet.

'You should have done that last night,' I say.

'I was too busy,' he replies.

I sit down with a sigh in front of his boarded-up fireplace. I don't like the sound of him being busy in bed with Trudy. I

172

don't want to ask him how she is today. Some other topic of conversation is called for.

'So,' I say, 'who are you today?'

'Huh?' says Eugene.

'Who are you?'

He stops scrubbing for a second.

'Who am I?'

'Yes. Did you find out? Did they tell you?'

'Who, Mum and Dad?'

'Oh, don't be so childish, calling them that.'

'What should I call them?'

'Mr and Mrs Bloom, I presume.'

Eugene laughs and looks back at the carpet.

'Well?' I say. 'Did they tell you who you are?'

Eugene shakes his head. 'They just said I am who I think I am. I'm the same person.'

'But what about your real parents? What about mine? They're different people. Did Garth and Gaynor say anything about them?'

'No,' Eugene shrugs, 'nothing. But why are you asking? On Sunday you didn't want to know.'

'Shock. It's sunk in now,' I say shortly.

Eugene points at the stain on the carpet. 'Can you still see it?' he asks.

'Only if I look.'

Eugene gets to his feet. 'Let's make another cup of tea,' he says, 'and phone them up for a little chat.'

'I'm never going to speak to them again,' I splutter. 'Those Blooms told us the biggest pigging lies in the history of pork pies . . .'

Suddenly, there's a bloodcurdling cry from the bedroom,

173

and I break off abruptly. It sounds like Trudy has just woken up. Maybe in her dreams she still had hair on her head.

'Sorry, I've got to go to her,' Eugene mutters. I don't stop him. I stand by the boarded-up fireplace and watch him leave the room, then I listen and wait. It doesn't seem to be an absolute emergency, because he doesn't run back out of the bedroom and phone for an ambulance, but I can hear a certain urgency in Trudy's tones.

After a while her high-pitched pleading and his pacific monosyllables seem to be coming to a crescendo. What are they doing on the crest of a wave? Slowly I draw closer to the door to the hall, and am dragged through it by a strong current of curiosity. I go with the flow and find myself right outside their bedroom at what turns out to be the crucial moment.

Oh, repulsive! I'm propelled from the door and into the kitchen, where the kettle flies at my hand, water pours from the tap, and tea bags jump into cups as if there is a poltergeist about.

Eugene and Trudy are having sex. Urgh! They're having sex. Urgh!

But by the time I've brewed up, they've finished. The bedroom door bangs and Trudy comes into the kitchen with a negligee on. I look up from my cup of tea, and drop it on the floor. The shroud of white nylon slipping from Trudy's shoulders reveals something that I didn't really want to see: it's another one of her lumps, growing like a third breast between the other two, blue-tinged translucent, with veins visible beneath tight-stretched skin.

I bend over to pick up bits of broken cup with a weird wind whistling in my ears, and that faraway feeling you get just before you faint.

'Is there tea in this pot, Grace?' asks Trudy. 'I want to take some in for Oogie.'

This brings me round a bit. Trudy sounds like her old self, using the nickname for Eugene that first alerted me to the fact that she was a force to be reckoned with. I'd thought that no other girl would ever be able to top my special name for him, Genie.

'Feel free,' I say, straightening up. She smiles at me! I see it briefly before turning away, because I don't think I can stomach the sight of her chest again, that boiled egg growing between the fried eggs of her breasts.

'How are you today?' she asks, in exactly the old Trudy's voice, and the same tone she used to use on me: unfailingly polite in the face of severe cold shouldering. I have to look at her.

'I'm fine, how are you?' I say.

'Oh, so-so,' she says, but she smiles again and it sparkles. 'Oogie deserves a nice cup of tea.'

I watch her make it. I watch her pour milk into a mug, and tea on top, then I watch her looking for the sugar. I watch her find the salt instead and put two heaped teaspoons in and stir it. She doesn't realise she's made a mistake. I watch her walk away, filled with nasty glee.

Then I stop her on the kitchen doorstep. 'Trudy,' I say, 'I'm sorry but, er, you put salt in it. Not sugar.'

I couldn't let her give it to him. Much as I'd have liked to be ready with a glass of life-saving water to take the briny taste away, I couldn't let Eugene walk into a booby trap. So Trudy stops dead in the doorway, but the excited light in her eyes dies more slowly. She stands there, almost as if she'd been turned to stone, except that she's sweating.

'Trudy?' I say. She's still looking at me, but it's not her any more. Her gaze is glazed. 'Eugene!' I shout. 'Help!' He comes from the bedroom, looking drained, and belting up a new dressing gown, a blue one. Blue isn't really his colour. He sees Trudy first and then me.

'Okay,' he says.

'I don't know what happened,' I say.

'She does it all the time,' he replies. He's calm and quiet, but I'm shaking. It was a shock, seeing Trudy slip away like that.

'I only told her there was salt in the tea,' I say.

'Salt in the tea?' says Eugene, and now there's a tear in his eye. 'What did you tell her that for?'

'Because it was true!' I say. Talk about being unjustly accused. Eugene thinks I'm the baddie here. He thinks I told Trudy there was salt in the tea when there wasn't, on purpose, to upset her. I take the cup out of her hand and thrust it at him. 'Taste it, if you don't believe me.'

Eugene does believe me. He doesn't taste the tea.

'Did she put it in?' he asks.

'Yes,' I say, 'she thought it was sugar.'

'Well,' he says, 'I'm going to take her back to bed now.' He picks her up and carries her down the hall, calling her 'his poor baby'.

That's not fair. I'm his baby. It's the first thing I can remember, being a baby and him being there, so I should have first claim on being his baby.

I'm still stewing about this when Eugene comes back into the kitchen having put Trudy to bed.

'Don't worry,' he says. 'It wasn't your fault. She does do silly things sometimes.'

He has misinterpreted my sulky demeanour. It's not surprising really, he's so tied up with his stupid girlfriend. But I can't let it go. I squeeze my anger tighter, and it bursts like a balloon.

'It's probably because you keep fucking her,' I shout. 'Don't you know when to stop? She's sick. And in my opinion, so are you.'

There is a brief moment of silence, before Eugene bursts into tears. Slowly he leans over the sink and cries as if he were vomiting. I've never seen him so wretched.

I didn't mean it! Well, I did mean it but I shouldn't have said it. It wouldn't have been so bad if I'd said it for the right reasons, like genuine concern for Trudy's health. But I only said it to hurt Eugene, to say 'fucking' loudly, to throw it in his face like an insult.

I wish I could take it back. I stand behind him at the sink and try and hold his spasms still.

'I'm sorry,' I say, 'I'm sorry.'

He turns and cries on my shoulder. I wrap my arms around him and even one of my legs. This is how we stood in the shower, only two days ago, and nearly had sex. I wouldn't believe how much trouble it's caused, if I couldn't feel his tears soaking through my shirt.

'I'm sorry,' I say. I've never seen Eugene cry like this before, not even when we were children. The sound of his sobbing reaches the pit of my stomach, and turns the whole world dark. But he shakes his head.

'It's not you,' he sniffs. 'It's Trudy. You're right, she is too sick to have sex. But she keeps asking for it. She keeps asking for it, and I can't say no.' Eugene's voice is thick with catarrh like lava erupting from the volcano of his emotions. 'It gives her a buzz,' he says, 'a burst of energy like the one just now when she came and made the tea. She couldn't have got up otherwise. And how can I say no to that?'

He keeps his face buried in my shoulder and cries some more. I hang on to him tightly kissing and caressing his hot head. His crying comes to a terrifying climax, then the sobbing slowly subsides and his breathing becomes even. It's an orgasm of sorts, but I'm not satisfied.

Over the next week or so, I see Eugene more than ever before, popping in for morning coffee or afternoon tea, staying for dinner and getting too drunk to go home. Sleeping on the sofa.

I get to know him again in a day-to-day way; we clean the windows, watch TV, wallpaper the hall. We talk all the time, putting the world to rights, the conversation covering ground as diverse as equatorial rainforests and polar ice caps. We talk like we used to, in a language that is almost unintelligible to others; but for all our rambling jabber, we do have a few pet subjects. One is whether or not we are really adopted. The other is Trudy.

First we have to go back to the beginning and study the ABC of our situation. We retrace our routes and go back to our roots. It's funny to be doing this so soon after Saturday night by the fireplace, when Eugene reminded me that there was a beginning and things hadn't always already begun. I'm beginning to see that it's all about change. Everything changed between us in front of the fire when he was thirteen and I was eleven, but I'd forgotten about that. And everything changed again when I remembered it. Then Garth and Gaynor dropped their bombshell about not being our mother and father and everything changed once more.

This is playing havoc with our sex life. We've gone from beating the shit out of each other in martial arts class and getting excessively drunk together before the age of consent, to developing complexes about each other's lovers and playing illicit games of footsie under dining tables; all because we thought we were brother and sister. When we finally arrived at the crux of this unconscious sexual behaviour, and attempted to consummate the relationship with real sex, it ended in tragedy. We lost our parents. And all because we're now adopted everything has changed between us again. We're living like an old married couple. Eugene shows no signs of fancying me.

But we have very interesting conversations. Sometimes we talk about Garth and Gaynor as if they're fictional characters, from a psychological thriller or a Shakespearean play, trying to work out what their motivation is. It's almost as if we're in the play with them and only they know the lines. It's an endless guessing game, not so much 'who-dun-it' as 'why-they-dun-it'.

On Sunday morning Eugene looks up from the newspaper and says:

'Does it matter?'

'What?' I say, mouth full of Marmite.

'If we're not their children. Do you think it makes a difference?'

'Yes.'

'But how? Do you feel any different? We still exist.'

'They lied to us, Eugene,' I say.

'No, they didn't,' he replies, 'they just didn't tell us the truth. We never actually asked them if we were adopted or not.'

'We shouldn't have had to ask. They should have told us sooner.'

'I can see why they didn't though.'

'Why?' I ask.

'Well, we wouldn't have believed them. It's the family resemblance. You and I are practically identical,' he smiles at me. 'The same teeth, jammed together like motorway pile-ups. Bent noses, broken cheekbones. It's no accident that we both look like car crashes.'

'That could just be due to our upbringing,' I say.

'We've all got red hair, Grace,' says Eugene. 'Their story can't possibly be true.'

'Then they lied to us!'

'Grace, whether we are adopted or not, they've lied to us. That's one idea you can safely start getting used to.'

'But why would they tell us we're adopted when we're not?'

'Because we had sex together. Well, we nearly had it together.'

'But why would we do that, if we were real brother and sister?'

'Because we wanted to.'

'But real brothers and sisters don't want to. Do they?'

'We did.'

'So maybe we're not related. Don't you see? We've always been different to the other boys and girls. We've always liked each other better. Being adopted would explain that.'

'Grace, your logic scares me. Your mind is dangerously mathematical.'

I look at the clock on the wall behind his head.

'I'll tell you what scares me,' I say, 'we should have given Trudy her breakfast half an hour ago.'

'Ooh, shit,' Eugene leaps to his feet. 'Look, I'll make it, you go and get her up. She must be still asleep.'

'I'd rather cook the eggs,' I say. 'It's the worst moment of the day, when she first wakes up. She always seems so shocked.' Every morning it gets worse, Trudy regains consciousness screaming or in pain. But I go anyway. On the kitchen doorstep I turn back to Eugene, as if a thought has just struck me. 'By-the-by,' I say, 'I think we should tell her the truth.'

'What truth?'

'Well, she still thinks I'm your sister.'

'So do I.'

'No, you don't.'

'I'm not saying anything about it to Trudy.'

'Then I will. It's not fair to keep her in the dark. It's patronising. She may be ill but she's still a person in her own right.'

'And she's still my girlfriend,' says Eugene.

I snatch up a saucepan.

'So you go and wake her,' I say, 'and I'll make the scrambled eggs.'

'Look here, Grace old girl,' he says, as he leaves the kitchen, 'I think Mum and Dad told us we were adopted so that we wouldn't fancy each other any more.' He smiles fondly at me. 'We wanted something we couldn't have, and if they told us we could have it, we wouldn't want it any more.'

I still think Trudy should be told the truth. It's on my mind the next day, when I hang out with her while Eugene goes to sign

181

on. It's got to the stage now where he doesn't like to leave her at home on her own.

'How's your kitten?' she asks me.

'The one you stuck your hair to?' I say, but she doesn't remember doing it now. 'Nod's still not very well, I'm afraid. Very weak. No miaow. Hardly any appetite. She still purrs; but Genie says cats do that even when they're dying, which is poignant because we associate purring with pleasure.'

'Pleasure,' nods Trudy.

'The other kittens are being very kind to her though,' I say. 'They keep her warm at night, and I even saw Wynken nudge the water saucer towards her once.'

'Once,' says Trudy.

'Or maybe twice,' I say. 'Trudy, what would you do if . . .'

'If . . .' says Trudy.

'If I told you that I'm not Eugene's sister,' I say.

She covers her eyes with her hands.

'I can't see,' she says. She's been rubbing her eyes for several days now. There's a problem with them. They're clouding over, whitening up, like an egg that's flipped to fry on both sides. But she's never said she can't see before.

'Let's have a look.' I take her hands away from her eyes.

'I can't see,' she says, though I've taken her hands away from her eyes. 'I can't see.'

Her eyes are white as lychees.

'I can't see. Let me out of here,' she says, getting off the sofa where we've been sitting and stumbling across the room. She crashes into the stereo stack-system, which unstacks itself noisily onto the floor. 'Ow!' howls Trudy.

I try and catch her. She falls into an armchair, then clambers out of it again frantically. 'Help!' she shouts. 'Get me out of here.' She staggers against a standard lamp, which falls over and takes her with it.

To my supreme relief Eugene arrives home at this moment. He rushes into the room and takes control of the situation.

'What's going on?' he says.

At the sound of his voice Trudy rises and glides directly into his arms. But once she gets there she sags, in a series of desperate sobs. I'm crying too, but mine's optional. Trudy has no choice. If she can't see any more, there's nothing else to do with her eyes but cry them out.

'What's the matter, Trudy?' Eugene asks her gently, but she can't answer. I'll have to say it.

'She can't s – ' I begin, but Trudy interrupts me with a burst of sudden energy.

'I want to tell him,' she says passionately, then kisses Eugene and says with pride, 'I've gone blind.'

After this, there's no looking back. Trudy needs to be watched round the clock. Community nurses and health visitors become regular fixtures in the flat. But the more symptoms Trudy exhibits, the less anyone is able to diagnose her. She's tested negative for all terminal illnesses on record, but she seems to be going ahead and dying anyway.

I turn up late one night, after a martial arts class, with some excess energy to work off.

'How are you?' I spring at Eugene as he opens the door. 'How's Three-Dee?' This is my new nickname for Trudy, to compensate for her loss of vision. 'Can I come in?' I bounce down the hall like I'm a bomb about to blow up.

'Sshh,' says Eugene, 'she's asleep.'

'Is everything okay?' I say.

He looks at me in a funny way.

'What?' I say.

He shakes his head and asks me if I'd like a drink.

The bottle of wine is all but empty before he opens up and tells me what's bothering him. By this time, I'm in no state to be an objective observer or an impartial ear. I'm lost in contemplation of his beauty. I'm having a hot flush.

'It's Trudy,' he says. 'She said something weird as I was putting her to bed.'

'Oh, yes?' I say cautiously. I'm not sure I really want to hear this.

'She said,' Eugene stops and shakes his head again. Then he stares at me hard. 'She said you weren't my real sister.'

I stare back at him.

'You didn't tell her that, did you?' he asks.

'Me? Oh dear, no!' I finish my glass of wine in one gulp.

'Then how does she know?'

'Well, maybe you haven't noticed,' I say in a deep voice, 'but since Trudy's been blind, she's gained more insight. She makes strange prophetic statements all the time.'

'Come off it,' Eugene says.

'It's true,' I say, but I sound a bit pissed. 'I think she is becoming clairvoyant.'

'Crap,' Eugene says. 'It's much more likely that she's spoken to Mum or Dad on the phone.'

'She couldn't have spoken to them on the phone because you or I have been with her the whole time, and I certainly haven't contacted them. Have you?' I demand.

He stares at me, daring him.

'No,' he says.

I still stare. If I don't see the family resemblance, this

contemplation of him no longer seems an unhealthy act of narcissism. I look at him through the wine haze. It's as if a mirror is melting between us. We are no longer reflections of each other. He's there in his own right, he'd be there even if I wasn't here. He is so much more beautiful than me.

A mirror is melting between us. I can feel the heat. I'm drawn into the distortion. When it clears I'll be able to see the truth. Eugene's expression still escapes me, it's elusive, on the other side of the haze. We are not one. There is something between us, stopping me reading his mind. He is on the other side of the haze, but I want him; I want him more than I want myself. So I'm going to go through it, through the haze. I'm not afraid. I don't care what happens as I move towards him.

I think what happens next is that I try to kiss Eugene. I must be drunk because it's all very clumsy. The sofa we're sitting on is suddenly as soft as a bouncy castle and it undulates crazily. I think that's why, when I try to kiss Eugene, our teeth crack together. He jumps to his feet. Again I try to follow him but only make it to my knees. I cling to his legs and try to haul myself up by his trousers.

Eugene fights to get free of me.

'Oogie,' I beg, accidentally using Trudy's nickname for him, 'if she died, then would you be with me?'

'I don't want her to die,' he says.

'But if she did, would you want to be with me?' I implore.

'I can't think about it, Grace,' he shrugs. 'I believe I'm your brother. In fact, since Mum and Dad told me we were adopted I feel more like your brother than ever before.'

'Well, I wish you'd start acting like it,' I retort.

I wake up next morning to find myself in a sleeping bag of a sulk on Eugene's sofa bed. I fight my way out, but as soon as I set foot on the carpet I know I've stepped out the wrong side. It irritates my soles. I sit down suddenly, woolly headed, and the bed folds up on me. With a groan its metal jaws spring closed. I fight my way out. It's going to be one of those days.

Flesh shrinking with the cold I get dressed but my clothes don't seem to fit. My breasts feel like boulders, knocking about in the rough sack of my bra. Putting on jeans seems like chaining myself to icy railings. Brushing my hair is an attempt to train a lion. It rears up roaring, electrified by the sight of the hairbrush. It's going to be one of those days.

I should leave straightaway. I should take myself off and sort myself out. I should commit myself to the asylum of my flat, and play with my kittens, and mark some maths.

Instead I go into the kitchen where Eugene and Trudy are preparing breakfast. Trudy's standing up at the stove, stirring scrambled eggs. She's obviously just had sex. I give her five minutes of relative normality before a rapid return to surreality.

I sit down at the kitchen table and pick up the newspaper. The print is blurred as if it's been raining outside this morning, but the song on the radio says it's raining in my heart. Out of the corner of one eye I see Eugene's face turning towards me, but I can't look back at him or I'll cry.

'Eggs, Grace?' Trudy says.

I don't answer her.

'Eggs?' she asks again.

Eugene clears his throat. I turn the page of the newspaper.

'Are you alright?' says Trudy. 'Is she alright, Oogie?'

Eugene clears his throat again.

'I think she's tired,' he says.

Trudy turns her boiled egg head and fixes a point two feet from my left breast with the bald glare of her boiled egg eyes.

'Poor darling,' she says, 'I hope we didn't keep you awake.'

I turn a page but it sounds like I'm trying to tear it out.

'What have you found? Something good?' says Trudy.

Still I don't reply. Eugene leans forward and whispers, 'Please talk to her. It's not her fault.'

'Fuck off,' I say, and stand up, and storm out.

I storm down the hall and into the living room and don't stop storming until my face is pressed against the window. If I want to go further, I'll have to jump through breaking glass. I stare out at the sky, and my eyes sting.

I'd never know I couldn't fly. One minute I'd be falling and the next minute I'd be dead; but death is just like zero, you can never actually go there and say you've been, so the last thing I'd know would last for ever, a recurring flight.

I sigh and bring my eyes back from the big oblivion of the grey city sky. I sharpen the focus so I can see my reflection in the glass. But I don't want to see myself. I am not what I want to see. I want to see if there's anyone standing behind me, if Eugene has followed the path of my storm. Reflected in its own window the living room looks unlived in, tidy and trim in contrast to the raggedly rough-edged rush of sky. And it's empty. There is no Eugene.

I'm turning away from the window and back to the door just as he walks in, damn it, just as my tears have dried up and I don't seem so devastated. But I pretend not to see him, I pretend he's invisible. If it works for Trudy it could work for me.

I look right through him and continue to turn on the spot, smooth, level-headed, like a ballerina. A blind ballerina, that's what I am. Suddenly I'm doing comedy, a cabaret circuit of the living room, with handicapped footwork and knock-kneed arabesques. I pirouette around the sofa and fall over in a perfect parody of Trudy.

'I think you'd better go now, Grace,' says Eugene. He's got the joke but he doesn't find it funny.

'No,' I say, in a voice which carries on taking the Michael Caine out of Trudy's wooden tones.

Eugene is standing beside me. I keep my head down. I can't look up at him. It's the only way to save the day, but I can't do it. If I looked into Eugene's eyes now, my gaze would not be straight. My eyes would roll around in my head like oranges and lemons. They'd tease him until they'd squeezed the truth of this tangle right out of him; how can Trudy be more beautiful than me?

'Go home, Grace,' Eugene says.

'No.' Why won't you send her to a home and keep me?

'Give me some space,' Eugene says.

No one has ever spoken to me like this before. They've always found me quite spacey enough, sometimes too spacey. I stand up, throw my feet into my shoes, snatch my handbag from the armchair, and leave the room. I still don't catch Eugene's eye, not until I turn in the doorway and give him a look which out-weirds one of Trudy's.

'I hope you catch what she's got,' I say. Then I walk away.

Nine

By the time I get back to my flat, my mood is black but the pool forming in my pants is red. My period has started, and this morning's bloody-mindedness all falls into place.

Like Trudy, love is blind; but the way I confronted Eugene was merely short-sighted. If I'd checked the calendar I would have seen what was coming; a rough patch on the path of my monthly cycle, a bit of a bumpy ride. If I'd realised it was only my hormones raging, the outburst need not have been entirely aimed at my ex-brother. What I felt was just the cosmic disappointment as another unfertilised egg went down the pan, and how could Eugene be to blame for that?

I sit on the toilet and deeply regret what I've done, but it's too late to be sorry. The times I most need to see where I'm coming from, I'm least likely to look. When I most need to hear what's on my mind, I'm least likely to listen. And what I most need to do now is run a nice hot bath, strip off my soiled clothes, and rest my body in supporting water. I should hold my head under till the tide of my mind is still for a moment before turning to more pleasant thoughts. I should treat myself to a watery orgasm with the shower attachment, just to relieve some pressure.

But instead of trying to make myself feel better, I make everything else seem worse. I notice how cold it is in my flat, how dirty the floor is, how bare the cupboards, how full the ashtrays. I focus on my sexless bed with the sheets so up-tightly tucked in; the stack of books to mark, the inches of dust to sweep away, the number of bills to pay. On a good day, I love having nobody to come home to; but today it looks like Nobody has trashed the place while I was out.

The kittens have been strangely quiet since my arrival. They normally do something to welcome me back, an all-singing all-dancing pet spectacular; but today they stay asleep. When I pick up their food bowl and see the caked-on crumbs I remember with a shock that I didn't come home to feed them yesterday. I was too busy trying to satisfy my own hunger at Eugene's.

I go down on my hands and knees at the open mouth of the swing-bin. They're all rolled up in there like one big ball of reclaimed wool, like four pairs of babies' booties that have been unravelled and rewound. I can see their ears sticking out of the mix-up in different colour tufts. I don't have a grandmother, but if I did this is exactly the sort of thing she'd have in her knitting basket.

'Hello,' I say softly.

They don't stir.

'Wakey, wakey,' I whisper and stroke the nearest curved back.

Wynken opens one eye. I tickle her head but she butts my hand away and tuts at me crossly.

'Sorry,' I say.

Blynken is coming round, too, pink tongue out and licking before she's fully conscious. She's lying on top of her brother and sisters, yawning and lapping at every part she can reach, until with a sudden movement she leaps onto the kitchen floor shivering and shaking herself as if to get rid of a nasty taste in her mouth. On the way out of bed she treads on Wankin's head and he wakes up, too, alert in an instant and chasing after her tail. It's all he ever thinks about, chasing the pretty girls' tails.

I wonder if they'll try and mate with each other when they're older. I'm surprised that I've never wondered whether animals have incestuous relationships with their brothers and sisters before. It's all I ever think about, myself.

Nod is still asleep. Wynken sits beside her miaowing loudly, filling the bin with a mournful howl, which really ought to have woken the littlest sister up by now. A prickling sensation ripples over my skin as I look at her and see no flicker of whiskers, no bristle of living fur. There's something wrong. I put my hand into the basket and Wynken spits at it. She's never done that before.

'Wynken,' I whisper, 'is Nod alright?'

Wynken gets up and walks away. She gives me a look as she goes. And then I see that Nod has already gone. Her eyes are open, but the spark in them is out. Nod is dead.

She must have gone in the night, all by herself, like a big brave kitten. Was she scared, did she struggle, wanting to stay and play, safely with the others? Why wasn't I here, breathing air on her, giving her water, massaging her heart? I could have held her back. She didn't need to go so prematurely and so alone.

Nod is dead. I don't know what that means, I mean I don't know where it leaves her; one minute she was here and the

191

next she is nowhere to be found. If I scoured the globe, if I got down on my hands and knees and climbed trees and shone a torch in cellars and shouted from the mountain tops and registered her disappearance with the Salvation Army, I'd never find Nod.

She is no longer in her body. It's barely recognisable as Nod's body any more. It's still soft and glossy and sweetly pretty, but now it's scary, too. It's sending shivers up and down my spine as if there's someone standing behind me, watching. Why are dead bodies scary? In horror stories, it's because there's a possibility that they might come back to life. But if they came back to life, they wouldn't be dead any more, so they wouldn't be scary.

When Eugene and I were at Glastonbury, a man looked at us strangely. He was a strange-looking man and he looked at us strangely for about an hour.

'What's wrong with him?' I shouted at Eugene, above the roar of the crowd. Poppins and the Pills were playing and we were in the midst of a gothic riot.

'Undead,' Eugene had replied confidently.

But when the music stopped the man came over and gave us a more plausible explanation for his strange behaviour. He could see people's auras, he said, and had been fascinated by ours which was very unusual. He said that instead of having one aura each, which is normal, we appeared to have only one between us; and that no matter how far apart we moved it still encompassed us both.

We believed him, though the fact that he was as keen to share his acid as his esoteric theories may have impaired our judgement somewhat; and to this day I swear that all living things are surrounded by a festival of light and colour that only a few can see.

Nod may have been an animal, but that didn't make her a lower life form. Each breath every sentient being takes is a spell of magic, a sparkle in the unrelieved darkness of the universe. Small things matter; sparrows are made of the same stuff as us, and are powered by energy from the same mysterious source. The spirit that animated my tiniest kitten has gone, and without it she is just meat or old machinery for eating meat.

I'm getting carried away. I have to leave the kitchen. I can't continue to meet the beyond-the-grave expression in Nod's eyes. I'm just delaying the onset of grief with philosophy and science fiction fantasies. I would be better to weep. So I collect up the remaining kittens and we go into the lounge.

I lose the rest of the day in sad contemplation, turning to stone on the sofa. Something like molten lava seeps from my heart and cools slowly to form a crust on the surface of my skin. At nightfall I smash my way out of it. I want a fuck.

You need an extremely good reason to think about sex at a time like this. Luckily, I have three.

1. Nod was my baby and now she's dead my body is urging me to make a new one.

2. Sex sometimes hurts and I want to get hurt because I hate myself for not looking after her properly.

3. It's the only way I'll be able to relax.

There's been the possibility of a shag for days. The little red light on my answer phone is flashing frantically, the tape's straining with messages. I've let them build up, till they equal the frequency of my heartbeat. I've waited till I'm panicking, before I press the play button and listen.

Hi, it's Nigel. Do you fancy coming round tonight?

Hi, it's Nigel. Where are you? Are you coming round tonight?

Grace, it's Kelly. Are you okay? You left in such a weird way yesterday. Can we get together? What about lunch tomorrow?

It's Nigel. Why weren't you in college today? What's the matter? Phone me.

It's Kelly. I came round at lunchtime and you weren't there. Maybe you were just pretending, or am I being paranoid? Aren't you speaking to me any more? Please give me a call.

Alright, Miss Bloom, it's Simeon. I know you said students shouldn't phone you at home except in an emergency, but I wanted to tell you that maths is meaningless without you. We had a stand-in teacher today and the class was so bad I think I've gone backwards. Any chance of some extra tuition?

Grace, speak to me. College said you phoned in sick. Where are you? At your parents' house? I think I'll try to reach you there.

Hello, it's your mother. Pick up the phone.

Grace, it's Nigel again. I rang your parents and they haven't seen you since last weekend. We had a bit of a sticky conversation. They both sounded very tense. No one mentioned your father's addiction but I think he might be in a state of withdrawal. He said he misses you. He said you left without saying goodbye and you might do something silly. Please get back to me if you possibly can. We need to talk.

Nigel again. On second thoughts, I'm going to come round and sit on your doorstep for a while, in case you show up.

It's Mum. Pick up the phone.

Hello, Grace, it's Kelly. Does this mean that our relationship is over? What are you afraid of?

Hey, babe. Like, Poppins and the Pills are playing a gig

tonight at Bliss City, and your name is on the guest list. Come round the back after if you want to go out with a pop star. Oh yeah, and I'm sorry about your cat.

It's Gaynor. Pick up the phone.

Grace, it's Nigel. I'm going to try and catch you at Eugene's. But I can't remember his number, it's . . . Oh fuck, I'll have to phone your parents again . . .

With a long bleep the answering machine reaches the end of its tape. Answer machine? All I get is questions.

As I listen to these messages in my cold dark room, the feeling that I could be dead instead of Nod creeps over me. I could be lying on the carpet, and I could have been dead for days, while the disembodied voices of my nearest and dearest serenade my final slumber. I could be stone cold and stiff. Why haven't they broken the door of my flat down already? Why aren't the police here?

I'm glad they're not, actually. I've already got some boys for my blues, all the better to bring me rudely back to life. I call Dave first because he's the worst, then Simeon, then Nigel.

I know I said I would give them all up, but I'm about to go on a full-scale alcoholic-style bender. I don't phone Kelly. I'm not addicted to her, because she hasn't got a dick. I just arrange to see the men, one after the other, in quick succession, insisting that they come on time and leave before the next is due to arrive. They don't know about each other. I tell them all lies, but it doesn't matter because they are all the same.

The binge begins. My bedroom is soon chock-full of cigarette smoke, as beery breathed as a pub. One by one the men come and make themselves at home.

'Hello, darling,' they say, 'did you miss me me me?' They're dying to tell me all about their promotion, detention, new tie, flat tyre, fantasy, hangover, goal. They go on for ages. Then the plot thickens: 'This bloke decided to have a go at me me me. I was just standing there minding my own business, and suddenly there's an envious penis in my face. He was big, too, but not as big as me me me. I showed him who's boss; me me me and a couple of mates.'

And finally they say, 'But that's enough about me me me, darling. How are you, alright? Did you miss me last night? Did you put a pillow between your legs and pretend that it was me me me?'

No, I only ever imagine that it's Eugene.

Yes, I only ever imagine that I actually tell them that.

I never talk back to the men. I realised a long time ago that they only listen when they want to hear what I'm saying. At the first sign of banned words, outlawed sentences or forbidden subjects they switch off. Their eyes go dead like Nod's.

They all say they love me, and they love it when I say I love them, too, but I know they don't love me really because I know they don't know me. When I try and tell them they can't love me because they don't know me because they never hear what I say, they insist that I'm talking nonsense.

They only want me for my body. But that's okay. I only want them for my body, too. I don't know how to handle it myself. I can turn myself on, but I need help to turn me off again. Otherwise, my tip gets like a dripping tap and keeps me awake all night. It gets stiff, and men's hands are stronger.

When I met Nigel he hadn't had sex for six years and he told me that the less you do it the less you want to. The urge subsides. But I feel about celibacy the way most people feel about being stuck in a lift; panicky and claustrophobic.

My body is a confined space, a solitary cell, but so long as someone is trying their key in my lock there's the chance I might get out of it. The problem is, there's only one right combination. Only Eugene's key fits. With him on the doorstep I could really feel at home in my body.

Without him, it's a jigsaw jumble. A jism jungle.

First Dave, then Simeon, then Nigel enter into the darkness. There's a lot of blood. I don't usually make love at this time of the month. It's impure sex, when my womb is full as the moon. There's no pain, but there's no pleasure either. I don't like blood with my sport, I can't feel foxy if he fucks me when I'm wounded.

He says it doesn't matter, and he says he doesn't mind. I've even heard it said that performing oral sex on menstruating women is one of the initiation rites of the Hell's Angels, as if it's the bravest thing a man can do. Personally, I think the woman would have to be braver. I find it tasteless, the very thought of things like that at a time like this.

The men attempt to turn me on. They're pert, they pout, pulling their stomachs in and sticking their chests out as if it's some plastic playboy, some silicone sex king I want. They wink and they wank, but they don't think or thank me for my clues to what really turns me on. They believe they've found a short cut when they thrust themselves between my thighs, but they'll never reach me from the outside.

Since I've lost my family, I don't feel safe. I used to take sexual risks, swinging on dicks like ropes from trees, never afraid of falling. I knew there would be someone to catch me. But now, I can't be so sure; I should hold on tighter or not swing at all. The choice is simple, but I'm completely stupid. I've taken the third option: hanging. It's sexual suicide.

When Eugene told me to go away, I went much further than

he meant. I went out of my mind. I left my body. My lovers, my substitute brothers, bend over it, bent on satisfaction. But I'm a bus ride away, watching through steamed-up windows.

The poor blurred boys, how it sounds as if I hate them. How I frown at their advancing foreheads and make cutting remarks about their stubble. I struggle against their strengths. I outstretch their arms, and knock their needs; but I love them really. I love the light in all their eyes. In Nigel's a wry light, worried grey, like twilight; in Simeon's a rosy but reluctant dawn; in Dave's a faraway distorted starlight. But only one of my lovers has eyes like the sun.

I watch the others come and go, doing insignificant things to my abandoned body. They feel like ants. After a while I can't feel them. I don't drink a drop of the beer and wine they bring me, but I'm drunk. I'm totally off my trolley, as it were; I'm Fucked Up Beyond All Recognition. I watch in confusion as three men blur into one, the only number that can be trusted, something less than the sum of their parts.

I try hard to tell the difference between them. It's not easy. They're all one, because they've all got one. They all give it to me. It's only when they take it back again, when they've finished, that I can start to draw distinctions.

Simeon bolts from my rabbit hole as soon as the sex is over. I think my orgasm scares him, he doesn't like the shouting. After all, I'm still his teacher, and he must be afraid of detention.

I'm definitely not going to see Simeon again. It's not doing either of us any good. He needs a real relationship before he gets fixed in time as a toy boy, because he withdraws from me so fast that he barely leaves the womb and may be in danger of never growing up.

Dave doesn't withdraw at all, but falls asleep before he gets that far, paralysed at the point of ejaculation. I know it's a biological fact that sex affects men's ability to stay awake, and I know that if women ate their mates afterwards like black widow spiders, the world would be a peaceful and prettier place; but nothing can reconcile me to the slump of a snoring body while I'm still tingling and invigorated.

Anyway, I'm not going to see Dave again. He's a better pop star than Mick Jagger because he *does* get satisfaction; but I'm just one of the minions who feed his ego and his libido. And he never fed my kitten!

But Nigel's as sweet as Thomas the Tank Engine as he pulls slowly out of my dark tunnel. After sex he holds me tightly as shudders judder along our bodies and steam billows between us. Our toes attract and repel each other like ticklish magnets. Our legs are interlocked, sticky with sweat, trembling with tension. We rub noses and touch tongues. We have children's conversations.

I must stop seeing Nigel soon. He's going to find out how I feel about Eugene. He's almost mastered my entire vocabulary and that's the only thing left to read in me.

This is the age of HIV, and sex ain't what it used to be. I can only dream of doing it without a condom, then slowly falling asleep with a man still inside me. Separation occurs quickly, and with some anxiety. It's time to choose quality over quantity; and settle down to monogamy. If I only had one lover we could stay together longer. We'd never have to come apart, because when a hole has something filling it perfectly, it's a solid whole. If me and Eugene joined up like that there would be union with no loss of individuality, merger without redundancies. But all negotiations between us have broken down, and I'm left asking myself endless questions.

Why was I so horrible about Trudy? I ought to admire him for his loyalty to her. Who am I to judge their relationship? I've made a complete mess of mine. Why did I want him to be more than my brother? Now I've lost him altogether. I've spent a whole day having sex with men I don't love, so why did I need to do something so obviously meaningless with Eugene? My body is sore but my soul is in torment: with him as my crutch, I never used to walk alone, but now I don't think I'll ever walk again.

I've been lying in bed for hours. Both dawn and dusk have altered the aspect of my room. I've had my spirits lifted and lowered and led a merry dance around the changing face of my furniture. Lunchtime and teatime have been and gone ignored, and the lines of the room are growing leaner, but the bed is a warm fat stomach, with me inside.

I'm too weak to get out. I lie on snuffly brushed cotton beneath soft blankets, on pillowcases edged with tired lace, and stare at myself in the mirror on the wall opposite. It's a heart-shaped mirror framed with flowers. Dave once said it means I love myself, and asked if I hear angels singing every time I see my reflection. I said no, it just shows me the face of Grace.

Now my sex binge is over I have to confront the truth of my addiction. Sickened, I swear I'm never going to do it again; but I know that alcoholics drink to forget how much they hate themselves for drinking. Guilt is my lover, since the men have left. When they were here, cavorting naked on top of the bedclothes, I wished they weren't; but now they've gone a sense of loneliness comes over me like a cover pulled up to my chin.

What on earth has happened? Apocalypse? I feel so alone, it seems all of humanity must have been wiped out without me noticing. I missed the blast. I was looking the other way, at myself in the mirror, narcissistic to the last.

And where is Eugene? Alive, or dead? In the old days I would have known, intuitively, if he were safe; but now it seems we've lost our telepathic contact. In my mind's eye I see myself making an urgent journey to his house across a devastated cityscape. Buses and streets are buried six feet under the earth's burnt crust. Blackened rubble with puddles of melted, smoking plastic and tangles of severed cables is the new terrain. Here and there, Coke cans glint in the darkness like dull jewels. I make my way by the bus stop signs, which stick out of the debris. Now and then, there's a pavement length of concrete pipe to walk along, or a bus rolled on its side like a red carpet; but mostly it's all scrambling up the sheer faces of what once were cinema screens and dodging the still tumbling tower blocks.

Human remains are recognisable in the rubble. Don't people look stupid when they've been killed by their own stupidity? Sets of teeth are smiling in silly delayed shock. Don't people look ugly when they've been killed by their own greed? Bones that once were fingers wag in the nuclear wind as if still trying to point the blame. Don't people look sad when they've lost everything they ever had? When they've blown it. When they've blown it up.

Of all the planets in the solar system, this was probably the only one with a stirring in its loins, the only one with lions and ice and the rhythm of life. The only one with mating rituals,

201

exotic fruit and rock'n'roll. Now there's only me, and a wind in the willowy steel supports of skyscrapers. Scraped skeletons and me, weeping. It's all my fault. I didn't notice the sun turn black, the moon bleed, the earth sink into the sea or the stars fall from the sky. I was unaware of the revelations. I was looking at myself, in a mirror. If I hadn't been so vain I could have done something glorious to save the day.

Somehow I manage to find my way to Eugene's house, which is still standing. The front door is underground, buried by the fallen civilisation, but his top-floor flat is now at ground level. It looks relatively unscathed. I struggle towards it across the surreal, uneven landscape, but the last few feet are made easy by an olive tree lying on its side, with some surviving doves huddling in its branches. I'm full of hope of finding my brother. The symbolic imagery bodes well.

Normally, dropping off and waking up are the best things about sleeping; normally they're the only times I know I'm doing it. I hardly ever remember my dreams. But this is different. I must have fallen asleep because it's definitely a dream, because I actually flew a stroke or two over the most dangerous terrain on the way; but I'm still awake and in control of more faculties than ever before. I'm awake in the dream, because I know it's happening; it's here and now, not something to dimly recall later, when I get back in control. I know that what I see when I look in the window is up to me.

I'd rather Trudy didn't put in a post-apocalyptic appearance, so I look through the window to Eugene's study, at the gable end of the house. It's a small room where he does big things, in his head and on his computer. He said he was working on something to do with the end of the world. Maybe he saw it coming and is prepared to save the day.

The window is heart shaped. It gives off a gold light. I press my face to it, and find that it's runny, like honey. My face goes right through. There's glass glockenspiel music in my ears.

Eugene is sitting at his computer, staring at the screen. He's bathed in the same golden light and serenaded by the same ghostly music. I can see half of his face and most of the map as, deep in concentration, he moves the mouse across it; but I can't quite work out which country is depicted. I look closer.

It's a map of Trudy. He's not trying to save the world after all; he's trying to save his girlfriend. There she is, her organs and arteries laid out like cities and roads, and he's covering every inch of her with his cursor. Along the bottom of the screen endless sentences are scrolling, as difficult to read as a doctor's prescription.

Eugene moves the mouse again and suddenly the mellow mood in his study is shattered. The ambient music flicks to a loud alarm and a red light flashes on the computer screen. The cursor rests on a withered chilli-shaped part of Trudy's body, illuminating it like an exclamation mark. At the bottom of the screen, the endless scrolling sentences have stopped and a single word is fixed in their place. APPENDIX. I always thought the appendix had no function, but Trudy's has sent Eugene's system into red alert.

I pull my head quickly through the sticky window, but this time the glass cuts me. Glass is splintering my ears and slitting my throat. Eugene's saving Trudy but I'm going to die. I'm crying tears of ground glass and honey, and screaming like a telephone into my pillow.

Hold on a minute. Hold on. It's not me screaming like a telephone. It's the telephone.

The surprise call is so timely that I actually answer it. It's such a welcome intervention to my dream that for once I reach out and snatch up the receiver, without waiting for the answer phone to find out who's at the other end of the lifeline.

'Hello?'

'Hello. It's your mother. It's Gaynor.'

The minute my guard is down, she rings. I flop back on the pillows, dizzy and still reeling from the dream, but reality is returning quickly.

'Are you there?' she asks.

'Hello.'

'How are you?'

'Fine.'

'You sound tired.'

'I was asleep.'

'But it's so early.'

'Is it?'

'Are you ill?'

'No. I don't think so. I don't know. I've just woken up.'

'What's wrong?'

'I was having a dream.'

'Oh yes?'

'You weren't in it.'

'Who was?'

'Grace?'

'Speak to me.'

'Grace!'

'Shut up.'

'But this is a telephone conversation. If I stop talking too it'll all be over.'

'Stop trying to act natural.'

'I'm not.'

'You're pretending nothing's happened.'

'I'm not.'

'What do you want then?'

'To talk to you.'

'Why?'

'Because I'm worried about you.'

'Why?'

'I've been phoning you for days. You never answer.'

'I've been at Eugene's.'

'How is he?'

'Oh, it's like that, is it?'

'What?'

'That's why you want to talk to me. To find out how he is.'

'Oh, Grace.'

'Are you still there?'

'Grace!'

'Is that my real name?'

'What?'

'Is Grace my real name?'

'Oh, God. I'm going to put your father on. I can't cope with you when you're like this.'

'He's not my father. He told me that himself. Get your story straight, you spastic!'

'Hello, Grace.'

'Oh. Hello, Dad.'

'Look, you've got to stop this. Your mother is in tears.'

'Fuck my mother. Bend her over the back of the sofa and give her one from me. She's not my mother.'

'Grace, please.'

'Who are my real parents?'

'We don't know.'

'Well, where did you get me from?'

'Listen, I love you. Isn't that all you need to know? I love you, and Gaynor loves you, and we both love Eugene, too.'

'But . . .'

'What?'

'But what?'

'Gracie, don't cry. Take a deep breath.'

'He doesn't love me!'

'Oh, Dad! He doesn't love me any more. He only loved me when I was his sister!'

Dad comes and picks me up in his car, half an hour after I put the phone down. I still call him Dad though I know his name is Garth now. He's going to take me home. I still call it home though I don't live there now. I shoo him out of my bedroom while I pack a small suitcase because it smells of sex. He doesn't seem to notice, but nevertheless I give him the nicer task of rounding up my kittens, because they're coming, too.

I must have forgotten about Nod, or else I wouldn't have sent my unsuspecting father to discover her sad remains. But she couldn't have been very far from my thoughts, because as soon as I hear the sound of Dad dropping the swing-bin I remember. Nod is dead.

It takes me ages to finish packing. I keep finding used condoms lying on the floor, and I can't manage to colour coordinate any outfits. Instead of attempting to match separate shades of blue and green and yellow, I put nothing but black and white in the suitcase. Then I tie back my unbrushable hair tightly and go out to face Dad.

He's standing by the front door with the wicker kitten-carrier in his hand and a big bright smile which draws my gaze up to his face. He doesn't look like a man who's just seen a dead cat. Either he's trying to hide it, or she's come back to life.

'Found them all?' I ask, trying to see into the basket.

'Yes,' he says, turning away.

Then I notice a bulge in his anorak pocket that wasn't there before. A pair of plastic bag handles are sticking over the top of the pocket like kitten ears. It's Nod.

All the way home in the car, he doesn't say a word about her. I don't either. I'm waiting for him to tell me that she's dead; wondering whether he's ever going to tell me at all. The longer he leaves it the more it seems to prove his adoption story is true; this is a man capable of keeping incredible secrets.

But I can't deny the family feeling between us. I know he loves me. Maybe he's waiting to tell me about Nod because he thinks I'm upset enough already and couldn't handle any further distress. If I loved him that much, I'd tell him I know she's dead; but I don't know how I feel about him until we've disposed of the body.

We arrive in the driveway and get out of the car, but instead of going through the front door he leads me round the side of the house and down the garden and into his shed at the bottom. It's a blustery day and trees tap on the plastic window pane as he speaks.

'Grace, one of your kittens has passed away.'

I look at the package in his pocket.

'I know,' I say.

He looks relieved. I'm not going to freak out or crack up.

'How did it happen?' he asks me gently. 'Was it just an accident?'

'No,' I say. 'It was my fault. I didn't look after her properly.'

As I speak Garth's expression changes. The gentleness gives way to something harder, blame, but it's not me he blames. He blames himself. I didn't look after my kitten properly because he didn't look after me properly, that's what he thinks. I neglected her because he neglected me.

I am his kitten. Knowing that is as much as I have ever known my father. Our relationship hasn't really changed. He turns to take a couple of spades from the tool rack. I sniff.

The air in the shed is what my dad smells of. There's creosote, the stuff that makes a man waterproof and protects his wooden heart. There's bits of metal machinery which, put together, work the way his brain works; cogs to help him cogitate. And there's white spirit, which strips the paint off the surface of situations, so he can see what's underneath.

'You can use the best one,' he says, handing me a shiny spade.

We dig a hole for Nod under a beech tree, and the wind whips up the fallen leaves as if it's giving her a final chance to chase them. Nod always wanted to play in a garden, but now all she can do is lay there. I get one last glimpse of grey and gold fur through a tear in the bag as I lower her into the earth. I wish I could go with her, into the organic darkness where all things end up as one.

Dad throws a handful of mud which rattles on the white plastic.

I'm grateful to him for helping me bury my dead, but I'd much rather do it myself. I look at him in silence, but some part of me must be saying that I want to be alone, because he hears it.

'I'll go indoors and put the kettle on,' he smiles. 'Come in for tea when you're ready.'

I stand beneath the screaming beech tree for ages, leaves flying in my face, trying to bring myself to fill the hole in the earth. I don't want this wound to heal. I want to leave it open and look at what's inside; because even though she's dead, Nod is more beautiful than most things still alive.

But it would be wrong to remember her as a rotting body, when her soul is fresh as the day she was born. So slowly, I shovel the earth on top of my almost human kitten, in order to forget her quickly. I politely do the last rite of passage, then I go into the house for tea.

Ten

I should have stayed outside in the garden. It was like standing on the very edge of existence, staring into a pit; but there's a stranger atmosphere in the house. It's as if a baby is about to be born. The moment I step inside I feel that I've come too soon.

Garth and Gaynor are whizzing around like they're possessed by aliens and talking in important voices on the telephone. They're too busy to stop and have tea with me. Their new book is out in a day or two.

Their last one was published three years ago. It was called *MUM AND DAD: Dumb and Mad?* I read my free copy fast and burned it furiously, but I can still remember the words on the back cover.

This book is about parenting in the 1990s. Due to a new age of psychological awareness, which has spawned such concepts as the Inner Child, we now realise that parents are children, too.

Please forgive us, for we know not what we do, say Garth and Gaynor Bloom. If parents are children, the children must be our teachers. The next generation are the future, and we must learn about it from them.

I can remember the words on the first page, too. Nuclear families are hostile environments, it said, and we should all be really nice to each other to make it easier to live together. But there can be no such thing as a happy family until each individual achieves personal happiness. Look after number one, it said, and if everyone else does the same, we'll all be okay. It's only when we forcibly try to make each other happy that disharmony occurs. Children, it said, should be allowed to bring themselves up, merely using their parents as advisers or libraries of information.

Then why, I wondered, did Garth and Gaynor Bloom stand on the edge of the swimming pool screaming ambiguous instructions while I tried to learn to swim? According to their principles, they should have just flung me in and left me to work it out for myself. After all, children float; a phrase they could have coined themselves.

I've tried very hard to forget what else my parents' book said. I was so embarrassed about it I didn't tell anyone except Nigel, who knew anyway and actually thought it was rather good. And once, I met someone in a pub who was reading it. In surprise I let slip my guilty secret: I am the daughter of Bloom. He said it must be great to have such a free-thinking easy-loving mum and dad. He said I must be very well balanced. I nearly fell over. I wanted to reply with a long and vitriolic diatribe against progressive parenting, but I kept it wound round my neck like a string of beads or poisonous berries. I was choking so much I drank nearly half his pint trying to stop.

I can't bear the thought of another book, but my parents' house is pregnant with prepublication atmosphere. Garth's holding his breath, and Gaynor's panting and panicking. I end up doing the hoovering. I thought I'd come to be looked after in my hour of need, but it looks like I'm running around after them. I rush from room to room with the vacuum cleaner screaming like a witch who's lost her broomstick, but they always seem to be one step ahead, avoiding me completely. They huddle in the hall while I'm doing the dining room, and disappear into the living room when I come out into the hall. They stay at arm's length all afternoon, beyond the reach of me and the lead of the hoover.

But in the evening Mum cooks fatty calf with Yorkshire pudding and Garth opens a bottle of wine. We sit down to eat, and they start to talk.

'What happened, then?' says Gaynor.

'What do you mean?'

'Between you and Eugene?'

'Nothing.'

'Well, why did we phone up to find you in hysterics, saying he only loved you when you were his sister?' says my father.

'Don't ask questions while I'm eating,' I say.

'Tomorrow,' says Gaynor, 'someone from *The Times* is coming to interview us.'

I laugh.

'Don't be rude,' she says.

Some food falls out of my mouth.

'I really think we should get this cleared up,' says Garth, looking at my mother. 'It sounds serious. So answer me properly, Grace. What happened between you and Eugene? The last time we saw you, you couldn't keep your hands off each other.' He turns his gaze on me.

'I'm glad you're not my real parents,' I say.

My father drops his fork. Gaynor reaches for her glass.

'It's the only good thing to come out of this mess,' I say.

'Why?' Garth asks.

'Because I don't like you very much,' I say, 'and now I don't have to pretend that I do. Couldn't keep our hands off each other, indeed.'

Garth bends double over his dinner, and Gaynor goes rigid. It's quite a violent reaction. I give a casual shrug and take another bite of beef. They haven't responded by the time I've finished my mouthful, so I speak again.

'When is *The Times* coming?'

'What?' Garth looks up hopefully.

'What time?'

'What's the time?' He looks disappointed.

'When will *The Times* come?'

'What times?' he says, shaking his head in bewilderment.

'Stop playing into her hands, Garth,' says Gaynor, snapping out of her trance. 'She's talking about the newspaper, but she's only doing it to confuse you. They're coming at one o'clock.'

'Why don't you like us?' says my father.

'Because you're crap,' I say. 'All you want to know is what happened between me and Eugene, and you only want to hear it when you're ready and not before. And finally it transpires that you don't even want to know how I am, not individually. You only want to know how Eugene and I are. Both of us, as a couple.'

Mum stands up angrily, but before she can speak, Dad grabs her by the wrist and pulls her back into her seat. While Gaynor gapes in silent shock at this treatment, Garth speaks to me.

'Sorry,' he says. 'You're right. We're crap.'

'I don't know how you had the nerve to write about good

213

parenting,' I add. 'Eugene and me are so fucked up and it's all your fault. You're like vultures, hovering over our heads the whole time, waiting and watching, like voyeurs.'

Dad replies with a taut little sentence which ties up the ends of the conversation so tightly that there's no room for me to squeeze in even a rapier-thin final word.

'You have every right to feel like that, Grace,' he says, with a look at Gaynor which warns her not to argue either.

We eat the rest of the meal in awkward silence, but as soon as they go to the kitchen to dish up the dessert, I hear them hurling abuse at each other like best china. I throw down my napkin and leave the table. I hate rhubarb anyway.

As I creak up the stairs, snatches of their conversation accompany me, in an ascending scale.

You shouldn't have
We couldn't have
Been and
Gone and
Done it now
Spoilt everything
With technical know-how
Stupid idea
Ground-breaking experiment
Not my fault
In it together
More's the pity
Oh
Don't you
Any more?

Although they don't name names, I assume it's me and Eugene they're shouting about. If they told us we were adopted to solve the problem of our incestuous relationship, they now need to come up with a solution to our subsequent estrangement. But it might just be a case of new book nerves. It's due for publication in a day or two, and their tone seems too academic for a family argument. I don't understand what they're talking about. My trust in them is shattered. They're so hooked on being psychological experts that they don't care about being real parents any more. They don't really care about me.

They've left an advance copy of their new book on the bedside table in the spare room, as if it's the bloody Bible. And I suppose the only way to know the truth is to read it; but it's been hard enough spending the day with the authors, without having to snuggle up to their subconscious imagery and therapeutic metaphors at night. Anyway, I've bought my own books with me, everything I could find in the library on adoption.

I go to bed and lie propped up on pillows with a manual about tracing your real parents open on my knee. My eyes move slowly and solemnly over its pages, but the sentence running through my head bears no relation to the words I'm actually reading. I am in blood stepp'd in so far, that, should I wade no more, returning were as tedious as go o'er.

I ignore it at first. It's easily done, what with Garth and Gaynor still audible in the background and the diagram of a family tree on my knee. The manual says it's simple to trace your birth parents. The hardest part is how to avoid hurting your adoptive ones. I try to concentrate, but Mum and Dad's argument and the mystery sentence keep interrupting.

I am in blood stepp'd in so far, so first find the name of your adoption agency, that should I wade no more, you tell me why we didn't see it coming, darling, returning were as tedious as go o'er. I am in blood stepp'd in so far, and here is a list of recognised adoption agencies in Great Britain, that should I wade no more, because we've got our heads stuck up each other's arses, returning were as tedious as go o'er.

It's Shakespeare, this is. I think it must be *Macbeth* because that's the only one I've ever read. I did it for O-level, but I can still remember some scenes clearly. This is the bit where he's up to his neck in shit, so implicated in his dirty deeds that to stop doing them will be as complicated as carrying on.

I, too, am stuck halfway across a river, thigh-high; and the people I thought were my parents on the bank behind me are now as far out of reach as my blood relations on the bank ahead. They're equally distant.

I shut the adoption book with a bang. Manuals like this are supposed to show you how to do it yourself, but it's not working for me. I've read thirty pages and I still haven't found out who my real parents are.

I turn off the bedside light, and lie down in the darkness. It's early, but I'm sleepy. Garth and Gaynor are still in the kitchen, tearing strips off each other as though their skin were wallpaper. I hear them through the floor as I float off along a long tunnel.

Satisfied now?

Didn't want it to turn out like this.

Take it back?

Too late for that.

After a while the darkness around me gives way to, not light exactly, but brighter darkness, and my floating reaches new heights. Gaynor and Garth are still launching microscopic attacks on each other, but from this distance their tiny fight definitely has nothing to do with me. I envisage the cord between me and my mother, the one which was umbilical but now seems unbelievable, breaking. And I don't feel a thing.

A complete absence of family and familiarity, of love and lovers in my life will be okay. If I don't get too close to anyone again, I'll never have anything to lose. I'll be above the sensory dimension, and pain and pleasure will both be beneath me, silly as plastic toys.

I should know better than to entertain such evocative thoughts on the way to sleep. The next thing that's going on is this crazy dream:

I'm Sindy and Eugene is Action Man. We're at the bottom of a toy box, where we've been tangled up since childhood. In the cramped and confined space it slowly becomes clear that he's got my left leg and I've got his right arm. We've been put together wrongly. but although our limbs are stiff and difficult to move, we start to struggle up through the sedimentary strata of the toy box, from soft fur and painted wood to nail polish remover, chemistry kits and computer bits; and onwards and upwards between the spokes of a big bicycle wheel where it starts to get light. Eventually we come out on top.

We turn to look at each other. He's a camp Action Man. One of his legs has twinkle toes. I'm a butch Sindy. One of my arms has Mr muscles. We're a right pair of freaks and fairies. We come from a funny family. No wonder we have to be our own best friends.

Eugene and I start to fight. We don't fancy each other. We're struggling for separation. We tear ourselves limb from limb in order to get our lives in order. I snatch his ankle, he grabs my wrist, we pull, wring and twist. There's a series of pops, like peas from pods, and then we no longer look so alike.

When all of Eugene's male members are present and correct, he gives me a cheery salute. Then he turns and walks off into a lollipop sunrise, across a beach made from the sandy covers of old school geography books. Only his slight limp shows that he's a war veteran, a real man.

He didn't stay and help me reconstruct myself. I'm left with a gaping hole that shows how hollow I am inside. Air the colour of the sunrise, factory pink, fills the space where a baby might grow if I had a father.

I wake up, with a start.

It's morning.

I must have lashed out in my sleep. The big pile of books on my bedside table has fallen to the floor with a crash. The only one left is the one that was on the bottom. It's my mum and dad's. The first thing I see when I open my eyes are the words written on its spine.

WHOOPS OEDIPUS: The Nuclear Family Explodes

I blink. This must still be part of my dream. I pull the book onto the pillow and it pops open, and words start jumping off the pages at me like a firework display. *Family favourites . . . Incestuous relationships . . . Ooh taboo!*

Oedipus was blind to the fact that the woman he loved was his mother; at least, that's his story and he's sticking to it. Feelings like his have always been disguised or denied; but they often turn normal family dramas into tragedies of miscommunication, in which it is better to hate than love too much. We show anger in place of admiration, ambivalence rather than affection, and live with secret abuse instead of mutual understanding. Biology tells us incest is wrong, but the laws which we've drawn between us and the objects of our original and deepest desires have bred a society of liars.

You what? Garth and Gaynor Bloom, you what? I don't like the look of this at all. I try to close the book, but it only opens wider. It opens at Chapter Five, which is called 'Sibling Ribaldry'.

'There was no beginning. It had always already begun. The love was there before we knew the words to express it.'

So said 'Jane', not her real name, when we asked how her sexual relationship with her older brother began. 'Jane', who sleeps with her brother to this day, went on to describe the development of their romance.

'We were happy to play with the children in our street. But we saw at once there were no other Kings and Queens, no other Doctors and Nurses, no other Mummies and Daddies. So we allowed our friends to join in the games, but only as courtiers, patients or pets.

'By the time we reached our early teens, we'd both realised that none of the kids at school turned us on. It was really as simple as that. We still didn't speak about it, but whenever I did my homework in his bedroom, or he played cards in mine, or we both rode our bikes fast down a steep hill, there'd be sparks flying and we just didn't get that with anyone else. I think we both felt a bit embarrassed about it; but only when we were apart. Whenever we were together there'd be this extra energy that made the rest of the world disappear. Then it seemed like we were right and everyone else was wrong, looking through windows to find their ideal mates when they should have been looking in the mirror at home.'

(Note here how Jane's comments are in accordance with that sense of 'self-satisfaction' discussed in Chapters One and Two. Because all her needs — intellectual, emotional and physical — are being met within the family, she feels no urge to look outside it for an 'other'.)

'When we eventually had sex we were so far gone we didn't care that it was illegal. In fact, I'd forgotten such a law existed. It was my brother who reminded me afterwards, but only as a joke.'

Through a process of reorientation, by playing and laughing about it, Jane and her brother come to terms with their unusual relationship. Before long it seems that they are the only sane ones in a world of blindingly stupid cupids. Rather than rushing around looking for the latest greatest love, they focus on their oldest flame, feed their original fire.

I don't realise I'm crying until a tear splashes on the last word of that sentence. But fire is preserved in print and cannot be extinguished.

'We can never tell anyone the truth about our relationship,' says Jane. 'But to be honest, we don't really care about other people. Sometimes I feel isolated, cut off from the rest of the world, but my brother is like a magnet to me and we'll never split up. It wouldn't be physically possible.'

At this point the bedroom door opens and Dad comes in

with breakfast on a tray. Before he knows what's hit him I've stood up in bed, and thrown the book at him.

It actually hits the teapot. China rattles and pages turn, churning like a mill wheel to guide the stream of liquid over the edge of the tray and on to the carpet. Garth is shocked. He looks at the book as it lands face up on the carpet, then he looks at me. He clears his throat, but before he can speak I start barking at him like a dog, mad words and shreds of sentences.

'In without knocking – don't you dare come – ever again.'

'Sorry,' he says.

'No privacy.'

'I know, I'm sorry.'

'Not fair. You've got a fucking force field around your personal space but you won't so much as knock on my bedroom door.'

'It won't happen again, Grace.'

'Do you think I'm just an extension of your personality?'

'What's up?' Gaynor has appeared in the doorway.

'I didn't knock,' Dad says.

'Grace, you're overreacting. Get off the bed,' Mum snaps.

A great rage is welling up inside me, overwhelming me, and I'm not sure if it's all mine. It is entering through the soles of my feet, shooting up my legs and into my stomach, as if my body is a straw sucking all the anger in the bed, the room, the house into my mouth.

'Grace?' I spit at my mother. 'Don't you mean ''Jane''?'

She looks blank for a moment, then she looks at the book on the floor.

'Oh,' she says.

'You knew about me and Eugene all along and you did

nothing to help us,' I shout. 'You studied us as if we were a psychological experiment.'

My father takes a step towards me. 'You've got it all wrong,' he says.

I've got this fury flowing through my body in an atomic stream, from my toes to the top of my head and the only way to let it out is to scream:

'I suppose you fancy yourselves as Doctor Frankenstein, but you're a pair of fucking monsters, with no sense of parental responsibility!'

Gaynor starts to cry.

'Go on then,' I say to her. 'See if I care.'

Dad takes another step towards me.

'Come down from there,' he says.

'Oh, no,' I shake my head. 'It's a position of power. Pick up the book and put it on the bed.'

He does so. I seem to be calming down a bit.

'Right. Now, rummage in the dressing gown pocket of your hideous Missus, and find her cigarette lighter,' I say.

'No.'

'Why not?'

'Because you're going to burn the book,' he says.

'Only Nazis burn books,' sniffs Gaynor, with a toss of her head. She doesn't seem to realise that if the book goes, I'll go too; up in flames, in protest.

'I'm not going to let you publish it,' I say. 'You can't state publicly that everyone in the family fancies each other. What will people think?'

'That's not your problem,' says Garth.

'It's our book,' says Gaynor.

'But it's related to me,' I reply. 'Anyone reading the book

222

will realise that somewhere in the Bloom house something must have been said, some look met, some feeling felt, some touch tried. They'll say we're out of our family tree. They'll talk about bringing back hanging.'

'We've been working on it for years,' says Garth.

'You can't stop us now,' says Gaynor.

'You'll be a laughing stock,' I tell them. 'You'll be burned at the stake.'

'We're prepared to take that risk,' Gaynor shrugs her shoulders, in her pear-drop yellow candlewick dressing gown.

'But it's my story,' I say. 'You're telling about me and Eugene. And you haven't even got it right. You said we would never split up. It wouldn't be physically possible. You said he was like a magnet to me.'

With these words, my body gives a final jerk and I slump abruptly on the bed. There is silence in the room. Garth and Gaynor are holding hands. They're holding each other up. What about me? My magnet doesn't love me any more.

'We can't stop the book,' Garth says.

'It's our baby, you see,' says Gaynor. She's appealing to me woman to woman, but that makes it worse. I'm supposed to be their baby. Now I'm in a state of sibling rivalry with the book.

Garth puts it gently in my hands. I look away, pulling a face.

'Read it, don't burn it,' he says. 'Read it all and don't say another word till you've finished. I'll bring you some more tea in a bit.'

'How can you bring me more tea if I haven't had any yet?' I ask.

He picks the lid of the teapot off the carpet and puts it on his head for a moment, giving me a funny look; a fatherly way of making me laugh. He and Gaynor leave the room, smiling. But before they've reached the foot of the stairs I hear another violent row breaking out.

I hit the book with a pillow. The book bounces in the air and I catch it in my other hand. I hit the pillow with the book. I'm not going to read the bloody thing. Nor am I going to sit listening to them bloody arguing. I've got to get out of here. I dress quickly and run down the stairs loudly, but it's nowhere near as quick and loud as they are shouting in the kitchen as I storm down the hall.

'Then our only choice is to tell them the truth,' Garth says.

'No, never,' says Gaynor.

I run out of the house and down the road and round the corner, holding my breath like a handful of shingle in my chest, a sharp stone stuck in my throat. I don't slow down until I reach the start of the park, where nothing but grass and trees lie in front of me.

The park is lit like a watercolour painting. The sky is grey all over, such a dull grey it makes me think that the light must be artificial. The air is full of water in disguise. It's thick and heavy, muffled with more of that uniform grey, like a school scarf, getting wetter with every breath. There is a crying out of crows in the bare black trees above my head, a meaningless screaming of ravens, a manifold closing in of sparrows. Beneath my feet the grass is long and wet and wishing as I walk.

I stop and listen. It sounded like two sets of footsteps splashing. Of course, I can't be alone here. I never was allowed to come to the park on my own. Eugene always came with me. It stands to reason he should be here today.

I'm approaching the paved part of the park, where there is a children's playground. The metal A shape of the swings frame, the O of the roundabout and the I of the slide are as familiar to me as my own handwriting. The red and blue and yellow and green of steps and seats and railings remind me of my very first paintings.

Though my mind's eye is watering, I can see us through it, Eugene and me; swinging, spinning and sliding in embarrassing anoraks. Our images leave traces, rainbow trails in the wet; visual echoes. I watch for a while then trudge towards the trees in the corner of the park. Hidden in the centre of the copse is an old stone edifice. We used to think it was the ruins of a temple, but now it just looks like a relic from the war. A paranoid folly, which was built for emergencies but never got used. Anyway, we used to call it the grotto and get up to no good there. Eugene introduced me to drink the day we shared a can of cider in the shelter of its walls, and tried to fill the entire place with fallen leaves so we could dive off the high board, which was all that remained of the roof. And we used to do great plays, improvising scenes of murder and mystery in this realistic location.

I stand there and listen to our ghosts. Shouting like Shakespeare, swashbuckling like Starsky and Hutch. We never played romantic roles. I suppose we had enough of that in real life, and were looking for escapism.

Eugene has got away. Until this moment his absence has been so tangible a presence that he might as well have been here with me, but now I know I'm on my own. I'm putting in a solo appearance, in a weird play of my own imagining; it's about a Siamese twin, surgically severed from the other, wondering which one of them has died. I walk sadly around the empty grotto.

There aren't as many fallen leaves as there used to be, but there's a lot of other stuff on the floor. Sticks and stones and bricks, bits of broken bottles and complete condoms. We never used to see things like that. The ground looks like a page of maths, with plus signs, minus signs, and numerous piles of berries. As I stare, a pattern seems to emerge, and it all starts to make sense. I pick up a stick and mark it, making a few adjustments, correcting the calculations in the earth.

$$a=b$$
$$a^2=ab$$
$$a^2-b^2=ab-b^2$$
$$(a+b)(a-b)=b(a-b)$$
$$a+b=b$$
$$1+1=1$$
$$2=1$$

Straight-line twigs make the plus, minus and equals signs; abstract shapes in man-made glass form letters and numbers. For the sensuous curves of the brackets or parentheses I use the condoms. I know it's unpleasant, but I'm in the grip of a great vision. I'm having a revelation, and anyway, I only touch them with the tip of a long stick.

By the time my work is finished, I've remembered why we used to call this place the temple. A feeling of peace has come over me. All my problems seem to be solved by the proof that $2=1$.

It is not infallible evidence. The maths is a bit tricky. I have to cancel by zero, and in theory that makes infinity.

But this is the practical answer. Garth and Gaynor may have told me and Eugene we were adopted because they thought it would help us out of a sticky incestuous situation. But surely they would never publish a book about incest using the story of me and Eugene as evidence, if they knew that we weren't really related. They couldn't stake their reputation and base their case on a blood brother and sister relationship if Eugene and I were not blood brother and sister.

Therefore, Garth and Gaynor Bloom's only crime was that they didn't try to stop the awful progress of our affair, but stood and watched and cleared the obstacles out of its path. They wrote a book about it behind our backs. They behaved like psychotherapists; they observed and they facilitated. And as this is exactly the way they urge parents to treat their children in the first book, *Dumb and Mad*, it probably means they are our real mum and dad.

Nevertheless, I'm full of joy as I leave the grotto and head for home across the park. On the way here my heart felt like a clenched fist in my chest, but now it's a bird flying free. The sun has burned a hole in the clouds and is shining through. I'm without a shadow of a doubt that Eugene is my brother. Now we can be friends again.

When I get home, I read the whole chapter 'Sibling Ribaldry'; but I'd think I was dreaming were it not for the solidity of my surroundings: the constant tick of the clock, the slow stroll of sunlight across the carpet, the steady procession of a late breakfast through my digestive tract. I'm back in bed as if I never got out of it. I pick up the thread of the text exactly where I left off, and scour it for more clues.

So do brothers and sisters really hate each other's guts, or is it all an act? Does the incest taboo between siblings exist in nature or only in nurture? Is it really 'God' who says no, or is the prohibition purely for social purposes?

We don't know. To any nature/nurture question science can only answer 50/50. It's six of one and half a dozen of the other, though this ambiguous result may well be telling us as much about our mathematics as the subject under analysis. We can only suggest that instances of sexual love between brothers and sisters are rarely recorded, and barely recalled, by many. Our culture is almost completely silent on the matter, yet we can only suppose, in the words of a cultural catchphrase, that silence speaks volumes.

In traditional psychoanalytic theory, siblings compete with each other for the attention and affection of their parents. But what if they don't care about the parents as much as they care for each other? Suppose a little boy walks into a room and finds his little sister in the arms of his father or mother, and suppose he slams the door and sulks till bedtime; traditional psychoanalytic theory would say he is jealous of his sister, he begrudges the extra cuddle she's received, and he fears that his father or mother love her more than they love him. But what if he knows his parents are a pair; he's done the Oedipus thing already, and teamed up with his tiny sibling. What if he's worried that his sister loves their parents more than she loves him?

It can happen that in the face of unstable or too strong parenting, the offspring will turn to each other for support, and find their primary love-object there. 'John', a man whose incestuous relationship with his sister has gone on in secret for many years, says that despite their parents' early attempts to separate them, encouraging individuation through sexual difference, the bond went deeper.

'The little girl belongs to Daddy, the little boy is

Mummy's, that was the idea we got; though sometimes at weekends my sister helped Mum in the kitchen, while I worked with Dad on the car. It sounds so old-fashioned now, like those books we used to read at school, with Spot the Dog.

'I don't think it was a generation gap thing, but I didn't feel linked to my parents in the way I felt it with my sister. If I stretched my arms out I could always reach her, but my mother seemed further away. I think it might be because we learnt to speak together. When we said "I" it signified two different people, but when we said "Me" we both meant the same thing.'

I like this. I don't like the way they've given Eugene, or 'John', all the deep and meaningful things to say while I, or 'Jane', drone on about how we'll be together for ever like a Mills and Boon romance. But I do like his neat little sutra; when we say 'I' it signifies two different people, but when we say 'Me' we both mean the same thing. There's always been a 'me-ness' between my and Eugene's 'I's, and perhaps that explains why we're so close. Garth and Gaynor Bloom could not possibly have made it up.

The mathematical problem that they pointed out, the fact that the answer is always 50/50, is because 2=1. I'll have to tell them that, as soon as I'm speaking to them again, which I think might be quite soon. I'm in a good mood because it looks more and more likely that Eugene is my real brother. We had a bad argument, and he told me to go away, but I've got him back. If he only loves me when I'm his sister, so what; I am his sister.

I'm ready to go downstairs now. It's nearly time for the

journalist and photographer to arrive, and I can't wait to meet them. I've always imagined the staff of *The Times* to be like the population of Heaven; a happy collection of luminaries and high-flyers, in assorted period costumes, sitting at desks in the clouds. Somehow I've got it into my head that the editor will be sending Freud or Jung to interview my parents for the psychoanalysis column.

I run down the stairs and the doorbell rings as I get to the bottom. Bingo! I smile and mime the words 'good afternoon' rapidly at my reflection in the hall mirror, then I open the door.

'Oh, it's you,' I say.

'Charmed, I'm sure,' says Angus Shanks. He's my parents' literary agent and he brushes past me in a neat grey suit with his tie flung over his shoulder like a feather boa. It looks very camp, but I think it must have flicked up there by accident in his rush to get here, because Mr Shanks is actually quite macho. He asked me out once, the first time we met. I said no, it wouldn't be appropriate because he was trying to publish my parents' book, but the real reason I refused his offer was my complete lack of attraction to him.

'Where are they?' he asks me.

'Not here yet,' I say.

'What?'

I look at my watch.

'There's five minutes to go,' I say.

But he's not listening to me. Mum and Dad's voices are rising and rising behind the living room door and he's striding down the hallway and bursting in on them.

I follow, saying, 'Oh, I thought you meant the people from *The Times*.'

Mum and Dad ought to be ready for them by now. They ought to have coffee and cakes on a side table and be sitting with their ankles crossed like royalty, making talk as small as corgis. But they're still in their dressing gowns and the room is a mess. I gasp when I see the state of things.

'Come on,' I say, 'tidy up. Quick. Get changed. *The Times* they are a-coming.'

Angus Shanks gives me a pitying look.

'No,' he says, 'they're not.'

'What?' I'm shuffling magazines into a neat pile, making sure there's a politically correct one on top.

'The interview's been cancelled,' says Angus.

'Why?'

He points at my parents. They're sitting in separate armchairs, looking like they're in a newsflash about a kidnapped baby.

'They called it off?' I ask. 'But why? They need the publicity.'

'Not if there is no book they don't,' says Angus Shanks.

'No book? Why not?'

He comes too close to me in a rush of breath.

'I don't know, do I? I'm trying to find out, aren't I? They phoned me half an hour ago saying I had to stop publication at all costs. The book must not come out. Now if you'll be so good as to piss off and get me a drink, I'm going to make them change their minds.'

'Er, okay,' I say, backing away. 'Tea or coffee?'

'I'd prefer a gin and tonic,' he replies, 'if you won't think too badly of me.'

I mix him a large one with stale tonic water from the sideboard in the dining room, then I stare out of the window and absent-mindedly drink it. I've scarcely had time to make another one before Shanks sidles round the door. His tie really clashes with the decor.

'The shit's in your court,' he says. 'Mr and Mrs B have been pricked by their conscience. They think it's not fair on you and Eugene, them broadcasting their theories of the new family to all and sundry. They think your friends won't want to know you any more.'

I laugh. I haven't really got any friends. I had a lot of lovers, but they were more like family: Nigel wanted me to have his babies, Simeon wanted to be my baby, Kelly wanted to be my mother, Dave wanted to be my brother.

'Anyway,' continues Angus, taking his drink, 'they're calling it off for the sake of your reputation. So what I want you to do is go in there and tell them everything's fine and you don't mind if they publish the book.'

I laugh again, though it sounds hollow in the cold dining room.

'Go on, Grace,' says Angus. 'It's no big deal. People won't exactly be queuing up to read it.'

'Is your tie meant to be like that?' I ask him.

He looks down at his chest, but his tie is still flung over his shoulder.

'It's very flamboyant,' I say.

He puts it back in place hurriedly, hardly liking to be seen touching it, as if it is a penis, in public.

'Help yourself to another drink,' I say, and sway into the hallway, feeling slightly drunk myself.

In the living room Garth and Gaynor are still in separate armchairs. This is serious. Normally they sit side by side on the sofa.

'Now look here, Mater and Pater,' I say, 'what's all this about calling the book off?' I seem to have picked up Angus Shanks's Oxbridge accent.

Dad looks up in surprise.

'Did he tell you that?' he says.

I nod.

'He had no right to,' says Dad.

'Oh, come on,' I reply rudely. 'If the book doesn't appear in the shops tomorrow his career will be down the toilet. He's going to do everything in his power to make you change your mind.'

Dad shakes his head.

'I won't be budged on the subject,' he says.

'Is it because of me,' I ask him.

'Yes,' says Gaynor.

I wasn't talking to her.

'Is it because I asked you not to?' I say to Dad again.

'Asked us? Told us!' Gaynor says. The loss of the book has been a big blow to her.

'Do you remember what my main objections were?' I say.

'A lot of shouting and crying,' Gaynor replies.

'Yes, but do you remember why?'

'I don't know. You said . . . you said we were . . . perverts.' This is not a word that fits easily into Gaynor's mouth. Her lips are too pursed for it.

'You said it wasn't true,' adds Dad. 'You said our theory was incorrect.'

'But,' I say, 'I don't know what's true and what's not, do I?'

Garth and Gaynor are silent.

'Because you've been lying to me, haven't you?' I say.

Still they don't respond.

'So tell me the truth,' I say. 'Once and for all, Eugene is my real brother, isn't he?'

They look at each other. They look at me.

'He is my brother, isn't he?' I say. I'm talking to them as if they're children. But frankly, that's how they've been behaving. Garth has finally decided to grow up.

'Yes,' he says, with a single nod of his head.

'Yes!' I say, flinging myself onto the sofa. 'Thank you.'

Gaynor sighs deeply. I lie down.

'And you two are my real mum and dad,' I say.

'Yes,' says Dad. In the opposite armchair my mother's body spasms as he speaks.

I close my eyes.

'And your son and daughter really were having an incestuous relationship,' I say.

'Yes,' says Dad. Mum jerks again. They must have strings attached.

'Then what you say in your book is true,' I conclude.

Mum draws a breath.

'What?' she says.

'You were right. What you wrote was right. You were wrong to write it. You should have tried to help in a real way instead. But now that it's written it would be wrong to pretend it wasn't. Someone's got to tell the truth, and it might as well be you.'

'But, Grace,' says Dad, 'you were worried what people will make of it. Your friends.' I don't want to dwell on this. It struck me in the dining room that I haven't really got any.

'What will yours think?' I ask him.

'Our what? Our friends?' he says. Then he looks at Mum. 'We haven't really got any,' he says.

'Rubbish! We got seventy Christmas cards last year,' Mum replies.

Angus Shanks appears anxiously in the doorway at this point, his drink much bigger than it was when I gave it to him.

'What's the score?' he says.

Eugene is my brother. Mum and Dad are my mum and dad. They're the maddest people on the planet, to think that they could pretend not to be my parents. It's the stupidest thing I ever heard, telling us we were adopted so we could carry on having incest, without fear of recrimination. They're mad, stupid, magic parents.

I stare into the sofa cushion as if it's a crystal ball. I'm still feeling a bit pissed.

'The mystic daughter has spoken,' I say, looking up at Angus Shanks. 'You shall go to the ball. *Whoops Oedipus* will be officially published, as of midnight.'

Eleven

I've got a white dress, which I've never worn. I bought it two years ago, but I didn't know why until today. Impulse buys can turn out to be premonitions, it's apparent. The dress is made of thin material like muslin, layer upon layer, so it's translucent but not transparent. It's full-length and flowing, with fine golden bindings winding round my waist and between my breasts in a Botticelli way. Sleeves hang in triangles, floating at my wrists. When I raise my arms they fly like wings.

I feel like an angel. I'll be in attendance at my parents' book launch, more than just a dutiful daughter. I am their muse, and I'll smile in the face of ugly truth. I'll watch as the monster emerges, and I won't run away.

Every beast must have its beauty, and every beauty needs a beast. I'll be at the book launch in my white dress, to show that even wicked witches and wizards can spawn fabulous fairy-tale daughters. If I've got to come out of the closet, I might as well come out proud, with my head held high.

I smooth my hair with a brush as rough as birch, and sigh for the passing of a moment of courage. My sleeves waft as I watch the brave face I've put on in the mirror. I remember the day I bought this pale, sad dress now. I wanted to wear it for my suicide, an occasion I planned whenever there were no joyous celebrations like weddings or christenings on the cards.

In the mirror, I put some bright red lipstick on, and though I've done it hundreds of times before, this if the first time it feels like I'm drawing myself a heart. I should paint them all over my body, to be safe and strong.

My parents call me, from the hall, through the walls. I leave my room with a backward glance at the bed, one last chance to see if I'm still lying there really, and this is all a dream or death. Then I glide downstairs in my dress.

'You look nice, dear,' says Mum, but she's only saying it, because she's actually looking at herself in the mirror of a little powder compact from her handbag.

'Yes, you do,' says Dad. He is looking at me, so I can see that he means it. 'You look like an angel.'

I smile and drift past him but he catches my wing to stop me.

'Listen,' he says, 'forewarned is forearmed. Eugene will be there today. With Trudy.'

'Thanks, Dad,' I say. 'Forewarned is foreskinned.'

He winces and lets go of my wrist, his hand falling to protect his trouser front, automatically.

'We don't want any trouble,' says Gaynor from the other end of the hallway.

'There won't be any. I was just kidding,' I say, rapidly moving towards her. 'You wouldn't have known that though, because you consistently fail to notice how the font of my forgiveness is never empty and the fountain of my love never runs dry.' I speak as fast as I walk, straight to where she's standing so screwed up, then past her and out of the front door, my wings flying behind me. 'Come on,' I say, 'you don't want to be late.'

I'm acting cool, but I'm actually so hot and sticky that after five minutes on the plastic seat of the car there's a damp patch on the back of my skirt.

When we arrive at the hotel I stride up and down on the pavement outside and stand around in a wide-legged stance to get as much dry air as possible up my skirt before we have to go inside. But Mum and Dad aren't hanging about. They're quickly swallowed up by a set of revolving doors, so I slowly follow them.

The hotel foyer is full of flowers, and there's a small knot of publishing professionals waiting for the Blooms. The ceiling is a great balloon of glass held in place by a network of golden wires and the sun shines through it, showing Angus Shanks in quite a good light as he rushes towards us in a bright green suit. He picks up my parents and practically carries them down a long carpeted corridor, while some sort of PR man drags me along behind. Abruptly we come to a parting of the ways, and without getting the chance to say goodbye or good luck to my mother and father, I'm led off in one direction while they're ushered in the other.

This enforced separation makes me feel like I've arrived at a concentration camp. The nameless PR man throws open a set of double doors, and even though I see a ballroom or banqueting hall of a warm pinky hue, and little round tables laid for cosy circles of people with lit candles, more flowers and free bottles of wine, a cold shiver runs down my spine. The ceiling is high, and at the front of the room there's a podium, where pictures of my parents are blown up to look like blurred photographs of the surface of the moon.

'That's your chair,' says the man, waving his hand at the foot of the podium. 'We've done a special table for the authors' family.' I look to find a frillier tablecloth with more wine than all the others, and Eugene and Trudy facing each other across the flowers and candles. I say they're facing each other, but Trudy has actually fixed me with a hostile stare, over Eugene's shoulder. I get closer but she still doesn't smile. She doesn't look very pleased to see me. Eugene's got his back to me, but I can tell he is tired and tense and has one of those headaches that feels like a hand clamped on the skull with a finger in each eye.

He jumps as I come up behind him, and nearly scares the life out of me as well. I can't meet his eye as I hang my handbag over the back of a chair and say my goodbyes to the PR man who suddenly seems like my only friend; but as I sit down, his image in the corner of my vision is lit up repeatedly, as if a flashcube is going off, or I'm getting a migraine, too. I still don't look at him as I reach out and pour myself a shaky glass of wine.

'Hello, Trudy,' I say, after a quick drink.

She doesn't reply. She must hate me, and I can't say I blame her really.

'She can't hear you,' says Eugene. His voice makes lights pop again, on the edge of my eyes and in the darkness inside me, but I still don't turn to look at him. I ignore him and give Trudy a stylised wave and smile as if I were the Queen or Marcel Marceau.

'She can't see you either,' says Eugene. 'She went blind, remember?'

I'd forgotten. I'm such a selfish cow. I'm so wrapped up in my own world I'd forgotten that Trudy can no longer see out of hers.

'Can't see and can't hear?' I say.

'No,' says Eugene.

'Oh, God,' I gasp.

'Grace,' says Eugene.

'What?'

'Look at me,' he says.

I can't. I'm looking at Trudy's ears. They're swollen florets, spongy forms, as if bits of her brain have come through the holes, then crusted over and collapsed in on themselves until the orifices are closed up.

'Oh, God,' I gasp. It's horrible, but I can't look away.

'Grace,' says Eugene.

'Yes?' I say, but I still can't tear my eyes from Trudy. There are tears in my eyes. I reach a hand across the table and take hold of one of hers. I don't realise until it's too late that her fingers are no longer separate. They've started to join together. My instinct is to snatch my hand away, but I fight it and merely flinch. Breathing deeply, I hold Trudy's awful claw long enough to give it a friendly and supportive squeeze, and then I let it go.

'Where?' Trudy says, and her hand follows mine across the table, groping like something from a swamp.

'Here,' says Eugene, catching Trudy's hand and holding it between both of his. I look at him now, now that he's looking at her; and my eyes spill two perfect painful teardrops at the expression Trudy will never see.

Suddenly it strikes me that, all my life, I've only loved things which are beautiful, nothing sick or ugly; things whose beauty reflects back at me exactly. I've always thought that stooping to conquer is bad for the posture. And in being loved, I have only wanted to be put on a pedestal; not needed, not deeply

240

touched, never worn down or messed up. But the look on Eugene's face as he looks at Trudy is showing me a new meaning of love and beauty: these things have got nothing to do with what you can see.

I'm looking so hard that I hardly notice Eugene turning towards me until a spark in his eye starts a fire in mine, and moist though they be, we're soon gazing at each other through a blaze. Not with my eyes but with my heart I see that our big argument meant nothing much; he will never stop loving Trudy, and he has never stopped loving me.

'There's a little something in my breast pocket for you,' he says. His hands are still tied up with Trudy so I have to take the envelope out myself. I slip my fingers into the silken lining of his rough linen jacket to get it. Eugene blushes and looks away.

It's lucky he looks away, because I think my face falls as I open the envelope and read the words on the cover of the card.

HAPPY BIRTHDAY SISTER

It's not my birthday. It's not my birthday for ages. What is Eugene playing at? But before I can ask him, a piece of folded-up paper falls out of the card and lands on the tablecloth. I pick it up and open it out into two pieces of paper, photocopied documents which I recognise immediately. They're birth certificates. I look at Eugene.

'See, ' he says. 'You are my sister. And Mum and Dad are our real parents.'

I read the words on the birth certificates. I have actually seen mine before, and Eugene's. The details have been there all along, unfolding like a game of Consequences: him, her, what they did, where they lived, the names they gave their bouncing babies, one boy and one girl, with two and a half years in between.

I sigh, and give a small smile, and say, 'I thought as much.'

'Me, too,' nods Eugene. Then he shakes his head and says, 'So they told us a lie. I wish I knew why.'

'You do,' I say.

'Why? To stop us fancying each other?'

'Or so that we could carry on,' I say.

Eugene slams his hands down on the table, and Trudy's go with him.

'Big bang,' says Trudy, but her dry, wood-splitting tones are drowned out by Eugene.

'I'm finding this very difficult to deal with,' he says. 'It's completely changed the way I feel about them. How dare they make such a drastic intervention in our lives. Our affair was none of their business. They preach about good parenting, but they don't know where to stop. Honestly, Grace, I can't get my head round their fucking unforgivable behaviour. What did they think they were doing, trying to ease our pain, like you can ease someone's pain with a giant redwood tree!'

'You can ease someone's pain with a giant redwood tree,' I say, 'if you sit them underneath it to lean back against the trunk and relax in the shade. They'll soon start to feel better.'

'Yes, but Mum and Dad brought it crashing down on top of us,' says Eugene.

'No, they just hid in its branches and jumped out at us as we walked past,' I say.

'No, they dragged us up to the top and threw us off,' he insists.

I let him have his own way.

'I can't get my head round how they thought we'd fall for it,' Eugene says. 'What a crass ploy, what a complete lack of common sense. They acted with no notion of normal social behaviour and a total disregard for human life.' I nod sagely, but he's not looking at me. He's directed his angry outburst at the blown-up photos of our parents on the podium. 'Are they a pair of assholes or what?' he asks out of the corner of his mouth.

'Yes,' I say, 'but I seem to have found the wherewithal to forgive them.'

'Where?' says Eugene.

'I don't know,' I shrug. 'In their new book.'

'You've read *Whoops Oedipus*?' he says.

'Yes.'

'What's it about?' he asks.

'Don't you know?' I say, aghast. 'Didn't they tell you?'

'No,' says Eugene.

'Oh, shit, you stupid people,' I say, to their pictures on the podium. 'What planet are you coming from? Okay, this is ground control,' I say to Eugene. 'I'd better fill you in quickly on the plot. Brace yourself for a shock.'

But it's too late. The platform is shaking. Garth and Gaynor Bloom are walking on stage to a round of polite applause from the audience. The presentation is about to begin.

I give a double take at the sight of my parents on the podium. Having been staring so long at the close-up photographic representations of them, their real selves seem unreal; in the same way that cartoons of politicians make their living models look like a joke.

'Ladies and gentlemen,' says a man in red braces and a bow tie, who has come to the front of the platform to make the formal introductions. 'It gives me great pleasure . . .'

I don't want to know what gives him great pleasure. I don't like the way his shirt buttons are straining across a stomach so

243

broad it makes his trouser region look tiny in comparison. I stop listening at this point, and start looking at my parents as if I'd never seen them before, trying to imagine how they'd look to a complete stranger.

The most noticeable thing about both of them is my mother's hair. It's wicked to say so, but women who pass forty without having their long hair cut off end up looking like witches. Not that I think it's necessarily a bad thing to look like a witch, but we're so used to seeing long flowing locks on a beautiful young woman that our eye is drawn at once to the face, and if it's old and wrinkled we can't help getting a shock akin to seeing something fly by on a broomstick.

My mother is wearing a black suit with a green silk blouse. My father's in a big red jumper and jeans with the creases ironed in. And even though his style is more casual than hers, and their colours clash, they still look like a couple; the sort of couple who couldn't ever have married anyone else. If they had never met, they both would have stayed single. They match each other, in the way that dog owners look like their pets.

It's time for them to speak. My father is getting to his feet and changing places awkwardly with the fat git at the front of the platform. He smiles at the audience.

'In two hours from now,' he says, 'when you've all bought your copies of *Whoops Oedipus* from the bookstall at the back of the hall, and rushed home to read it, you will see that it begins with the briefest of introductions. In most books the introduction tells you what it's all about, but this one is different. The introduction to *Whoops Oedipus* only says what the book is not about.'

He clears his throat and continues in a slightly different tone of voice, to signal a quotation.

'We would like to address the issue of sexuality in families. This does not mean sexual abuse. As far as we are concerned sexual abuse is sexual abuse whichever way you look at it and whatever social relationships are involved. At the back of our book is a bibliography of studies of incest. None of them have been able to draw distinctions between abusive and non-abusive situations, except to make the vague suggestion that sexual interactions between brother and sister are "not as bad" as those between parent and child. Clearly a closer look at both implicit and explicit sexual practice in families is long overdue. We will find that there are great differences between incestuous relationships and sexual abuse.'

My attention it torn away from Dad's text by Eugene who seems to be trying to stand up and get Trudy to stand up at the same time. I catch him before the scraping of chair legs causes a distraction to the rest of the audience, and manage to keep him in his place by holding his left hand in my right and Trudy's right in my left. He is already clasping her other hand, so we've formed a ring around the table, a complete circle of shoulders, elbows and wrists. Eugene has to stop pulling; he might be torn himself but he's not going to tear Trudy in two. I squeeze Eugene's hand tightly, and will him to stay and be strong. People may point their fingers at us, but they'll only be able to talk behind our backs if we leave.

Fuck me, if I can't read my brother's mind. 'Incest,' he is saying, 'they've written a book about incest. But that's our story. How did they know?' He's thinking exactly what I thought when I first saw *Whoops Oedipus*. We make eye contact.

'I'd now like to read an extract from the chapter entitled "Daddy's Little Girl",' says Garth Bloom on the podium. He finds his place in the book, and smiles over our heads at the audience proper.

'If she wasn't his little girl, she'd be his ideal woman. Why do we find this so shocking? It's only natural to prefer things which are the same as us to things which are different. Flesh of our flesh is much less threatening than the skin of a stranger. But the joys of the identical have been denied us by the machinations of a society which must grow, which needs us to mate with the members of other families in order to establish a gene pool of fit survivors.

'Father/daughter sexual relationships are neither biologically nor psychologically advisable. But the incest taboo works on a sociological level, too. Girls and women are seen as objects, given by their own family to another's at marriage, bearing children to continue their husband's family name. Fathers are not allowed to keep their daughters, but must swap them for wives for their sons, in order to maintain their own line of descent. They are something to exchange, to have but not to hold.

'The man in the street feels fine about this. He's happy to watch his little girl grow up and then let her go. It's not good to hang on. But still he may get a shock when he sees a child the spitting image of himself suddenly take on the shape of a young woman. Or what if this daughter resembles his wife, who doesn't really love or want her husband any more, but still looks on her daddy as king of the world and adores him more than her mother ever

246

did? The shock sets in stronger. Then when his teenage girl goes off with some young hoodlum who doesn't deserve her and doesn't look back, Dad is left feeling jealous. But he can't show it, because if people knew he was jealous of his daughter's boyfriend they'd think the worst of him. They'd think he was perverted. So he has to wait up till she comes home from the date and lay into her for being so late. He has to shout and swear and maybe even slap her, to stop the shock.'

I think I'm going to faint. My father's words rush over me like a frightening hot flush. I start swaying and say to myself that if I don't lose concentration soon I'll lose consciousness completely. With a great effort I divert my mind from the stream of Dad's reading. When it's free, the first thing I see is the glass of wine on the table in front of me. I'd love a drink but I wouldn't like to let go of Eugene and Trudy's hands. So I bend my head and partake of my wine by putting my face in the glass and sucking. I kiss the liquid, and swallow a mouthful. Eugene thinks this a splendid idea. He tries it, too; and soon we're bobbing up and down like a couple of emus, with Trudy a strange and silent Rod Hull sitting between us.

Genie and I aren't making much noise. We're not slurping so loudly that I can't hear when Garth stops speaking and Gaynor starts. She's reading from the chapter called 'Mummy's Boy'. She's making such a tit of herself I can hardly bear to look, but I can't help but listen.

'Most mothers love their sons, everyone knows that, but what a lot of people don't realise is that many mothers are also in love with their sons. With her baby at her breast, many women achieve a state of union with another soul, which all the world of romance and adult relationships attempts to reconstruct. The bliss of oneness, which centuries of religious endeavour have striven to find, starts and ends with the Madonna and child.

'But a woman's marriage with her son is doomed to separation. Mother has pulled this rabbit out of a hat, she's produced it as if by magic from nowhere; she's warmed it with her lifeblood, fed it on the contents of her own stomach, pumped it full of the air she breathes. This is literally flesh of her flesh. But the child's birth is only one end of a long and rocky road; at the other end, he tells her to leave him alone because he didn't ask to be born. Mother journeys on, carrying the burden of guilt on one shoulder and the child on the other; and labours to bring him to a state of self-sufficiency, though in doing so she makes herself redundant.

'Motherhood is a sacrifice with no cause but our own satisfaction. We invent a child to love us, but then it meets someone else and goes off with them. All we wanted was a lover who wouldn't leave us before we were ready to leave him. But every time we take our nipples from our baby son's lips we're one whisper nearer the ultimate no, the point at which we must cover up our breasts, never to offer them to the boy again.'

A shudder goes through Eugene's body, and because his hands are still attached to mine and Trudy's all three of us do an involuntary Mexican wave around the table. I'm feeling a bit drunk now, and a bit as if we're in a pub with a couple of undesirables attempting to pick us up. Garth and Gaynor are saying some very dodgy things on the topic of parents and their children, which makes me wonder if it wouldn't be a good idea to leave after all.

I've nearly got to the bottom of my glass of wine and so has Eugene, and the people at the next table have noticed our slurping noises and are staring crossly. But it's beyond our control; if we've got bad table manners it's because we were badly brought up. Dad is staring down at us from the podium. He dare not glare in front of all these people.

He and our mother seem farther away now, one step removed from where Eugene and I are. There's more than a generation gap between us. They're talking about parents, up there on the platform, and that's got nothing to do with me. I'm just a child; I'm innocent. With every word they say Garth and Gaynor Bloom are incriminating themselves. And like a baby born addicted to its mother's nicotine habit, I am not responsible for my needs. It's probably just the wine, but a smug glow of well-being is coming over me. I stick my face in my glass and drink the final gulp loudly. Catching sight of Trudy over the rim, I mentally toast her, hoping she will get well soon.

Gaynor finishes speaking. She bows like a beheading, to show that it's all over. The audience applaud. Then the man with barrel belly and braces stands up beaming and asks if there are any questions for Mr and Mrs Bloom. The audience fall silent. Beside me, Eugene can hardly contain himself. I feel angry energy flowing from his hand to mine as his feelings explode, though he struggles to save his own questions till the family are in private. However, the general public seem reluctant to start discussing the matter. My parents have spent two years writing their book and no one has a word to say in response. Just when it looks like it's all been a silly waste of time, someone sticks their hand up behind us.

'Aren't you confusing sexual love with a purely parental love?' asks a man with untidy hair and a red face.

Mum and Dad exchange glances.

'Maybe,' says Dad, cautiously.

'Well, doesn't that invalidate your theory?' asks the man.

'I don't think so,' says Dad. 'Our theory is that it may be possible to confuse sexual love with parental love.'

The questioner tuts crossly. Someone else puts their hand up, a woman in a tight business-like suit, with red lipstick and big blonde hair.

'The presupposition of heterosexuality invalidates your theory,' she says.

'Pardon?' says Dad.

But Mum heard the first time.

'No, it doesn't,' she replies. 'Desire is as desire does. You see, we talk about heterosexual parents because that's the dominant experience, but there's nothing to stop a homosexual father feeling a shocking ambiguous love for his son.'

'That's enough!' comes a sudden shout from the back of the hall. 'I forbid you to say any more!'

Everyone turns to stare as an old man stands up and points his finger furiously at the platform, an old man with rusty grey hair and a face so freckled it's a uniform russet colour.

His words have all the impact of an assassination attempt on my parents. Mum clutches her chest, her face an instant picture of dismay, and Dad steps automatically in front of her. Angus Shanks appears on the podium, peering at the audience with his hand shielding his eyes. His movements are jerky and uncoordinated and his mind is confused. Though logic is telling him it was only a comment from the floor, intuition makes him react as if to a gunshot. He covers Garth and Gaynor and looks questioningly at the old man.

Who is he? A religious freak come to censure those who speak of a sin so deadly it isn't even included in the ten commandments? Or an irrelevant vagrant who's come in off the street, tempted by the promise of free wine?

Angus Shanks shuffles his feet, as do most of the audience at this moment. It's a funny thing about the detached and semi-detached classes. They'll do anything to avoid a conversation with a homeless person. And should a wandering soul sit down next to them on a tube train or bus, they'll do anything to avoid a confrontation; like suddenly deciding to travel in completely the opposite direction, or be French, or be attacked by a giant newspaper. I don't know if this principle applies in homeowners' own homes, but it seems well worth a try. If I were a vagabond looking for a roof for the night, I'd just walk into some commuter's living room and settle down on the sofa. He'd either pretend not to notice, or get up and run away.

But whatever Angus Shanks may think, the doddery old codger addressing my parents has a tiny, tidy home of his own; a current bun of a cottage in the country, a long way away from this city. He's ventured here today on a matter of national importance. And he's brought his wife.

She has struggled to her feet now too, a pepper-pot-shaped lady, with faded ginger hair and a handbag. She threads her way between the tables and chairs like a lace-maker's bobbin, through the throng of people, her eyes fixed on my parents on the platform.

'Garth, Gaynor, get down from there,' she says. 'Come on,

quick.' Then, with a twitch of her stiff little figure, she is standing on the stage. 'Get off! Shoo!' she says to my mum and dad, clapping her hands at them as if they were a couple of chickens, heedless of Angus Shanks's attempts to catch her.

'Ladies and gentlemen,' she says, turning to the audience, 'go home please, all of you, run along there. Spend the rest of the day in prayer. Try to forget you ever heard the names of Garth and Gaynor Bloom, for they have been taken in vain.'

At this, Mum gives a gasp, followed by a succession of half-breaths which smack of hyperventilation. Angus stops trying to get the old woman off the stage and turns his attentions to Mum instead, a solicitous arm extended, ready to escort her to safety. But Dad gets in the way, standing like a stone in the middle of the chaos, staring at the old one in disbelief.

'What do you want?' he says.

'An end to your book,' she replies.

'Why?' he says.

'Because it's time to stop your lies.' The old woman looks from Dad to Mum and seems to give a shudder of disgust. 'Didn't you hear me?' She turns to the audience and takes her feelings out on them, 'I said everyone was to go home. Get out of here, you bunch of slugs and slow-coaches. Please leave at once. There is no book to buy. There is no book.'

Suddenly there's a scream from the back of the hall. I look over my shoulder to see a lot of arm-waving and some smoke. Grey clouds are rising in a column towards the ceiling, fanned by the flapping. Men in suits come running from behind the stage, the vents at the backs of their jackets gaping, their ties flying like little flags in the confusion.

There's a fire. The piles of *Whoops Oedipus*, waiting on a table to be sold, are on fire. The girl from the publishers, who was

252

going to sell them, is struggling with the old man and a box of matches, while the plumes of smoke reach the ceiling. And then the alarm is set off, a supersonic scream that gets the entire audience to its feet and through the exit in less than sixty seconds; not because the fire suddenly seems much worse, but because the sound of the siren is painful to the ears.

Luckily it doesn't last much longer than a minute. Angus Shanks went like lightning to find a fire extinguisher, and is now striking the knob and directing the jet of fast white foam at the base of the flames. Hurrah! It looks like he's saved the day. After a few more seconds the smoke clears away and the alarm stops. There's silence in the hall, except for the dripping of water, and the odd glass of wine which got knocked over in the exodus.

Then the double doors burst open at the back of the room and everyone from the hotel manager to the fire brigade to the chambermaids rushes in to see what all the fuss is about.

Eugene, Trudy and I are still at our table at the front. A casual observer could be forgiven for thinking that all three of us are blind and deaf, for although Trudy is the only bald one, none of us turned a hair during the arson attack. We just held hands in a circle. But my heart is pounding like a drum in the jungle, and fear is wound like a creeper round my throat.

Who is that old man? And who is his partner, the old woman who's flaring up again on the platform? I look at her face. It's blotchy, breaking out all over in a strange rosy bloom. Her cheeks are wobbling, but her chin is grim. I've never seen her before, I'm sure of that, but somehow she looks familiar. She looks – oh, bloody hell – she's looking at me.

The old woman is looking at me in much the same way as I'm looking at her, as if waiting for a name to appear from behind a cloud of amnesia. She looks at me for ages, a frown between her eyes as they slowly but surely clear. Then she turns abruptly to Mum and Dad.

'Is that your daughter?' she asks.

Dad looks at me.

'Yes. That's Grace,' he says.

'And that's Eugene,' says Mum, pointing out my brother. They sound like a couple of kids, showing us off as if we were their best toys.

'You don't deserve such beautiful children,' says the old woman.

Mum and Dad take a step backwards which brings them close to the edge of the platform. They're already close to tears. They're holding hands but not helping each other, being equally weak and watery. Seeing them like this brings out an urge in me to protect them.

'Why not?' I say, standing up and addressing the old woman. 'How do you know they don't deserve us? Who are you?'

'Grace,' she says my name as if she's trying it out for the first time, 'I'm your grandmother.'

'How can you be?' I say. 'I've never met you before.'

'That's as maybe,' says the old woman, and presses her lips together till there's nothing to them but a thin white line.

'So whose mother are you?' I ask her. 'Mum's or Dad's?'

For a moment, her blue eyes have got such a cold hard stare in them she doesn't look like a mother at all. Then she softens slightly, and her lips go pink again.

'Don't you know?' she says.

There's a crash behind me as Eugene ejects like a rocket from his chair, and it falls, a spent fuel tank, to the floor.

254

'That does it,' he shouts, 'I can't take any more. Come on down, you two, come on down,' he talks to my parents like a deranged game show host, 'and you, too, you insinuating old woman. Get off the platform and start talking straight to me, or there'll be a serious family misfortune.'

Eugene has finally flipped; but even in the midst of his fit he manages to hold out a hand to help them all step down. He never completely loses control.

'This family is so full of secrets we're going to make ourselves sick,' he says.

'Oh, no,' says Mum, reaching the floor, 'no one's going to be sick.'

'Shut up,' Eugene hisses at her. 'You said our grandparents were dead!' He's helping the old lady climb off the podium now, but at these words she loses her footing and falls on top of him. He catches her, and carries her clear, in a fireman's lift.

'Dead?' she says to Mum over Eugene's shoulder. 'Well then, we've come back to haunt you.' Eugene puts her down. 'You're a good boy,' she says to him.

'So what's the story?' says Eugene, as Dad steps off the platform. 'Is this our grandmother?'

Dad looks at her.

'Yes,' he says.

'Don't, Garth,' says Mum.

'So,' says Eugene, 'whose mother is she?'

'What?' says Dad.

'Whose mother is she? Yours or Gaynor's?'

'Don't, Garth,' says Mum.

Dad gasps.

'Don't,' says Mum.

Dad is looking at the old woman in a daze.

'She . . . She . . .' he says.

'Don't say it,' says Mum.

'Jesus Christ . . .' says Dad. His head is in his hands.

'Whose mother is she?' says Eugene.

'Don't tell him,' Mum barks at Dad, then whines to Eugene. 'She's no one's mother.'

'I can't say that,' cries Dad. 'I love you, Gaynor, and I'll go to great lengths to keep you happy, but I can't stand here in front of her and say she's no one's mother.'

'Whose mother is she?' says Eugene.

Garth sighs desperately.

'I'll have to tell him now,' he says to Mum.

'Don't you dare,' she says, an hysterical edge to her voice.

'But there's no going back,' he says.

'We don't need to go back,' says Mum. 'We're fine where we are. She's no one's mother,' she smiles at Eugene.

'They're not going to believe you,' Dad says to her.

'They did last time,' she says. 'Didn't you?' she asks Eugene. 'Didn't you believe it when we said you were adopted?'

'For God's sake, Gaynor, spare a thought for people's feelings,' Dad shouts. 'You're losing all sense of perspective. It's time to re-prioritise.'

'My priorities are the same as they've always been,' says Mum. 'It's yours that have changed, or else you wouldn't even entertain the idea that Eugene and Grace's grandparents may not be entirely dead.'

'I don't want to lie any more,' says Dad.

'But think of the truth,' says Mum.

'I am,' says Dad, 'and do you know what? It's not so bad as the lying.'

'Garth,' Mum says calmly, 'I'll kill you if you tell them.'

'But my death,' Garth replies, 'would completely defeat the object.'

Mum jumps on him. Not in a nice way. Like a wild animal. Not in a sexy way. She goes at him like something from a spring, all nails, teeth and kneecaps. She attacks him with a scream in his face and a vicious clawing. Her hair bristles and she barely seems to touch the ground during the onslaught. But Dad defends himself fairly easily, as a man tends to be able to under such circumstances, and Eugene moves to restrain Mum from behind, so the fight looks like a foregone conclusion.

I turn to look at the old lady standing beside me instead, and find that she's already looking at me.

'Whose mother are you?' I ask her, politely.

'Do you really want me to tell you?' she says.

'It would be rude not to,' I reply.

The old lady looks nice suddenly, and sad.

'Now that it comes to it,' she says, 'I can't bear for you to know.'

'This is scaring me,' I blurt out. 'I'm really scared. My stomach is . . .'

'Don't worry. It can wait till later,' the old lady says kindly and puts her arm round me.

'Please tell me now,' I say, 'because I think I'm going to be sick anyway. Whose mother are you?'

'Both of them,' she sighs. 'Both of the little devils. I'm Garth's mother, and I'm Gaynor's mother.'

I think I knew she was going to say that, but I still burst into tears.

'Have you got any other children?' I wail.

Before she can answer there's the sound of someone

clearing their throat very commandingly behind us. We turn around. A strange man, conveniently wearing a badge which introduces him as the hotel manager, has approached our family group.

'Mr and Mrs Bloom?' he asks.

'I'm Mrs Bloom,' says the old woman, 'and that's my husband over there, between those policemen.'

'Ah, no, I meant the younger Mr and Mrs Bloom actually,' says the hotel manager, and looks at Mum and Dad, who have just finished fighting.

'That's not their names,' says my grandmother, and the manager looks at her in surprise. 'Oh, they're Garth and Gaynor Bloom alright,' she goes on, 'but they're not Mr and Mrs. They're brother and sister. They're Mr and Miss.'

'My mistake,' says the hotel manager, turning back to them, 'I do apologise. Mr and Miss Bloom, if you'd care to accompany me to my office . . .'

I don't know if they do go off with him or not, across the floor of the ballroom. I've suddenly got tunnel vision, and Eugene's face is at the end of it. My lovely Eugene in agony; his fine features steaming, nostrils arched and brow lowered, as he lets the pain take the strain.

I lurch towards him, across the floor of the ballroom, as if we're going to do a cha-cha-cha; but the light goes out at the end of my tunnel before I can get there. Eugene is lost from sight.

We're both in darkness. Our mother and father are sister and brother.

I don't know how long it is before I start seeing things again. Then there's some confusion as to whether the white shape swimming in front of me is a literary agent or a toilet bowl. They've both got the same name: A. Shanks. I think I'm right in saying that Angus holds my hair out of the way while I'm sick in Armitage, because my mother and father are sister and brother.

I don't know how long it is before my head stops spinning. In fact, when I first come round it seems that I've gone back in time. I'm lying on a little bed, and there's Eugene in a twin one only an arm's stretch away, while Dad sits on a stool in the middle, telling us a bedtime story.

'When Gaynor fell pregnant with you, Eugene, our parents wanted to know who the father was,' Dad says. 'We could have lied, of course, for we'd kept our relationship a secret all along, and if we'd just said it was some lad from the village they'd have been none the wiser. But the baby was changing the way we felt about ourselves. It was almost as if the sins of our flesh were absolved in this new life form. It sounds crazy now, but we saw the pregnancy as a sort of biological blessing.

'So we were in a state of euphoria when we told our mum and dad that I was the father of Gaynor's baby,' says Garth, and he laughs. 'I don't know how we expected them to react. We naively thought they'd be pleased, I believe. Needless to say they weren't.'

'What did they say?' asks Eugene.

'Oh, well, you know, it ranged from gobsmacked silence to screaming heebee-jeebees that lasted for days,' says Dad. 'It was a living nightmare. I think it put Gaynor off telling the truth for ever. Anyway, first they said she had to abort the baby; and twenty-five years ago this was not the easy surgical termination it is today. There were none of these vaginal vacuum cleaners; you had to hook it out with a coat hanger while fully conscious. Women died of it. The only alternative was that your mum could go off and live with some nuns for the length of her confinement, and then have the baby adopted, if a baby it was; for as our parents persistently pointed out, the thing growing inside her stemmed from an unnatural act and may well turn out to be deformed and unfinished.'

'So what happened?' asks Eugene.

'We ran away,' says Dad. 'We wanted to be together and we wanted to have our baby. And in those days a small family could live on the student grant I received, so we came to the city and set ourselves up as the young Mr and Mrs Bloom. We didn't see our parents from that day to this. Once you were born, Eugene, we rejoiced that we hadn't had you aborted or adopted. You were so bonny and bouncing, not a bone or a chromosome out of place. In time we couldn't resist the temptation to have a little brother or sister for you; and Grace turned out to be well worth the risk.'

'Is she awake?' asks Eugene, raising himself on an elbow to see me.

'Yes,' Dad smiles.

I can't respond to their sweetness. I'm still feeling sick.

'Are you alright?' Dad says.

I can't even shake my head. I'm lying paralysed upon the hotel bed.

'Anyway, it wasn't till we started writing books that things went seriously wrong,' says Dad. 'We'd severed from our parents, and our amazing babies were growing up, and we just felt so damn sure of ourselves we could hardly keep our relationship a secret. That chapter in the book, "Sibling Ribaldry", it wasn't about you two at all, it was our story. Your mother and I are Jane and John; the picture of a perfect incestuous relationship, to show people the other side of the coin. Believe me, we didn't even know that you two were sleeping together too until after the book was finished. Well, then, of course, our house of cards came tumbling down, our paper construction had to be torn up and started again.'

'You rewrote it?' asks Eugene.

'Not the book,' says Dad. 'Reality. The book was the last of our worries when we discovered that you and Grace were in love. But we applied its theories to your sexual practice and told you that you were adopted, hoping that if we relieved you of social pressure, your problem would resolve itself naturally.'

'You were wrong,' says Eugene.

'I know,' Dad replies, 'and I wish I had torn the bloody book up now, because it's brought nothing but trouble. Our mother and father saw us talking about it on television last week and that's how they tracked us down. They've been fuming for years, so I can't really blame them for setting a fire today. When they heard we were masquerading as man and wife and had two children they couldn't contain their anger. One child may be an accident, but to have another under such circumstances is downright irresponsible. All they wanted were some nice normal grandchildren, and they felt we've deprived them of that. They'd never admit to it, but I think they've been grieving deeply for us, ever since we ran away from home in the middle of the night.'

There's a knock at the door of the anonymous hotel room and Dad breaks off abruptly.

'Come in,' he calls.

The door opens slowly, and the old lady who has turned out

to be his mother shuffles in, leading Trudy by the hand. Trudy looks like she's won the lottery; her pockets are stuffed with sweets and biscuits and an enormous lollipop is crammed in her mouth.

'She's been crying for you,' the old lady says to Eugene, and she's clearly telling the truth because the channels of tears are visible in the chocolate and cream on Trudy's face.

'Oh, Trudy, it's alright, I'm here now,' says Eugene, leaping off the bed. He takes her from the old lady and puts his arms around her.

'Pyjamas please,' says Trudy, plaintively.

'Thanks ever so much for your help. I'm really grateful,' Eugene says to our grandmother, and then he looks at me. 'Grace, can you come and help me wash her face?'

I get off the bed at once. No matter how paralysed I am, when Eugene needs me I jump. Mini-miracles like this occur between us every day; it's all part of the power of our love. I follow him into the bathroom beaming, but get a shock like a bucket of water as I overhear what my grandmother says to my father when she thinks I'm out of earshot.

'Your two ought to be like Trudy, and that's a fact.'

'That's not very nice,' says Dad.

'She's turning into an egg, isn't she?' insists the old woman. 'She's smoothing over and sealing up. If you ask me, it's nature's way of telling you the eggs that were Grace and Eugene should never have been fertilised.'

'Don't be ridiculous,' says Dad.

With a quivering bottom lip I join Eugene and his girlfriend at the sink. Eugene's not a happy bunny either. He looks at me all wide-eyed and worried.

'We're in trouble now,' he says. 'Trudy's not supposed to have sugar.'

Twelve

We have to leave the hotel soon after that because Trudy starts saying she wants to fly. Luckily, there's a park nearby and we all have a go on the swings, because we think this might be the sensation Trudy's looking for. We sit three abreast, me on a red swing, Eugene on a blue one and Trudy in the middle on yellow.

We're swinging out of sync with each other, so I only hear snatches of what Eugene's shouting as we pass at points on our individual arcs.

'God, why . . . do this to us? . . . Fucking . . . Richard the third! . . . Ought to have . . . abortion . . . to be born . . . No wonder . . . so weird . . . Inbreeding . . . bleeding royal family . . . what a shock . . . knock . . . feather!'

I say nothing but kick out harder and try to swing right over the top. I've never gone over the top before. I've never gone over the rainbow, or flown off on the end of a kite string, or the parrot-headed handle of an umbrella.

'Mum and Dad . . . brother and sister . . . aaaa . . . aarrgh!' screams Eugene.

Between us, Trudy keeps the momentum going steadily.

She's forgotten almost everything these last few weeks, but her body remembers how to swing. She seems to do it automatically, working her legs with an inbuilt rhythm, leaning back in the seat and straining at the chains as she moves through the air like a pendulum; naturally at one with the laws of physics, without using her brain. And Trudy is laughing. It's a laugh that would make people weep to hear it, but she doesn't have such mixed feelings any more; she's wholeheartedly happy.

We're not alone in the park. There are a couple of young children, making more noise than us. The little girl is at the top of the slide going 'Mum, Mummy, Mum, Mummy,' and waiting for her mother's undivided attention before descending. She's wearing a pink bobble hat and a brightly patterned anorak that looks as if it could inflate like a parachute once she starts travelling downwards at speed. The other child is a younger boy, completely encased in a green waterproof. He is involved in something of a struggle with his mother. I can see his legs moving fast as a cartoon character as he tries to run away from her, but unfortunately he is held in midair, suspended a few inches above the ground while she fumbles with his coat fastenings, and he screams in fury at getting nowhere.

Next to his ungodly cries, the little girl's repeated pleas from the top of the slide sound almost angelic. Nevertheless, Mum sees fit to glance up briefly from the details of her son's all-in-one and shout, 'Just shut up and do it, Crystal. Callum wants to go home for his tea.'

'Watch me then,' says Crystal. 'Watch me, Mum, Mummy, watch me!'

'Alright, just hurry up,' says her mother.

I watch as Crystal wriggles readily at the top of the slide, tosses back the bobble on her hat, and elaborately lets go of the railings. She starts to slide, slowly at first, then faster and faster, but before she has even stopped at the bottom she's looking for her mother, looking for her mother's approval. Crystal's face falls, faster than the slide; as fast as if she'd simply jumped over the side. Her mother is miles away, past the roundabout, past the swings, running after that little shit Callum. She's grabbing him and grappling with his zipper, his ripcord, his ring-pull; his tag, his toggle, his wiggle, his woggle, whatever it is she wants from him.

'Mum?' says the poor little girl sitting at the foot of the slide. 'Did you see me?' She sighs and stands up and seems to be about to run up the steps to the top again, when her mother shouts, 'Crystal! Get here!' in a tone most people wouldn't use on a dog. So then she starts to trudge towards them with the shifting, hurt and homeless look of someone who's only four and three-quarters but pretty sure that her mother likes her little brother better.

It could have been a scene from my parents' book. I don't know whether Eugene noticed or not. I've switched off from him for a moment, and got wrapped up in my own blanketless fog and sweet-tealess shock. Now I'm trying to shake it. As Crystal passes us I call out to her.

'You slid splendidly!' I say.

She gives me a worried glance over her shoulder and runs after her mother in the gathering darkness.

My swing comes to a halt and the chains rattle as I stand to release the small plastic seat beneath me. I leave its moist surface with a sigh like a limpet losing its suction grip on a rock.

Trudy is slowing down, too. She must be getting tired. I

stand and rub my hips which hurt where the chains were digging in, and watch her flying feet come back down to earth.

'A hundred bedtimes have come and gone,' she says, 'and I still haven't got my pyjamas on.'

I go home with Eugene and Trudy and help him put her to bed in their big double. He can still do it single-handedly but she's getting harder and harder to manage, so it's easier with two. Sometimes she's incontinent, and then the quilt has to be washed.

We ease her between sheets which smell of musk and medicine. Eugene holds her shoulders and I take her feet. They are ice cold and lemon-yellow, like lollies on the thin sticks of her legs. Her rough skin snags on the brushed cotton.

As Eugene pulls the covers up to her chin and tucks her in, Trudy speaks.

'I can't hear anything,' she says. 'I can't hear ANYTHING. I can't even hear me. Am I still here?'

Eugene bends and kisses her on the lips.

'Eugene?' she says.

He takes her head in his hands and gently makes her nod it, as if to say yes.

'Where are we?' she asks.

Eugene looks at her helplessly. Her eyes have clouded over and her ears have folded up. The main avenues of communication are closed. Even her voice has broken; its box has rusted, the hinges are hammered, and the vocal cords are all out of tune. But she still sounds like Trudy. His original girlfriend is still in there, stuck out of sight, captive in her own head. She's asking him to get her out of there. Eugene looks at me.

'What can I tell her?' he says.

I shrug. And Eugene takes Trudy by the shoulders and makes her shrug them, as if to say, I don't know.

'Was it an accident?' says Trudy. 'Am I ill? You took me to the hospital. I didn't have to work there but I could smell the disinfectant.'

Trudy was a nurse once. She realises there's something wrong. But even as she speaks, that capable part of her is slipping away, leaving her to the mercy of the sisters of the night shift.

'Oh, it's falling. The dark is on the march again,' says Trudy. 'Mummy!'

The cold terror which grips her now is catching. Eugene and I have to fight its effects on ourselves before we can calm Trudy down. The whole room is full of icy shivers which keep touching our spines and making us turn around suddenly.

'When this happened last night,' says Eugene, trying to sound blasé about it, 'and the night before, I lay down on the bed next to her and sang. Even though she can't hear, she seems to find it soothing, because she went to sleep really quickly.'

I need no second bidding. I'm in that bed before you can say medley of Beatles songs, with the covers pulled up to my chin. Eugene gets in on the other side of Trudy. She's hot, and as we warm up, too, the ghosties and ghoulies simply melt away. After about ten minutes the medley of Beatles songs gives way to a medley of songs in general, which ranges from classical to rap, and ends in a sort of Gregorian chant cum shamanic trance with Eugene booming the bass and me wailing like a weird woman, with loads of nasal harmony.

When we finish, we finish together, each knowing somehow that the other has come to the climax. In the silence that follows I swear I can feel all three of our hearts beating. I open my eyes and blink in the bedside light. Blimey! I'm shagged out. Beside me, Trudy is asleep. Beyond her, Eugene is sitting up briskly and slipping out from under the quilt.

'Hey, where are you going?' I ask him.

'For a drink,' he says.

Hey, that's a good idea. But I get out of bed more slowly. I take my time, properly planting my feet on the floor, perfectly balancing the line of my spine. Then I bend over to cover Trudy up again. She seems to be sleeping peacefully now, though I can still see some tears drying on her temples.

Trudy ought to have temples built to honour her name. She ought to have a splendid spire and an altar at the end of her nave. Maybe it's because I'm on my knees at her feet tucking the covers in and she looks like she's being crucified that I can see her as a Jesus figure. Perhaps it's because things are starting to reach biblical proportions between me and Eugene that Trudy seems a bit symbolic. I stand by the bed for ages and contemplate her like a prayer.

Trudy, my cross-eyed bear.

Eugene is on his second can of beer by the time I go into the lounge.

'Is she alright?' he asks, without looking at me.

'Has she had her appendix out?' I say.

He looks at me.

'What?' he says.

'Has she had her appendix out?'

'Er, yes,' he says. 'Why?'

'Well,' I answer slowly, 'it just occurs to me. If you're looking for a mystery virus, you should look everywhere.'

'But the appendix is a blind alley,' replies Eugene. 'It's a dead end. It doesn't do anything.'

'Medical science tells us the appendix is useless,' I say, 'but that's not necessarily the ultimate answer. What if it used to do something vital to our functioning? Or what if it does something we don't understand yet?'

'I hear what you're saying,' Eugene takes a long swig of his drink, 'but I can't see it helping Trudy. You're just clutching at straws.'

'But it's the only part of her that hasn't been examined,' I say desperately.

'Grace, if only you knew,' says Eugene; 'what matters now is that you care. That means more to me, and Trudy.'

He crushes his empty beer can. I feel something compact inside me as I watch, something to do with his words. I feel like his sister, suddenly; it's a sensation which used to come easily, but has grown unfamiliar through lack of practice. It's about us being together to help someone else.

'Do you still sleep with her?' I ask.

'No,' he says, 'she's got a prolapsed vagina.'

'What?'

'The world's falling out of her bottom.' Eugene cracks open another can.

I know what a prolapsed vagina is. Someone at work had it. My confusion is because I didn't really mean sex when I asked Eugene where he slept.

'I mean can you still sleep in the same bed, actually,' I say. 'Is it uncomfortable for you, or her?'

'She doesn't want sex any more,' says Eugene.

'These prolapses can be rectified, I mean put back in the right place,' I say, helpfully.

'I think it's better out than in,' says Eugene. 'Do you want a drink?'

'Yes, and a fag.' I reach for my handbag. I don't smoke much. I never used to smoke at all. But since the family outing I've kept a packet in my pocket, in case of emergencies. It never makes me feel better. If anything, it makes me feel worse. But at least it takes my mind off the edge, loses it in a cloud of grey fog.

Today it looks like even Eugene is tempted by the weed. He eyes me needily as I put a cigarette in my mouth and rummage in my bag for a lighter. Before I can find it I have to bring out the wad of white paper on top. I've forgotten what this is until I start unfolding it, then I remember with a shock.

It's our birth certificates, photocopied shiny white and single-sided. I stare at them in horrified fascination. This morning they seemed to be the end of the story, bringing the matter of who was related to whom to a close. Eugene and I were brother and sister, and Mum and Dad were our mum and dad. But now I see an opening, a new beginning; in the place where our mother's maiden name is meant to be, there's nothing but empty space.

'Look at that,' I point it out to Eugene. 'How come we didn't notice it before?'

He cracks open two more cans, one for me and one for him, like a couple of gunshots to the head.

'Because we're stupid,' he says, 'congenitally stupid. We're so stupid we should be in a home. We thought we were so clever, didn't we, going away to university; but for all our academic abilities we're still a couple of cretins.'

Oh dear. Eugene's getting drunk. He's hard to handle under

271

the influence of alcohol, slipping through the fingers of reason, into the mire.

'Would you care to commit suicide with me, Grace?' he says.

I stand up.

'Coffee?' I say.

'No, I don't think you heard me correctly,' Eugene takes another swig of beer. 'We used to be so beautiful.'

I smile at him. Is it his unpredictability I find most attractive of all, or is it his predictions? I'm still wearing my white dress, the one I bought to commit suicide in.

'You haven't changed,' I say.

'Me?' he says, getting off the sofa. 'I've gone through a hundred and eighty degrees in the last few weeks and ended up facing completely the opposite direction.'

'I'll go and put the kettle on,' I say. 'I expect you'd like to come down from there.' He is standing on the glass-topped coffee table.

'Grace,' he says, 'let's kill ourselves.'

'No.' I'm getting a bit irritated now.

'But we never should have been born.'

'So?'

'Our whole lives have been a lie.'

I stab out my cigarette in the ashtray.

'But our love hasn't,' I say.

'How do we know that? We've never really loved anyone except each other. How do we know our love isn't a symptom of our sickness?'

'Because we're not sick.' I pick up the ashtray and head briskly for the kitchen. 'See Trudy, she's sick. You're just pissed. I'm going to empty this.'

'Once you seemed so beautiful,' says Eugene, 'that it hurt to look at you. I had to squint as if your skin was a source of light, strong as the sun. Your softness could make me cry. Now I look at you and think maybe you're a horrible monster. Your mother and father are brother and sister, and so are mine. Maybe my eyesight is defective.'

I turn and throw the ashtray at him. He doesn't see it coming.

'Look at your girlfriend,' I say. 'She's a real stunner.'

I storm into the hall and start to put my coat on, but the front doorbell rings warningly, as if I'm causing so much static in the atmosphere it's triggered a reaction and set off an alarm. Goddammit, I've done it again, just when I thought I wasn't going to do it any more. I've got out of an argument with Eugene by hitting him where it hurts: Trudy. I've slyly brought her in to a completely different conversation and set her up for the punchline. It's so unfair. Eugene's threatening suicide and I'm in a huff because he said I might be ugly. He's probably right: at this moment in time I seem very unattractive indeed. I stop putting my coat on and decide to stay and apologise instead. The doorbell rings again. I run back into the living room.

'There's someone at the door,' I say.

Eugene is climbing off the table.

'I know,' he replies.

I fall into an armchair, full of foreboding as I listen to him answering the door. I've got a feeling we're about to be visited by the sins of our father. But then I hear Eugene greeting our guest. He gives a loud cheer, chirpy as a cockney chimney sweep.

'It's Davey Poppins!'

And before there is time to say supercalifragilisticexpialido-
cious, Dave is in my face, trying not to look surprised to see
me. It's hard for him to do this, his standard expression being
one of mild surprise.

'Alright, Grace,' he says.

'Alright, Dave.'

He thrusts a brace of drinks at me, more cans of lager.

'How are you doing?'

'Fine,' I say, 'how are you?'

'Great,' Dave replies, and laughs in a way I don't find funny.
'Never felt better.'

Eugene taps me on the shoulder.

'Kindly furnish me with a beer,' he says.

I give him one.

'Sounds like you want her to shake it up and spray it all over
you, that. Furnish,' Dave smirks.

'Why not,' says Eugene, opening his can, 'she's already
decorated me with the ashtray.' He makes a show of dusting
some fine grey powder off his dark lapel.

'Sisterly love, huh?' says Dave.

The next thing he knows, my brother's got him by the collar
of his scruffy psychedelic shirt.

'What do you mean by that?' asks Eugene, menacingly.

Dave looks to me for explanation. But my lips are sealed.
This situation is built on secrets, down to its very foundations.
If Eugene knew I'd slept with Dave recently the walls would
shake. If Dave knew I'd slept with Eugene the whole house
would fall down. Stiffly, I shrug it off, and shift the blame to
Eugene.

'He's drunk,' I say.

Dave shrugs Eugene off, but talks to him gently.

'How's Trudy, mate?'

Eugene sighs.

'She's about as psychedelic as your shirt,' he says.

'What?'

'She's blind and deaf, but she has hallucinations, because she's losing her marbles, but more are growing on her skin. And her fanny, my friend, is billowing in the wind, her fanny is billowing in the wind,' finishes Eugene.

But Dave has turned and walked away mid-sentence, his eyes glazed over, temporarily taking on some of Trudy's symptoms in an attempt to become immune to them. He sits down on the sofa, shaking his head as if to clear the air of the subject.

'I've got a new girlfriend,' he says.

Eugene shudders at Dave's easy dismissal of Trudy. This was how I felt when Dave didn't look after my kitten. I hold my hand out to Eugene, full of sympathy, but when he sees it he recoils. He goes and sits down on the sofa next to Dave.

Dave's looking at me. 'I've got a new girlfriend,' he says.

I don't like Dave any more, so I don't care about his new girlfriend for my sake; it's for Eugene, and the fact that Dave doesn't care about Trudy. I'm inclined to ask Dave to leave. But Eugene has rallied. He told me once that the way he talks to Dave is just to let him drone on about whatever bee is currently in his bonnet, instead of watching him wriggle around with ants in his pants, barely disguising his boredom at Eugene's topics of conversation.

'So, who is the lucky lady?' asks Eugene.

'You don't know her,' Dave says, 'I met her at a gig. She's an artist, right, but it ain't fine art, it's really rough. She's done this piece called *River Thames* made out of used condoms. It's not the original spunk in them, obviously. It's glue. It's a load of old johnnies stuck to the page like waves.'

'Sounds rather unsavoury,' says Eugene.

'Oh, no, she's sweet, man,' says Dave. 'She's got long black hair and, like, Chinese eyes. I call her Yoko, but just for a joke, because her real name is Tracy. We have excellent sex.'

'What do you use for contraception?' says Eugene, with a raised eyebrow. 'Paint?' The more he drinks, the dryer he gets.

'She's on the pill, mate,' says Dave, missing the point completely.

'Do you love her?' I ask him, suddenly.

'If you saw her,' says Dave, 'you'd love her, too. She's only little, but her tits are big. I love women like that. Top-heavy. Do you know what I mean, Eugene? Drives me wild. She hardly ever wears a bra either. When we met at the gig all she had on was tiny silver shorts and a stars-and-stripes waistcoat. She was dancing around at the front of the crowd, and I kept having to look twice. I played like a plonker that night, my mind was right off it.'

'But do you love her?' I ask Dave again.

'Yeah, I love her,' says Dave. 'She makes a lot of noise when I fuck her.'

I look at Eugene. He's drinking so much he's going to spew. I'm feeling pretty ill, too.

'Dave,' I say, 'just so I know we're talking about the same thing when we say the word love, imagine this. Your chick is sick. She's in bed, but you can't shag her. You can't touch her skin because it's scaly and flakes off, you can't suck her tits because they could be full of poison. Her big brown eyes stop looking at you like Bambi, and slowly go blind as bird's eggs.

276

Her sweet lisp and desirable overbite start to sound as if she wants your blood. Imagine that. And the question is this: do you still love her? Would you still want her? Will you look after her, and watch her die; holding her as she goes with as much feeling as you hold her when she comes?'

Dave is quite shocked by this speech. He doesn't say anything for ages, though his lips move silently as if he's still working his way through it. While we wait, Eugene cracks open another can, and raises it to me in a brief and somewhat begrudging toast. Then at last Dave looks up at us.

'I'll be disarmingly honest,' he says. 'If that's what love is, I don't feel it for Tracy. If that's what love is, I don't even feel it for my mother. You're a better man than me, Eugene,' he adds, charmingly. 'Even Grace is a better man than me.'

Dave and I have eye contact for a moment. I see him wondering if he actually got to know me all those times we had sex together. I see him trying to work out if it ever actually meant anything at all. He gives up and averts his gaze.

'Look,' he says, 'I only came round for a few tinnies with me old mate Eugene. I didn't expect the Spanish Inquisition.'

'You shouldn't have sat in the comfy chair,' I say coldly.

'I just don't deal well with doom and gloom,' says Dave. Then he takes a tape out of his jeans pocket. 'Now, who wants to hear my new song?'

I wish Dave wasn't such a good musician. I can't help being seduced a bit by his bluesy new groove, even though the only mental picture it gives me is Yoko, oh, no, Tracy bouncing around with no bra on. But if something in the way Dave talks makes me prefer his girlfriend whom I've never even met, it's nothing to how he makes me feel about my brother. There was a time they used to merge in my mind's eye; naughty thoughts of one transferred to the body of the other. I used to layer Dave's countenance on Eugene's; a superimposition to make, or fake, the acceptable face of my fantasies.

I only fancied my brother's friend because he was the next best thing to my brother. I slept with him secretly, making him swear not to tell Eugene because I was supposed to be true to Nigel; but all I cared about was Eugene finding out, even though I secretly wanted him to know. And now that I've realised this I'm free. Now that I don't fancy Dave any more I can just let him be himself, an old mate of my Eugene, a master of music and masturbation. He has no hold on me.

Genie, on the other hand, is finding it harder to leave Dave alone.

'Tell me the truth, once and for all,' he says. 'What are we like?'

'Uh?' says Dave, playing air-guitar with an empty head.

'Are we okay?' says Eugene.

Dave stops pretending to play, or pretends to stop playing. His soundtrack continues.

'What?' he says.

'Are we alright?' says Eugene.

'What, you two?' Dave says.

I can see why Eugene's asking. He's sitting on the arm of my armchair, which is thick-skinned and sagging and covered in Trudy's hair. I'm wearing my long white angel dress with one of Trudy's old navy blue nursing cardigans over the top. Even though our physical bodies are not touching I can feel us mixed up together in the atmosphere; an invisible meeting of water colours in the air, a ring of words around us, advertising *Something's Wrong*. We've just had a terrible argument and we're hardly talking to each other, but we're still deep in telepathic communication. Even though Eugene is desensitised by drink I know he can feel it too.

'What are we like? Come on,' he urges Dave.

'You're very strange, as it goes,' Dave admits. 'You're two of the strangest people I know, and that's saying something.'

'How are we strange?' says Eugene.

Dave scratches his head.

'I don't know,' he says.

'Do we look funny?' says Eugene.

Dave looks at us hard.

'You do now,' he says. 'You don't normally.'

'What's the difference?' asks Eugene. He's really slurring his words.

'It's because you're both together,' Dave says. 'When you're separate you're two people. When you're together you are one.' He rubs his eyes. 'Hark at me. Getting myself right at it. I don't know what I'm talking about, actually,' he adds with a carefree trill on his imaginary guitar.

'And do we behave strangely?' asks Eugene.

Dave tuts, and pretends not to hear.

'Dave,' says Eugene.

Dave fingers the air faster.

'Dave,' says Eugene, again.

'For fuck's sake, mate,' says Dave, exasperated. 'Yes, you behave strangely. So does she behave strangely, even though she's not saying anything. It's silly, both of you sitting there and only one of you speaking.'

'Do we scare you?' asks Eugene.

'You could do,' says Dave.

'No, I mean, are we scary?' asks Eugene.

'You could be,' says Dave.

'What about when we were kids, did we seem normal?' asks Eugene.

'No,' says Dave, 'I was the only normal one.'

'What was wrong with us?' asks Eugene.

'I don't know,' says Dave. 'You're paranoid or something.'

'Paranoid?' says Eugene, in dull surprise. 'You mean this isn't really happening?'

Dave looks at me and shrugs helplessly.

'What's happening, Grace?' he asks.

'Nothing,' I say. 'He's just had too much to drink.'

'No, I haven't,' says Eugene, taking another swig.

'Guys, I've got to go now,' says Dave. He gets up and turns the music off. 'I'll have to take this with me. I promised it to Tracy. She'll cop the needle if I leave it behind.'

Eugene mutters something in the silence that follows.

'What?' says Dave.

'Women,' says Eugene. 'Can't live with 'em if they can't live without you.'

'Yeah, look, I'm sorry about yours, mate,' says Dave awkwardly as he walks toward the door.

'Don't worry,' says my brother. 'It's nearly over.'

Dave visibly shivers. He thinks Eugene's talking about Trudy, but I can tell by the way that Eugene's looking at me, he isn't. He's talking about me. He's talking like he doesn't want to see me any more.

I hurry Dave into the hall and help him out of the front door.

'Catch you later, Grace.'

'Yes. Bye.'

'See you around.'

'Okay. Bye.'

'Hang on, how's your kitten?'

'Dead, thanks. Bye.'

Dave keeps talking through the ever-decreasing gap, as I close the door.

'Have you told Eugene about us?' he says.

'No, Dave, I never will and if you do I'll kill you. Bye.'

As soon as I get the front door shut my body breaks out in uncontrollable shaking. I go to the toilet, but I don't sit down. I stand and stare at myself in the mirror, then turn both taps on and listen to the water splashing in the sink, letting it run for a long time. I gain relief from this, for the tears and the piss I can't release.

I think I've blown it properly this time. Eugene's never going to trust me again. Trudy has turned into a test of character, a cross to bear. Every time I make a nasty comment about her, I look a little worse in his eyes. Now he'll scrutinise each act of kindness and spontaneous gesture of caring, to find my ulterior motive. And that's the real reason he can no longer stand the sight of me; not the switching between family and friend, but the switching between friend and foe.

When I get back to the living room Eugene is asleep on the sofa. I go up close and look at his closed eyelids. There's no rapid movement behind them so he's not even dreaming. I'm glad to see him resting at last. It's been such a long day. The book launch at the hotel seems like a lifetime ago; and our grandparents' revelations, his fire and her brimstone. It's been a bit like another family outing, only this time it all came out.

The word *karma* appears in my mind, lit up in red letters. I look at the clock on the video machine and decide to leave. It's only nine o'clock and this place is like the grave. I put my coat on in the hall and this time the doorbell does not ring and Dave Poppins does not appear. I do up the buttons in silence surrounded by a sense of inevitability that makes the smallest of details seem significant. Then I pop in to say goodbye to Trudy in case I never see her alive again. It's dark in her room and there are sounds in the darkness; not where she is, but on the periphery. I creep towards the bed in the centre. Trudy is still, but as I bend to kiss her I sense something moving over the surface of her skin: not her breathing, but her breath being held. With the kiss the sensation stops, and Trudy gives a deep peaceful sigh.

'Bye,' I whisper.

She turns on her side and snuffles into the covers.

I get a spare quilt out of the linen cupboard, the one I use when I sleep on the sofa, and it's silky slithering masks the sound of the darkness closing in. I leave the room and cover up Eugene, who snores beerily.

Then I leave his flat, and assume that I'm going home because I don't know where else I'm going, but it soon becomes apparent that I'm not catching the bus to my house. I'm catching the bus to Nigel's.

I haven't been to Nigel's for ages. The trip that used to be a daily drudge or tedious trudge now seems somehow special. The bus is lit up like a carriage in a procession, and people and rainy pavements and gay shop windows move past the windows as if they've got some higher purpose. It strikes me that it must be nearly Christmas. There're more children around than usual, that always happens at this time of the year.

I start to think about babies. I know it sounds crazy, but it's actually very normal for a woman of my age to sit on the back seat of a warm bus and think about babies. Especially so close to Christmas when the bus is packed with happy families who've been late-night shopping. I shake myself. I'm an atheist. These people are celebrating commercialism. And it's wrong for me to think about offspring under any circumstances.

But I can't stop. It just seems to be happening naturally. I get off the bus and walk down the road to Nigel's, a road lined with illuminated windows, safe houses, where grown-ups and children live together in the proper way. This is the place where married people go to be mummies and daddies. It may be hard financially, but it's biologically easy. One day follows another in an orderly queue, at the same pace children take to grow out of their school shoes. Life here glows with a boring beauty, an ordinary ecstasy. When can I move in?

I try to dismiss the idea as I draw closer to Nigel's home. I'm not seriously considering living here, just looking for a little normality. A cup of tea and a conversation about maths and the sixth-form college staff's personal politics. I just want to spend a couple of hours in the company of someone who isn't, isn't pretending not to be, and isn't suddenly turning out to be, a member of the Bloom family.

Nigel's so keen to start a family of his own, though, that toasted teacakes by the fire will quickly turn to talk of ticking body clocks and knitting booties. I've just been expecting the inevitable, I suppose, brooding on reproduction all the way here. I've just been experimenting with a different way of life.

The light's not on in his living room. The light's not on and the curtains aren't drawn. This does not bode well. This bodes badly. As I open Nigel's gate and walk up Nigel's path I see that the house is not in total darkness, the hall and landing lights are on; but Nigel always leaves the hall and landing lights on in case of burglars. Oh, Nigel! I ring the doorbell, suddenly feeling the cold that I hadn't noticed till now. There's no answer, nothing,

283

no inner stirring, toilet flushing or gas cooking abruptly arrested. He's not here. I ring the bell again. The ice-blue door does not open. I am unable to enter.

'Oh, Nigel!' I say aloud.

If only I had a key, but I've always refused Nigel's offer of a key, protesting innocently, 'Why would I want to be in your house if you're not there?' If I had a key tonight I'd be in his house though he's not there. I'd sit alone by the fire, and eat all the toasted teacakes myself. It's not that there's a long walk back to my flat. It's just that it's freezing.

My flat is freezing cold and completely devoid of kittens. As soon as I get home I realise that this is the real reason I didn't want to return. The sudden urge to have babies with Nigel was just an excuse to stay out a bit longer. It seemed like an alternative avenue on the map of my fate, a standard happy ending that would be well worth exploring; but when I found that Nigel's house was empty and the dream was a decoy, it didn't come as much of a surprise. Now I stand in my kitchen by the empty red bin, swinging its top sadly. My kittens are still on vacation, staying with their inhuman grandparents, out in the suburbs. How am I going to get them back?

I sit down to think, but it's so cold I can hardly sit still. So I walk around to think, but I'm still shivering. I start picking things up and putting things down to think, but I'm so cold they keep slipping out of my grip. Then I throw things around, smash things on the ground to think; a vase of dead red roses and a plaster cast model of Sleeping Beauty that I really love.

Only one thing is clear. I need an agent. I don't want to have any contact with the two people who produced me, Garth and Gaynor Bloom. I don't want to see them, I don't want to speak to them, I don't want to know them.

I do not want to go to their house to collect Wynken, Blynken and Wankin; nor do I bloody bleedin want them to bring Wynken, Blynken and Wankin to mine.

I love those cats so much I would die for them, but it would be better to lose them for ever than murder my mother and father. This is not a gross exaggeration. My anger feels sharp as a knife in my hand, explosive as a bomb, poisonous in my mind. I know for sure that should we meet I would literally apply it to my parents, because they've been cheating and lying and brother and sister all along. So, even though it's human beings I want to kill, I telephone the RSPCA. It's nearly midnight by now so I have to leave a message on their answer phone. I give them my name and Mum and Dad's address, then say that there are three dream kittens in need of a good home and could they be taken in tomorrow?

Ten minutes later, I phone back and leave another message about how I've heard that if the animals they take in are not passed on to nice members of the public within the week they're put down. If this is so, could they please let me know when Wynken, Blynken and Wankin's time is up so that I can come and save them?

Half an hour later, after I've broken some more of my most precious ornaments, I phone back and say, ignore the last message, I never want to see another kitten again as long as I live.

Then I think about committing suicide.

Then I make a mug of hot milk and honey and go to bed with a good book.

Thirteen

The telephone rings at nine the next morning and wakes me up. I reach out to get it and knock the lamp off my bedside table. It's Genie.

'What are you doing?' he says.

'Nothing,' I reply.

'Have you got to go to work?'

'No.'

'How big is your pile of marking?'

'Negligible.'

That's a lie, but Eugene sighs like it's what he wanted to hear. And not only is my pile of marking so high I can see it from where I'm lying, I can also vaguely recall the phone ringing earlier this morning, about eight o'clock, and the secretary of the sixth-form college leaving me a message. I didn't wake up properly, but came round enough to hear her on the answer phone, asking just how sick I am exactly, before sinking back to sleep and dreams of my job in jeopardy.

Yes, now I remember standing naked but for the bondage of briefcase straps in front of a maths class containing Simeon, Nigel and Eugene, who are chanting something like this:

One two is two, two twos are four, you used to have five lovers, but you haven't any more. Three twos are six, four twos are eight, you could have salvaged one love, but you left it far too late. Five twos are ten, six twos are twelve, no one loves you, Grace, because you only love yourself.

I shake my head and try to concentrate on the real conversation. I'm quite surprised to hear that Eugene is still talking to me, after yesterday's interaction from hell. Maybe my bit of sniping in the evening has faded into insignificance beside the cataclysmic events of the afternoon. But there's definitely something amiss. I detect deep concern behind his casual tone.

'So do you have plans for today?' he is asking.

'Why? What's the matter?'

'Nothing, I just wondered if you had anything on.'

'Only a spot of Chanel Number Five,' I say.

'What?'

'I'm in bed.'

'Oh. Sorry.' He still sounds like he's hiding something.

'Are you alright?' I ask him.

'Absolutely fine.'

'Why are you phoning me then?'

'Well, I, er, I wondered if you'd like to come over. For coffee.'

'Is it Trudy?'

'What?'

'I know there's something wrong. Is it Trudy?'

'No, it's not her.'

'What then?'

'Nothing. I don't want to worry you. Just come round.'

'Is it you?'

'No, I . . .'

'Are you ill?'

'No, I just don't feel very well.'

'What's wrong?'

'Nothing. I don't want to worry you.'

'Is it . . .'

'It's not . . .'

'Catching?'

'What Trudy's got.'

I go in a taxi. The driver tries to talk to me like they always do, but I don't listen. I'm still in a sort of dream state so nothing he says makes sense, anyway. All I can think of is Eugene having what Trudy's got. Her nameless illness may well be sexually transmitted; one of those diseases that makes love worth dying for, whether you like it or not.

The taxi driver drones on, but all I can think about is Eugene, the one sun shining out of a world of arseholes. If he were to go blind, or deaf, or slowly become dumb, I'd never want to see and hear again either. I'd go with him into the darkness, or into the fire; I'd go anywhere so long as he didn't have to go alone. This must be love, the sort I see between him and Trudy and admire so much; so why does it seem so despicably turned in on itself when it's between me and him? It's not immutable, carved in grave stone: if he were in pain my priorities would change.

'No, keep it,' I say, as the driver tries to give me a handful of coins in return for a ten-pound note.

'This is a rainy day, love,' he replies, as I slam the cab door shut behind me.

I run up the stairs to Eugene's flat, and bang on his door, as fast and hard as my heart is pounding.

'How are you?' I ask breathlessly, as soon as he opens it.

'I've been sick,' he says. He stands on the doorstep, his shoulders drooping, his bottom lip stuck out, half old man, half tiny child. 'And my head. Hurts. Oh, Grace. Help.'

'Let's get you to bed,' I say, and step inside.

I tuck him up next to Trudy who's having a lie-in this morning. She's semi-conscious, slumped on the pillow half-smiling, but Eugene is almost crying with his pain.

'When did this start?' I ask him.

'I woke up like it,' he says. 'Dizzy and disorientated. And I must have lost my memory, because I don't know what happened last night. My brain feels . . . damaged.'

Simultaneously, we steal a look at Trudy, as if to compare her symptoms with his. Eugene gives a sob.

'But you know what's worse,' he says, 'I was dreaming. I perchanced to dream about you. And in this dream I realised that we've never actually had sex. We're so screwed up by our so-called incestuous relationship, we keep forgetting that we've never really done it.'

'Haven't we?' I say.

'No,' says Eugene. 'Not properly. The first time, when I was thirteen and you were eleven, was an accident. It couldn't have been sex because we didn't know what sex was yet. And the next time was that lost weekend, when Mum and Dad came back too soon from their conference. We were inches away from it, remember?'

'We stopped to get a condom,' I say, slapping the counterpane as it all starts coming back.

'But before there was time to put it on,' says Eugene, 'they barged in and interrupted us. And the next morning, in the shower, the same thing happened again.'

'That's when Mum discovered us,' I say.

'Yes,' Eugene shouts triumphantly, 'but the illicit relationship we seemed to be having had not actually been consummated! I have never come inside you!' He winces as the volume of his words hit his headache. 'Ow!'

'Would you like a glass of water?' I ask him.

'Yes,' he says. 'That's another thing that's wrong with me. I'm really dehydrated.' He sighs deeply.

When I return with a full pint in my hand, he is still doing the same sigh, and the conversation picks up exactly where it left off.

'Which is why,' he says, 'if I'm to die, let me donate my organ to you.'

'You prat,' I say. 'You're not dying. You've just got a hangover.' I've just seen the number of empty lager cans in his kitchen.

Eugene's face falls.

'A hangover?' he says.

'Probably,' I say. 'How much did you drink last night?'

'I don't know,' he says. 'I can't remember. My last memory is of lying on the bed with you and Trudy, singing some eternal dirge, some infernal funereal song. I kind of thought I'd died already.'

'Dave Poppins came round,' I remind him.

'Oh,' says Eugene. 'Yes.'

'You remember?'

'Sort of.' Eugene frowns, and his eyes go far away as he tries to recall the events of yesterday. 'Did I tell him,' he struggles to say, 'that our mother and father are brother and sister?'

'No, you didn't,' I say, 'but you dropped some bloody big hints.'

'Ooops,' says Eugene. He downs the pint of water in one. 'So the sickness, and the headache, and the memory loss, are all part of the hangover thing, are they? I'm not really going to die?'

'No, you're not,' I say. 'Honestly! Haven't you ever been hungover before?'

'Not like this,' replies my brother. 'I never drink that much. I normally just feel a bit stupid.'

'Well, I hope you're feeling very stupid today,' I say.

I get up abruptly and leave the room. I want to be alone for a while, but Eugene follows me into the lounge, dragging his feet and clinging to a pillow. I turn on him crossly.

'You woke up on the sofa,' I say, 'stinking of beer, with a pile of dead cans on the table; and instead of simply assuming you'd had too much to drink, you made an emergency phone call implying that you'd caught Trudy's terminal illness. It nearly scared me to death.'

'Sorry,' Eugene mumbles.

'I've given away my kittens!' I shout. 'Yesterday, when Mum and Dad turned out to be brother and sister it looked like you didn't love me any more, even though you said I seemed as sick and ugly as Trudy. I was so confused, I even went to Nigel's! You talked about committing suicide last night, but you don't remember that, do you? You were too drunk. But I thought about suicide when I was alone and cold and sober.'

'You went to Nigel's?' says Eugene.

I don't reply.

'Did you go to Nigel's?' says Eugene. 'Last night?'

'Yes. So?'

'I don't believe it,' says Eugene. 'You're so fickle. There was I asleep and still dreaming about you, after all we've been through, and now we know who we really are; and you're out having a casual sexual encounter with your old maths teacher.'

'It wasn't like that,' I protest.

'Oh, is it serious?' says Eugene. 'Well, excuse me for waking up feeling like death and realising that my dying wish is still to have sex with you, my sister. Blood is thicker than water, but semen is thicker still.'

'Stop . . .' I say, but Eugene carries on.

'You're more than my sister, when I think what Garth and Gaynor's dodgy genetic engineering must have made of us. Yet you act so shallow,' he says, 'sloping off to see Nigel in the middle of our family crisis.'

'He wasn't there.' I finally get a word in edgeways.

'Oh, dear,' says Eugene, 'how sad, never mind.'

'Come on, be fair.'

'I am being fair, Grace. You always go on about how you feel and now it's my turn. You've given me a whole heap of shit about Trudy.'

'I know,' I say. 'I won't any more.'

'I'll believe that when I see it,' he says. 'You'll still be making snide remarks at her funeral.'

'You bastard, I won't! I love Trudy . . .' I break off abruptly and, although my words are true, the expression on my face is more ambiguous as I catch sight of the woman herself, gliding past the lounge doorway in a yellowy nightgown, and down the hall to the front door.

'Holy cow! Where's she going?' I gasp.

Eugene looks at his watch.

'It's nearly time for the nurse,' he says.

The doorbell rings. Eugene claps his hand to his mouth and speaks shakily through his fingers.

'This is the third time she's done that!' he says. Then he hurries out of the room. In the hall I can hear his girlfriend struggling to open the front door.

The nurse breezes in, bright as Trudy in another lifetime. She even looks a bit like Trudy used to, blonde hair and blue eyes; and she flirts mildly with Eugene as they discuss Trudy's mysterious new habit of predicting her daily arrival.

We all go into the kitchen and cook the inevitable eggs and feed them to Trudy, the unenviable egg. The nurse confirms that Eugene is severely hungover but not terminally ill, then takes Trudy off to the bathroom while he and I do the washing-up.

'You're not going to die,' I say.

'No,' he smiles, red-faced, up to his elbows in soap suds.

'So how do you feel?' I ask, trying to keep my face straight.

His breaks into a laugh.

'Stupid,' he says, 'very, very stupid.'

We make a bit of a song and dance about this, skidding around the kitchen on flicked foam, singing the words 'very, very stupid' in a variety of funny accents. The soap suds get everywhere. I see them staying on his nose and eyelashes like snowflakes, and start to dance better, more like Julie Andrews, singing about her favourite things. On the line 'Raindrops on roses' I come face to face with Eugene who is spinning the other way round the kitchen table; but when we get to 'whiskers on kittens' I stop and turn away sadly, a tear in my eye.

'So tell me, hypothetically,' I say, panting slightly, 'now

that you're not going to die, would you still want to consummate our incestuous relationship?'

'Yes,' says Eugene. He does not hesitate. 'But I tried to say no,' he goes on. 'I always try. Sometimes I can get it to stick at no for five whole minutes, but it always goes back to yes again in the end.'

'You would?' I say, incredulously. 'You would do it with me?'

'Yes,' says Eugene. 'But only once.'

The nurse and Trudy come back from the bathroom. They sit down at the table to have coffee, except that Trudy's not allowed to have coffee any more. Eugene and I go instantly into customer service mode, making herbal tea and no further reference to *The Sound of Music* or theoretical sex.

As I put a cup of camomile in front of Trudy she says something.

'Injured newts and turtles?' I repeat. 'What on earth does that mean?'

'Ninja Mutant Turtles,' says the nurse. 'She thinks they're coming to rescue her.'

I stare at the nurse thoughtfully for a moment, while Eugene hands her a coffee.

'Do you know anything about the appendix?' I ask her.

'What appendix?' she says.

'Any appendix, Trudy's appendix,' I say impatiently. 'Appendices in general. What did they teach you at nursing school?'

She shakes her head, stirring sugar into her coffee.

'Trudy's appendix has been removed,' she says. 'You can tell by the scar.'

'Okay,' I say slowly. 'Do you think there's any chance it could be a clue to a cure?'

The nurse looks at me over the rim of her cup.

'I think there's more chance of the Mutant Turtles turning up,' she says.

Eugene laughs hysterically at this, and goes right over the top with offers to refill her coffee cup, but one helping is enough for the nurse. When she's finished it she takes Trudy for a lie down, saying she'll sit by the bedside and write up some notes.

I wait till I hear the bedroom door shut behind them, then turn to Eugene.

'Only once?' I say.

'Yes,' he replies.

'You'd only want to have sex with me once?' I say. 'Why?'

'Because more,' says Eugene, 'would be too much. If we did it twice, we'd do it every day for the rest of our lives, and we'd end up like Mum and Dad.'

'No, we wouldn't,' I say. 'We'd never be like them. We wouldn't have kids, for a start.'

'But I want kids,' says Eugene. 'You want kids. Don't you?'

'No,' I say. 'What would I want to have children for? There are too many already. We don't need any more. Anyway we'd have each other. We could just be two grown-ups together. I could do my maths and make cakes and you could save the world. I know you've got it all worked out on your computer. Or I could get some more kittens, and this time I wouldn't need to have them adopted, not if you were looking after me.'

'You want kids,' says Eugene.

'I don't.'

'You haven't really abandoned your kittens,' he adds.

'I have.'

'We'll never be able to have children together,' he says. 'The DNA wouldn't let us. We may appear to be relatively normal, but our genes must be defective. The next generation would be like disgusting slugs crawling in primordial slime.'

'We'd have Trudy!'

'Grace, can you please try and take this seriously,' says Eugene. 'Trudy is not a child. She's not going to grow up.'

'I'm sorry, I just thought it might satisfy your urge to nurture . . .' I say, but Eugene interrupts me.

'You are really pushing your luck,' he says. 'Do you know how special today is? It's more important than Day One. It's Day Dot. Zero hour. Do you remember why? When I woke up this morning I realised that we've never actually finished having sex; and I've now managed to convince myself that our relationship is innocent, completely unconsummated.

'This is our chance,' he continues, 'to wipe the slate clean. To start from scratch. To no longer be at home to the call of incest, unlike our mum and dad. We should learn from their mistakes, Grace, not merely repeat the pattern of their behaviour.' He smiles at me like a politician in the middle of an election speech. 'It is not too late to change. A willing spirit can outweigh a lot of weak flesh. Let's make a clean breast of things.'

He almost has me convinced, but his lip twitches on the last sentence, then his façade breaks down completely.

'Oh, bollocks,' he laughs, 'that clean breast slipped in there before I saw it coming. I wasn't going to mention any more bodily parts.'

'Alternatively,' I say sweetly, shocked that he might never

talk dirty to me again, 'we could just do it once. We could do it on your very sensible assumption that once will be enough.'

'It should last a lifetime,' says Eugene.

'Any more would be too much,' I reply.

'It will be an ultimate union,' says Eugene.

'Perfect bliss,' I say, 'I quite agree.'

I don't really. I want to go on screwing Eugene for ever. I don't believe in perfection. Things can go on getting better and better. I'm a mathematician; I know less isn't more.

And I don't believe this is Day Zero. I don't believe in Nothing at all. There has always been something going on between us, although Eugene might swear that we're still technically innocent.

But I'll let him have his way in the argument, because then he'll let me have my way with him; and I'm secretly hoping that when he sees where we go, on the sexual journey into ourselves and each other, he'll realise that there is only one way.

'So, do you want to do it now?' he says.

'Certainly not,' I say. 'If it's only going to be the once, timing is everything.'

'And the venue will be very important, too,' he says.

'You're right,' I say. 'So where do you want to do it? Not here.'

'And not at your flat,' he adds.

'We need a significant location,' I say.

At this very moment the phone rings. Eugene turns and runs into the hall to answer it.

'Wait a minute!' I shout, running after him. I'm normally more laid-back about answering phone calls, quite choosy about whether I even lift the receiver; but Eugene has always been a slave to that imperious ring, as if he expects at any minute to be summoned by the Queen.

'Yes?' he says, into the mouthpiece. His face turns red and his mouth opens wide, then snaps shut. 'Hello, yes, fine, thank you,' he mutters.

The muted tones at the other end of the line sound like Garth Bloom. I bet the RSPCA have turned up and he can't believe I've told them to take the kittens away.

Eugene laughs nervously on the phone.

'Er, I'll have to check it with Grace,' he says.

'Yes,' I mouth at him, large and clear, hovering at the edge of his line of vision.

'Oh, well, she's here actually,' he says. 'Hold on a moment.' He holds his hand over the receiver and says. 'It's . . .'

'I know. Say yes.'

'Are you sure?'

'Yes! Go on, quickly, before I change my mind,' I say.

Eugene gives me an agonised look, and returns to the phone conversation. 'Yes, that's fine,' he says, then says fine again a few more times, and finally, 'Okay, lovely, thanks, bye.' Then there's a click as the call is disconnected. 'Do you know what you're doing?' Eugene points the handset at me, and I hear the dialling tone.

'I've thought about it very carefully,' I say. 'Getting rid of the kittens is the only way I can get through to Mum and Dad. They are more deeply entrenched in their own little world than we realised, and only dramatic gestures will have any effect on them. I need them to know how hurt I feel, how totally blown apart yesterday's revelations have left me, and the kittens have to be sacrificed; but don't worry, I'll probably go and rescue them from the refuge tomorrow.'

'No, you won't,' says Eugene. 'Grace, you sad old cow, that phone call had nothing to do with your kittens. It wasn't Dad, it was Grandad. We've just agreed to go and visit him and Grandma in their cottage in the country tomorrow.'

Fourteen

At three o'clock the next day Eugene and I walk down the
platform at Paddington Station, him clutching a small suitcase,
me carrying both our coats over one arm, looking for all the
world like a pair of 1950s newlyweds. We catch a real old-
fashioned train to the country, one with doors that don't open
automatically.

We sit facing each other in a quiet compartment, his long
legs in smart pressed trousers stretching from his seat to the
floor under mine in an elegant straight line. My legs, in tights,
are twitching. We sit face to face and stare at each other
without saying a word, to the rhythm of the old-fashioned
train.

We've done so much talking, but for the first time ever, it
seems that we're really speaking. Now I know what goes on in
the gaps between our gabbled words, in the pauses that
punctuate our speech. Now I know why we always see what
each other means without ever saying it. In the silence, I hear a
whole truth, which sentences only scissor into snippets and can
never fully explain. When I look at Eugene and leave
everything unsaid there is no such thing as lying.

We have been under many illusions in our lives, and been very disillusioned. We have called ourselves brother and sister, and had those names taken away from us. We have called ourselves Bloom, and also had that identity removed. We have called ourselves children of a man and woman, lawful husband and wife, bonded by love but not blood, then found that we are born of a brother and sister. And so we are brother and sister again, recaptured in the thrall of an incestuous attraction.

As the journey continues, Eugene's expressions pass in a long procession. There is a beginning. The slow dawn of recognition, with several false starts. I look at Eugene and see him simultaneously as a stranger and myself. He flickers, we flicker, between the two. Frowns cross his face like thunder clouds in time-lapse photography, casting shadows, casting doubt, but only the shadows of doubt. For soon the sky clears and the sun comes out. Eugene's eyes are blue and through them the sun comes stronger, harder, hotter, brighter, fierce and glaring, highly excited. There used to be a fireguard in front of it. There used to be bars between us and the fire.

As the train carries us cross country Eugene's expressions press on, their procession across his face never-ending and always changing; but behind the flickering black stripes of his eyelashes, the crystal fire burns steadily. His gaze holds mine until my eyes are pools of melted eyes. Tears are brimming in them. They start to waterfall, cascading in the sparkle of his sunshine; but I can still see him clearly through the cataract, shimmering in the spray like a fairy-tale character, the handsome prince, bewitched.

He's my brother. I can't kiss him. It would be like kissing a frog. But could it possibly break the spell, and wake the part of him that isn't related to me at all? The part of him that is beyond a name, not a Bloom; nobody's child, nobody's brother, nobody's lover. That's who he really is. Just a man, with the body of Adonis and a mind of his own.

We stare at each other all the way to our grandparents' house. It's an eye test, a trust exercise. From station to station, we don't look away while our lives flash before us; the same life, from two different angles. Through the kaleidoscopic shifting I can see that, eventually, we've got nothing to hide. There are no more secrets because there were never any secrets, if only we'd known it. No balonius, to our own selves we were true.

Now I can see that Eugene loves me. I've always looked in the wrong way before and ended up worrying that he loves me too much or not enough; but perhaps that's what I was looking for, because I thought he was my brother. Now I know he is my brother, I know he loves me. He loves Trudy, too, but that makes it better, not worse, because it means he knows what love is.

We tumble off the train at a tiny station with a name that sounds vaguely ominous. The cold winter sun is wasting no time in setting, and dusk is gathering as we stand on the platform and straighten ourselves out. I feel drowsy from the journey, and dream-like, as I clumsily do up my coat buttons and look around. Of course I feel as if I've been here before, but whether this is genuine *déjà vu* or just my imagination I can't be sure. The station's look is clichéd; I've seen it in a hundred films, the scene of a hundred brief encounters. Everything from the obligatory hanging greenery to the parochial vending kiosk is exactly as I would have predicted; yet the cold, still, dream-clear platform that has so suddenly supplanted the hot, rocking, eternal journey of the train is a shock.

'How do we get to their house?' I stammer.

'They're meeting us,' Eugene replies. He picks up the suitcase. 'Come on.'

We have to go over an old-fashioned footbridge to get out of the station. I get the feeling that our grandparents are watching us from somewhere, though we can't see them. The bridge is made of wrought iron, painted dark green, and I can't help thinking we must make rather a picturesque couple, coming across it, with our ginger hair. Then I realise that we must remind them so strongly of our mum and dad that they probably can't see us at all. My legs are shaking so much they get the whole bridge going.

Out of the station entrance is a flight of steps, and at the bottom of the steps an old-fashioned car is parked. We walk towards it. Some inappropriate music is stuck repetitively in my head, which makes the descent seem like the introduction to a cabaret spectacular.

But after such a big build-up, the meeting with our grandparents is low key and ordinary. We say hello and how do you do as they drive us to their small red-brick villa-style Victorian house with a tiled roof, set back from the country lane and surrounded by a walled garden. We walk down its well-kept path, through the freshly painted front door into a flagstoned hall, and into a little living room where we find tea things already laid out on a low table.

'Sit down,' says our grandfather, who stands by the mantelpiece, quietly filling a pipe. 'So they told you we were dead, eh?'

Eugene nods mutely, beside me on a flowery sofa. I look at

our grandmother in the armchair opposite, leaning to pour the tea. She's crying; single tears run one after the other down her cheeks, in a silent and constant stream.

'Did they say how it happened?' asks our grandfather.

'Fire,' Eugene clears his throat apologetically. 'And floods. They said Mum's parents had gone up in a house fire, and Dad's got swept away in a flash flood, all in the same tragic year.'

'Didn't that ever strike you as odd?' our grandfather says.

'It's the first thing I can remember,' says Eugene. 'They told me when I was tiny, perhaps even before Grace was born. I didn't know if it was odd or not; I had nothing to compare it with.'

My grandmother hands me a cup of tea, in flowery china.

'I don't suppose you've brought any photos of yourselves as babies?' she asks.

'Oh, no,' I say. 'Sorry. We should have thought of that. But we haven't been thinking straight these last few days. We'll send you some in the post.'

'When are your birthdays?' she asks, handing tea to Eugene.

'November the fifteenth,' he says. 'And Grace's is in May.'

'So she is — let me see — two and a half years younger?' says the old lady. 'There's exactly the same difference between your mother and father.'

I'm staring at the tea tray with a frown on my face as I realise that I've missed Eugene's birthday. November the fifteenth has passed and the poor boy didn't get a present or even a piece of cake. Grandfather sees me staring, but he thinks I'm looking at the plate of biscuits.

'Go on, Grace,' he says, 'help yourself. I bet you've never seen anything like them before.'

'Are they home-made?' I ask.

'My wife's shortcake is the talk of the women's institute,' he says.

'Wow!' I laugh. 'Look at this, Genie. Biscuits made by hand!'

Our grandmother is shaking her head, half in modesty, half in despair.

'You could have been brought up on those,' she says. 'Your parents were. They should have kept in touch. Children need their grandparents, to show them the old ways, and keep the continuity going.'

After the tea and biscuits, which are the best I've ever tasted, Grandmother collects up the plates and cups and says she'd better get herself back to the kitchen if supper is to be on the table by seven. Grandfather yawns and stretches and says he'll go and check the chickens before it gets dark.

'You're going to check some chickens?' says Eugene. 'That sounds interesting. Can I come, too?'

'Of course you can, young man,' Grandad beams.

'They're his pride and joy,' says our grandmother, bustling out of the room with a loaded tea tray.

As soon as she is gone I realise that Eugene and Grandad are both looking at me expectantly, and though I'm feeling so full and sleepy I could sit on the sofa indefinitely, I leap up and reach for my coat.

'Where do you think you're going?' says Eugene.

'To see the chickens,' I say.

'Oh!' says Grandad, and laughs in surprise.

'Wouldn't it be nicer to help, er, Granny, in the kitchen?' says Eugene.

'You're right,' I say. 'It would be polite.'

And so my brother is installed in a flowery apron while I try on a selection of spare Wellington boots to see which fit for a trip to the bottom of the garden. The grandparents are strangely delighted by our modern behaviour, and use the term role reversal as if it were a high-tech invention of the nineteen nineties; like modems or road rage. In their day, granddaughters helped in the kitchen, not having the necessary hormones to walk down the garden and feed a few hens.

Eugene is quite taken with the quaint scene. He's happily camping it up with a potato peeler as Grandad and I leave by the back door and wander through the wet grass to a hen coop behind a compost heap.

The chickens are boring and smelly, which is just how I imagined they would be; but they still seem preferable to a tête-à-tête with my mother's mother. Coming towards me with their ruffled feathers and lurid coloured combs the chickens seem slightly evil; and even though I'm sure my poor grandmother is a paragon of goodness, she still frightens me more.

In conversation with her all sorts of things could come out, but Grandad merely tells me the names of his hens: Gilda, Gwen, Prudence and Penny. He explains the little differences in their personalities, and describes the group dynamics.

'Have you got a cock?' I ask him, keeping a completely straight face, but making a mental note to scream with laughter later. I can't wait to tell Eugene that our grandfather does not have a cock, but his next-door neighbour owns a splendid specimen, which he is willing to lend whenever fertilisation is required.

'In fact, see those two little black ones?' says Grandad, pointing out a pair of smaller hens behind the group of big red ones. 'They're Bertie's daughters.'

'Bertie is your neighbour's cock?' I ask, loving every minute of it.

'That's right, Bertie Rooster,' says Grandad. 'And those little black ones were born last year. They're called Shirley and Bassey. Beautiful eggs.'

'Isn't that a bit racist?'

Grandad laughs. 'Don't be silly, love,' he says. 'You can't be racist to animals. Now come over here and see if there are some eggs for dinner.'

He makes me put my hand through a hole in the hen coop wall and into a warm nest of straw.

'I'm not going to get bitten, am I?' I ask anxiously.

'No, they're all out in the run,' says Grandad. 'And anyway, hens don't bite. Do you, my darlings?'

I feel around and find two warm egg shapes. They make me jump when I touch them, even though I was expecting them.

'Good girlie, good Bassey,' my grandfather clucks dodgily.

I bring the eggs out one at a time and show him carefully. They're big and brown.

'Lovely,' he says. 'I don't know what your grandmother's doing for dinner but if there's no room for eggs on the menu you can always have them for breakfast.'

'Or,' I say, 'we could take them home for Trudy. She's very partial to eggs.'

'Listen, there'll be plenty more where those came from tomorrow,' says Grandad.

He locks the little wooden door over the egg-stealing hole and says his goodbyes to every chicken by name before we turn and walk back up the garden to the house.

'It's just struck me,' I gasp as we go, 'that I don't know what your name is, or your wife's. I'm managing to say Grandad now, but I don't know what you're really called.'

'Well, isn't that a sorry state of affairs?' he says, and puts his arm around my shoulders. 'We should have had this conversation when you were three years old. There's so much we've missed out on, so much to catch up.

'My real name is Ernest,' he says. 'And your grandmother's is Gladys. I used to call her Glad, you know, but that all stopped when Garth and Gaynor ran away.'

Back in the kitchen Eugene is serenely stirring something in a saucepan. He smiles when he sees us.

'Granny has popped upstairs,' he says.

Grandad and I take off our boots by the back door.

'I bet I know what she's gone for,' Grandad grunts. 'She's been holding onto it for years.'

The kitchen has a tiled floor and I slide in my stockinged feet, feeling like a child. The kitchen is steamy with the dinner cooking; the smell is appetising.

Granny comes in with a battered cardboard box.

'Oh, you're back,' she says. 'Did you enjoy the chickens?'

I nod enthusiastically. I can't wait to tell Eugene about the cock.

'Good,' says Granny. She puts the box on the table. 'Look, here is something I've been keeping, in case today ever came. I kept if just for Eugene, though I didn't know his name, because I didn't even know that Grace had been born. But now you can share it between you, to piece together your past.'

She puts her hand into the box and pulls out a sad-faced piggy bank, big and pink but looking very old.

'There's a story attached to this,' she says. 'It belonged to your mother. It stood on her dressing table and she used to put her pocket money in it every week. Occasionally she'd take some out, to buy a book or sweets, but more often she'd just hoard it, saving it all up for something special. Christmas 1969, that's the last time I remember her asking her father to help get every last copper out. He had a knack of doing it with his penknife. By spring the next year it must have been full of coins again, and she was pregnant with Eugene. She was only sixteen, still a child, more interested in sweets than lipstick; but one June morning, when I went to wake her up, the piggy bank was lying on her bed empty, and she had left home.'

Granny is crying again, tears falling down her face, but she seems not to notice.

'Gaynor had taken her pocket money and run away,' she says, 'carrying an unimaginable responsibility in her belly. She hadn't left a note. But I found one ray of hope in the desolate situation: the piggy bank was not broken. She had taken her savings out carefully: she was determined, not desperate. This small sign that she and her brother might somehow manage to survive was all that could console me. And so, once a year from that day forth, at about the time I imagined the baby was born, I've put some money in this piggy bank. A pound for every year of his life. A pound for every year we've lived without our children. On your fifth birthday, Eugene, I put in five pounds; on your tenth, ten pounds; on your twentieth, twenty pounds. We estimate that there is a few hundred in there now.'

'Three hundred and fifty-one, to be exact,' I say.

'Of course you must share it with him,' Granny says to me. 'If we'd known when you'd been born, we would have started another.'

'But some of it is in the old pound notes,' says Grandad. 'I don't know whether they're still valid.'

'Your bank will change them,' I say.

Eugene holds his hands out to slow the conversation down.

'We don't want your money,' he says. 'I mean, it's not the money that counts. We're just happy to have met you at last.'

Grandad chuckles delightedly.

'You haven't got the money yet,' he says. 'You'll have to break the piggy bank first.'

'No,' gasps Eugene.

'Yes,' says Grandad, 'it's easy enough to get coins out when you've got the knack, but all those notes are another matter.'

'Well, they must stay inside then,' says Eugene. 'We can't break the piggy bank. Not when it was so important that it was in one piece.'

'But that doesn't matter any more,' says Granny. 'Don't you see? It mattered when we didn't know if you were alive or dead or, God forbid, in a mental hospital somewhere in between. Its being in one piece was important when we lost our son, our daughter and our grandchild to an unbelievable story of,' she whispers the word, 'incest, and we didn't know the ending. This smooth pink porcelain was the eggshell of our hope. But now you're here, in the flesh, we can smash it up and get the money out.'

'No,' says Eugene.

'I'll do it,' I say. 'Not for the money!' I add as he kicks me unsubtly on the ankle. 'It'll be like breaking a spell.'

'Yes!' says Granny, with witchy glee. 'Grace knows what I mean.'

Eventually we come to a compromise because Eugene insists on breaking the piggy bank carefully, so he can stick it back together again with glue. He goes at it with a hammer and chisel, gently as Michelangelo on David's delicate bits. He does it at the kitchen table, on a piece of newspaper. As first born he has the right the choose the method of death. I personally would have thrown it against a wall, screaming; which probably isn't in the spirit of the occasion.

When Eugene cracks the pig in half it's like a shell hatching, though the crumpled notes come out like a hundred dusty butterfly wings. There's a lot of pound notes, once common-place, now quaint and old-fashioned; and they give the impression that the history of the unbroken piggy bank amounts to more than a quarter of a century. We let them flutter around the kitchen, and in light conversation, reflect on the meaningless of money, without devaluing our grandparents' gift to us.

Soon we start to get in Granny's way as the time for serving dinner is upon her. She sends us to sit in the dining room, where a gleaming oval table is immaculately laid.

'This is so weird,' whispers Eugene.

I nod, in a high-backed velvet-covered dining chair. It's very comfortable.

'Do you suppose there'll be any wine?' he says.

I finger the silver cutlery and shake my head.

'I fear not,' I say.

'Do you think we should ask them what Mum and Dad were like as children?'

I shrug.

'Don't you want to know?' he asks.

'They seem so ordinary,' I say. 'Just nice, normal Granny and Grandad.'

'They're quite posh,' says Eugene.

'Sshh,' I whisper. 'No, they're not. This stuff's not real, it's just imitation antique. You put it together yourself. I've seen it in shops, and it's not very expensive. I've looked at the prices, because actually I quite fancy it myself.'

'Is it all a façade, then?' says Eugene.

'What?'

'This good old English ordinariness,' he says. 'God, I could do with a drink.'

'No, I think it's really them,' I say. 'They're average, in an excellent way.'

'But they were different at the book launch.' Eugene drums on the table with his cutlery. 'Grandad started a fire and Granny got up on stage.'

'That was just shyness,' I say. 'They were out of their milieu and unsure how to approach Garth and Gaynor.'

'Shyness?' Eugene shrieks, and hits his side plate with his knife like a cymbal. 'They were showing their true selves.' Then he points his knife at me. 'Or they were hiding a lie.'

'Hiding a lie?'

'Yes,' says Eugene. 'What is behind the façade? I'll tell you what I see. It's just like looking in a mirror. Ernest and Gladys, another brother and sister Bloom.' He puts down his knife, picks up his glass, and stares at it intently for a while, as if it were a crystal ball; but then he looks up at me and says, 'This is not a wine glass, is it?'

At nine o'clock, Granny and Grandad go to bed. I can't believe it's so early. They say they go to bed at this time every night.

'What time do you get up in the morning?' I say. 'Four o'clock?'

'It's different in the country,' Granny says, 'you work with the natural rhythms. You sleep when it's dark, and wake when it's light.' She smiles from her armchair, replete with

312

shepherd's pie, then gets to her feet. 'We'll show you your rooms. They were Garth and Gaynor's.'

They still are Garth and Gaynor's. They're not quite the *Marie-Célestes* I expected them to be, with coffee cups half-drunk and homework half-done and some sixties song still revolving eternally on the turntable, but their shapes and space and light and shadow are like portraits of my mother's and father's faces.

And there are photographs of them on the dressing tables. In Garth's room a black and white one in a silver frame of two children in the snow. Boots and gloves and coats and hats, and two chubby faces looking startled at the camera as a shared toboggan ride down a short slope ends in disaster at the photographer's feet. And in Gaynor's room a colour photo in a gold frame showing a sunny beach, blue sky and sea, and the adolescent bodies of two skinny redheads as brown as they're ever going to be. Posed together on a towel for the camera, they have obviously got bored of the birdie; and turning to talk to each other instead, get photographed in the animated profiles I know so well.

These are my parents when they're younger than me. I look more closely. They could be my little brother and sister. My mum was only sixteen when she had Eugene, just nineteen when she had me. I think she must have lied to us about her age, because she always seemed much older than that.

It's amazing. She was just a child and she ran away from home to have Eugene. Dad was only two years older, so they must have supported each other. I've been so angry with them for not looking after me properly, but it's a wonder they were able to look after me at all.

Our grandparents suggest that Eugene sleeps in Garth's

313

room and I sleep in Mum's and I see no reason not to go along with their sense of tradition. They also see us to our separate rooms as if we are going to sleep straight away, but it's only just gone nine o'clock, and I see no reason to stay put. The night is younger than we.

I tiptoe along the dimly lit landing to Eugene or my father's room, and tap on the door. He opens it quickly and quietly, and I tiptoe inside.

The room is painted in three shades of green, darkening into shadows at the skirting board. The floor squeaks.

'Does the bed?' I say.

'What?' whispers Eugene, and looks at it.

Our suitcase is lying on the counterpane, like old-fashioned honeymoon luggage. All our belongings are in there, his things and mine, romantically entangled; pyjamas, toothbrushes and socks. There are no condoms.

If we're only going to do it once, we want to do it properly, as it was originally meant to be done, with maximum moistness. I want to feel Eugene make his deposit, not have him masked in dry rubber and making a quick withdrawal. I want to smell our sexual juices in synthesis, not some synthetic fruit flavour. This is the moment we've been waiting for all our lives, so why should we commit spermicide now?

Our sex will be safe enough. We've both been tested for HIV this year. Eugene did it when they were trying to find out what was wrong with Trudy, and I did it when I finally admitted to myself that my behaviour could be termed promiscuous. Anyway, we both failed the test, the results were negative, and neither of us have had unprotected sex since then. On top of this, my period has just finished, so there's no danger of pregnancy.

'Oh,' says Eugene, opening the suitcase. 'I know what you've come for. Your nightie.'

'I wasn't planning to wear one,' I say.

Eugene stops rummaging. He straightens up and looks me in the eye.

'What do you mean?' he says.

'I'm not going to wear it.'

'Why?'

'If we're only going to do it once, we want to do it properly, as it was originally meant to be done,' I say. 'Let's get naked.'

'No!' says Eugene. 'Not here!' He stares at me in disbelief. 'We can't!'

'We can.'

'Grace, it would be too terrible. In Dad's old room?'

'You might have been conceived in here,' I say, as the thought suddenly strikes me. 'Wow!'

Although we're making many exclamations, we're not talking much above a whisper, but Eugene hisses at me to stop.

'No,' he says, 'if Granny or Grandad found out, they'd have a heart attack.'

'They've seen it all before,' I say. 'You even suggested they were brother and sister themselves.'

'I didn't!' whispers Eugene.

'You did.'

'When?'

'Before dinner.'

'To their faces?' He gasps in horror.

'No, silly, to me,' I say. 'Wow, what if you were conceived in this room?' I sit down on the bed. 'At some point in the space-time continuum it's still happening.'

'Pardon?' says Eugene.

'Right here, on this bed, the ghosts of Garth and Gaynor are still going at it, hammer and tongs.' I stand up again.

Eugene's gone pale. He picks a book out of the suitcase and clutches it for security, distractedly stroking its pages.

'In the time-space beyond cause and effect,' I say, 'it's still happening. Do you know what I mean?'

'Yes, you're making me feel sick,' says Eugene. He hands me my book. 'It's stuff like this gives you ideas like that. Science fiction? You'd better check your facts.'

I smile at the picture on the cover. Jean-Luc Picard smiles calmly and confidently back.

'It could be true,' I say.

'Grace, when will you realise?' says Eugene. 'There's no such thing as *Star Trek*.'

'Is.'

'Isn't'

'Is.'

'Listen,' Eugene insists, 'let's not argue. Tonight let's just turn in separately, and read our own separate books, and believe whatever the bloody hell we like. I'm tired.'

I think about this for a moment, then nod my head in agreement.

'Yes?' he says.

'Yes,' I reply.

Eugene is surprised that I go so easily, give in without a fight. He kisses me on the cheek. I creep back along the landing, clutching my nightie and toothbrush and reading material.

In Gaynor's room I look at the photograph again. Seeing my parents as children I feel differently towards them. They look more like me and Genie. I've been so angry with them for not loving us enough, and for loving us too much; but when I see who they really are, two kids on a beach towel who got so close they made two more kids who couldn't let go either, I realise that love can't be quantified, because all there is is love. Eugene and I are made of love, so are Garth and Gaynor. It's bigger than all of us. It gave my young mum and dad, two skinny weirdo redheads, the strength to raise two relatively normal offspring. It helped the teenage ginger gits create new lives, and generate experiences which truly touch on beauty.

I don't read my book. I put my nightie on, turn the light off and lie down under the covers with my eyes open. I breathe deeply. Gradually the room stops spinning. The merry-go-round of the last few weeks of my life, with the principal characters waving from colourful horses and key scenes painted on the backdrop, slowly comes to a halt. I find a place of pure rest, in the still centre.

Then the bedroom door handle starts to turn. It's silent but I see the movement out of the corner of one eye. I see a tall thin black shadow which gets broader as the door opens further, and the shape of my brother slips into the room.

He comes towards the bed in a rush and I lift the quilt like a wing to take him under. It's dark and we don't speak. We lie down together, in a cocoon of brushed cotton. All the fuss and worry has been about nothing, because when me and Eugene finally have sex with each other, it's so much better than sex that it's something else altogether.

It's difficult to describe. Much of the time I'm lost in personal pleasure, and most of what happens is too private to tell. But I'm dimly aware of swimming when the bed disappears, and we drift out of context in some kind of sea. My body is moving in waves, which end in my mouth, which is joined to Eugene's by a kiss, which makes my waves turn into his. We've waving at each other, slowly at first then faster and faster; until the waves get so fast they all catch up with the one in front and become a big wave. I'm lifted on its peak, making a noise like a mermaid, a strange siren song, half-human, half-animal, unintelligible to mortal ears but irresistible to sailors. The bedclothes are heavy as if they're full of water, but they fall off, trawl off, before we're dragged down. With the use of a modern role reversal technique, Eugene saves me from drowning. He lifts me on top of him, into his lap.

His one enters my nothing, filling the hole in my zero, making it whole. He and she, he and me, fit together to form something solid, a shape with no spaces or sticking-out places. Now we have slotted together like pieces of a puzzle, I can see the complete picture. In two halves, we were broken; fragments frantically trying to feel at one with ourselves. But being penetrated by Eugene proves that my maths is true, just like I always knew. Two equals one. $2=1$. This is the meaning of love.

When he comes inside me a bright white column of light is raised to the roof. My back arches like stone. I get the fleeting impression of a civilisation being founded beneath us.

When he stops moving I feel it, too. An explosion of power, the back-draught of his ejaculation, somewhat delayed. It sends thrills through my body, and fills me with a spreading fern pattern which flickers like Christmas tree lights. If I were dead this would bring me surging back to life, but because I'm alive already my heart misses a beat. I gasp, and go into an awesome orgasm, an outing in space to a clock-stopping place. I've got my eyes shut but I can still see Eugene looking at me, and his face is framed by the stars.

This isn't sex. I know what sex is, and this isn't it. I've

known good sex, excellent sex, and this has surpassed it. I've already lost the best bits, the memories escaped as fast as they were made, through the holes that got blown in my mind; but I recall enough to realise that Eugene and I have gone one rung higher up the ladder on the scale of human bliss. Incest is much taboo about nothing, because it is nothing to do with sex. When it is over, when the rocket has burnt out, I come back down to earth with a sinking feeling, on an anticlimax which opens out like a parachute. My smile spins to the ground like a sycamore seed, and gets there faster.

I cannot say the exact moment his penis leaves my safekeeping, for the sensation remains long after the substance has gone; but gradually Eugene slips away from me and separation occurs. I am surgically resealed, hermetically whole. Now that my hole is my own again, it feels unbearably lonely and long. We remain joined together like a pair of Siamese twins, attached at the lips, nipples, and hips; but it seems his thoughts are receding, on the other side of his forehead; shrinking away from me like his spent flesh.

Now we've done it once, I want to do it again. I want to do it again at once. The perfect union and ultimate bliss Eugene promised me has been a big hit, and I'm the type of personality to become an instant addict. Instead of relaxing and enjoying the afterglow, experiencing it fully enough to last eternity, I'm already plotting a way to recapture the moment and get him back inside me.

'Are you asleep?' I ask Eugene.

'No,' he says, 'but I'm dreaming.'

'What about?' I ask him.

'This,' he says.

'Is it nice?' I ask him.

'Sssh,' he whispers, and smiles with his eyes shut.

This makes me feel more alone than ever. I wish I could get back inside him. My arms tighten around his waist. We've been brought together by blood, and stuck together by sweat and tears. Now semen oozes gluey between us, too.

'Talk to me,' I say.

'Okay.' Eugene opens his eyes with great effort. He smiles when he sees my face. 'I've just remembered the first time I saw you. The first time it really registered that you were a proper person.'

'Tell me,' I say.

'It was summertime,' Eugene speaks lazily. 'You must have been just two years old. I was three and a half. It was in the garden. In the middle of some game I was playing I stumbled across you on the lawn. You were sitting amongst the daisies in a little white dress and bonnet, doing nothing but looking around you. You looked at me as I came up to you. And I looked at you. We stared at each other for ages. I thought you should speak first. I didn't realise you couldn't. In the end, I broke the silence myself.'

'What did you say?' I ask him.

Eugene replies slowly, dredging the depths of his memory to find the first words he spoke to me.

'You smell,' he says.

'What?' I reply, not knowing whether to laugh or cry. 'What did you say?'

'You smell,' he says.

I decide to cry.

'I didn't mean it,' Eugene tries to reassure me. 'I was just sulking, or showing off. Don't take it seriously.'

He gives me a hug, but I sob into his shoulder. 'I smelled!'

'You didn't really,' Eugene protests.

'That was the first thing you ever said to me,' I sniff.

'It might not have been,' says Eugene. 'It's just the first thing I remember. It was the worst insult I could think of at the time.'

I'm not really as upset as I'm pretending to be, because he's holding me so tightly in his arms; but I don't let the subject drop for some time. I wonder aloud if my feelings were stunted by this early rejection, and thus the normal sibling relationship failed to grow.

'No,' says Eugene, kissing me.

'But when you said I smelled it must have had some effect.'

'You were preverbal, baby. You wouldn't have understood my language.'

'It might have sunk in subconsciously,' I say.

'Grace,' says Eugene, kissing me again, 'just be grateful I noticed your smell at all. Most big brothers wouldn't. Maybe even then, your junior pheromones were working on me; the juices were starting to flow.'

We're going to have sex again. All the signs are there. A new heat is rising between us, and we're getting a second wind. His hands move over my body in an upwardly direction. The kisses get deeper. Before long, we're being very rude to each other, much ruder than when we were kids. There's a lot of lingering fingering. A bit of biting. Animal noises. But when I press my thigh between Eugene's legs, I feel a mouse where there should be a monster. What can the matter be?

It doesn't matter. This is not a race. Our pace, after the initial urgency, is slow and luxurious. We've got all the time in the world. I lie back on the pillows. Why worry about the resurrection when he's kissing my feet. Why wait for seven inches of flesh to swell when he can make a start with a single finger. I lie back on the pillows and let Eugene take care of the tonguing and the timing.

An hour goes past. I never thought I'd see the day he'd give me more attention than I can take. By now I'm so full of desire that I could sing like Pavarotti. The empty space inside me has swollen to the size of the Albert Hall, and I'm desperate to fit Eugene in for the next performance.

I make a frenzied attempt at insertion.

'Oh, come on, do it, please, please do it!' I beg him.

'But we've done it already,' he replies.

'Do it again, do it again!' I moan, completely losing control of myself.

'You agreed we'd only do it once,' he says. 'Grace, you promised!'

'I didn't mean it,' I wail.

Eugene moves away from me, and we separate like Velcro; our nearly fusing nuclei now achieve fission with an almost audible ripping. Every cell in my body screams after him as he goes. He jumps out of bed and takes my heart with him; I can feel its strings tugging and snapping as he gets further away. I can see sparks in the air between us, where the vital links are broken.

Eugene stares at me in the darkness.

'God, you liar,' he says.

'It was only a little white one,' I splutter. 'I thought you'd thank me for it eventually.'

'Didn't you understand?' he says. 'Loving and losing, loving and leaving, or never loving at all. I wouldn't have done it otherwise.'

'Yes, I understood.'

'So why were you trying to do it again?' he asks.

'Why were *you*?' I say. 'The first time finished ages ago. You shouldn't have started all the new foreplay if you didn't want to do it again. You should have left straightaway.'

'That wasn't new foreplay,' Eugene shouts, 'that was old afterplay. I was finishing the job properly. I know what you women are like. You're not satisfied till you've had at least fifty orgasms. A man can't do that with his dick.'

He picks his pyjama trousers off the floor and starts to put them on, but before he can properly pull them up I've dived out of bed and pulled them down again in a sort of rugby tackle.

'Get off, Grace!' Eugene steps backwards but I'm clinging to his ankles, crying.

'You think I smell,' I say. 'You hate me.'

'Don't be silly,' Eugene kicks his legs to loosen my grip. 'If I hated you we wouldn't be in this stupid situation.'

'Then come back to bed with me again,' I say. 'Wasn't it better than anything else you've ever experienced? We could make it last for ever, if you stay with me.'

'I can't,' Eugene frees one of his legs and struggles off, dragging me round the room on the end of his other one. 'If we stayed together I would hate you. We'd be like Mum and Dad.'

'Mum and Dad don't hate each other,' I say desperately. 'They might not love anyone else, but they don't hate each other.'

'If you don't love everyone, you can't love anyone,' says Eugene. He takes me by the hands and makes me stand on my feet. 'We agreed, Grace,' he says. 'Be brave.'

'No,' I howl, 'I can't. I love you but I don't love myself!' I sink to my knees and cling to his. But he heaves me to my feet again.

'We can still be friends,' he says.

'We can't,' I say. 'A friend is someone I haven't fucked yet.'

My sentence has a sharp edge, like a scream. It's the angry wind that augurs a storm. We're right in the middle of a moor which is murderous dark and dirty. The ground crouches and the sky is shuddering. Should there be lightning, Eugene and I are the highest things for miles around. We'll be struck, for sure.

'Let me go, Grace,' he says. 'This isn't love. Love would let me go.'

That was it. Lightning forks in flashes, and strikes twice. It gets me and my brother. We step back from each other with shock. I clutch my blasted heart.

I feel my being is burning up. The milky flesh speckled with peachy freckles, the flesh that's covered me since childhood, is consumed with flame, and underneath is a blackened metal frame. I'm turning out to be a mechanoid, a robot like Arnold Schwarzenegger in *The Terminator*.

Eugene is smoking. There was a packet of cigarettes and a lighter on the dressing table. We'd left them there earlier, when our grandparents showed us the rooms. They said we could smoke in here, but only if the window was open and we were leaning out, like Gaynor used to.

I lurch towards Eugene. My legs are stiff and I can hear joints clicking. I raise my arm to him like a crowbar, but he sees me coming and catches the blow. My reactions are slow, as if I'm operated by remote control. He said if I loved him, I'd let him go; but my computations tell me all the love would go with him, and I'd be left unable to function.

324

'Grace, I'm going back to Garth's room now,' Eugene says.

'But it isn't over yet.'

'I can't wait till the end. It looks like you want to kill me.' He lets go of my arm, but I point its still-rigid finger at him as he backs away.

'There's no escape,' I say. 'I'll see you in the morning.'

Eugene laughs.

'Every time the going gets tough, you do this mad Arnie thing,' he says.

'Sorry,' I say.

'That's okay. We deal with the situation in our own ways,' Genie replies.

'You'd better not walk back along the landing till you've finished your fag,' I say.

'Why are you such an angry robot?' he asks.

'Because you're abusing my joystick with confusing commands!' I say. 'Earlier this evening, I settled on separate beds; but you came after me and got into my peaceful space. I was prepared to let it lie, but you couldn't rest till you'd got it all ruffled and raised up again. It's not the stiffness of *my* resolve that's in question here.'

There is a timid knock on the door, and before we can think to answer, someone bravely opens it.

'What's all the shouting?' says Granny. 'Are you two alright?'

She flicks a switch, and Eugene and I are illuminated in frozen poses; he in pyjama bottoms, me naked, the bedclothes covering the floor in disarray and a pall of smoke at the ceiling. It probably looks like a scene from a Greek myth. Eugene is accosting me, half-dressed; half-man, half-beast. I have unconsciously adopted the stance of Botticelli's newborn

Venus: one hand covering my breasts, the other shyly hiding my pubic hair. Our fixed positions tell a story with a whole range of emotions, from tragic to comic: and for Granny, also ironic. She's seen it before; Garth and Gaynor acted it out a generation earlier.

Our grandmother gets a good, long look at us, but her face does not change an inch. In horror I anticipate her having a heart attack, but her features remain passive. I expect her to speak, but she doesn't say a word. Her hand is still on the doorknob, and as she slowly backs out of the room the door shuts automatically.

We hear her walking heavily along the landing to Grandad; one step, two steps, three steps, four. There is a long pause, then a loud thud. Granny has fallen. We rush for the door. On the landing, Granny is lying against the wall. In the dim night light she doesn't seem to be dead, but she's certainly unconscious.

Eugene runs and knocks on Grandad's door, I run back to Gaynor's room. I put on my nightie and a cardigan and some socks. I smooth my hair then go back out on the landing. Grandad is bending over Granny, and Eugene is running downstairs to phone an ambulance. Grandad is crying Granny's name, and trying to cuddle her. I rush back into my bedroom and bring out the quilt to cover her up. Grandad is distraught. I've never heard anyone say 'Glad! Glad!' in such a sad voice before.

Eugene runs back up the stairs and says we should all get dressed so we can go to the hospital with Gladys in the ambulance. Grandad hardly seems capable, so Eugene goes with him. I throw myself into my jeans, and don't miss them, which surprises me because I can't feel my legs at all. Granny continues to lay on the landing, in a frighteningly unnatural position, until the ambulance arrives. Grandad is dressed, at the cost of Eugene still being half-naked, but the ambulance people say there isn't room for all of us anyway, and only Grandad can go. Me and Eugene must follow by car. Grandad says we can use his, but he doesn't know where the keys are. The ambulance crew are talking in urgent technical terms all around us, so we say don't worry, we'll find them. Then Granny is taken downstairs on a stretcher, out of the front door and into the ambulance.

It rushes whitely off into the night, blue lights flashing. It doesn't have sirens blaring, but I suppose on a country road in the middle of nowhere, that would just be showing off. It's also the middle of the night.

Eugene and I go back into the house and get dressed properly. It's freezing cold, and my own hands feel like ice when they touch my skin. They're next to useless as we rush from room to room looking for Grandad's car keys. We try obvious places first: mantelpieces, hooks in the hallway, coat pockets. But it is like looking for a needle in a haystack; they could be hidden anywhere. We haven't quite sussed out yet how eccentric Grandad is; for all we know he may secretly keep his key in a warm, straw nest in the chicken coop. Not feeling up to going down the garden, I search harder in the house; and eventually find them on his chest of drawers, with some small change and a pair of spectacles.

Eugene drives. Neither of us are particularly impressive behind the wheel, but he has at least passed his test. I always fail to grasp the fact that the other cars and bikes and pedestrians with pushchairs are real, and not just simulations in a virtual reality game who can never actually be killed. I don't trust myself to drive seriously enough. To me, only people who can guarantee one hundred per cent concentration, and a sharply focused mind which won't waver for a second, should be allowed to drive. I've seen some right cretins sitting behind steering wheels and they seem to know what they're doing, so perhaps with me it's a genetic disability.

Eugene is not totally in control of the car either. We crunch and shudder and stall our way to the hospital, following the directions that the ambulance driver gave us as he staggered and grunted our grandmother downstairs on a stretcher.

It's miles away and there's nowhere to park so it's an hour before we run into the emergency department. Grandad leaps out at us, sitting with his head in his hands on an orange plastic chair in the middle of many others. We rush up to him and sit down, one on either side.

'How is she?' I ask.

'She's had a heart attack,' he says.

'Is she going to be alright?'

'She died,' he says, 'and they brought her back to life. Her heart stopped in the ambulance and they started it again.'

We get coffee and soak up the atmosphere of the emergency department all night. We're not allowed to see Granny, but we get a strong sense of the gravity of the situation from the other accidents and emergencies going on all around us. This is a place on the edge of life and death, and the people in it are going through crisis. Some of them cry and scream regrets and recriminations; some just sit on the orange plastic seats as if it's a dream.

Grandad is traumatised.

'What happened?' he keeps saying. 'I woke up and she wasn't there. She was lying on the landing.'

'Mmm,' I say, sympathetically.

'The ambulance man said she must have gone to the bathroom, but she'd gone the wrong way!' Grandad says.

By four in the morning Granny is settled in intensive care. We're not allowed to see her, though the doctor lets Grandad look through the glass door. She's in a critical condition, having recently come back to life. He says there's a bank of flashing lights, and an electronic bleep for every beat of her heart.

I suggest we go home to get some rest, and he reluctantly agrees to leave Granny to the nurses, who promise to phone in a further emergency. We drive in exhausted silence, and climb the stairs to bed on our last legs. We all collapse with our clothes on, it seems; for when the phone rings two hours later we all appear fully dressed on the landing within seconds. Eugene makes it downstairs to the phone first.

The news is bad. After saying yes twice, Eugene says oh, no, and then no again, several times in quick succession. He listens and nods and says we're on our way, then hangs up. Grandad and I have got to the bottom of the stairs by now and Eugene holds his hands out to us.

'It's not Granny,' he says, 'it's Trudy. That was her nurse, at home. Trudy took a turn for the worse and was rushed into hospital overnight. They're going to try an emergency transplant on her. Grandad,' Eugene's voice breaks as the old man opens his arms to hug him, 'I'm sorry to leave you like this, but I must go to her.'

Grandad understands. He makes a bit of breakfast while we're packing then gives us a lift to the station on his way to see Granny. He seems stronger this morning, and very supportive, but as soon as he has seen us off, Eugene turns to me and says I should have stayed with him.

'What?' I ask, three steps behind on the climb to the station entrance.

'You could have stayed with Grandad.'

'Why?'

'Well, we didn't both need to rush off and see Trudy. You could have looked after him.'

'He's alright,' I say.

'Who's going to cook and clean and keep his spirits up?'

'I only met him three days ago. I think he's a nice man, but I haven't formed a lasting family bond yet,' I say, striding down the platform.

'I know,' says Eugene, 'I just thought it would be nice. After all, we are responsible for nearly killing his wife.'

The train sidles noisily up beside us, drowning out what Eugene's saying, but I can read his lips. We get in and slam the door. Several other doors slam, along the length of the train; but the name of the station is still being announced, slowly and unclearly, over the Tannoy. Yesterday it sounded vaguely ominous, something like Sodom; today it sounds like Gomorrah.

The train thunders out of the station. Yesterday, Eugene and I sat opposite each other, and I was facing forwards. Today, I sit down on the seat beside him so we're both going backwards. The view from the window speeds away from us, a road running parallel to the railway line, with cars which could be Grandad's rushing to the hospital. I take hold of Eugene's hand.

'Don't,' he says. 'We've given our granny a heart attack. It's got to stop.'

'How?' I ask.

He takes back his hand.

'We've got to say goodbye,' he says.

'Goodbye,' I say in a funny voice, a bit Goofy.

'Not like that,' says Eugene. 'It's got to be natural.'

I laugh.

'What's a natural goodbye?' I ask.

'We'll come to a parting of the ways,' he says.

'How will we know it?'

'Well, there'll be two different paths to take, and you'll go in one direction and I'll go in the other,' he says. 'For instance, what are you doing when you get off this train?'

'Going to the hospital to see Trudy.'

'Oh,' he says, 'that's where I'm going, too. Never mind, the T-junction will come in time.'

'Okay,' I say.

We get off the train and go to the hospital to see Trudy. It's hard to find her, and even harder to find out what they're doing to her. All they say is that they're attempting a last-ditch transplant operation. They don't let us see her.

Eugene and I spend the whole day and some of the evening sitting on orange plastic chairs in the waiting room. For light relief, I phone Grandad in his waiting room, to find out how Granny is. There is no change. She hasn't died again, but she's not showing much life either.

Eugene is right. It is our fault she is ill. We might have killed her. He doesn't say I told you so, though. He doesn't say anything, all day long. We sit side by side, lost in our own thoughts. We don't share them. We're huddled up, hoarding our own guilt.

I remember that I haven't told him about Grandad's cock

331

yet, but this doesn't seem an appropriate moment to bring it up. I remember that I missed his twenty-sixth birthday, but I don't think he's in the mood to be reminded of it now.

Trudy's special nurse comes and sits with us for a while. She says they're waiting for a donor, and a doctor who's flying in from Russia. She brings us some tea, then disappears again. Eugene and I sit in silence some more. After about an hour I say, 'What's a doctor coming from Russia for?'

'Jet lag?' Eugene shrugs. 'Maybe none of the local doctors are tired enough to perform the operation properly.'

A couple of hours later, he turns to me again.

'Grace,' he says.

'Yes?' I reply.

'Nothing,' he says after a pause.

Twenty minutes after that he sighs deeply and says, 'It smells here, doesn't it?'

At nine o'clock in the evening he stretches and yawns, and gets up stiffly. The orange plastic chair seems to scream with relief. Eugene looks out into the corridor, checks left and right. The last sighting of a nurse was at ten past eight, when one came and told us that nothing will happen tonight and if we go home they might let us see Trudy in the morning.

'I'm going,' says Eugene.

'I'll come, too,' I say.

'Oh,' he looks slightly surprised. 'So this is not the parting of the ways either.'

It is possible to go left or right from here; though right is the way out and left leads into a ward. Unless one of us wants to stay in this hospital for ever, our journey together must last a little bit longer. We walk along shiny scrubbed-up corridors of many lights.

'Thanks for today,' says Eugene.

'What?' I say. 'It wasn't one of my best. The conversation didn't exactly sparkle.'

'But I got a lot of thinking done,' he says.

We burst through the glass double-doors of the hospital and come out to a dark rainy street, with orange lamplight splashes on the pavement. Cars and buses pass in a slow wet procession, a constant dazzle of headlights and hiss of windscreen wipers.

Eugene stands in the rain, shouting, with a smile on his face.

'Where are you going now?' he says.

'Where are you going?' I ask.

'Home,' he says. 'I'm going to sit down at my computer and bloody well invade Poland. I had been working on a way to save the African rhinos, but my plans have changed.' He does the zip of his jacket up and smiles tightly.

'Can I come with you?' I say.

'No,' he says, 'it's the parting of the ways.'

The rain is really heavy. It's soaking through my sheepskin hair and getting my head wet.

'Are you sure?' I say.

'Absolutely,' says Eugene. 'So are you going to the bus stop?'

'I don't know. I could do.'

'Well, do you want to get on a bus?'

'I don't know where I'm going.'

'You have to accept it, Grace,' he says. 'Our paths are diverging. You can't come with me this time.'

'Okay,' I say. 'And you have to accept that I have no other destination planned.'

'You're just going to roam the streets then, are you?' he says.

'I daresay I'll get somewhere eventually.'

'Unless someone gets you first,' he says, nastily.

'Well, if you put it like that,' I reply, looking at my watch, 'there's still time to catch the last martial arts class. I could kick bricks and throw my weight around.'

Eugene strides off and I skip after him, sidestepping a puddle.

'The bus stops are over there,' he calls over his shoulder, gesturing dramatically in the rain. Then he stops and turns to me completely, suddenly looking like Laurence Olivier in the final scene of a film.

'I never wanted to say our goodbyes somewhere so tawdry and awful, my darling,' he says.

'Let's go somewhere else then. Let's go to my place, or our old temple in the park, or Glastonbury,' I suggest, sure that there can still be a happy ending.

The rain is like rapturous applause. I can hardly see through the deafening downpour, or hear through the wind. A tree on either side of us bows low, scooping up tributes of litter tossed into the street.

'Grace, we could go round the world saying goodbye to each other and never get anywhere,' shouts Eugene. 'Look, I've got to cross over the road. My bus will be along in a minute or three.'

Eugene stops at the kerb. He looks right, then left, where he finds me in his face. Our car-crash features, all noses and cheekbones, are in collision. He is still beautiful. So maybe I am, too. He is still desirable, so maybe I am, too.

'Can I come?' I say.

'No, stay here,' he says. 'Stay till you know where you really want to go. Let's not say goodbye at a bus stop.'

'It wouldn't stop anyway,' I say. 'This thing had no beginning. I can't see how it's going to end.'

I can see a bus coming over his shoulder. A big red one.

'It's a natural transition,' Eugene smiles sadly, 'not really an end. We only have to say goodbye with our physical bodies. We just have to stop having sex.'

'There's a bus coming,' I say.

'Oh, shit!' He starts to run.

'I'm coming, too,' I say.

I start to run with him because we're part of each other and there's nothing he can do to stop me coming, too.

I start to run with him, because the big red bus is going to get to the bus stop before us, because there's a big red bus we haven't seen yet coming the other way.

At about the same time as this Garth and Gaynor Bloom are going to bed. They go to bed at about the same time every night. They lie themselves down in a double, though they can't really be said to be sleeping together any more. For the last six years or so, since their children left home, sex has only happened on high days and holidays.

This would normally be one of those magic nights. Their new book has been launched. That would normally call for a pat on the back and a kiss on the arse, a bit of slap and tickle. Gaynor Bloom puts on a seductive negligee and waits for her brother to come upstairs.

He's down in the kitchen, putting the kittens in their wicker basket. The RSPCA came to take them away, but he wouldn't let them go. He said Grace might change her mind and come back for the tiny trio herself. He couldn't believe she'd give them up for ever, just because she didn't want to see her mother and father again.

But Gaynor Bloom, who would have given anything not to have seen her mother and father again, begs to disagree. It was a living nightmare at the book launch, Mum and Dad turning up like that to haunt them, and her having to tell Eugene his grandparents weren't dead. She crosses her fingers, closes her eyes and opens her legs; and waits for her brother to stop fucking around with saucers of milk and straw.

Downstairs in the kitchen, Garth has spilt some milk on the floor. He's crying. He can't believe Grace doesn't want to see him any more. Blindly, he reaches for today's newspaper, which he hasn't had the heart to read, and uses it to mop up the milk.

The third page he pulls out has his own name printed in one of the headlines. He looks twice.

GARTH AND GAYNOR BLOOM – EVANGELISTS OF THE NEW FAMILY

Underneath is an article about the book. He doesn't read it, but a few choice words leap out at him nevertheless. His eye wanders to the photograph next to the piece. It has nothing to do with him and Gaynor. It's a picture of candyfloss clouds floating in a Botticelli-blue sky, with streaks of molten gold on the horizon. It's advertising something.

If Garth and Gaynor Bloom are evangelists of a new family, he thinks, Grace and Eugene are the angels.

The telephone rings. Gaynor answers it at the bedside, with immaculately polished fingernails and cocoa in the corners of her lips. She starts to scream. Eugene is phoning from the hospital, because he and Grace have been in a road accident.

Gaynor shouts for Garth and he's there at once, having

legged it up the stairs at the first sign of trouble. He heard her gasp the word 'hospital', and assumes it's to do with Trudy. They get dressed in a whirl, trivial things like nylon negligees and newspaper reviews instantly lost to the wind of their changing, as Gaynor tells him that their children have been run over by a bus. They go in the car, but get to the hospital quicker than Superwoman and Superman could fly; like a streak of red lightning, powered by an energy only parents understand. The adrenalin rush soon dies away, but Garth and Gaynor Bloom continue to demonstrate a superhuman strength, as they take up their positions on the orange plastic chairs.

They sit in the emergency department so long that their next book is conceived there. It's the third in a trilogy about the nuclear family: *Fission, Fusion and Fallout*.

Fifteen

Just as there is no beginning, so there is no end.

There was darkness for a while, in the middle of my story; there was a big red bus, and a lot of lights.

So this is an appendix. It's not a proper chapter. It's apocryphal, which means I wouldn't swear it was true. I honestly couldn't say whether what happens next is true or not.

The last thing I remember was the bus, but it didn't stop there. A lot of faces followed, some familiar, some strange, expressing some unspeakable pain. One face in particular was so constant and so close to me I thought it must be mine.

I marvelled at his eyeballs, prized them like marbles. I loved his hair as if it were my teddy bear. His mouth I associated with music, and couldn't keep my hands off it, tinkering with his teeth the way I tinkled on the keys of my tiny plastic piano. He moved around me with such ease of mobility I assumed he could fly.

I don't remember dying. It must be like being born, rushing along hospital corridors on a trolley, with doctors conferring in urgent terms, and a nurse wheeling a drip. Or perhaps I am not dead.

'What's that?'
    'Oxygen.'
    'What's it oxygen for?'
    'So you can breathe.'
    'Why can't I breathe?'

These beatific snippets of conversations are keeping me alive. I know who I'm having them with. He's there every time I open my eyes. He was there at the bus stop, he was there at the start; and perhaps the fact that he's still there means this story didn't end with a bang. I can't speak properly because of the mask over my mouth; but at certain times of the day or night, on certain combinations of medication, I can keep up my end of the dialogue.

'How's Trudy?'
    'She's getting better. The transplant was a great success.'
    'They gave her my appendix, didn't they? I'm so glad.'

On another occasion I am visited by my grandmother. She appears at my bedside, glowing with health, and says she has a message for me.

'Do not be afraid of dying, Grace,' she says, smiling. 'When I had my heart attack I died for a while and it was fine. It's a breathtakingly beautiful country, and as soon as you arrive there you realise it's home.'

I struggle to ask her a question, something that comes from

a drab place, with a dull haste. It hardly seems to make sense now that I'm always wearing a nightie.

'Did you tell Grandad
you saw me and my brother
undressed in the bedroom
that once was our mother's?'

'I didn't,' Granny says.

She didn't see us, or she didn't tell him? I try to question her further, but my mouth can't form the verse. Somehow I feel that my grandmother must be addressed in poetry, because she's been dead and white.

Every day I have an audience with my parents. They're the ones who got me into this mess, and they still think they can get me out of it by lying. They're blatantly reading aloud from a book, but pretending to use their own words. I can see the title in rainbow coloured letters: *Positive Affirmations for the Terminally Ill*.

'Grace, you're fine,' they say. 'You're full of life.'

'And you two are up to your old tricks again,' I growl through the tube in my throat, but I'm not really angry any more. I've still got a photograph of them as children. I don't know whether it's on the table by the bed, or in my head, but I can see it all the time, and it reminds me not to judge them too harshly.

One day, Dad appears to me looking just like a little boy. With a naughty expression he opens his coat to reveal a kitten, a large kitten, more of a small cat.

'It's Wynken,' he says.

I can see that. I wink back.

If I'm not dead yet, it must be a miracle. I'm in very bad shape. I lie down all the time and there's a big hole in my

340

stomach. I don't eat anything and never seem to go to the toilet.

There are a lot of nurses but the main one is Trudy. She looks brilliant in her blue uniform, back at work and fit and well. It's because I donated my appendix to her, after the accident. It was obviously meant to be; she was at death's door waiting for a donor and I was run over by a bus outside. Her hair has grown back, flowing and golden, and when she leans over to tuck me in, it tickles my face.

The transplant has taken, though it seems that Trudy must be taking a lot of anti-rejection medicine, because she's growing very fat in the tummy. I comment on it while she's changing my dressings one day.

'Are you on drugs?' I say.

'No,' she smiles, 'but you are.'

'It's just that you seem swollen,' I explain.

'I'm pregnant,' she says.

'Grace? I know you can't hear me. But I need to talk. It was all my fault. You were only little, but I was big enough to know better. We should never have slept together. Not the first time, not the second time, not the third time; none of the times we pretended it hadn't happened when it had. And though I said we were theoretically innocent, I felt practically guilty of murder. Granny's heart attack was fateful, Grace, it was a warning; something had to stop. So I, control-freak of the century, tried to force things to a logical conclusion. I was determined that we would say goodbye outside the hospital, that we wouldn't go a step further together. I'm sorry now.

'Grace? I wish you could hear me. The doctors say it can still go either way. You could still make a complete recovery. It's somehow up to you. See, this doesn't have to be the end. It wasn't a natural goodbye at the bus stop, I made it happen. I was stupid, and I hate myself, and I really need you to get better and love me again.

'Grace, I hope you can hear me. You're an auntie.'

Just as there was no beginning, so there is no end. Before the accident, before the bus came, we sat in the hospital, waiting. We sat side by side in a stew, not speaking, while Trudy's life was at stake. Now it's me who could be dead or alive, but Eugene's voice is going on and on in the darkness. His words are the shape of my world, his love is my language. And when the baby starts to cry I hear another voice, which might be mine, saying goodness gracious; it's already started all over again.

Alison Habens

DREAMHOUSE

Celia Small has been planning her engagement party for years. Now the big day has arrived, her best fantasy is about to come true.

But two of her hated housemates are also having parties tonight, and their impromptu affairs are quite at odds with Celia's prim, family arrangements. With three parties in one house, Celia is set for the worst night of her life.

Led astray by a drug-dealing White Rabbit and a trail of dodgy jam tarts, Celia wanders like an accidental Alice into a weird Wonderland of drugs and dressing-up, psychedelia and social deviance, on a one-way trip of self-discovery.

'A truly astonishing feat of the imagination, supported by a dazzling display of wit and wordplay . . . One of the best first novels to appear this year' *Sunday Times*

'Curious and magical . . . Alison Habens has a refreshingly playful love of language, and is endlessly inventive' *The Times*

'Like Carroll, Habens has a talent for playfulness so deft that it conceals its craft' *Independent on Sunday*

Lois-Ann Yamanaka

WILD MEAT
AND THE BULLY BURGERS

Growing up in Hawaii, Lovey Nariyoshi is having the
worst year of her life. Overweight and unpopular, she's
sick of being poor and settling for home-made and
second-best. Her family thinks she's uppity and her
schoolteacher scorns the way she talks. For, above all,
Lovey is a Japanese-American: not white, not *haole* —
and from the food she eats to the pidgin she speaks,
nothing in her life fits the standard model of success.

Heartbreaking and hilarious by turns, written in a
language that explodes off the page, *Wild Meat and the
Bully Burgers* introduces one of the most vibrant new
voices in fiction today.

'Fortunate reader. Here is a rare book . . . Yamanaka is
brilliant'   *E. Annie Proulx*

'Wildly funny and rich, as inventive as it is authentic.
Yamanaka's is much more than "just" an ethnic novel. It
is a novel of our time, as it is truly experienced and
lived'   *Gish Jen*

'A vibrant, funny, bittersweet, sassy joyride of a novel'
                                          Jessica Hagedorn